The Scent of Deception

By: Lori Campbell

Dedicated to: My husband, Frank, who never thought it was just silly that I was writing.

1. Rise and Shine

The day started like every other with the not so subtle burn in my throat as I awoke. I could feel it cracking with every breath that forced its way down. The experience was probably much like trying to breath in a sandstorm. It had been too long since I had satiated my thirst and my throat ached like I had never had a drink in my life. It was going to be a long day.

I grimaced as the alarm clock screamed and thought how often the need to feed pressed itself on me lately. Usually human food was enough to keep me in good spirits and health for two or three months at a time, but now it seemed that the burn was becoming unbearable in barely a month's time. It demanded my attention the minute I became stressed. So, like every other normal person, I blamed my job.

Being the personal assistant to Ms. Georgia Stone took an intolerable toll on my self-control. Unfortunately for her, that meant the likelihood of me losing my temper was much higher and that usually led to blood being spilled. Fortunately though, through years of practice, I had conditioned my body to be governed by my mind instead of my instincts. I was more controlled than others that felt this same craving, but no matter how I looked at it, today was going to be trying.

Today was the day we prepared to go to where no Philadelphia news crew had ever dared go before, the untamed wilds of Alaska. Apparently the Air Force had developed a new aircraft that would "modernize warfare for the next generation." The reason for Alaska being the site for this revolutionary unveiling, in the middle of winter, escaped me. But my feelings were less than amiable about it. Aside from the climate, it would mean that I would have the pleasure of spending an ungodly amount of time stuck in an airplane with the one woman I could not stand. I could only imagine the tirade when she realized that it was going to be far too cold to wear anything under three layers.

It also didn't help that Alaska just happened to be the last place anyone had seen my so-called father. It wouldn't have been possible to be *less* enthused at the prospect of running into him. Of course he didn't even care that I, his abomination, existed at all. In all fairness though, I shouldn't exist. I'm sure he thought after his brief tryst with my mother there wasn't a chance that I would. He was wrong.

I searched my closet, behind the skirts there was one clean pair of pants, thank god. As I stared into the mirror at the eyeliner that wouldn't go where I wanted it to, I couldn't help thinking that there must be more of my kind, but I suppose we are few and far between. We, the dhamphirs, the unexpected offspring between a male vampire and a mortal female. Freaks in a world of monsters, and yet somehow here I am and headed towards the one man to blame for my misery. But alas, the three hundred something year old vampire that sired me was not my main concern on such a sunny Philadelphia morning. No, my mind became occupied wondering how the inevitable fall out from a thirty year old woman's latest break up was going to darken my beautiful day.

Of course it wasn't really a surprise. After one hundred years of walking the earth, I had learned a few things about humans, and for the most part they weren't terribly difficult to read. News anchor Georgia Stone was truly one of the easier ones to predict. She was so full of herself, one of those women who would always do what would make her happy regardless of the consequences, and today was no different. She had wined and dined her way to the anchor position with the station's lead anchorman and now it was time for her to move on up to the next person who could advance her career. It put me in mind of Evita, although Georgia needn't tell anyone to not cry for her. No one I knew would.

I walked to the bus stop in the beautiful December air. The wind nipped at my cheeks and I felt the blood move to warm them. The air smelled of snow, a nice crisp smell that made me smile as I waited for the bus. The humans near me, however, were no cause for joy. I had been this way for 100 years, but the stares and the sharp intake of breath that assaulted me every day on the street still tweaked my nerves. The reaction of these little nothings was not because they had any inclination of what I was, they reacted to what they considered my beauty. The most insignificant weapon in my extensive arsenal. It disgusted me that these humans saw me as an object of desire when they should have fled in terror. It frightened me a little to know what I could do in a moment to their frail bodies, but then again, it wasn't like I actually existed to them.

As usual, the bus was late and arrived smelling like stale beer and vomit. I just tried to not to breath as I made my way towards the back of the bus, as far away from the other passengers as possible. When it was this necessary to hunt it was always a challenge to be around warm blooded food sources. The scent distracted me and the sound of the pounding heartbeats hummed in the air making my mouth water. I tried hard to concentrate on what was waiting for me at the station, but the constant thump of their hearts kept grabbing my attention.

Suddenly someone's heartbeat rapidly changed and drew my eyes reluctantly to the host. As his eyes caught mine, his heart started racing and I could almost taste the sweat that was beginning to bead up on his brow. My body tensed for a leap. I looked away. Control yourself, control yourself. I chanted the words in my head as he stirred in his seat. The slight movement wafted his smell through the bus and I gripped the edges of my seat to keep myself from jumping up and quenching this unbearable thirst. His blood was pumping so close to the surface. Stop it. I concentrated on regulating my breathing and focusing on the cars next to us, but the bus was moving so slowly. I wanted to jump up and run away. Yet all things shall pass and after what seemed like an eternity, the bus lurched to a stop in front of the WJDR building.

He was already standing when the bus stopped. He fidgeted nervously by the front exit door. Every movement made my senses tingle. He tried to be subtle as he checked my position at the back door, but it was all to obvious he was watching me. I focused all my energy on not giving in to the urges that were so hard to overcome. His heart was working overtime bursting against his ribcage and pumping that sweet sustenance to the surface. My breathing started to intensify as I smelled the blood racing just below that thin layer of skin. I could make sure it would be quick for him; he wouldn't even know what happened. Stop it. There's no better way for you to blow cover than to drain the blood of that little punk in broad daylight.

I had been so distracted by his blood it took me a minute to realize what he was so jacked up about. I chuckled under my breath, a sound no human ear would notice, as I heard his breath hitch. He tensed his muscles to pounce. The little hoodlum was going to try to steal my purse. The thought was so ridiculous I nearly snorted in amusement. I smiled to myself at the many different ways this could end for him and a little girl standing beside me cringed away in fear. I smiled, baring all of my gleaming teeth at the child, and her eyes widened immensely. My little thief seemed to take no notice of the fear I inflicted upon the child and just kept glancing at my purse nervously. Then the doors opened to my waking hell. I evaluated my choices and decided it would be best to just embarrass, not kill, him. I stepped onto the pavement with a sigh.

Two steps from the bus door he picked up the pace, grabbed the bag, and ran. Or rather he tried to run. As soon as the purse strap reached its end I pulled slightly and sent the would-be thief flying to the pavement straight on his back. I could hear the breath escape his lungs in one long whoosh. The warm pulsing temptation was only a few feet away and it called desperately to me. I leaned towards him fighting to clear my mind of the scent and trying to stop my mouth from watering. It took me a few seconds, but once in control of my cravings, I smiled in satisfaction at my command. I could have thrown him so hard into the bus it would have shattered the windows or drained every last drop of his blood from miserable thieving body, but I hadn't. It was a little victory in the day that left me with some hope that the rest of the day might not be a total disaster.

My light blue sunglasses slipped down my nose so that he had an unobstructed view of my pale blue eyes. He stared directly into them and I could see the fear begin to mount until it spilled out in the form of tears. I didn't need to say a word. I could feel the fire in my eyes. The hunger and the absolute need smoldered just below the surface and he knew it, sensed it, without ever needing me to put it into words. I was dangerous. I was a monster. And my baby blues were the scariest sight he had ever seen. I have to admit that I enjoyed the moment of terror that made the little hoodlum shake on the pavement. I growled involuntarily. He scrambled to his feet frantically and scampered away into the crowd.

The whole scarring scene hadn't attracted much attention from what I could tell. Until I heard a faint chuckle. I surveyed the crowd to find a man standing on the steps of the building. He was apparently deeply amused. He was no immediate threat even though he was tall, muscular, and definitely armed. The scent of gunpowder wafted faintly from his side, he had discharged his weapons fairly recently. Judging by the hair and clothing choice, he was a serviceman. In my quick assessment, his face struck me as being quite handsome. His hair, a sandy blonde color, was cut in the military fashion shorn close against the head. His eyes, aside from being so smugly amused were a deep brown above his thin lips set in his broad square jaw. He was handsome. In a rugged outdoors sort of way. But he was just another human and therefore completely off limits for me. The whole intimate relationships with humans thing never ended well.

I straightened up and pushed my sunglasses into their proper position. No need to frighten everyone to death before I could get my facade in order. I slung my purse over my shoulder and made my way up the stairs towards the huge glass doors. I walked past the mystery man, his blood pumping with adrenaline. I took a deep breath and my mouth begin to water. Then I smelled it, the acidic scent of a vampire still lingered on his clothing, it wasn't fresh but it was distinctive. I took a breath again to confirm that the smell of lye soap and spice was purely superficial. It was. He was just a human, but he obviously was very closely involved with one of them. I let the unfamiliar scent register in my perfect memory. Granted it wasn't as though I had met every vampire that ever existed, but I had met the few that lived nearby. It wasn't one of them and judging by his attire my mystery human wasn't from around here. His sweater was far too thick and his boots had too much tread for the barely covered streets of Philly.

I caught his eye as I walked by and the look he gave me made me shiver. The way his eyes appraised me wasn't normal. My stomach lurched sickeningly as I realized I knew that look. In fact, I looked that way often. He was a predator and I, the prey. An unfamiliar sensation ran down my spine. Obviously, I wasn't helpless, nor was this the first time I had been the object of a hunt, but this was different, wrong. Maybe it was the scent that still lingered in my nostrils. I suddenly felt the tension settle back into my shoulders and the back of my neck, but I didn't have much time to ponder the intentions of the man by the door or the mystery vampire he was involved with. A different kind of monster was waiting inside the building and I was less than thrilled about the prospect of facing any of them.

I had barely walked through the sliding glass doors when Jane, the production assistant, sprinted to my side. I could almost taste the panic. I knew before her mouth ever opened that today Georgia had sashayed in and thrown the news crew into a tizzy. After their brief and torrid affair, John Taine, the head anchor, had divorced his wife. I had overheard him planning to make a present of the signed papers to Georgia after their romantic dinner out last night. I also knew that yesterday Georgia had hooked a much bigger fish in the way of network executive Stanley Jackson. But I would let poor Jane explain, she looked like she would burst if she didn't get it out.

"Oh my god, Nora, you are my savior," she cried grabbing my hands. I could feel her pulse through her dark skin. I held my breath for a moment to compose myself. Normally humans shied away from my touch as if there was something in it that just wasn't quite right, but Jane never seemed bothered by it. From the moment I met her she was the only person in the entire building that I feared would find out my little secret. The way she looked at me with those curious brown eyes made me wonder sometimes if she knew already and was too afraid to speak up. However, I was apparently nowhere near as threatening as Georgia when she had a fit.

When I first met her, I thought Jane had been in the television business too long to be floored by anything, but today the fear was pounding through her veins. In fact, the entire building seemed to be buzzing. The adrenaline, frenzy, and stress were so palpable I could almost pluck it from the air. I suppressed the growl that was growing in my throat and tried not to think about how very long eight hours was while Jane described in detail the entire Georgia-John break-up scene. The elevator doors slid closed with an ominous thud.

"It was so bad this morning," she started.

I pressed the number 5 on the elevator wall and nodded encouragingly.

"Georgia walked in and we all knew that something was wrong. She just looked evil, you know?"

I nodded again and tried to look concerned.

"She just walked up to John and dropped his house key into his coffee and smiled," Jane fretted wringing her hands unhappily, "She didn't say a word. She just walked away and left John standing in the center of the studio. He hasn't been a normal color since. He was paler than you at first and then turned this scary crimson red color. It was just horrible." She shuddered. I hadn't missed the "paler than you" comment and it made me smirk as she continued to blather on about the screaming match that ensued.

She finally stopped talking and I took a deep breath. Her eyebrows knitted together, confused, when it registered that I was smiling. I quickly wiped the smirk off my face, shook my head and sighed, "Leave it to Georgia to destroy the morning news." Jane made a quiet little nervous sound which I assumed was meant to be a laugh. She was truly concerned about the outcome of this miniscule and ultimately meaningless little drama. It was so bad that I was beginning to think she would have permanent lines etched into her face. She cared more than anything that the news went off without a hitch and every time Georgia did anything that could in any way jeopardize the show Jane was distraught. Unfortunately for Jane, Georgia constantly did things that could put the show in jeopardy. Georgia was a one-woman wrecking crew when she wanted to be, and she wanted to be often.

Jane gave me her penetrating stare and I suddenly felt uneasy. She was one of the only humans who could do that to me. It was like she was examining everything that was in my heart and I didn't want to know what she was seeing. I looked up at the glowing numbers above the stainless steel doors and sighed. I self-consciously shoved my hands into my pockets and rocked back on my heels. "It'll be alright" I murmured furrowing my brow, but I couldn't pull off the whole concerned look. "This isn't the first time Georgia's broken somebody on the news crew's heart" I smiled trying to reassure her, but she didn't seem too sure.

"She's never broken the heart of anchor," she countered.

"She's broken the hearts of pretty much the rest of the crew, of course with the exception of Carter and Oliver," I laughed.

“That’s not the only issue here.”

“I know,” I looked at her seriously, “I’ll handle it when we get there.”

Jane folded her arms and slumped back against the railing exhaling slowly. She looked very annoyed as she stared daggers at my reflection in the doors. I smiled, but closed my eyes and took a deep breath to settle myself. Being trapped in an elevator with that warm sustenance so close was nearly unbearable. I considered just leaving after an hour and claim to be sick. I’m sure I could fake it. I mean seriously how hard could it be? But before I could lay the foundations for my ruse, the elevator’s door opened to the scene I had been expecting and dreading for days, the Georgia-John aftermath.

The personal assistants were all in a flurry trying desperately to make each one of their divas happy. John’s personal assistant, Michael, was staring angrily at me as I stepped out of the elevator. Like it was my job to police what Georgia did outside of the building! Georgia was sitting in a make-up chair with a martyred expression as the girls primped and prodded and made her look beautiful. Jane nearly bowled over Mary, the coffee girl, as she bolted out of the elevator. I suppressed a laugh at the sight. I looked around at nothing but knitted brows, angry mouths, and glowering eyes. They were everywhere and everyone seemed to be wearing a matching set.

The technical crew was the only exception. They moved in a manner that can only be described as fluid. It was like watching a dance. The lights moved one way, the cameras moved another, and all of them swirled together to create the morning news. Without them my day would be devoid of all art forms.

“Nora” rang out loud and clear, almost before my foot hit the cheap tan linoleum outside of the elevator.

There was no mistaking that grating voice. Georgia the bane of my existence, for this decade anyway, was already screeching at the top of her lungs. Jane grimaced beside me and I snorted in contempt.

“Nora.”

The tone of her voice made me want to growl. She was demanding and superior and she had only said one word. I needed a new job. As soon as she noticed that I wasn’t rushing to her side,

Georgia swung her arm across the counter causing the many lipstick tubes to clatter across the floor like a hailstorm. She sauntered towards me, shoving Janet, the beautician, out of the way.

"Nora, tell this woman that I only wear 'Passion Paradise' shade lipstick and that I will not wear whatever other hideous shade these social rejects are attempting to subject me to."

I forced myself to smile and fought the urge to roll my eyes at Jane who looked more and more every minute as though she were going to faint. Without even looking at her I could hear her heartbeat fluttering in her ribcage. I never understood why people treated Georgia as though she were the most important part of the production instead of the very replaceable anchorwoman she was. What was worse was how Georgia strutted around like she deserved all of the attention for reading off a teleprompter. Her attitude made me want to vomit. You would have thought the world was coming to an end the way she huffed and stomped about over a lipstick shade. Janet looked absolutely exasperated and I was calculating the odds as to whether Janet or Jane would faint first.

"Janet," I said stepping past Georgia, "What's the reason for the change?"

Janet fidgeted with the tube of lipstick that had started this fiasco, nearly dropping it several times. Her big hazel eyes were wide in apology. "It wasn't my idea," she whined softly; I thought the poor girl was going to break into tears.

"I'm not mad," I said softly, forcing my voice to sound soft and velvet smooth.

"It was Mr. Taine's idea," Janet cringed as Georgia huffed, but continued in a barely shaking voice, "He said that Ms. Stone was looking too pale with Passion Paradise and 'his angel needed to look like one.'"

Georgia screeched out a howl that made even me jump in surprise. "You fat heifer, since when do you take beauty tips from that asshole, John?"

In a very uncharacteristic move, Georgia lunged at Janet who dropped the tube of lipstick and cowered against the wall. I easily caught Georgia around the waist and held her back. I swear this was like patrolling kindergarteners. "Georgia," I reprimanded gently, "Janet was just trying to make you look as beautiful as possible, but I'm sure that she can use Passion Paradise if that's what you really want."

Georgia put away her claws and sat in the beautician's chair with a murderous glare for Janet. I smiled reassuringly at Janet and whispered for her to do whatever she thought was best. I must have gotten my expression under control or I was nowhere near as scary as Georgia on a bad day because Janet smiled at me thankfully and went back to her station.

Janet did, however, change out whatever shade she was originally going to use for the Passion Paradise. I tried not to, but I couldn't help smirking to myself. Georgia didn't realize that John was right; her beloved "Passion Paradise" really did make her look washed out under the lights. Her complete and total vanity just made that fact more satisfying.

To be honest, Georgia could have been beautiful. Her hair was a thick golden blonde. It highlighted her emerald green eyes and dark red lips. However, her physical appearance was not the issue with Georgia's beauty, it was deeper than that. Her smile, although sparkling white and perfectly straight, was empty and her eyes were malicious. Her actions and her words were only to achieve her own ends. She was one of the most selfish people I had ever met. So, although it was admittedly stupid and juvenile, I must say I secretly liked it when she looked less than her best. I guess you could consider that my vice, well one of them at least.

With all of the excitement the broadcast was expected to be a total disaster. But they were all far more professional than I had given them credit for. John had gotten his color and temper under control by the time Georgia placed herself next to him. Georgia was so pleased with her Passion Paradise that she barely noticed John existed. She primped her hair and fiddled with her shirt as though he was no more than a shadow made by the bright lights. I watched from behind the cameras as John's face began to pale, then darken to a near fuchsia color. He opened his mouth several times, but no sound actually came out of his mouth. Just when I thought he was actually going to form the words and let them escape from that cavern he considered a mouth, I got the signal in my earphones.

John cleared his throat and Georgia dabbed at her lipstick. When the cameras turned on you wouldn't have known that anything was wrong. John and Georgia both were flawless, made the requisite banter with one another, and once Georgia even patted John on the hand. Jane was beaming from ear to ear, pleased as punch that her little corner of the world was not going to disintegrate today. Afterward, of course, it was not quite so friendly. John accosted Georgia near the refreshment table.

"What was that all about?" he growled, grabbing her arm.

"What?" she hissed, pulling her arm away forcibly.

"That whole scene this morning…couldn't you have waited until we were alone?"

Georgia rolled her eyes and let out a huff turning back to the fruit platter.

"I thought it was just a little inappropriate, you know."

"Nobody cares about you, John," she snorted, tossing her long hair over her shoulder.

"I cared about you. I put my job on the line to get you promoted to anchor. I divorced my wife for you."

Georgia's smile reminded me of a villain from a 1950's movie. "Why do you think I chose you, Johnny boy?"

John's face drained of color as the realization dawned on him, "This was your plan? This entire time, you were just using me to get ahead?"

"Please," she huffed, "Don't think you are anything to tempt me."

"I thought…"

"Well that's your issue right there, you thought."

John's mouth hit the floor as he stammered incoherently.

Georgia sighed and sidled over to my side. "Nora," she grumbled dismissively waving her hand, "I need you to make it very clear to this idiot that I am done with him."

She turned on her stiletto heel and crossed her arms like a child confronted with broccoli. With her nose that high in the air it was amazing to me that she didn't tip over. Poor John, on the other hand, looked horrible. His face went stark white and his fists started to shake as he stared at Georgia's back. I wondered idly if he was wishing he had a knife. I think a lot of people felt that way about her.

Yet, looking properly enraged, he simply hissed the word "bitch" under his breath and stalked away. I could smell the salty tears as they rolled down his cheeks in time with his angry footsteps. I felt bad for the poor guy; although he should have known that Georgia's only intention was her own advancement. He was, after all, the fifth in line of Georgia's broken hearts club. But even with the trail of destruction that she continued to leave where she went, his heartbreak seemed genuine. It never ceased to amaze me how completely she was able to blind the men she was involved with. Their common sense seemed to completely dissolve with a simple smile from her. She smiled happily at my appalled expression and snickered, "He'll survive." I just stared, amazed in the knowledge that I was the lesser of the monsters in the room.

"I need you to pack up all my things from my dressing room," she prattled grabbing my arm and dragging me along behind her.

"I need to get the papers together before we head up to Alaska tomorrow," I countered gently pulling my arm back. What I considered gentle nearly knocked her off her feet, I smiled on the inside.

Unfortunately, it barely fazed her train of thought. "No problem, you'll just have to miss the party with the crew tonight."

I started to object, but then realized how perfect this excuse was. No one would ever doubt that I had gotten stuck in the office doing Georgia's bidding. I pretended to put up a fight for a few minutes then huffed, "Fine," and stomped away. I could almost see her smiling behind me. She always thought I did her bidding because I wanted to make her happy. She was so delusional in her own little world.

A few moments later, I was standing in the doorway of Georgia's dressing room and just staring at the mess. You would have thought that she would be able to get dressed at home, but of course not. The dressing room was one of the perks of sleeping with Charlie Kingsley, the building coordinator. For the three months she put into getting this rather miniscule closet, she didn't take care of it. There were heels scattered across the blue carpet and shirts thrown carelessly across the brown suede couch. In short, Georgia was a slob. The only good thing in this situation was that my "condition" left me with the ability to move much faster than an average human. In twenty minutes, I had packed Georgia's bag of "work clothes."

Of course, I packed the skimpiest clothes I could find; Georgia never liked to wear anything that fully covered her body. Low cut blouses, short shorts, tight pants, and belly shirts comprised most of her wardrobe. Not surprisingly she was hired by a male employee in the Human Resources Department. However, as skimpy as her clothes were, the sheer volume of them made up for the lack of fabric. With all of the clothes she had stuffed into her dressing room, I shuddered at even the thought of what her closet at home looked like.

I quickly shoved the duffel bag under a pile of clothes just in case Georgia came by to see if I had been there already and went to speak with Terri Bentley, the travel coordinator extraordinaire. She was the person who thought ahead enough to issue us every possible piece of documentation we would ever need. She even made sure that each of us had our passports, even though we were traveling in the United States. When I asked her about it she replied condescendingly, "What if there's bad weather and you have to stop in Canada?" I swear that woman thought through every worse case scenario.

I knew the standard traveling papers were issued and signed before I even stepped through the office doors. Terri was always one step ahead of the game, and I loved that. Most people who worked here avoided her office at all costs. She wasn't exactly the most personable employee, but I liked the way she handled business and left the drama to the rest of the peons. It meant that I never had to stand in her office for thirty minutes listening to the latest gossip before I got what I needed. I swung open the heavy oak door and stepped onto the gray marble-esque tile that Terri insisted her office be covered in. She didn't even look up as I walked in.

"Papers are in the folder." She waved her hand dismissively towards the counter.

"What would we do without you, Terri?"

She harrumphed and grumbled, "Well, you wouldn't be going anywhere that's for sure." I laughed and she snorted wagging her finger at me, "Have fun, and don't forget that I need all of the receipts for everything. Don't let Georgia anywhere with the company credit card."

I snorted and huffed, "Have you ever known me to let Georgia anywhere without supervision?"

Terri just grumbled and went back to her computer. I had been dismissed.

The door swung shut behind me and I was free. I was nearly skipping as I made my way back to Georgia's dressing room to grab the duffel bags. With the work done and the morning news wrapped up the crew should have left, but Carter Greyson and Oliver Green were standing at Georgia's dressing room door when I got there. Carter was worrying his bottom lip and Oliver kept spinning his ring around his finger nervously. I was not going to like the reason behind their obvious tension. "Boys, what's going on?" I asked cautiously, walking past them and opening Georgia's door. Jake cleared his throat nervously as I walked through the doorway and that's when I saw it. Amazingly, it looked even worse than before I cleaned it. I stopped in the doorway stunned.

"What?" I stammered.

Oliver cleared his throat hesitantly, "John thought…"

I held up my hand to stop him and smirked, "'John thought' was enough of an explanation."

Carter spoke up, "We came to help you clean up, but we didn't want to go in without you."

"I thought burning it would be the best option," Oliver sneered.

I snickered and shook my head. Carter and Oliver had arrived at the station nearly six months ago and we immediately hit it off. They really were good guys and I was glad they were the two we were bringing with us to Alaska.

"It's alright guys," I said smiling, "You should get to the party. Don't want to miss all the good gossip; I'm counting on you to tell me about it tomorrow on the plane."

They both looked relieved. Carter smiled and turned to go, but Oliver turned back hesitantly, "Are you sure you don't want help? We would rather have you see the spectacle first hand you know."

I smiled and told them I wasn't really missing anything and to go on without me. Carter didn't need to be told twice, he grabbed Oliver's arm, and blew me a kiss over his shoulder as he took off down the hallway.

After they left, I surveyed the mess. Granted, it had never been very clean to begin with, but this was ridiculous. John had never struck me as the most intelligent person, but this was just plain dumb. I mean seriously? Are you kidding me? Throw her stuff around the room? It wasn't like he thought she was really the one who would clean it up. I growled and rolled my head around my shoulders. I thought I heard the click of a camera shutter and spun around, too quickly. It wasn't human enough. I surveyed the hallway, but there was no one in sight. I took a deep breath and caught the lingering scent of the mystery man I had seen earlier. I moved as quickly as possible while still attempting to maintain my cover, but he was nowhere in sight. Even the scent seemed to dissipate into the air as I moved forward. It unnerved me, but there was nothing I could do about it now. He and his mystery agenda would just have to wait.

My thoughts were consumed by it as I returned to the disaster zone. I slumped against the doorframe. I was not looking forward to this monstrous undertaking. I glanced behind me again to make sure whoever was after me was not still watching from around a corner and closed the door quietly. I slowly checked the room for any hidden surveillance and found none. I breathed a sigh of relief. It would take a normal person upwards of an hour to clean this mess, it only took me ten minutes to flit around the room and put it all back in order. Then it was off to the task that had been on my mind since I woke up. I was off to hunt.

2. Thrill of the Hunt

Hunting was always a frightening ordeal. Finding prey was easy enough, but I needed to stop feeding before I killed my victim and I needed to make sure no one saw what was going on. The latter was important for obvious reasons. I can't imagine my already crippled social life would survive a rumor that someone saw me draining the blood from a hobo's neck. I guess I didn't really need to keep my victim alive, but I always felt so guilty if they died. There were only two in the last 100 years who didn't survive, but the memories are less than pleasant.

Honestly, I hadn't meant to kill the first man, I didn't even know who he was. But even after sixty years, that day still played through my mind. It was Mid-march in Connecticut, quite cold outside. I, unfortunately, am just as susceptible to hot and cold as any human, but I've never been rolling in the dough so all I had was a threadbare coat as I walked home that night. At that time in my terribly long life, I was a maid for a fairly wealthy family. I can still remember being so frustrated about the preparations for the stupid party we were throwing for the daughter of my wealthy employer, Katie Rose. John Rose, Katie's father, had arranged for the son of the wealthiest man in town to marry his precious little peacock. She would strut and preen as though the world lived only to serve her. It's kind of been a theme in my employers. Her father saw to it that no one disillusioned his princess. So, when Katie's eye fell on the young and handsome Cameron Walters, he was acquired with no more ado than if Mr. Rose were acquiring a new Thoroughbred stallion for his stables.

The infamous Cameron Walters was to be married into the Rose family in late December. This little event that we had been working interminably on for about a month was merely an engagement gala. It was awkward being forced to deal with the princess and the snake. There wasn't a maid or single girl in town that hadn't felt the uncomfortable stares of the young Walters. I still remember when he cornered me in the kitchen the first time he had been invited over for dinner. He made my skin crawl, but at least he knew better than to make another advance. He had reached for me and I nearly broke his wrist in my defense. The thought of the look in his eyes still made me shudder.

Through my reveries about the upcoming annoyance and forced exposure to the sleaziest man I had ever met, I had noted a man stepping out of a local bar. He was alone and his feet scraped against the sidewalk as he stumbled forward. He was quite shnookered and I wrote him off as essentially harmless. I could smell the alcohol in his blood from twenty feet away and from the drunken swearing, I figured he was more interested in yelling at his wife when he got home than in bothering me. I put him out of my mind and the memories of how Cameron had attempted to seduce me and Katie's supreme arrogance saturated my thoughts. They made my blood boil and for some reason I tended to dwell on the negative in upcoming events rather than hope for the best. I puzzled at how I didn't feel any sort of attraction to him, not like any of the other women seemed to. The other girls seemed to fall all over him, even Katie, who was not unattractive or undesired, seemed completely smitten by that jackal. She didn't even seem to notice how he cozied up to anything with breasts. I was so baffled by this that I was caught off guard by the drunk I had moments before dismissed from my thoughts.

He grabbed my arm and threw me into an alleyway before I even had time to scream. He was on top of me before I thought to react. All I could think was how incredibly absurd this situation was as his body pinned mine to the ground and his heavy hand clamped over my mouth. The scent of the whiskey that emanated from every pore of his body was suffocating. He made a growling throaty laugh that seemed to come from deep in his soul and he smiled sickeningly when he noticed my widened eyes. He just didn't realize it was amazement instead of fear that gave me those unbelieving baby blues. I was completely in shock that this puny little human thought he could take advantage of me, but I must admit that my disbelief put me on my heels and I did not react as I should have.

When his clumsy fingers grasped at my coat it snapped me out of my shock and I acted. With a movement that was far too quick for his weak human eyes to notice I turned the tables and he was pinned below me. Now it was my turn to stare into his startled eyes, they were both surprised and excited. He smiled and tried to grab my wrists, he thought I was receptive. He laughed and for a moment I was taken aback. I couldn't imagine what he found funny about this situation. Again my disbelief stinted my reaction time. The drunk reached down and pulled a knife out of his boot. Without thinking my upper lip pulled back from my teeth and I growled savagely. I was so angry that he thought he could take advantage of me! That he found this so funny! That he thought he could threaten me! That I sunk my teeth into his neck. I felt the knife plunge into my side and it only succeeded in upsetting me more. I didn't realize that I had gone too far until it was too late. His body was limp and lifeless below me.

The sight revolted me so much I didn't even notice the wound on my side as it healed. I shivered in the cold and scampered back away from the corpse. I wasn't sure how long I sat against the wall of the building staring at my hideous work, but it had to have been hours. His eyes were open, staring at me, judging me, watching me in all my horror. All of the annoyances that had plagued my thoughts on my walk home seemed decades away. I couldn't take it anymore, I ran. I ran and left his body to be discovered by someone else, anyone else. I just needed to get away.

The next morning another bar patron found his drained body and reported it to the police. They refused to release any information to the public about how he had been killed, but there were rumors. Some said there was a psychopath on the loose that slashed his throat, others said there was a monstrous animal on the loose that had ripped his throat out. It was all gross exaggeration. I had never been that sloppy or vicious. The rest of the women on the Rose house staff were all afraid to walk home on their own and I traveled in the pack with them, not wanting to stand out from the crowd. Only I knew the only thing to fear out there was me. The murder continued to go unsolved and my conscious continued to nag at me that there was something fundamentally wrong in my make-up if I was able to do such a horrible deed.

It was raining the day of the funeral. I don't know why, but something compelled me to go and watch the ceremony. I stood apart from everyone, pretending to look at a different gravestone while the ceremony took place. I watched as the wife laid flowers on the casket before it was lowered and I could see the fear and sorrow in the eyes of her son. Their heartbreak was tangible. I watched as the mother's shoulders hunched protectively around her son while neighbors shook their hands and whispered their condolences, but I knew that when they went home that place in their hearts would be empty.

Yet it was my victim's son that I couldn't look away from. The boy was maybe ten years old and was suddenly forced to be the man of the house. It was more responsibility than he should have to endure, and I was the cause. The guilt crashed over me in waves. It weighed down on my chest to the point that I couldn't breath. I gasped for air as the tears started flowing down my cheeks. I don't know how long I stood there crying. My eyes adjusted to the dark almost imperceptibly, but the realization that the night creatures were creating a symphony around me drove the vision of that child standing over his father's grave from my mind. I ran.

But that was decades ago and tonight I needed to feed. I finished putting on my make-up, but the creature in the mirror wasn't me. It was some dark perversion of me. The woman in the mirror's blue eyes stared at me and fiddled with her blue top, but there was something in her eyes that made me turn away in fear and disgust. This was me, the monster, and tonight I needed to be for the safety of everyone else tomorrow.

It was in a dark state of mind that I walked into a local bar. And what to my wandering eyes should appear, but my little wanna-be thief from this morning. I felt a dark laugh build up in my throat as I stood there. I had found my evening meal. He was sitting at the end of the bar hitting on a girl in a rust orange dress. Perhaps it was a bit hypocritical for me to sneer at the woman's short dress since I was in a miniskirt and low top, but I did anyway. Her dark eyes kept darting back and forth like she was looking for someone to save her. I smiled and a business man in a suit nearly walked into the door he was so busy staring. I found myself a stool at the bar and ordered a martini. Truth be told, I have never liked martinis. My preferred drink was a nice daiquiri or Amaretto Sour, but the martini completed the look. I glanced around me coquettishly at the men who were staring at my legs. I was in awe of this monster that could sit among all of this deliciously close sustenance and control herself, the one who could turn a man's head with only a smile. She was a fearsome creature to behold.

My little thief flirted unsuccessfully with the rust clad woman. She shifted her weight from one foot to the other nervously. She was trapped between my prey and the wall. She kept looking desperately at a couple of girls who were sitting in a booth across the room. I assumed they were supposed to be her friends, but they just giggled and waved at her while the thief slurred his advances. With friends like that... The burn in my throat flared as the bartender passed a little too closely by me. I needed to make my move before my self-control reached its end. So I stood up with my martini and strolled down the length of the bar.

As I strode past the bar in my stiletto heels, every man there ran his eyes over my legs. I hate it when men do that. I strolled casually towards my little thief while the burn throbbed in my throat almost unbearably. I sidled up beside the little jerk and whispered, "Remember me," in his ear. He stiffened quickly and stared through the girl in the rust dress. She was frozen in place staring at me with a frightened look. I smiled, hoping that she would take the opportunity to slip away. She apparently wasn't that smart. She stared at me and her expression went from being shocked and amazed to being offended. Her eyes held that competitive gleam that I was so used to seeing in Georgia's.

It never ceased to amaze me how these women survived since they were constantly trying to tear out each others throats. The best part of that was that she didn't even want the sniveling excuse for a man in front of her, but she didn't want his attention taken away from her. I could feel the eyes of her catty friends behind me staring daggers and every man in the place was beginning to wonder why this little runt was getting the attention and they were being ignored.

The girl stared for a moment longer before she opened her mouth to speak. "Run along dear," my voice barely concealed the underlying threat. I felt the pulse of my little thief quicken at my voice. I hadn't spoken to him before, but somehow he instinctively feared the sound. The girl, however, didn't and I noticed that the bar was becoming more and more interested in our little exchange.

I leaned over to my thief and whispered, "Why don't we get out of here." It wasn't a question and the spike in his amazingly tempting blood proved that he already knew that. His breathing hitched as he turned to face me. Amazingly enough the rust clad woman still didn't take the hint as she sneered, "I think we were having a conversation." The whiny tone of her voice grated on my ears. It sounded like a mouse suddenly felt like chiming into the repartee. I laughed and the sound seemed to engulf the entire room. My little thief was enthralled, his eyes held nothing but childlike admiration and awe. I sighed and shook my head at the tenacious woman saying, "Well if he'd prefer hamburger instead of filet mignon I suppose I'll leave." My prey bolted up out of his seat and grabbed my arm before I had a chance to fully turn around.

I smiled quietly and proceeded to walk out the door with my prey following me like a little puppy. It was almost too easy. I took his hand and stepped out into the night. My eyes adjusted quickly to the dark, but my little thief stumbled over every crack in the pavement catching himself on my arm every time. The constant tripping and tugging was beginning to wear on my nerves as we approached the sage green sedan that was his. He stumbled to his door and attempted to open it by scratching his keys across the paint. My stomach turned wondering how many nights he had gotten behind the wheel in this condition. A growl rumbled deep in chest at the thought of how many innocent people he had put in danger with his inability to regulate his addiction.

The lock popped up and I gently took his hand. I cooed, "Why don't you let me drive?" He nodded and went to kiss me. I ducked out of the way of his alcohol soaked breath and laughed, "Not yet," as I took the keys. He stumbled around to the other side of the car as I cranked it up and "Play That Funky Music White Boy" blasted out of the speakers. He turned the radio off with a blush and said, "Just drive to the light and turn left." I sped out of his parking spot and took the turn at 70. My thief hastily tried to buckle his seat belt as we wheeled through the next couple of turns. Unfortunately, he couldn't control his innards and threw up on the thin tan carpet.

The smell gagged me and I had no choice but to roll down the window. Even though the heightened senses were usually a bonus to this whole half breed thing, the downside was horrendously obvious. I nearly had to stick my head out the window to breath. Luckily we were only a block away from his driveway…correction, his parent's driveway. I stepped out of the car and stared at the family of garden gnomes that stared back with unblinking black eyes. The thief touched my elbow and in my surprise I pinned him up against the car with a growl. His eyes widened in fear and tears were rolling down his face as he looked at me, but his jaw was set. He knew in that instant, just as he had known earlier that I could kill him without breaking a sweat. He recognized me now where he hadn't in the bar and the fear dampened his blue jeans, but even through the scent of urine I was focused only on the terror in his face. I was truly a monster to inspire such horror.

My lips were curled back, my teeth bared, the sweet pulsation of blood was barely inches away and I couldn't do it. I wanted to so badly, but I couldn't get past his fear. I stepped back and the man slid down the side of the car into a pile on the asphalt driveway. He didn't speak, but stared defiantly, the salty tears wetting his cheeks. I took a few more steps back nearly tripping over the family of gnomes and whispered gruffly, "Know you just nearly died." He didn't move, just stared at me as I walked away.

I hardly waited until I was out of sight before I started running. I pushed myself to run faster and faster, but the fear and revulsion just followed. I ran into an alleyway and started heaving. I had wasted too much time on a failed conquest. I was exhausted from the long day and the lack of blood was making me more and more weak. I gasped for air and tried to calm the hysteria that was rising in my chest. A few deep breaths later and I pushed away from the wall. I slunk home very dejectedly through the back alleyways of Philadelphia. I grabbed a couple of rats next to a dumpster outside my apartment building. I hated the way they tasted, but at least they dulled the burning. I knew it would be enough to get me through the 7:00 flight, but I was not happy about it. I would have to feed my first night in Alaska and that could pose its own set of issues.

I got home and went to the refrigerator. A drink of cold water felt good, but this wasn't a surface thing. This burn was deeper, and it was nearly impossible to ever quench it entirely. I walked to the bedroom discarding clothes as I went. I pulled on my silk pajamas and snuggled myself down into the covers. It was cold in my apartment, and I was chilled from the run home. I curled into a ball and snuggled my warmth away from the outside. I closed my eyes and hoped desperately that I would be able to sleep uninterrupted tonight.

I was running. I was running and it was freezing cold outside. The lack of blood made me weak and this dream always followed failed conquests. There was wind whipping through trees and snow was beginning to fall. I couldn't feel my toes in the arctic winter. I hurt. It wasn't physical. My toes only registered as a thought, not a feeling. It felt like a hole had been ripped through my chest. I could feel my heart beating, but it might as well have been an empty void. I felt broken inside. In the dream my throat hurt, but not any worse than normal. I knew the part that was coming up, the part that would wake me up in a cold sweat. I was reaching the cliff. I felt my toes reach the end of solid ground and looked down into a dark abyss. I couldn't tell what was in the abyss, but I jumped. I didn't know why, but I knew I had to.

I sat straight up and a vase flew off my dresser and shattered against the door. This is why I hated this dream. Every time I had it I broke something else. I made a note to deal with the pile of glass tomorrow and sank back into the deep dreamless blackness that always followed the "running dream."

3. Place your seats in their upright and locked positions

The next morning brought the same ache in my throat only intensified by the new one in my head. I hadn't slept well, my head and body screamed, I was about to travel with Georgia which was always an ordeal, and I was cranky. The day sucked before I ever rolled back the covers. I slapped the off button on the clock alarm with extreme prejudice and thanked silently whoever invented indoor plumbing. The nearly burning hot water of the shower massaged away the aches in my body. At least this was a good moment.

All my issues started to melt away as I turned the nozzle head to massage. I nearly purred as the water pummeled my body. I stood there contemplating the undertaking ahead until the hot water started to run cold. It was time and the chill of my apartment sent shivers down my back as I pulled my bathrobe around my shoulders. I wondered if the sudden chill was the air or my thoughts about my intended destination.

I stood in the warm air of my hair dryer much longer than I had thought and had to rush through my makeup. Inevitably as I rushed I managed to smear my mascara beneath my eye, the racoons would have been jealous. I quickly threw all of my toiletries in my carry on as my buzzer rang. Perfect timing, it was my cab.

I ran into the bedroom to get dressed and saw that my cell was blinking. It was Jane, "911-GS on rampage." The tension settled back between my shoulders as I pushed my sunglasses on top of my head. I took a last look around my apartment, making sure I had turned off the iron and the lights, before I grabbed my bag and locked the door. I hated that feeling when I left on a trip, the one where I think I forgot something and usually realized later that I had.

Still, I ran out the front door of my apartment building going over in my head the usual suspects for being left behind and nearly knocked over the old woman who lived in the apartment below me. I apologized politely, but she just glared. She knew there was something wrong with me and the way she acted threw me off. The human part of me usually put people at ease. In fact, people were usually attracted to me unless I was trying to be otherwise. But she would always skirt around me, even if I was trying to be sweet and charming. I am pretty sure she was Romanian. All the apartments in Philadelphia and the half-vampire entity picks the one with a Romanian who believes in monsters living below her. Can you say ironic?

I chuckled to myself as I handed my bags to the cabbie. Thankfully there was nothing breakable in there as he chucked it into the trunk like he was throwing shot-put. I jumped into the back and told him to floor it to the airport. He grunted in acknowledgment and I was slammed against the uncomfortable back seat as he literally put the accelerator to the ugly gray carpet and we catapulted into the street. Luckily, the streets were nearly empty at this hour in the morning. I slumped back in the seat as I wondered how incredibly horrid Georgia was planning on being today. I should have known that she had been far too calm yesterday. The storm was bound to come. The cabbie flew through traffic lights as I reluctantly flipped open my phone and called Jane. Her voice was shaken as she answered.

“What happened now?” I asked trying not to sound as annoyed as I felt.

“I don’t know,” she whispered, “Georgia just keeps muttering about 'that damn asshole’ and no one knows who she’s talking about.”

“Well, what happened last night at the party?”

“She met up with the liaison the Air Force sent down..um...” it sounded like she was flipping through notes, “Sgt. Timothy Bracken. Oh my god Nora, he was hot, but anyway they seemed to hit it off, but he’s not here yet. Maybe that’s who she means?”

“Did John do anything to mess up her little thing last night?”

“No, John was nowhere to be seen, so I don’t think she means him unless he called her or something.”

“How bad is it?”

“It’s been worse, but she is raising hell with everyone. We’re all standing in front of the Delta counter and I’m afraid they’ll ban her from the flight if you don’t get here soon and calm her down.”

The cab made the all to familiar turn into the airport and I grimaced, "We're pulling into the terminal now, I'll be there in a minute."

I clicked the phone shut as the cab driver pulled into the terminal drop off lane. He just held out his hand without a word. Gotta love that Philly hospitality. I gave him forty dollars on a thirty-two dollar tab and he just shoved it all in his pocket. I muttered "keep the change" rather than deal with him as I climbed out and looked up at the cloudy sky. As I was pulling my bags from the trunk a light snow began to fall, it was beautiful. In all of this crazy morning, the one thing I was sure of was the December I was leaving behind was going to be nothing compared to the December I would be arriving to in Alaska.

Since finding out about the trip I had researched Alaska. I am a complete nerd. I can't go anywhere without thoroughly researching it. I found out many interesting tidbits, information about the aurora borealis, local wildlife, weather patterns, and I realized the average temperature was -7 degrees Fahrenheit. Not exactly Tahiti. I felt like an absolute idiot walking around in a brisk Philadelphia morning in an overstuffed parka, but the less I had to check the better. A man scurrying towards the cab rolled his eyes at me and huffed as he pulled the door shut behind him. I frowned and tried to gently close the cab trunk. I succeeded in making the car shudder. It was going to be a very long day.

Yet the upcoming weather situation and the rude people in the airport were low on the list of priorities right now. Again Georgia had managed to steal the spotlight. What should have been a wonderful trip to a place none of us had ever seen before was being turned into a nightmare by her antics. I was tired, I was cranky, I was thirsty, and I was not about to deal with any more of her crap. I took a deep breath as the sliding doors to the terminal opened. I heard Georgia before I saw her.

"NORA," I grimaced and felt my eyes start to burn, "Get over here NOW!" I shouldered my bag and stalked towards the Delta counter. I didn't bother to attempt to control myself as I glowered at the selfish child that stood there tapping her foot with a look of superiority on her face. I had had enough and I was ready to explode. There was a growl growing in the back of my throat as I towered over Georgia. I felt my lips pull back into a snarl and for what I believed was the first time in her life Georgia shrank in fear. I could hear the heartbeats around us spike and I could smell the fear fueled adrenaline pump through their veins.

Georgia's reaction was no different and her bottom lip started to quiver. Her warm blood was pumping just below her skin barely inches away, but I knew I couldn't fulfill that need here. Besides, at this point I was sure that I would kill her. My instincts were pretty well governed by my consciousness, but not even my conscious self was entirely sold on leaving her to live. My eyes and my throat both felt as though they were on fire. My teeth ground together as I hissed "What Georgia? What could be so important that you would ruin everybody's morning? We are already going to have a long flight and you can't help but be a bitch to start it off. What do you want?"

Her eyes grew wide for a second and the color completely drained from her face. She tried to say something but all that came out was a terrified squeak. My nostrils flared and I snapped straight up in a move that I realized was too quick to be fully human. I needed to calm down. I took a deep breath through my mouth so I didn't have the temptation of her blood in my head and stepped back from the trembling little twit. I felt slightly bad that I had been so forceful. She was, after all, only human. I rolled my head around to loosen my shoulders. It didn't relax any of the sheep that surrounded me, but it made me feel so much better. I took a another deep breath that registered the faint scent of vampire and that snapped me out of the rage I felt welling up inside of me. She wasn't here, but her scent certainly was.

I turned on my heel and stalked to the ticket counter. The color hadn't returned to Georgia's face yet, and every other member of this little expedition was frozen in their place staring after me. It was getting to be time for me to move on. I wasn't going to be able to handle dealing with this for much longer. But the much more pressing issue was the possibility of what that vampire scent meant. I knew that man from yesterday was the key to what was going on, but I couldn't figure out what I was supposed to know. My brows knitted together as I thought of the mystery. I didn't even realize that I was still my fairly scary self at the moment.

As I dropped my purse on the gray laminate counter I took in the look of horror on the Delta clerk's face. I tried to wipe all traces of hostility off my face. "I'm sorry about this," I whispered in the velvety smooth voice reserved for these situations, "Sometimes she can just get so out of hand. I'm sure you've had a boss like that before?" The girl's face relaxed and her mouth twitched at the corners as she nodded. I smiled and handed her all of the necessary paperwork. As she handed me the boarding passes her eyes lit up, but she wasn't looking at me. She was looking just over my shoulder. This is why I hate crowded places; it is very hard to hear individuals.

I sniffed over my shoulder and caught a whiff of the same vampire scent I had smelled a moment ago. It was stronger now, less than 2 hours old at most. He had seen his vampire sweetheart recently. Stupid human, I wondered if he knew he was playing with death. I turned around and saw the face I had been expecting and the expression on that face answered my earlier question. He knew exactly what he was doing and the strange glimmer in his eyes frightened me. I wasn't sure what he and his vampire friend were up to, but I knew I was playing a pivotal role in it and had a feeling I wasn't going to like it.

Air Force liaison, Sgt. Timothy Bracken, stood before me in his uniform. My eyes narrowed despite my attempt to control my expression. I figured it would be more diplomatic to be polite, so I curled my lips back in what was supposed to be a smile. His eyes widened in fear and the breath caught in his throat so I figured I hadn't achieved the disarming demeanor I had been aiming for. However, I was enjoying the thought of his fear. He had no idea who he was messing with. I must give him credit though, he composed his expression in a second. He held his hand out to me and I took it as he introduced himself. He almost seemed surprised at my touch as if he wasn't sure I was really real. His voice, however, was haughty and superior as he announced his name, like I didn't already know who he was from the stripes and name tag.

Not surprisingly, Georgia was not to be ignored for long. She seemed to overcome her fear of me as she came bounding over to the dashing young sergeant, with nothing but smiles. The attendant at the counter was as, if not more, impressed by the young man. I could feel the heartbeats pounding around him. The young attendant at the counter nearly hyperventilated when Sgt. Bracken turned his dark eyes and too perfect smile in her direction. Georgia, however, was the one who surprised me with the small spike in heart rate when he smiled at her.

I figured she would have had no reaction due to the many admirers she had in the past, but I could tell by her smile she was positive that every reaction she had to him, he was having tenfold towards her. She was wrong. It was as though he didn't even notice the near panting of the human women around him. His heartbeat remained steady except for an occasional adrenaline rush when he looked in my direction. It wasn't attraction from the expression on his face. He was hunting.

His eyes were appraising as they quickly moved over my body. He was quick, but it still made me squirm to have someone so obviously see though my pretenses. He knew what I was and that frightened me. What was more frightening was that from his expression, he liked it. It had taken no more than 30 seconds for him to introduce himself to me, but every tick of my watch felt like an eternity. The acidic smell, his eyes, and the way every woman seemed magnetically drawn to him put me on edge. Who was this man? Even the make-up woman Janet, whom I hadn't seen with a man in the three years she had been working with us, was ogling him. It wasn't normal. Granted he was handsome, but he wasn't any more handsome than any of the other men Georgia had paraded around with. He *was* entirely human, but there was something unnatural about him at the same time. I had chills.

I walked past him as politely as I could manage and handed the boarding passes to their respective owners. Oliver and Carter were taking stock of the equipment and making sure everything was in order. Carter wagged his eyebrows at me like a villain in a fifties movie. I rolled my eyes and Oliver snickered.

"Everything alright boss?" Oliver asked, trying to gauge my reaction to the morning's festivities.

I sighed, "It's about as alright as it's gonna get boys."

Oliver laughed, "Well it seems that the young ladies are quite taken with your friend there."

"Please," I snorted, "Pretty boy over there wishes he was my type."

Carter laughed, "Why don't we get pretty boy to help us carry these things?"

I shook my head and slung a camera bag over my shoulder.

"What and ruin his hair?" Oliver said in mock horror.

I couldn't help but smile.

Oliver and Carter were both big burly men, and they made me laugh just about every time I spoke to them. I would be sad to leave them when the time came. Too bad I couldn't bring them with me, but I couldn't even let them know what I was. I grunted picking up another bag of equipment, it wasn't actually heavy, but I shouldn't be able to lift these things without some sort of physical reaction. "Let's just get this stuff past security," I sighed, "That should only take us a couple of hours." Carter groaned and Oliver sighed heavily, but we all grabbed bags and cases. We also all noticed that the good Sergeant, Georgia, and Janet didn't so much as pick up their own things. I made a point to leave everything that wasn't mine or equipment related lying on the tile floor.

We looked at one another incredulously as we heard Georgia's giggles and Janet's sighs as the dashing Sergeant regaled them with stories about Alaska and the beauty of the Aurora Borealis, although "its beauty is nothing in comparison to Ms. Stone's." He made me want to vomit, and for once I heard Georgia's heart skip a beat at the compliment. I didn't understand why. She never had a response like that to anyone, let alone a man. Oliver made a gagging face and Carter rolled his eyes. This young man was unbelievable.

I turned and called for Janet sharply. Although my voice was no where near as rough as before, Georgia's eyes widened slightly and Janet cringed. Apparently my outburst this morning was going to have some lingering side effects. I smiled to myself as Georgia positioned herself next to Sgt. Bracken in a way that he would be forced to protect her if I attacked. Janet dropped her head and slunk to my side, picking up her bags as she did. Georgia cooed for the sergeant to pick up her bags as she walked past us all to the security checkpoint. Her expression was a strange mixture of defiance and fear. I glared and she quickly adverted her eyes.

Timothy smiled and then pulled a move I didn't expect. He looked straight into my eyes, smile wide and innocent, and then asked Oliver and Carter in sickeningly sweet voice, "Can I help you gentlemen carry these?" His eyes never left mine. He was mocking me, testing me, trying to see how far he could push me. I wondered if he knew how thirsty I was because now he was first in line to be my meal. He took one of the heavier cases from Carter who looked at me quizzically and took one of the cases I had been holding. I smiled as gratefully as I could manage. I hadn't expect the Sergeant to publicly engage me like that.

He was toying with me. He wanted to see how much I would reveal when provoked, and he was trying to provoke me. Quite a clever little monkey. Whomever the vampire was controlling this, they had picked a good little puppet. I could feel my lips twitch into a little half smile as I place my bags on the security counter and reached into my purse for the proper documentation. This was going to be a game. The only part that bothered me was that I didn't know what the stakes were. I like to know what I'm playing for before the starting gun, but I had no choice in this one. I thought about just asking him, but figured that he would play dumb anyway. This little intrigue was going to make for an interesting trip.

As we approached the security counter, the female guard gave Sgt. Bracken the same stricken look the Delta clerk had. I almost expected her to pick him out for a "random" pat down. I rolled my eyes and took a deep breath.

Luckily for me, security didn't seem to be in on the plan to make this the longest day of my very long existence. All the bags were checked through with no fuss and even with a warm smile for me from one of the younger men. I was actually flattered. I felt myself blush slightly. I was always overshadowed by Georgia's flamboyancy. I smiled back at the young man shyly and heard a faint snicker behind me. It was so low I couldn't be sure but I had a feeling it was Sgt. Bracken.

The plane ride was a nightmare. First, I was seated nowhere near either Carter or Oliver. I wasn't even seated near Georgia, Janet, or the annoying Sergeant Bracken, who seemed to have every stewardess wrapped around his finger. I was seated behind the wing where the sound of the engine thrummed through the cabin like a parade in full force. My chair vibrated with the concussion. I was hoping I could just block out this day by catching a little sleep, but as soon as my seat tipped the screaming behind me began.

The shrill voice of a child trilled, “Mommy, she’s going to crush me with her seat.” I growled under my breath and snapped my seat into its upright and locked position. Then the kicking started. I glanced back with a glare that would have made most adults soil themselves but this child seemed oblivious. He was only too happy to screech at the top of his lungs about how he didn’t want to go to New York, as he continued to run up and down the back of my seat. I could feel my patience reaching its end the more Mommy dearest cooed, “Now Tommy, stop that,” “Sweetie, you’re making the nice lady uncomfortable,” “I’ll get you whatever you want honey, just please stop kicking the back of the nice lady’s seat.”

A shiver went down my spine and suddenly there was no more kicking. I knew before I even looked back there what I had done. I snarled under my breath, I hated when this happened and I didn’t need to risk everything in front of the vampire’s spy. I snapped my head around and glared at the little monster in the making. His mother was hysterically patting his head and shoulders whispering, “Honey, Sweetie, what’s wrong?” “Can you move honey?” The kid looked as though he had been hit by a shock wave. I smiled on the inside, but I whispered “Is he alright?” anyway and tried to look as concerned as possible.

The mother looked at me in horror. Her eyes were wide and her bottom lip trembled. Tears were welling up into her eyes and it looked like she was about to break down. I felt a swell of disgust hit me. It was the mother’s fault the kid was so obnoxious, but then again I couldn’t keep the kid pinned to the seat for the *entire* flight anyway. I sighed and felt goosebumps race down my arms. The child began to squirm and tears rolled down his cheeks. The mother glowed as the relief flowed through her. She pulled her son into her lap and rocked him back and forth, cooing incoherently.

I turned and rolled my eyes as the mother continued to fret over her little hooligan. There was still an hour until we landed. I closed my eyes but I doubted seriously that I would be able to go to sleep, even for a quick catnap. I could feel his eyes on me. He had been watching me almost from the moment we had boarded.

They were a few rows ahead of me and somehow Georgia had finagled her way into a seat right next to her latest target. The good Sergeant had been playing the attentive admirer role for Georgia when necessary, it amazed me that she didn't notice the absolute disinterest that colored his voice. Or that his attention was focused solely on me. I didn't like the feeling. So, as childish as it was, when he turned to glance at me I looked him dead in the face and stuck out my tongue. He looked taken aback, so I smiled widely and bared my teeth. He snorted and turned back to face the front of the plane. I closed my eyes in childish satisfaction and the next thing I knew we were landing in New York.

It felt so wonderful to stand up and stretch. We got off the plane and almost immediately Carter and Oliver were at my side. I slumped my head against Oliver's shoulder and sighed dramatically. Carter snickered, "So I saw your little friend there. How was your impromptu massage?" I glared and Oliver laughed and put his arm around my shoulders as we wandered through John F. Kennedy International Airport looking for our next gate. It was a blessing that Terri had made all of the arrangements. She was always good at getting connecting flights that lined up with the least amount of wait time. We were only sitting at the gate for twenty minutes before boarding started. It was just enough time for me to scarf down one of the delicious soft pretzels I had nabbed in the airport in Philly.

For this leg of the journey the airline gods smiled upon me, I was conveniently seated next to Carter in the middle of the plane, and far away from Sergeant Bracken and any children. As soon as we took off Carter started talking about what I had missed the night before. I really wished I hadn't missed it now that my brilliant plan to hunt had fallen through. But if someone was going to tell it, I was glad it was him.

He started with, "Oh my God, Nora, you will never believe what you missed last night." I smiled and leaned back in my seat knowing that I wouldn't have to supply much of the conversation as he continued, "So, after Olly and I left you at Georgia's dressing room, we went to the lobby and met up with the rest of the crew. Georgia was nowhere to be seen and we were all thrilled.

Honestly, I'm amazed that she wasn't connected to Janet like glue. You know how much she hates to miss a party in her honor," he rolled his eyes, "So we high-tailed it out of there before she could show up and just to be sure we were free of her we changed the location of the party to a little bar downtown."

He caught the expression on my face and snorted, "Of course, it was my idea." He smiled impishly and I laughed. "So, things were going so well, I couldn't believe it. We were all having fun, the bar was full and there were so many people all laughing and dancing and just enjoying themselves. No one even noticed that Georgia was missing, or if they did, they were as happy about her absence as I was. Oh, and the bartender was soooooo hot and he made us all these drinks that he said were the 'house special' and they were just absolutely amazing." He closed his eyes and "mmmed" at the memory.

Then he opened his eyes but he seemed really annoyed. "Well, that is when *she* showed up. She walked in wearing a skirt that barely covered her huge ass and a shirt that barely hit her nipples. She looked like a cheap hooker." I snickered. "You think I'm exaggerating, but I'm not. Seriously, she wouldn't even have been able to work a main street the way she looked; her pimp would have stuck her in an alley so that she didn't scare the customers. But seriously that was nothing compared to her attitude. She walked straight in and pushed Janet off her bar stool. She actually hit the floor, it wasn't like a little light push it was a full out shove. Poor Janet was just absolutely astonished." My eyes narrowed as only this morning Janet had made sure to assure me she had no idea what was making Georgia so testy. Carter didn't seem to notice my reaction. "So, Janet is sitting on the dirty bar floor and everyone is just staring at all of it. Like I am sure that there was still music playing, but I swear no one even heard it. Then Georgia started going off on Janet about how she was "such a bitch" and "how dare she tell her the wrong bar."

"It was insane. I felt bad about it because it was my idea, but we were all so stunned by her sudden entrance that no one could find their voice. The entire bar was silent. I finally snapped out of it and opened my mouth to tell her exactly where she could get off, but before I could make a sound the *dashing* Sergeant Bracken strolled on in. Suddenly Georgia is nothing but smiles and flirting. It was like flipping a light switch. She went from evil Godzilla to sweet debutante in an instant. Of course, once Georgia set her sights on him there was no getting near either of them. They spent the entire night over in the corner of the bar just making goo-goo eyes at one another, but the night was completely ruined. The entire atmosphere was changed. There was no more party and happy and dancing like before. Oh, and poor Janet barely lifted her eyes from the bar all night."

My eyebrows knitted together as I glanced over my shoulder at Janet who was staring out the window. I didn't blame her for not telling me what had happened now. Carter continued, "Don't worry too much about our little Janet, about eleven this guy came over to her and bought her a drink. They started talking and about twelve they left together. She looked pretty happy when she got out of the cab this morning at the airport." He winked and I smiled at him. "The best part of the night though was quiet little Bill Whistler."

I pulled up his picture in my head. Bill Whistler was maybe five feet tall on a good day, hence the nickname "Little Bill," with thick soled shoes and the coke-bottle glasses that were fodder for jokes at every turn. I don't think I had heard Whistler say ten words in the year that I had known him. He may have been quiet and quirky, but for all his bad eyesight, he had a knack for finding just the right way to place the lights to get the best shots. It never ceased to amaze me. His pictures were utterly breathtaking.

"It was just a little after twelve when Bill walks up to Georgia and says, 'Why don't you go back to hell where you came from?'" I stared incredulously. "I swear I am so not making this up…Okay he had had several shots of tequila and a few other little things. But that is not the point. You should have seen it. I mean no one knew what to say. We all just stared with our mouths open. The entire place was in awe. Georgia turned the same color as her hideous lipstick and Sergeant Bracken was almost laughing…Seriously, he was biting his bottom lip and his mouth was twitching. It was great. Oh but it gets better, Bill was no where *near* done. He starts telling her how everyone hates working with her because she's such a bitch, she looks like a whore, and he then has the balls to ends it with telling her we changed the place we were partying right before we left to avoid having to see her 'skanktastic face.'"

My jaw hit the floor. Of all the people we worked with, I didn't think *Bill* would ever have the guts to stand up to a kitten, and here he went and told off the one person who everyone in the office seemed to live in fear and awe of. Carter just nodded at my expression and leaned back in his seat, satisfied with his ability to thrill me with this little story. At least now I knew who Georgia had been railing about this morning. He added slyly, "Oh, and soon after that the good Sergeant excused himself and Georgia went home alone." I couldn't help but smile.

All I could utter was "Wow." I knew it was a poor reaction to such an epic occurrence, but it was the only word I could think of. However, Carter seemed to be satisfied with it. He looked behind him at Georgia and her obvious attempts to make Sergeant Bracken want her like every other man who seemed to lay eyes on her. It obviously wasn't working. He smiled politely and paid the appropriate amount of attention, but his body language screamed uninterested. Amazingly, she didn't seem to notice as she continued to throw herself at him. Carter looked at me and smiled, "Do you think she'll ever get the hint?" I shook my head and turned the conversation to the weather we would be facing when we arrived in Fairbanks. He immediately started to talk about the frigid cold and lack of proper entertainment and pretty much did most of the talking, but I preferred it that way. I calmly smiled and nodded when it was appropriate, never having to pay too close attention. It was perfect.

The flight to Seattle seemed ions shorter than the flight to New York. I blamed the company. We rushed through the airport again with barely enough time to grab a quick cappuccino from the Starbucks before the first boarding call sounded. I made a mental note to get something nice for Terri. If it wasn't for her we could have been sitting in the terminal forever. The next flight out to Alaska didn't leave for another four hours, far to long to be subjected to watching the sickening display of flirtation between Georgia and her uninterested beau.

From Seattle to Anchorage I was seated next to a complete and total stranger. Even if I hadn't been able to smell the steroids in his veins, the bulging muscles with veins standing out upon them would have awakened my suspicions. The muscles in his arms seemed to leap of their own free will under his extra shmedium tee. If I had been human, I would have worried he would hit me in one of his uncontrollable movements. As it was, I was supremely unconcerned and leaned back my seat. This time I slept. My body couldn't take it anymore.

I drifted, my head sagged heavily, and there was only darkness. I slept dreamlessly and woke only when the stewardess came by and asked us all to buckle our seat belts. I glanced furtively around me. There was nothing broken, nothing had moved. I breathed a sigh of relief as the landing gear shifted beneath the floorboards.

Unfortunately, the layover in Anchorage was considerably longer than any of the others. I understood but that didn't mean I had to like the hour of uncomfortable seats, ugly carpet, and grumbling passengers. Oliver and Carter sat near me whispering and throwing some obviously disgusted looks at Georgia, but I couldn't sit still and listen to them. There was something that felt wrong in the air.

I kept taking deep breaths through my nose, testing the air looking for a scent. I didn't know what I was looking for, but I was hoping to find it. But, I didn't smell anything out of place. I couldn't help it though, I just wasn't at ease. I had to get up and move. I wandered past Georgia and Sergeant Bracken. She smiled coyly at him to gain his attention. He had been staring at me and from the quick glare that Georgia shot my way I could tell she didn't like the implications of that.

I wandered through the terminal, worried and anxious. I stopped at a little sandwich shop and got a roll to munch on as I observed the mannerisms of everyone around me. I found myself assessing whether or not they were a threat but none of them seemed to be. I tried to relax but nothing I did seemed to work. I wandered back to Oliver and Carter and slumped into a seat near them. Oliver glanced up at me with a look that was fatherly and concerned. I smiled as best I could, but I couldn't shake the feeling that I was being watched. And unfortunately, it wasn't Sergeant Bracken. I didn't like it.

The trip from Anchorage to Fairbanks was fairly quick and absolutely beautiful. At least from what I could see from the plane window it was beautiful. We landed at four in the afternoon and there was a sparkling white blanket of snow covering the ground and the limbs of the trees. I was wrong, it wasn't beautiful, it was breathtaking. We were all in awe of the beauty as we stared through the thick panes of the airplane windows. Yet, from the way the breath of the grounds crew was billowing out of their mouths, we were in store for a horrendously cold day.

4. Some Enchanted Evening

We stepped out of the terminal and I realized that I had been wrong yet again. It wasn't cold. "Cold" was no where near intense enough to describe the atrocity that awaited us, freezing wasn't even a strong enough word to describe it. Frigid came close. Carter, Oliver, and I all stood staring at the cold that was almost visible. The wordless horror was plain in our dropped jaws. None of us were willing to take the first steps. Instead we stood and watched as a couple of privates from base ran the equipment to the van. Finally, I cleared my throat, they looked at me and nodded. Then we took off running and literally jumped into the back of the car. My nostrils felt frozen from the few moments I had spent outside, but the ridiculous act of leaping into the car sent us all into peals of laughter. We all huddled into the seat for warmth, but their warm blood was a double edged sword.

Janet was the next one to come out of the terminal. In an attempt to look as though she would not be controlled by the temperature she walked slowly towards the car. She took about three steps out into the freezing cold and quickly jumped into the backseat. She breathed a sigh of relief when she realized that the heat had been running for a while before we got there. The look on her face made me giggle more and soon she joined in as well. But then Georgia came out wearing Sgt. Bracken's jacket and walking as though it were a sunny warm day. The laughing stopped. Carter muttered something about her cold heart before she stepped into the car.

Georgia settled into the car next to Sergeant Bracken and gave us all a disdainful glance. We knew what that look meant. Don't speak and ruin my time. So of course Carter couldn't resist the chance to be cheeky and say "Wow Georgia, you're taking the cold in stride." He smiled sweetly and Georgia glared at him as though she wanted him to die a slow and painful death. In fact, I'm pretty sure she was hatching plots for all of our deaths in her spare time. I nudged Carter in the ribs and Oliver sighed agitatedly. He seemed ill at ease. He kept glancing back at the van that held all of our equipment. I laughed "It's the Air Force Oliver, where do you think they're gonna go?"

The young man driving the car tilted his head in my direction when he heard my voice. I noticed and wondered what the motive behind his interest was. Even the thought of it made me feel bad, I shouldn't assume there was something amiss in his actions just because Sergeant Bracken kept staring at me with an expectant look on his face. It seemed there was no escaping *his* attention. I decided the best way to deal with it was to focus on the important task of figuring out "must have" shots and possible issues. At least that way whatever the young man overheard would be nothing of a compromising nature.

It was not long before Georgia noticed the young Private's apparent interest in my conversation with Oliver about our itinerary. She quickly turned her attention from Sgt. Bracken, who was too preoccupied with a phone call to be of much use to her and turned all of her charm on the unsuspecting young man.

"Private Tenor," she cooed batting her eyes and smiling seductively, "You're the one assigned to keep me out of trouble aren't you?"

The young man smiled nervously and gulped.

"You'll have your work cut out for you, I like causing trouble," she winked.

The poor young man turned scarlet and concentrated very hard on the road ahead.

Georgia turned from him and smiled at me. It was a smug look that screamed triumph. She was taunting me. She turned her attention back towards the young man who was gasping for air like a fish out of water. I could hear his heartbeat accelerate when he caught her eye. He was making little gurgling sounds, far too nervous to form a coherent thought. It was obvious what he was thinking as she continued to lavish her attention on him.

Honestly, most men fell all over themselves, but I never understood it. I had watched as she flirted with man after man and their reaction was always the same. Even the random men on the streets took a second glance at her when they walked by. Now I can admit that she wasn't ugly on the outside. She was ugly; hideous really, in a way most men didn't see or didn't care about. She wasn't a real person either, physically or emotionally.

To begin her breasts were fake, well everything above an A cup, her nose and long eyelashes were compliments of a

Philadelphia plastic surgeon, and even her name wasn't real. Her real name was Prudence Steinman. The only thing that was real about her appearance, the only thing she apparently hadn't felt the need to change, was her green eyes. The only reason it hadn't been changed, I was fairly certain, was that she couldn't find a doctor who would do that, and I'm sure contacts would just be too much trouble for such a busy diva. She was so worried about her appearance and what people thought of her that it destroyed her basic humanity. I was more human than she was and I was born half monster.

It turned from her new little friend and smiled at me. She didn't need to say a word, the challenge was clear in her eyes and she stared intensely, daring me to accept. I turned my head towards the window with a slight smile, refusing to be drawn in to her petty little game. She opened her mouth to speak, but at that exact moment Sgt. Bracken snapped his phone shut and smiled at me. Georgia's breath caught in her throat as the object of her current obsession was smiling at me. I could almost smell the rage boiling in her blood as Sergeant Bracken smiled a sickeningly sweet smile and informed me, "Captain William Dixon, is looking forward to making your acquaintance." I smiled politely and looked impatiently out the window as we pulled up to our hotel.

We were staying at the Regency. It was an older hotel that honestly wasn't much to look at, but then again, we never really stayed in five star hotels. It wouldn't be economical. So we were subjected to bad wallpaper and ugly low-pile carpet time and time again. It could be worse I suppose, but Terri always made sure we had rooms on the same floor. More often than not, we had to awkwardly ignore the strange man who stumbled out of Georgia's room in the early morning and pretend that we didn't hear every thrust through the thin walls. Of course, she didn't find there to be anything wrong with it and was always completely unapologetic when she joined us for the day's work.

This time Georgia's insatiable appetite for men started even before we were given our keys. The young Private Tenor had already been talked into carrying Georgia's bags inside. Sergeant Bracken just smiled enigmatically. I couldn't tell if he was angry, jealous, or just being a jerk as he ordered Private Tenor to wait in the car. The young man obeyed without question, dropping his head like a scolded pup. Sergeant Bracken excused himself as I dealt with the clerk.

Welcome back to my never ending day, the clerk was honestly a moron. I reiterated time and time again that we had specifically asked for rooms near each other. And time and time again he stared at me like I was speaking another language. So, Georgia decided to strut up and announce that it didn't matter anyway and smiled at the young man with a look that could not be mistaken. He smiled smugly in my direction as if to say, "See?" But when I snatched the keys out of his hand his eyes widened and every trace of smugness fled from his now ashen cheeks. Georgia didn't seem to notice as she walked towards her room.

I stalked down to my room and slammed the door. I was frustrated beyond words. I threw my bags down on the bed so hard that they bounced off and hit the wall. I kicked them for good measure before walking into the bathroom with my overnight bag. I just needed to brush my teeth before we left. The mint taste of the toothpaste in my mouth always helped to make everything less desirable, especially blood.

Then there it was, a whirlpool tub. I was looking forward to a long bath already, but unfortunately my day was nowhere near over. Yet even through the burning in my throat and the aches that coursed through my body I was amazingly alert. It really surprised me. I expected to be completely exhausted. The thought that I would start to lose my control had been weighing heavily on my mind, but everything was completely clear and in sharp focus. I looked longingly at the tub as I brushed my teeth, but resisted the impulse and went back into the main room with the two double beds.

I glanced at the clock and realized that I had taken more time than I had originally thought. I shuffled quickly through my bag looking for all the documentation that would get us through the checkpoints on the air force base and ran down to the lobby. Oliver, Carter and Sgt. Bracken were waiting on me. I smiled and laughed, "Why thank you for waiting gentlemen." Carter and Oliver smiled, but Sgt. Bracken just stared at me, it was just plain creepy. We headed out to the car that was waiting, but Georgia was nowhere to be seen. Private Tenor went to find out where Georgia was hiding.

When Bracken finally spoke he said, “There’s a wonderful little Italian place in Fairbanks.” He smiled at me and I wasn’t exactly sure what was going through his mind for a moment, but then he said it, “Do you think Ms. Stone would like to have Italian tonight?” The side of my mouth twitched up into an involuntary smile as his lips curled into a sneer. It was just another attempt to taunt me into some sort of reaction, but it wasn’t going to work. He seriously wasn’t my type in more ways than one. “Sergeant Bracken,” I cooed as sickeningly sweet as possible, “I doubt very much that you could suggest *anything* that Georgia wouldn’t be up for.” Carter tried to hide his laughing behind a fake cough that no one fell for, but Oliver tried to help it seem much more real by pounding on his back.

It was then that Georgia came flouncing out of the hotel with Private Tenor on her arm. She was reapplying her lipstick and Private Tenor looked like he had just committed the most deadly of deadly sins. Carter rolled his eyes at me and Oliver looked out of the opposite window in disapproval while Georgia didn’t seem bothered in the least by whatever she had done to the poor kid. She whispered something in his ear as he opened the door for her and his skin blanched. I don’t think he knew that whatever moment of carnal pleasure he had just indulged in came with a price tag. Now he owed her for keeping her mouth shut and at some point she would call in that favor and he wasn’t going to like it. I almost felt sorry for him, he was only human.

We arrived at the base through the snow framed streets and were ushered through the outer security checkpoints. The frigid air assaulted us as soon as the car door was cracked open. It was like a predator waiting to attack at the slightest opportunity. What in the world had possessed me to think this was a good idea? Everyone hurried from the car to the promised warmth of the nearest building. It did not disappoint. We had been in the arctic air for a grand total of maybe 30 seconds and already we were all rubbing our arms and making whimpering complaints of how cold it was outside. In the back of my mind I couldn't help but wonder how I would be able to hunt.

I looked up into the high vaulted ceilings and down the columns that looked to be marble. It wasn’t, but the effect was beautiful. Still this was not what I had expected from a military base. I looked around at the hustle and bustle that was going on in the great hallway. There were plenty of Air Force minions running around. They all seemed to be busy. Heads down, arms full of papers, and scuffling shoes created an intricate dance through the lobby. It reminded me of the tech crew at the station. I smiled and Carter nudged me playfully. He motioned with his eyes for me to look over my shoulder. That's when I saw him. He was hurrying towards us with a deep smile. I felt my heart skip a beat.

He wasn't a terribly tall man, six-two, but tall enough for me to be forced to look up at him. I knew what he was the second I had seen him, but he was different somehow. He moved towards us, even walking at human pace he was fluid and graceful. That was definitely not a trait I had managed to pick up. He was smiling. His lips look soft. His eyes held the same pull that most vampires seem to have, that look that makes every heart about them pulse with that undercurrent of desire. This was stronger than anything I had ever felt before. I felt my face flush and dropped my eyes. I knew he could hear my heart beat feverishly in my chest, but there was nothing I could do to quiet it.

His eyes flashed to mine in question. He had heard my heart irregularity but it took me a minute to understand that the confused look on his face was because he heard a heartbeat at all. He knew that I wasn't human. I took a deep breath, trying to be subtle and failing miserably. He didn't have the sharp smell I had become used to, in fact he smelled quite good, like roses, but he was a vampire nonetheless. He was hungry too. He had deep purplish shadows below his eyes and his eyes were so dark they bordered on black. Mine are usually paler the hungrier I am, but most full-blooded vampires have darker eyes the less blood they have in their systems. I tried to be nonchalant as I assessed him from the distance. His skin was as pale as mine, but even I could feel the heat flowing through my body. I knew he would feel, or at least smell, it. My pulse was completely out of control.

My entire appraisal of him took less than five seconds, and all the while I could feel his eyes on my body. The blush burned deeper and I broke off from the intensity of his stare to fiddle with the papers in my hand. As he approached I made a point of avoiding eye contact by being overly involved with finding a pen in my purse. Oliver and Carter snickered and bumped me like the big brothers I never had or wanted. I didn't need their ribbing, my reaction confused me enough by itself. My stomach tightened, my breathing accelerated slightly, and I could not force my heart to behave properly. I had never reacted this way to anyone before. Granted, he was incredibly handsome, but I had dealt with handsome men before. I had never felt this draw to anyone, this intense longing in my body for him. I knew my eyebrows were knitted together and I couldn't control the expression. I was quite befuddled.

He walked up to our little party and nodded to Bracken. Bracken gave him a look that was troubling. It was almost as if he was saying, "It's all yours." The man didn't smile back. He introduced himself as Lieutenant Charles Sullivan and my heart skipped a beat at the sound of his voice. It was like velvet against my skin. He explained that he was the press liaison for Captain Dixon. He shook my hand and I couldn't meet eyes as he spoke. A shiver ran through my body. It wasn't a chill; it was more substantial, like I had touched a live voltage wire. His presence excited me in ways I had never felt before and that frightened me more than I cared to admit.

His hands were cold as they took mine, but that was to be expected. I was sure that mine must have felt like fire against his. His skin was smooth in my hands, his eyes were warm and his scent was inviting. I knew that was just part of his arsenal, his bag of tricks to catch his prey, but I couldn't help falling deeper into the scent with every breath. He smelled fresh and clean, with a hint of roses. Roses were my favorite flower and that only helped to draw me in further. My consciousness ordered me to get it together and I tried my best to obey, but when he spoke again my heart stopped. His voice was just so beautiful, deep, musical, and velvety smooth. The sound seemed to wrap itself around me.

I kicked myself for letting a total stranger have such control over me, especially one that could hear every heartbeat that thudded against my ribs. I knew that my voice was going to come out weak when I tried to speak. I could feel the muscles in my throat tighten before I even tried. "Get a grip, Get a grip" the mantra just continued to chant through my mind. I looked up and smiled as confidently as possible. I introduced myself calmly and my voice came out confident and strong, effectually hiding my inner turmoil. I was so relieved that I sounded confident that I nearly laughed. I felt my smile widen and I recklessly looked into Lieutenant Sullivan's eyes. "Whoa" was the only word that bounced through my mind. Carter's conspicuous laugh at my side broke the trance that I seemed to be in. I looked away from Lieutenant Sullivan's intoxicating eyes and patted Carter on the back with a concerned look. I could feel Lieutenant Sullivan smiling; it was like a warm summer's day.

Sgt. Bracken took control of the party for a moment and started to lead us to the meeting room. Lieutenant Sullivan tried to be inconspicuous as he surveyed me from the corner of his eye, but his gaze had an almost physical effect on me. My body felt warm and my skin felt like it was tingling. I wanted desperately to look at him, to see what his reaction was as he stared, but I lacked the gumption. It didn't help that the only thing I could think about was having his lips pressed against mine as we were led into a large room. They ushered us through two sets of huge oak doors into a room that held news agencies from around the country and a lavish fruit spread. Lt. Sullivan excused himself with a smile and disappeared into the crowded room.

Relief flowed through me as soon as Lt. Sullivan was nowhere in sight. I didn't understand why my feelings towards this complete stranger were so strong. It frightened me and I chided myself for being so transparent. I needed to collect my thoughts and the absence of his perfectly delicious body was definitely a help in that aspect. As long as he was in sight, he was all I could think of.

I helped myself to some grapes as Carter scoped out the room. He was already nodding and smiling at people from around the US. I glanced around and recognized a few of the faces from other coverage events and smiled politely when I caught their eye. They responded in kind. Carter noticed the coolness of the exchanges and made the comment that I mustn't be as popular as he was. The more I stared around the room, the more I noticed the agitation. The restlessness was almost tangible as the divas and the crews milled aimlessly around the room. I wondered how long the Fairbanks and Anchorage stations had been waiting as yet another crew was shown in. They looked more annoyed than anyone else.

I continued to look around, purposefully focusing on details to keep my mind off of Lt. Sullivan. I took a deep breath and nearly choked on the scent of fruit and cheap cologne. One of the men who wandered near me was actually wearing Axe Body Spray and a well tailored Italian suit. The dichotomy managed to amuse me for a moment. The perfume seemed to be a little more high end than the cologne and the shirts a little more low cut. Chanel No. 5 and Prada mingled in the air and the garish makeup on several of the divas would have made a drag queen blush. So, I decided to focus on the décor more than the people as frankly some of them were beginning to frighten me.

Rather than focusing on the scent of blood, I concentrated on the sandy brown carpet and the pictures of seascapes set against a very pale blue wall with some white wainscoting. It looked like a beach-side cottage. I'm sure it was their attempt to bring the warm memories of the beach to this land of ice and snow, but the memory of the cold was so vivid in my mind that the décor did little to persuade me otherwise.

As my eyes continued to wander, I noticed that Georgia was standing in a corner monopolizing Sgt. Bracken's attention and I swear her shirt got lower as the minutes ticked by. She hadn't noticed my embarrassing reaction to Lt. Sullivan for which I was thankful, but the reason gave me the strangest sensation. She hadn't noticed my sudden and violent reaction because she didn't consider me competition. She didn't think that I would figure as an issue if she chose to change from Bracken to Sullivan. The challenge that flashed in her eyes when she looked at me screamed it. I was nothing; take a man from her if I dared. I was insulted and infuriated.

I also made it my mission to avoid eye contact with both Carter and Oliver. I didn't want them to see the emotions plastered all over my face. But I knew they had noticed Lt. Sullivan, and I knew that they would be more than happy to embarrass me when the opportunity presented itself; so, I readjusted my expression to try to look uninterested and detached. From the moment I walked in this place I didn't feel right. I was beginning to long for the boring press introduction.

As if in answer to my thoughts a black haired young woman with dark brown eyes and candy apple red nails entered and called for our attention. She announced that her name was Ms. Lena Watters, press liaison to Captain Dixon. She reeked of her own importance to the point it was impossible to ignore. Her nose was tilted in the air and her high cheekbones accented her pointed chin giving her an "I'm more important than you" expression. She reminded me of a witch. Her pursed lips barely moved as she announced that we would all be receiving a press packet as we entered the conference room and that this was not the time for questions, this was simply a quick introduction. Carter muttered something under his breath about it being a day for introductions and wagged his eyebrows at me.

However, he was apparently not the only party interested in me. Ms. Watters couldn't take her eyes off of me as we moved through the flock of reporters trying to file through the double doors. Even Oliver noticed the hostility that was poorly concealed in her stare. He moved slightly in front of me taking an almost protective stance and it seemed for a moment to break her fixation. I gently patted his forearm and smiled thankfully at him. The only other thing I could do was wonder what I had done to earn her disapproval already.

We walked towards the two uniformed men standing at the open doors. They looked supremely and disinterestedly bored. I almost laughed at their attitude. If it wasn't for all of the sudden intrigue that seemed to be surrounding me, I would have felt the same way as, like cattle, we were herded into a large auditorium-looking room. Ms. Watters was handing out blue folders with the air force seal emblazoned on the front and an aloof smile on her face. As we approached her, however, her demeanor changed.

She and Georgia exchanged a glance that silently acknowledged the other was competition, but it was warm and fuzzy compared to the hostility she directed at me. Oliver, hero that he was, attempted to stare her down as we passed, but she didn't even noticed his existence. Her eyes were only for me. I didn't return the stare as, without my conscious permission, my eyes covered the conference room searching for Lt. Sullivan. He was nowhere in sight, thankfully. I concentrated on the set up. This was nothing like it would be at the real reveal. No one had a microphone on the podium, no one would be fighting for real attention today, and all of the information given right now was what any of us who had ever done this before already knew.

I steered our crew towards an open row in the back. I needed my completely erratic heartbeat to be skewed by all the other heartbeats in the room, even though I knew it wouldn't matter. He would be able to hear every stutter, every beat, even in this crowded room he would be able to zero in on me if he truly wanted to. I wasn't quite sure if he really did. Part of me, that I was trying to ignore, desperately wanted him to find me in the crowd, yet my far more practical side was wary at best. I wasn't a hundred percent sure that I wasn't food.

The back-feed from the microphone quieted the room. My stomach turned as I sunk into my chair, I wasn't loving the new sensations. Ms. Watters puffed out her chest and her black skirt seemed to creep up her thighs revealing the snaps of a garter belt as Lt. Sullivan's eyes flitted past her. Her heart pounded so loudly that the sound echoed above every other in the room. I smiled and shook my head slightly, at least that was one of the mysteries of Alaska solved.

Carter nudged me in the ribs and motioned with his eyes for me to look towards the stage. I didn't need to look to see what he wanted me to, the intensity of Lt. Sullivan's stare had been palpable. When our eyes met he flashed the most beautiful smile I had ever seen. My face grew warm and my legs felt weak as the soft scent of roses seemed to fill the room. I wanted to look away, but couldn't. I was impressed as Lt. Sullivan continued to talk to everyone without breaking stride. I don't think if I tried to speak at that moment I could have done so coherently. I was lost in his eyes. Jokingly, Carter put his arm around my shoulders.

My startled look made them both laugh, but Carter removed his arm as a low growl rumbled through my teeth. I concentrated on the sandy brown carpet and tried to will the pink blush to fade from my face to no avail. Oliver leaned over and whispered, "You know there's nothing saying you can't have a good time while you're here." I glared and hissed back, "I don't know what you're talking about." He snorted, "Of course you don't," and opened his press packet looking over the top of it surreptitiously.

I flipped mine open and sank down into my chair. I didn't raise my eyes again through the entire presentation. I went through the press packet and pretended to be totally absorbed by the normal procedures, the map of the base, the itinerary, the blah…blah…blah. In all honesty I couldn't keep myself focused on anything but him. His voice wrapped around me as he continued to go through procedures and I could feel his eyes searching for mine. I had never felt this forceful of a desire before. I didn't want to be so obsessed by this practically complete stranger, but there wasn't much that was able to distract me at the moment. The décor had already held my attention for as long as possible and I already knew what was in the packet. It was the same everywhere we went. I flipped to the next page and saw to my dismay that tomorrow night there was a semi-formal dinner to give the Air Force a chance to show off their hospitality. The only thing I hated about being put on assignment at a military base was the food. It wasn't exactly restaurant quality, heck half the time I wasn't sure it was human food.

My wandering mind was brought back to the present when Lt. Sullivan introduced Captain Dixon. I raised my eyes without thinking and immediately wished I hadn't. Lt. Sullivan still had his eyes on me and the breath stopped in my throat. He smiled and quickly mouthed the word "Hi." I couldn't help but smile back. As he moved off the stage, I was struck at how graceful he was. It was barely movement at all, he was so fluid. His seat was situated near Lena Watters and she tried to rub her breasts against him as she leaned over to whisper something in his ear. His eyes never left mine. However, Ms. Watters seemed to have the same issue as Georgia; she was not to be ignored. She nagged at him until he broke the trance he had me caught in. He looked at Ms. Watters with a polite smile and I quickly dropped my eyes to the press packet. I never thought I would be thankful for a rival.

Captain Dixon was speaking, but I barely paid attention to what was being said. I kept fighting the urge to look up at Sullivan. I couldn't help it, the thought was ever present. I couldn't concentrate on anything else. Luckily for me it was the same old same old as far as press conferences were concerned so I didn't miss anything. Welcome to the base, we are so happy to have you all here, if you need anything contact Ms. Watters or Lt.

Sullivan, and enjoy our beautiful city. It was the same wherever we went. The press packets were filled with information and had everything that we *needed.* They always did and this one was surprisingly thorough.

Captain Dixon dismissed us all with an obviously rehearsed wish for us all to enjoy ourselves and there was a mass exodus towards the door. The more of these I went to the more I was convinced that people hated the press. I kept my eyes on the carpet as the herd moved out of the room, hoping beyond hope that *he* would not make a sudden appearance and ruin my carefully prepared façade. In this manner I made my way into the hallway with the rest of the sheeple being jostled about like baggage at an airport. I sighed as the congestion around me ebbed, I had never been comfortable in large crowds anyway, but the burn in my throat wasn't helped at all by the warm bodies. I turned to ask Carter where the equipment had been taken. He wasn't interested in work at all and made no qualms about it. He wanted a play by play of my emotions and the looks between Lt. Sullivan and me during the introduction and I knew there would be no business done until I obliged him.

"He's attractive," I sighed.

Carter laughed, "I think it was a little more than just *attractive.*"

I nudged him in the ribs, "I have complete control over my emotions…"

Oliver interrupted, "I could tell by your blushing cheeks."

I smacked him lightly and growled, "I can control myself, so can we please go over important things?"

Carter sighed, "What's more important than a hunky Air Force Lieutenant?"

Oliver laughed.

I blushed.

Carter snickered, "Okay, let us go over the *important stuff.*" Quotation fingers included.

I really did like these two, but at this moment they were the two most annoying men I had ever met. After a little coercing and a few threats, we finally were talking about the technical aspects of this assignment. We were going over a list of "must have" shots and laughing at Oliver's impression of Georgia hanging all over

Sgt. Bracken when I caught a very strong scent. It was the same smell that had lingered on Sgt. Bracken when I first saw him, the female vampire's smell. But this wasn't some rubbed off scent, this was pure. She was here. She had to have passed within inches of me for the scent to have been that strong. There was no way a scent that strong had carried from across the room. She had to have moved fast to get away before I turned. Apparently she didn't care if someone noticed her and that made me even more nervous. The scent was already becoming skewed by the many human scents that were circulating in the air, I couldn't track it. A growl rumbled in my throat.

Carter touched my arm and the warmth of his touch made me jump. He chuckled, but the noise was off, nervous. Oliver's eyes were concerned. They had never seen me on edge before and apparently it was unsettling. Here I felt completely out of my element. I must have looked a mess. The thought that I looked horrid the first time that Lt. Sullivan laid eyes on me suddenly dawned on me and the vampire who was stalking me through Sgt. Bracken faded into my subconscious. Thankfully, I didn't have time to dwell on it as Carter and Oliver drug me to the car. That snap of cold air was enough to wake the dead or at least clear my mind.

5. Helpful Stranger

I stood in my room staring at the suitcase laying on the bed and wondering what I was going to do about the thirst welling up inside me. I tried to focus on the landscaped watercolor hanging over the red and tan paisley comforter. It looked like it was meant to mimic a Native American painting. The subject was by no means original, reindeer on a snowy hill, but the overall feel of the piece was reverent. But, it held my interest for about five seconds. The standard twenty-six inch television that only had fifteen channels and the ugly blue carpet also held no interest for me. My mind was far too occupied with other concerns.

A new place presented me with new difficulties. Especially a new place where I was positive other vampires roamed. It's dangerous to encroach on another vampire's territory without permission. I knew I could survive on deer or bear or mountain lion, heck even the rats of the city sewers would dull the burning. But here I didn't even know where it would be safe to do that. A fleeting thought that it would be exhilarating to hunt with Lt. Sullivan flitted across my mind, but was suppressed by the sudden desire for blood.

I grasped my throat with my hand and tried to will the burning to dull, but it had been far too long without blood for it to be quieted by my willpower. Frustrated, I shoved the suitcase to the floor with a thud and threw myself across the bed dejectedly. I had no idea what I was going to do. The wicked part of my mind came up with the plan to sample some of Georgia's blood and I smirked at the visual. The look of horror that would cross her face as my canines elongated was wickedly amusing. I laughed out loud and despite my constant struggle to behave myself and be good I truly considered walking to her doorway and putting her out of my misery.

I took a deep breath to banish the thought and sat straight up on the bed. Lt. Sullivan was walking to my door. His sweet scent registered even though he had barely stepped into the hallway. I knew that if I could smell him I was already on his radar. My heart was thudding like a drum and would not behave for the life of me. It was a beacon to his all too sensitive ears. I could almost hear him smiling. Should I open the door before he gets here? Should I wait and pretend that I didn't know? How much did he know about me? How much did I want him to know? My mind raced and the emotions I was feeling ricocheted around my chest relentlessly.

The footsteps stopped at my door. I darted across the room with superhuman speed and swung open the door before his hand had fallen against the wood. Admittedly, I was showing off just a little bit, I wanted him to know that I wasn't a simple human. I wanted him to know that I was something special, but I must have looked quite flustered. As soon as his eyes connected to mine the blood stained my cheeks. I could feel the wild excitement in my eyes as he just stood there looking absolutely gorgeous in his blue jeans and white tee shirt. His black leather jacket was carelessly thrown open doing nothing to cover his absolutely perfectly sculpted body and my breath caught in my throat. The shirt was a little small and his abs and chest were perfectly outlined. I fought the urge to run my fingers down his six pack. A little late, but the thought registered that I didn't know what this beautiful stranger's intentions were. His expression was completely blank.

"Can I help you Lieutenant?" I asked realizing with chagrin that I sounded a little breathless. Maybe he hadn't noticed. His carefully composed facade broke and he chuckled. It made my heart quiver. This was becoming an unhealthy infatuation. I had only known of the man for a few hours and already the slightest sound of his voice set my body on fire. I tried to focus realizing that I still had no idea why he had shown up on my doorstep not that it mattered as long as he was here.

"I actually came by to see what I could do for you," he smiled, walking through the door. He brushed by me and the slight brush of his arm against mine sent a shock through my body. I wanted to lean in and press my body against him, but instead I pulled away slightly. I didn't want to present myself as desperate although that was certainly how I felt. The scent of roses wafted in after him as though he had thought to bring some ambiance with him.

"I'm glad that you came. I was actually hoping," *That you were desperately attracted to me*, "That you could tell me where a good place to eat would be." I immediately dropped my eyes. It was a little embarrassing and definitely the first time I had ever asked that question with this type of food in mind. His smoldering gaze made my heart jump, I couldn't meet it and still hope to be able to control my thoughts. I was reacting to him like a teenager in high school. Hopefully by not looking straight into his eyes I could hide my thoughts. I didn't want him to know what was swirling around in there.

I saw from the corner of my eye as the edge of his mouth twitch up into a playful smile as he said, "I know a terrific little restaurant downtown, or were you thinking something a little more nonconformist." His eyes gleamed mischievously as he ducked down to catch mine. I pursed my lips, marshaling my thoughts, and took a deep breath through my nose. I knew my eyes held the desperation I was feeling, but this was a desperate need for blood. A gentle laugh slipped through his lips as he looked at my perplexed expression. It took my breath away. "I know what you meant," he whispered, stepping towards me. His face was so close to mine. I wanted to move forward, to taste his lips, but I willed my hormones to stay in check. That didn't stop me from feeling light headed, however. I'm sure the lack of blood didn't help.

He hesitated for a moment. Like he wasn't sure what to do. He leaned forward infinitesimally, but then suddenly pulled back. I could feel the hurt and disappointment splatter all over my face for a split second. His mouth twitched up into a smile. I don't know why he found it amusing, but he seemed to. I looked away from him like an angry child. How dare he find it amusing to toy with me? Maybe he was just part of the army of stalkers I seemed to be amassing with every second. And of course, that thought stuck in my head. Why else would he take an interest in me? Why had Sergeant Bracken given him that look? Georgia was right, I wasn't competition, I was nothing. Scratch that, I was pissed.

His eyes turned almost frantic for a moment. "I meant I can show you where it would be safe to hunt…I need to hunt anyway…If you wanted to…" he seemed to get more and more confounded as he continued. His calm confidence seemed to melt away. I don't think he ever needed to run a pitch this long before. I'm sure that all he had to do was motion to Ms. Watters before she fell into his arms, but now I wasn't so sure why he was feigning interest in me and a small voice in the back of my head was screaming that whatever it was that was going on in this small town was anything but friendly. I wanted to be safe, but I wanted to be with him. It was making my head ache. Besides, he still hadn't gotten around to saying what he meant to say. I forced my mouth up at the corners as I decided I was going to take a chance and see where this course would lead me. His eyes lightened and the calm returned to his face.

"Why Lieutenant," I smirked, "Are you asking me out on a date?"

He laughed and smiled impishly. "I guess you could say that."

"Why the interest in a complete stranger?"

"I'm just a nice guy," he smiled.

"Well then, what exactly did you have in mind?"

He smiled, "I hope you don't mind wildlife. I try to stay away from the humans in town. It might draw some unwanted attention."

I nodded, dropping my eyes. He started towards the door, but I hesitated. One of the all-to-apparent disadvantages of being a half breed in this harsh and unforgiving environment, was a susceptibility to the weather. I had nearly frozen to death just running to the car earlier that day. True, I was always warmer after a hunt, but I doubted the extreme cold I had felt earlier would afford any sort of warmth for me blood-filled or otherwise. "Um...Lieutenant?" I stammered, "What should I wear?"

The look on his face was something between confusion, curiosity, and amusement. I was fairly sure that he had never met a damphir before, and I blushed realizing that he probably didn't understand what I was talking about. I cleared my throat and muttered, "I am...sensitive." His eyebrows knitted together as he cocked his head to the side. I was starting to fidget, "You know...I'm half human...I get cold in cold weather." I hadn't fidgeted like this in decades. He just continued to stare at me as I messed with the bottom of my shirt. "I'm sure you can smell my blood and hear my heartbeat..." He didn't say anything and I was beginning to wonder if he thought I was crazy. I took a deep breath and tried to think of the best way to phrase what I was.

As I opened my mouth to speak he stepped forward. My breath caught in my throat and I froze as he moved. His hand reached out and pushed a stray strand of hair out of my face. A strange expression quickly flashed across his face, but was gone in half a second. "I'm sorry," I whispered, "I'm just not used to being around people who move that quickly." He smiled, but his eyes were off. I wasn't sure exactly what it was, but there was definitely something that wasn't right. Without understanding why, I felt the sudden urge to reach out and stroke his face, let him know that whatever it was that was bothering him could be solved. I just wanted him to be happy. Where did that come from?

"Do you have anything like under armor?" he suggested taking a step back and nervously clearing his throat. I nodded and rifled through my suitcase looking for the black shirt I was positive I packed. I couldn't look into his eyes as I stepped into the bathroom to change. I was panicked and excited and my heart was whirling into overdrive. I didn't have any idea what I was doing. I didn't know if he liked me, if he wanted to feed on me, or if I was nothing but a charity case in his eyes, a poor hungry stranger all alone in a strange place. Again the thought that he was just another part of whatever was after me here in this barren land crept into my head and ruined the hope of his desperate love and admiration for me.

I struggled to control my breathing as I slipped my shirt over my head. I looked into the mirror and stared into my own eyes. I barely recognized the stranger that was staring back at me. My cheeks were flushed, my eyes were wild, and my lips were quivering. I took a deep breath and knew that I was already in too deep. Whatever was going on, I was in this thing for the ride.

When I came back out he was sitting on the edge of the hideous comforter. He looked gorgeous and I couldn't believe that I was about to go out into the wild with this...vampire. I wondered quickly if I would be coming back from this excursion. I still wasn't sure if there was enough human blood in my veins for me to smell appetizing. I nervously cleared my throat and announced, "Ready when you are Lieutenant." He shook his head and sighed. He moved to my side and in a blink was so close I could almost taste the fresh rose scent that seemed to ooze from his body. Without meaning to I found myself leaning towards him. He didn't move away as he teased, "My name is Charles, Nora." My heart fluttered. I moved back and smiled nervously. It didn't escape his notice.

He smiled impishly and laughed, "Worried?" I swallowed hard and attempted to look a little less desperate. I blushed again and headed for the door without answering. I wasn't prepared for his reaction. He grabbed my arm and swung me around so that I stumbled into his chest. The feeling that coursed through my body was new and intense and amazing. I didn't think I would ever get enough of it. His fingers wrapped around my face as he lifted my chin so that I was forced to look at him. He rubbed his nose against my neck and took a deep breath. Every last breath escaped my lungs and I bit my bottom lip quickly. I could feel him smile near the base of my throat and I went stiff. He took a deep breath and leaned back to look me in the eye. "You don't smell like food, you know." He breathed in through his nose and smiled. I tried to step back, but he slipped his hand around my waist and held me fast against his chest. I liked the feeling. "You smell like a meadow after a spring rain," he laughed letting me lean back to look into his eyes. I searched his face and he let me go quickly dropping his eyes and stepping away.

I cleared my throat and tried to beat back the blush that I felt creeping across my cheeks. I was sure that I was reading too deeply into every interaction. He mustn't feel the same about me or he wouldn't have stepped back so abruptly. He stepped aside opening the door a quick and fluid movement and let me walk into the hallway first. He made sure that my door was closed and offered me his arm. I laughed and slipped my arm through his.

"So," he asked as we strolled along, "how fast can you run?"

"You wanna race me down the hallway?" I snorted at him.

"I'm just hoping you can keep up, I hate to be slowed down."

I rolled my eyes and smirked.

"You think I'm kidding?"

"I doubt that I'll be the one having trouble keeping up."

"Is that so?" he asked credulously.

"You have no idea," I surprised myself with the easy banter I felt slipping through my lips.

"Do you always think so highly of yourself?"

I smiled, "Is it wrong if I'm not exaggerating?"

"I haven't met anyone who is as fast as me."

I sneered extending my hand towards him, "Hi, my name is Nora,"

He smiled and pulled me along the hallway with him. "You think you're so special."

I pretended to primp my hair, "Think?"

A strange expression crossed his face as he muttered, "You have no idea."

My head snapped around when I heard Georgia's door open. Lt. Sullivan followed my gaze in time to see Private Tenor stepping into the hallway. He stopped dead when he saw us. On second thought, I don't even think he even registered that I was standing there, but Georgia who stepped out behind him in nothing but a silky bathrobe looked me dead in the eye. Any intimidation that I had effected upon her earlier that morning had apparently worn off. She looked as though she was ready to kill me. I could almost feel the hatred rolling off of her in waves. Lt. Sullivan didn't miss the exchange and put his arm around my waist protectively as we turned the corner.

I looked into his eyes frantically and apparently the sight amused him to the point of snickering. I stepped back indignantly and growled under my breath. He held up his hands, palms towards me as though he was surrendering, but still snickered under his breath.

"What is so funny?"

"You," he laughed.

"May I ask how exactly?" I was hurt and angry and I could feel the muscles in my jaw tighten.

"You are very possibly one of the most powerful beings in the world."

My eyebrows knitted together in frustration.

He sighed, "You could snap her neck in less than a second and yet you defer to her."

"Don't you defer to humans, Lieutenant?"

"Not because I fear their reactions." He stared at me intensely and I could feel my insides turn to jello. "You actually care."

"I care how she'll treat everyone I work with if she's pissed off."

His mouth lifted into a half smile as he shook his head and muttered, “You are the strangest creature I have ever met.”

I stood there staring into his all-to-perfect face. He had a peculiar look in his eyes. With a shock I realized it was admiration. I was completely caught off guard. I had never expected anyone to look at me like that let alone someone like him. My face was suddenly on fire. I quickly stepped out into the cold and skidded to a halt. Ms. Lena Watters was stepping out of her car several spaces away from where we were and her eyes were nothing but disgust cast in my direction. This was just my lucky day.

Charles didn’t even seem to notice. He laughed at my expression as he followed me into the cold. Acting as though it was a fairly common occurrence he took my hand and led me towards a huge jeep with huge off-road tires. I wasn’t the only one who was caught off guard by the sudden hand holding. Ms. Watters turned about four shades of red before Charles looked up and nodded in acknowledgment. That was the only encouragement that she needed. In a moment she was upon us, trying desperately to look alluring in her fur trimmed parka. I politely tried to pull my hand away, but Charles tightened his grip and growled playfully under his breath.

“So where are you off to?” she cooed. Her body language obviously excluded me.

“Business,” he laughed squeezing my hand.

“Oh,” she stammered, he hadn’t left an opening for her to continue and she was not ready to let him go anywhere with me.

“You look great, Charles.” She tried to step between us, but he maneuvered around her.

“Good night, Lena.” His voice was cold and almost sharp, a huge change from how he had been speaking to me all night. She was hurt for a moment, but then her competitive nature won out. I had seen that look before and I had a feeling it wouldn't be the last either.

Charles tugged on my arm and led me towards his vehicle. I smiled and whispered, “Impressive.” We walked hand in hand with Ms. Watter’s stares burning holes in our backs and I couldn’t have been more pleased with myself. Charles put his hand around my waist and lifted me into the jeep effortlessly, winking as he closed the door. I put on my seatbelt and felt a little smile play around the edge of my mouth. He jumped into the driver's seat and muttered sarcastically, "Say goodnight to Ms. Watters darling."

I chimed in with my best schoolgirl voice, "Good Night Ms. Watters."

He laughed.

The Jeep bounced down the road weaving in and out of traffic at such a speed that I was amazed it stayed upright. I held onto the "Oh, Shit" handle and enjoyed the ride as much as I could. I wasn't used to being in a vehicle with someone else driving, let alone someone else who drove like me. I took deep breaths and every time his sweet scent registered in my head it calmed me. He looked over a few times as if there was something he wanted to say, but he couldn't quite get it out. We swerved down a little side road and then found ourselves bouncing mercilessly down a small dirt trail.

"So, how well do you know Ms. Watters?" I finally asked to break the silence.

"Not as well as she'd like," he scoffed back

"Oh, really?"

"Don't act like your surprised, you knew the moment she glared at you that I was the reason why."

"Not that exact moment," I spat.

"Hey," his voice was soft and genuine, "She's got nothing on you."

I laughed, "Except that she smells so delicious."

His eyes roamed over my body hungrily but then a playful smile broke across his face as he laughed, "You're right, she's much more appealing than you."

I sniffed in fake anger and looked out the window at the trees that were whizzing by way too quickly.

He sighed and added seriously, "Look. Lena and Georgia seem to have a lot in common from what I can tell, and that doesn't appeal to me."

I smiled, "Why should it matter to me if they appeal to you?"

He looked confused and focused back on the road.

I laughed, "You can eat whomever you choose, it's no never mind to me."

He snorted and half-smiled.

I sighed and added sincerely, "Thank you for doing this. I knew I couldn't last much longer and I wasn't sure how many vampires there were in this area. I wouldn't want to step on any toes."

He looked taken aback, "What…" he thought better of it, "You're welcome."

"So where are we going?" I inquired enthusiastically.

The look in his eyes sent a shiver down through my body, "To a little place in the middle of nowhere so we can have some privacy."

We were there almost before the words left his lips. A rustic little hunting cabin covered in snow appeared in the bouncing headlights. It looked like a postcard with the spruce trees around it dusted in white. It was beautiful. I was speechless. I laughed when I realized that my mouth was literally hanging open at the sight. The sound broke the silence and bounced through the whiteness, startling me. Charles just stared at me with an amazed smile on his face.

"You're going to kill me aren't you?" I laughed.

"What?"

"Isn't this the type of place that powerful men take poor unsuspecting young women? You know, the type of place where they're never found again."

"Come into my lair," he snarled playfully and jumped out of the jeep. Before the door even clicked shut he was standing in the snow by the passenger side. I was impressed and actually wondered if I really could keep up. With a movement that was almost too quick for me to see he swept me into his arms and darted into the cottage. I knew he could feel my heart rate jump off the charts by his close contact. It was utterly delicious. In the warmth of the house he set me on my feet but didn't step back, keeping me close against his hard body.

I snorted, "Show off" and pushed away, knowing that I would be much more coherent without his body against mine. He laughed and motioned to the huge French doors that opened into the wilderness that stretched for miles upon miles, the challenge was plain on his face. I smiled impishly and strolled slowly towards the back door. I steeled myself against the cold and swung the door open to the white wonderland. Charles hadn't moved from the front door as I threw over my shoulder, "Try to keep up." I darted out the door and into the wilderness. I could hear his laugh behind me.

6. Experience Alaska

Hunting was interesting. It was freezing, literally. I did my best to keep my shivers in check as we sprinted into the woods, but I knew he noticed the few times I couldn't control it. The air froze in my nostrils and made me sneeze as I sprinted over the snowbanks. Charles glanced back a couple of times with an almost pained look, but he didn't say a word. I just glared every time as he had easily overtaken me in the woods and was running several paces ahead.

I took another ice-filled breath and suddenly caught a scent. I stopped dead in my tracks and tried to find the scent again. Charles skidded to a halt and turned back to me. A slow smile spread across my face and the air almost felt warmer as I imagined the blood. "The stag's mine," I teased taking off running. I heard him chuckle as he took off. We raced through the snow barely leaving tracks behind us. My blood was racing now and the joyous warmth spread through my body. The burn in my throat flared up as I imagined the warm liquid quenching my thirst.

I let my instincts reign as I took in the scent. I flew through the woods with Charles right behind me. Even as focused as I was on the hunt, I was aware of him just a step behind me and I knew in the back of my mind, with some annoyance I might add, that he was letting me beat him to the herd. But this wasn't right. A second scent accosted my senses, wolves. I heard a growl behind me and Charles snarled, "The alpha's mine." I smiled as we rushed through the brush.

There was barely a pause as we reached the clearing and I leaped at the second largest wolf in the pack. She didn't put up much of a fight, she was weak from hunger. In only a moment I had drained her of blood. This was the one advantage to hunting animals, you could drink until you were satisfied and didn't need to worry about the devastation you would leave behind if you lost control. Otherwise they didn't taste very good, much like broccoli, and this one was malnourished so it was really more like tofu. I pushed the lifeless predator off of my body. I closed my eyes and enjoyed the warmth the blood created in my limbs.

Charles sunk his teeth into the Alpha's neck. There wasn't a single drop of blood on the white snow bank beneath him. He moved so quickly it was as though he floated above the ground, never touching it. Snow had started falling during our run and it clung to him and glistened like gems. Even in the ferocity of the kill he was gorgeous, beautiful. I was absorbed.

I caught the scent just as the wolf I hadn't seen leaped from the brush. I didn't have time to react before it crashed into me. The impact threw me into a tree. My rib snapped. I sunk my teeth into his throat as his teeth punctured my shoulder. The wound was deep, the blood broke the surface, and I was vaguely aware that this was bad. I, however, had the upper hand in strength and drained the blood from the wolf in an instant, dropping it in disgust. I looked up to see Charles running towards me. A horrific sound, somewhere between a scream and growl, erupted through my clenched teeth. Charles was at my side in a blink of an eye. I tried to push him away, to tell him there was too much blood, but he scooped me up in his arms and was running through the woods faster than I ever could hope to. Show Off.

The only thing I could think of to do was to wrap my arm around his neck and hold on. I unconsciously shifted my weight so that I wouldn't push my bloody shoulder against his clean shirt and gasped at the pain in my side; it wasn't finished healing. Still, his scent calmed me, and I almost felt sleepy wrapped in his arms and warm from the fresh kill. The scent of my blood snapped me out of that happy little fantasy. I was bleeding in the arms of a vampire. This was not the best position to be in. I tried to protest and have him set me down, but he just growled every time I suggested it. Sooner than I had realized, Charles was slipping me into his jeep. I felt an impossibly warm sensation where his arms had held me.

"Lieutenant," I whispered reaching out to him, he caught my arm and looked into my eyes with such force that it knocked the breath out of me. There was an electric charge flowing through me and my breath quickened. He quickly dropped his hand and looked away quickly muttering, "I'm taking you to the hospital. I can't believe I took you out here…this was a mistake."

"Lieutenant," I started, but he placed his fingers on my lips and whispered, "What's my name?" I didn't know if I could speak, but I whispered "Charles" against his fingers. God my voice sounded so very weak, but I was thrilled that his fingers were touching my face. He pulled his hand back like I had burned him. I took a deep breath.

"Charles," I assured him, "I don't need a doctor. I'm fine."

"You didn't yell like that because it tickled."

I smiled, "I'm already completely healed."

His brow furrowed and he looked confused as he muttered, "I don't understand."

"Well," I blushed, "I'm a freak."

I looked out from under my eyelashes to gauge his reaction, but he only looked curious. Of course he was curious. Who wouldn't be curious about a freak of nature? I cleared my throat and continued, "I'm half human, remember. I can die. I can bleed. My bones can break. I have to breathe air. I need human food..." All the words came out in a rush. I lifted my eyes from the floor of the jeep and let my voice trail off. He was staring at me again with that same strange expression I couldn't place.

He finally asked, "You can die?"

I nodded.

"And you can be injured?"

I nodded again.

"What hurts you?"

I smirked, "Well, a forceful knife thrust has about the same effect as it would on a human, but I heal much much faster."

"What just happened to you?"

"I didn't make sure of my surroundings and I got caught off guard."

"What happened?"

"That wolf broke my rib," I laughed.

Charles looked appalled, "You need a doctor."

I grabbed his hand to stop him from walking away and was thrilled at my own bold behavior, "I'm fine."

He snorted at my assertion and tried to pull away, but I held fast. I looked into his eyes, willing him to trust me as I pulled his hand closer. He looked nervous, but I smiled as reassuringly as I could. He didn't pull away. I placed his had against my ribs. He looked confused as he felt along my side. I felt electric. His fingers searched my side for the break I knew wasn't there anymore. He placed his other hand on my other side and continued the process of searching for my injury. He poked and watched my face for a reaction that would betray some pain. It was a little tender when he found the right spot, but it wasn't nearly as painful as it had been before.

He looked confused as he probed my sides. I watched his face intently as he struggled to figure out why he couldn't feel the break. His face was flawless, just like every other vampire I had ever met before. Somehow, there was more to him. I couldn't figure it out. He was obviously handsome, but there was something about the way his mouth twitched and the way his forehead wrinkled. He touched where the break had happened again and I winced mentally making sure that I didn't show any outward signs. I could heal quickly, but it normally took an hour or two for me to recover completely from a broken bone.

I started to shiver as the cold air wrapped around the inside of the jeep and blushed again at my humanity. Charles feeling my body quake under his hands looked into my eyes and paused. It seemed as though he was unsure of what to do next. I was sitting in the open door of the jeep his face just inches away from my own. I felt the urge to lean forward and kiss him again. I took an uneven breath and leaned infinitesimally forward, but before I knew it, he was pulling a jacket out of the duffel bag he had retrieved earlier and stepping back. I tried not to let the embarrassment show on my face.

"Why do you have a jacket?" I mumbled as he thrust it into my lap and walked around to the driver's side door. The jeep roared to life. He didn't answer my question. In fact he was suspiciously quiet, and that was when the thought suddenly dawned on me, "Did you bring it for me?" I tried not to smile at the thought. He didn't answer me and refused to meet my questioning stare. I stared, waiting for some sort of answer, some sort of sign that he had or hadn't brought that lovely warm jacket with me in mind.

He cleared his throat in an almost nervous manner and asked if I was still thirsty. The smile broke through as I answered, "No, I'm not thirsty anymore, but I am a little hungry." The jeep bumped down the road. He didn't look at me and I dropped my head ashamed, worried that I had done or said something to upset him. I saw him glance over at me and then a quiet laugh shook his shoulders. "You look like you've committed a murder," he chuckled. I looked over and our eyes met, a shiver ran through me. It wasn't from the cold, but from the look on his face. His eyes were a lighter green, not hungry, but not satisfied. The hunger in his eyes seemed to be something else. Something much more primal.

I had to look away before the emotion growing in me made it known on my face. He smiled. Softly he brushed the hair back from my cheeks and asked where I wanted to eat. I felt my confidence return somewhat or maybe I just figured that I should pretend if nothing else.

I tossed my hair back and smiled impishly, "Just take me to your favorite place."

He laughed and the sound was sweetly musical. "How does some local cuisine sound?" he smiled playfully.

"Sounds delicious, I assume it's no one I know?" I bit my bottom lip as he shot a look in my direction, but it was wickedly playful. My heart trembled.

He smiled, "I was thinking maybe Café Alexis."

I sniffed, "How absolutely mundane after the appetizers."

He laughed.

Cafe Alexis was a modest and unassuming place. Small, but it smelled delicious. The outside was completely brick with windows that looked thick enough to hold back an atmosphere. Two large oaken doors with black iron hardware locked away the cold as Charles handed me out of the jeep. He swung open the doors and the warmth from inside the restaurant spilled out and wrapped around us.

Barely a moment after we walked in, it became obvious that I was not the only person who found Charles Sullivan attractive. Most of the heads in the restaurant turned. I blushed and Charles took my hand as he ushered me to the hostess stand. He winked. He actually winked at me and my heart stuttered. The hostess didn't notice, in fact her eyes never left his face. She was an attractive young woman. Her facial structure and skin tone hinted that she was of Native descent. She held her head high and her black hair almost sparked in the low light of the dining area. Charles smiled at her and she positively glowed back. I felt the stab of jealousy accost me as we were led to our table. I was so glad when a male waiter introduced himself, but apparently

Charles was not. He shot the waiter a nasty look when he smiled all too warmly at me. The poor man shuddered, but bravely stood by and asked for our orders.

We *both* ordered. I raised my eyebrow when he set down his menu and smiled at me. I was completely fascinated. I had never gone to eat with a vampire, but I imagined that it was not the ordinary course of action to order a full course meal. In fact, I seriously wondered if he had ever been to a restaurant since the change.

"Why are you ordering?" I asked taking a sip of my Coke.

He smiled, "It's all part of my elaborate cover. I push it around a little bit, make it look like I've eaten. No one has actually caught on."

I laughed and took another sip of my soda, "Clever cover."

"So," he finally said, "Tell me more about yourself."

"Like what?" I was immediately nervous. I didn't like to talk about me.

He looked at me with a piercing penetrating gaze, "Everything."

I looked away and took a deep breath.

"I want to get to know you better."

"It's not that interesting."

"It is to me," his eyes smoldered. I could smell the roses through the food.

"A girl shouldn't tell all on the first date," I gulped trying to sound playful and failing miserably, "You already know quite a bit about me."

"Not as much as I want to."

The waiter saved me with the breadsticks. I shoved one in my mouth immediately.

Charles wasn't happy and he grumbled under his breath.

"What?" I teased, "Are you always used to getting your way with only a smile?"

He pursed his lips together and thought about it for a moment.

"Well," I snickered, "Doesn't Ms. Watters usually give you everything you want as soon as you turn on the charm?"

"Actually," he finally mused, "they *all* do."

I huffed and nibbled on my piece of bread.

He smiled, "All of them except you."

I dropped my eyes and mumbled, "I already told you I was a freak."

He looked taken aback, but didn't say anything.

Thank the heavens for quick service, just at that moment the waiter brought us our entrées. He bought me several precious moments as I chewed the chicken parm. Charles was silent for several minutes as I ate; he did just as he had said he would and pushed the food around on his plate. The food was surprisingly good. I smiled foolishly through my full mouth and Charles chuckled. He rested his head on his hands and stared into my eyes. I got lost in the depth of those gorgeous green oceans and almost choked on my pasta. He chuckled softly as I gulped down my food.

It seemed like forever as he stared and I felt that same desire to kiss him swell within me. I was now, however, completely in control of my hormones. The blood had saturated my system and given me back every ounce of my will power. He broke the spell by clearing his throat and dropping his eyes. The waiter returned and filled my Coke. I noticed the glare when the waiter turned his back on Charles and focused completely on me. I was flattered. The waiter tried to ascertain if I needed anything and I smiled politely that I was fine. Still he hesitated and I heard a low growl in Charles' throat. It was much too low for the waiter to hear, but he still looked over his shoulder uncomfortably and walked away quickly.

"How long have you worked for Georgia?" Charles finally asked, not looking up from his plate. I wanted him to look up, to let me get lost in those eyes again, but at the same time was grateful that he didn't. The break from his mesmerizing stare allowed me to formulate a coherent thought.

"Too long," I answered with a grim laugh, "It will be four years in March, but I don't know that I will be able to keep from killing her for that long."

He laughed and I cleared my throat.

"So, how old are you?"

He smiled, "If I was a woman you wouldn't ask that question."

"But you're not," I countered, looking up at him from under my eyelashes.

He muttered something I couldn't make out before he said more clearly, "I turn 150 years old on January first."

"New Year's Baby."

"How about you?"

"Well, I am a woman and I don't have to answer that," I turned my head away from him in mock indignation.

He pouted, jutting his bottom lip out. He looked adorable.

I rolled my eyes and answered, "I'll be 101 in June."

"Well," he laughed raising his untouched Coke to me, "You don't look a day over twenty-five."

I blushed and muttered for him to shut up.

He smiled and it took my breath away. I looked at his barely touched meal and muttered, "Guess you weren't as hungry as you thought." He smiled back at me and hoped that my smile was half as dazzling as his. The waiter must have thought so because he was at our table in a second. Charles didn't even pretend to be polite as he asked for the check. I smirked a little. It felt really good to have someone act jealous because of me. I blushed. He offered me his hand, and I took it with a pleasure as he helped me from my seat flashing a smile that made my heart jump. The waiter came towards me with a flirtatious grin and Charles put a protective arm around my waist as he escorted me to the jeep.

"Jealous much?" I whispered as we walked out the door.

His arm tightened around my waist, "It's not what you think."

How would he know what I thought? How would he know if it was what I desperately wanted it to be? He knew that I was attracted to him and I couldn't be sure that the feeling had been reciprocated. I gave him as incredulous a look I could manage while staring into his eyes and he shook his head but continued, "You're a very special woman and I wouldn't want anything to deprive me of you."

I blushed as he helped me into the jeep, completely confused as to what he was talking about. I didn't know what to think as he drove me back to my hotel. He was taking a very keen interest in me and I was afraid that I was letting my imagination take control of a “nothing but friendly” situation. But when he glanced at me, I couldn’t help but feel it was something else.

He walked me in to the hotel and insisted on accompanying me to my room. He didn’t say a word as we walked down the hallway. I laughed when we reached my door. “Thank you for a wonderful evening.” I spun around to face him but didn’t realize he was so close. I turned straight into his chest and the blush I had become so familiar with in the last few hours stained my cheeks once again, but he didn’t step back like I had expected him to. I was suddenly trapped between my door and his rock hard, perfectly sculpted body. I stopped breathing.

He very slowly lifted his hand, almost like he was afraid to move too quickly and frighten me. He touched my cheek. His fingers were cold, but I felt warm where he touched me and my knees felt weak. I fought against the urge to lean my head into his hand as his fingers traced down my jawline and I could feel the electricity flowing through me. My breath was starting to come in short ragged breaths. I had never felt this absolute longing before and I couldn’t get enough of the sensation. He drew his fingers to my chin and lifted my eyes to his. His eyes were smoldering with desire and I swallowed hard. I wanted him to kiss me. I wanted him to feel the same desire I felt. He leaned in and I came forward slightly as he bent his head towards me. He was just about to touch my lips when he hesitated and kissed my forehead. He whispered, “Sleep well” and looked away quickly.

I took a deep breath filling my lungs with as much of his scent as I could sustain as he stepped away and disappeared down the hallway without ever looking back. I fumbled with the key to my room and I dropped it several times. Once the door was finally open, I threw myself down on the bed and kicked off my shoes. My insides were a mess. I was so exhilarated that I could barely breathe. I replayed every look, every word, every moment of the night in my head as I lay there. I reveled in the thought that he might actually care for me. I tripped through my own surprisingly girlish fantasies. I had felt desire before, but never like this. This was more than just a carnal desire, this was a deeper feeling. Almost what I imagine love would feel like, but I’m sure I must have been mistaken. No one can fall in love in the space of a few hours. Can they?

Then the terrible thought that he was just playing with me, like Sgt. Bracken, stabbed into my inflated ego and my all too willing heart. I didn't believe it, I wouldn't believe it. Behind my closed eyes I saw his face and smelled his scent. It was as though he were standing next to me. I didn't open my eyes. I wanted to believe my over active imagination. That he had the same violent reaction to me that I had to him.

The corners of my mouth twitched upwards as I heard his breathing. I had been so lost in my own thoughts that I hadn't heard how he had slipped in. He stopped breathing when I smiled, trying to be silent, but I already knew he was there and he knew it. I didn't open my eyes; I didn't want him to go. I don't know how long I laid there like that, him not breathing and me in bed. I listened to him as he sat down on the opposite bed. I could feel his eyes on me. It was strange, even with all of the doubt that surrounded him, I felt safer with him there beside me. I could feel him smile. He knew I wasn't asleep and I couldn't help but laugh. I chuckled, "Good night Charles," and heard his low musical laugh as I drifted off.

The nightmare was new that night. I was running as I had been before, but this time I ran until I was standing in the middle of a large room covered in lights. They were very bright. They hurt my eyes they were so bright. I squinted against them and all I could see were shapes. There were dark figures against the lights, but I couldn't make out any of their faces. All I could see were gleaming teeth. Pointed teeth, vampire teeth, but also human teeth, all twisted in grotesque smiles. They were smiling at me, looking at me, examining me. I was terrified. I was vaguely aware that I was screaming, but there was nothing that I could do. I was paralyzed in my dream. I tried to move to run, but I couldn't. I screamed again and the sound of myself screaming woke me up.

I didn't know that I talked in my sleep, let alone that I screamed. I bolted straight up in bed and stared in wide eyed horror at the set of teeth that stared back at me. Sharp pointed vampire teeth gleamed in the dark. I jumped back against the wall with a defensive growl, but then I recognized the figure standing there. Relief.

Charles was at the edge of my bed his arms extended completely unsure of what to do. I didn't stop to think of the consequences of my actions, I just wanted him to comfort me. I realized as I jumped into his arms that nothing was thrown across the room. I didn't want him to know how much more of a freak I was. Then I noticed what used to be a picture frame lying in a pile of splintered glass and wood. I tried to pull back afraid that he had seen what I had done, but his arms closed around me and pulled me down on the bed. I didn't fight him. I'm not sure that I could have if I wanted to. He was so much stronger than me, I don't think that I could have fought him off. That realization frightened me horribly, but excited me at the same time. I had never met a person who could match me let alone excel me. I was exhilarated and exhausted at the same time.

He shifted me around until I was sitting on his lap. I buried my head in his shoulder and only then did I realize that I was crying. That dream had truly shook me to the core of my being. I closed my eyes for a second and saw those gleaming white teeth. My eyes quickly flew open. They were not friendly whoever they were, they were after me, and I didn't know how to escape. It was too real. I might as well have been sitting in that room with all those hostile teeth glaring at me. His cold fingers closed around my chin and brought my eyes up to his. He looked absolutely tortured. My throat was thick with sleep and tears as I whispered, "How long have you been here?"

"I never left, you're adorable when you're sleeping," he whispered with a soft smile, but then his voice changed. It became darker, "You started screaming about five minutes ago. I didn't know what to do," his voice became hard, "You looked so terrified...I couldn't...I never felt so helpless. I didn't know what would make you feel better and I so desperately wanted you to wake up and know you were safe..." his voice trailed off as he wiped the tears from my cheeks with his thumb. He pressed my head against his shoulder again and told me to go to sleep. He looked ashamed when he looked away. I didn't understand why. I started to ask, but he gently kissed my hair and my thoughts scattered. I didn't want to close my eyes again, I was afraid of what I would see. Charles ran his fingers through my hair and whispered soothingly, "It'll be alright."

I closed my eyes and heard him breathing rhythmically. I decided that I didn't care why he was here, why he was worried about me, why he was holding me. I just cared that he was here, holding me. It was like laying amongst flowers. I felt his cheek lean against my hair and his breath was sweet. Before I knew what was happening I felt my eyelids droop and my consciousness fade. I fell into a deep dreamless sleep.

7. One Thing After Another

When the alarm went off I was completely alone. I wondered if I had dreamed the whole thing. My imagination must have run wild after the long night. That was the only explanation. Then I realized that I was wrapped up in the ugly comforter and laying horizontally across the bed. I couldn't have been dreaming, I knew I didn't go to sleep that way and there was no way that I had scooted around enough to pull that off. Part of me was elated that he had stayed and part of me didn't even understand why I had let him.

Puzzling out my feelings, however, would have to wait, as the hard pounding on the door commenced. I didn't even need the strong scent of Hypnotic Poison that wafted through the cracks to know that it was Georgia on the other side, eager to go shopping and find a dress that would wow all of these "little people." She would be all bubbly and happy this morning with the prospect of being the most revered and envied woman at the dinner tonight. I, of course, would smile and compliment her as I picked something very understated and simple. She would turn heads and wow everyone that she saw while I sat with Oliver and Carter in the corner, sipping champagne and longing for the moment we could escape.

I glanced in the mirror before I answered the door and smiled at my completely disheveled appearance. I would let Georgia make her own inferences about what went on last night; I didn't even bother to try and make myself look presentable. Thankfully, that fact did not go unnoticed. Oh, life's little victories. Georgia took in my attire and messy hair with a completely disgusted look. Her nose even wrinkled slightly. She demanded I get ready and we go shopping, "not that we'll find anything decent in this horrid little place." I doubted what she had in mind would be considered decent in any company, let alone the Air Force. I mumbled for her to give me a minute to get ready and closed the door in her face.

She wasn't very happy that I was not already waiting for her to knock on my door or my rude dismissal; I could hear her breathing spike indignantly. Still she stood by for a moment, tapping her foot in the hallway as I stared in the mirror. I really did look an absolute mess. Finally, in a barely civil tone Georgia announced to the door that she would be getting breakfast in the dining room. I could hear her angry steps marching down the hallway. I wiggled my finger through the hole the wolf had left in my shirt and huffed. I actually liked that shirt. I guess it could have been worse. I ran my hand over the smooth skin on my shoulder. There wasn't a scratch to betray what had happened. I stretched a little and the rib was fine as well.

I took my time gathering my things, childishly making Georgia wait as long as possible. I took all of my make-up into the bathroom with my plush light blue bathrobe and fuzzy matching slippers. I set everything on the counter and arranged it particularly. Once I was convinced that I had everything in order, I stepped into the shower and let the hot water do its work.

I had a feeling this was the only warmth I was going to be dealing with today. I let it rush over me, caressing me, wrapping me in its comfort. I needed all the comfort I could get. Today was going to be horrible. Georgia had this little game she liked to play every time I was subjected to her company. She would parade through hundreds and hundreds of dresses and make me watch as she pranced and turned and spun and flaunted everything her mamma, and her plastic surgeon, gave her. I had to smile and pretend to care; all the while wishing I could melt into the floor and escape the misery. Then as soon as I picked up a dress she would immediately start to berate me. "Oh, dear that color is just horrible for your complexion." "You really don't have the body to pull that off." "You really shouldn't wear a neckline like that, it makes you look…well, you know." However, I always knew that the dresses she hated the most looked the best. For some reason she never figured that out in her infinite narcissism. It obviously made her feel better about herself to put others down, but I hated being on the receiving end of that. I tried not to let the thought bother me as the water started to run cold. That was my cue; it was time for me to step out.

I looked in the mirror, ready to start a new day. Or at least I was going to pretend. I still couldn't get the dream out of my mind and the feeling of Charles holding me through the night kept nagging at the edges of my consciousness. I pulled on my terry cloth robe and snuggled into it against the sudden cold air that assaulted me. I loved hot showers, but could never stand the sudden chill that assaults you as soon as you step into the air. I stood at the mirror and stared at the darkening circles under my eyes. My eye color had returned to its normal hue of blue that only seemed enhanced by the purplish bruise-like shadows beneath them. I sighed as I carefully pulled back my hair and applied my lipstick and eye-shadow. I snuggled myself back into my robe before I stepped out of the bathroom. Within a second I was back inside and had slammed the door shut.

"What are you doing?" I gasped. Charles' intoxicating laugh slipped through the door. I must have been red from head to toe. I had just stepped out of the shower and he was standing there. Just standing there. Looking at me. Me! I was wearing a huge fuzzy robe and matching slippers. I must have looked ridiculous. If nothing else I definitely looked like a lunatic.

"I just wanted to talk to you while you were lucid," he laughed.

"Charles, I'm kind of indecent at the moment if you didn't notice." I childishly slammed my fist against the door.

He laughed roguishly, "Oh, I noticed," the short silence that followed was charged with implications, "you know I like the whole fuzzy robe and wet hair look on you."

I huffed, "I hate you."

I could tell he was fake pouting, "Do you really?"

I huffed, "If I say 'yes' will you go away."

"No, I will be here forever."

I sighed, "No, I don't really hate you, but I am extremely annoyed with you at the moment." I wanted so badly to be mad at him, but I wasn't. I was elated.

"Well, if it makes you feel any better, last night you were much more indecent." His voice was thick with innuendos.

I made an indignant sound and swung open the door and pushed past him. He leaned against the wall with the most insufferable smile on his face. I grimaced at him and made a show of slamming the drawers on the hotel dresser shut and throwing my clothes on the bed. He just watched smiling.

"You aren't going to talk to me?" he finally asked.

"No," I said stubbornly. For some reason he brought out the most childish reactions in me. It was the most frustrating feeling in the world. He snickered even though I glared at him as forcefully as possible, which unfortunately wasn't nearly as forceful as I had intended. I'm sure the wet hair and fuzzy slippers diminished the effect a bit. It also didn't help that I made the mistake of looking into his beautifully light green eyes and all my thoughts scattered horrendously.

He stepped forward, his eyes sparkling mischievously. "Do you want me to leave you alone? Never come back? Pretend you don't exist?" He fake pouted at me and my scowl melted into a smile despite myself. I growled under my breath, his smug smile just rankled me. "That's what I thought," he gloated. I huffed and gathered my clothes into my arms.

"What was it that you broke into my room to tell me?" I snorted walking back into the bathroom.

I made a point to slam the door and he laughed, "You're so cute when you're mad."

I harrumphed and muttered under my breath. I heard him slump against the door as I got dressed.

"I came here to ask you out on a date tonight?" I was flattered for a moment and then I realized that tonight was the night of the press dinner. He was messing with me. Well, if he was going to mess with me then it was only fair that I got to mess with him too.

I smirked and answered, "Well, I don't know. Why should I spend this evening with a man like you? One who obviously has no qualms about breaking into my room?"

He pushed off from the door almost angrily and I smiled as I put on my outfit. I heard him gently place both hands on the door. His voice became intoxicatingly melodic I had to concentrate on my breathing. He whispered seductively, "Because for some odd reason neither of us seems to be able to leave the other one alone." My heart skipped a beat thinking that perhaps he had as difficult a time staying away from me as I had staying away from him. I took a deep breath and swung open the door.

"I think that seems to be one sided," I brushed past him and picked up my purse and slipped on my jacket. I smiled to myself when I heard his playful growl. I turned to face him and in a lightening fast movement he was inches from me. I fell back against the dresser, but instead of backing up as I expected him to he leaned in closer. My heart kicked into overdrive and my breath came out in ragged short gasps.

I was practically sitting on the dresser. Charles placed his hands against the faux wood. He was so close his nose was nearly touching mine. My heart raced against my ribs and every breath brought the sweet scent of roses to fill my lungs. I was torn. Should I lean in or pull away? Was I prepared for this? It took me a minute to realize that my mouth was hanging open and my eyes were wide. I closed my eyes, shook my head, and attempted to reassemble my expression.

As soon as darkness filled my eyes he brushed his lips against my jaw line. My body reacted electrically. I didn't dare open my eyes as his lips moved from my jaw to my neck. I began to feel dizzy as his lips moved up under my chin, but he didn't kiss my lips. He was only inches away from my face. He dragged his fingers across my lips. I parted them slightly allowing myself to be pulled into his charm while a voice in my head screamed that this was wrong. Something wasn't right. I didn't care. Charles was here and he wanted me as much as I wanted him. He leaned close and whispered breathlessly in my ear, "Completely one-sided, but all you have to do is tell me to go away."

I hadn't realized that at some point I started to hold my breath. It suddenly whooshed out as I pushed him back. My pulse was still erratic and my breathing hadn't come back under control yet. He smiled, but didn't resist my rebuff. "Go away," I smiled, "I have to go meet Georgia and subject myself to hours of shopping."

He laughed and pushed a few stray strands of hair behind my ear. "Doesn't that sound like fun?"

I snorted and looked down. His eyes were searching for something in mine and I was afraid to return the gaze. He ducked down until I couldn't avoid his gaze any more. I could feel myself blushing as he stared into my eyes. He pulled out metallic blue cell phone lingering just slightly as he shoved it deep into my back pocket. "My number's in there," he laughed, "If you need anything, like directions or fresh wolf, call me." I rolled my eyes, but I was completely jumbled inside. I was thrilled that he seemed to care so much and a little confused as to why he was handing me a cell phone. I finished getting together my gloves and hat.

Charles stood by the door dangling my purse from his fingers and smilingly impishly. I tried not to return his smile, but I couldn't help it. I couldn't help but smile at his amazingly cute and breathtaking smirk. I reached for my purse, but he wouldn't release it.

"So, are you going to dance with me tonight?" he asked tugging my purse as I tried to take it from him.

"Are you going to hold my purse hostage until I say yes?" I tried to make my face look severe. It didn't work out too well. I'm sure I looked much more like a child than an angry grown-up.

I could see that reflection in his smug little smirk as he whispered, "Possibly."

I rolled my eyes and sighed, "Well then I guess I better do some shopping for myself. Any suggestions?"

He let my purse fall into my hands as his eyes roam all over my body. The feeling was almost tangible. I felt the blush rush over my face. "I would suggest blue, to bring out your eyes," he purred, "And make sure it doesn't cover too much." He traced his fingers down my collarbone and I shivered underneath his icy touch. His temperature didn't have anything to do with the jolt that ran through my body. I disengaged myself from his eyes and mumbled that I needed to go and deal with Georgia. I wasn't quite sure if it was coherent or not, but he must have gotten the gist as he stepped back and let me go.

I heard the door click shut behind me. He wasn't following me, but I looked over my shoulder anyway. Nothing. I went to the lobby to meet with Georgia and was taken by surprise to see Sgt. Bracken speaking with her. He smiled as I walked over. It wasn't a very pleasant smile, quite honestly it frightened me. There was something sadistic behind his fake civility. He was waiting for something to happen and I was fairly certain I wasn't going to like it when it did.

"Ms. Bell," he cooed in a harsh voice. I smiled warily and extended my hand. I quickly scanned the room looking for the scent from the female vampire he had seen no more than a half an hour ago. It was still fairly strong. I'm surprised that Georgia didn't realize he was seeing another woman, she seemed to be able to zone in on that with any other man. The only other people in the room were the concierge and Lena Watters, still staring daggers in my direction. It was really something that I was beginning to get used to. I didn't think that she was ever a pleasant person. In fact, I'm pretty sure that the human shell she wore was incapable of being pleasant. But I smiled politely in her face and felt the phone in my pocket.

"Are you joining us for this little excursion?" I tried to sound polite, but was convinced it didn't come out that way.

However, he smiled and shook his head with mock sadness. "I'm afraid I will have to defer to the ladies as far as that is concerned. I have no head for fashion." I smiled, but my eyes narrowed. There was something going on. Whoever was pulling this marionette's strings was keeping well out of sight. I took a deep breath and analyzed the scent again. This time there was a faint perfume to the smell. It was definitely artificial and I racked my brain as to why a vampire would need perfume. I took another deep breath and suddenly realized why that smell was so familiar. It wasn't the mystery vampire's at all. It was Georgia's. Hypnotic Poison, her favorite. It was a much older smell than the vampire's, from last night at least.

Georgia, unable to bear being out of the spotlight asserted herself yet again. She loudly cleared her throat and took Sgt. Bracken's hand. He politely kissed it and gave her a devilishly charming look that almost made her knees give out. I wanted to burst out laughing. The irony of Georgia falling for the one guy who was ultimately unavailable did not escape me. Honestly, it served her right. She always messed with other people's emotions, so it was only fair that she be messed with too.

She was obviously displeased by the smug look I felt creep across my face. In a huff, she picked up her jacket and shouldered me out of the way hissing, "Let's go." I tried not to laugh at her expression. Instead I smiled at Sgt. Bracken and excused myself, there was no need for me to be uncivil. So, with a deep breath I was as ready as I was ever going to be to brave the shopping world with the world's worst companion.

As if sensing my reluctance, Georgia was nothing if not miserable the entire time we were out. Being used to the plentiful shopping options in Philadelphia, the three stores that sold dresses were a great disappointment to the diva and we ended up in the

Sears desperately seeking through racks and racks of frilly prom dresses. Honestly, everything about the situation was distasteful to Georgia and the service left the most to be desired in her eyes. The salesclerk was actually very pleasant and did point out the area where the dresses were held. However, in order to placate the diva in any way, you would be required to stand at the dressing room door with armfuls of clothes. I envied that the girl could walk away and never have to think of this again except as lunch room gossip. I, on the other hand, would have to deal with the repercussions of this day for the next three or four.

It was plain that in Georgia's eyes I was there as consultant and nothing else, but that was not why I was in such a foul mood. I had important business to handle today. I needed to impress a vampire who, for some odd reason, I couldn't get off my mind. I kept feeling the urge to reach back and touch the blue phone in my pocket. I still couldn't figure out why he had given me a phone. And every single dress I looked at had something wrong with it. They were too poofy, too short, too long, too see-through, too everything. I couldn't find a single thing that I thought Charles would find attractive. On top of that disappointment, I constantly had to reassure Georgia that she looked beautiful in anything she tried on which was perhaps the most depressing part of the afternoon.

Mostly I lied through my teeth. Georgia deliberately picked out the shortest, most revealing outfit she could find. Her first dress was two sizes to small around the bust and she nearly popped out of the strapless top just spinning around. Her second dress barely ended below her butt cheeks. She pretty much looked like a whore in most everything she tried on. However, she wasn't the only one who preferred that sort of attire. After about the fifth dress Georgia paraded out in, there was an unexpected squeal of delight. As if my day wasn't painful enough, it was our very own Ms. Lena Watters. She found her way over to us and of course she and Georgia found common ground immediately. They were both searching for the absolute perfect dress for tonight's little gala. I smiled as best I could.

Lena gave me one of the most thinly veiled hostile stares I have ever seen. She sneered an introduction at me and I responded with what I hoped was a polite smile. I attempted to distract

Georgia with another dress, one that I knew she would approve of, but to no avail. Lena butted right in and offered to help us both find dresses that were designed to impress. I could see it in her eyes; she was determined to stay with us. As soon as Georgia walked into the dressing room, Lena turned her attention to me.

She smiled an obviously fake smile and said, "So, you ever been to Alaska before?"

I smiled politely and indicated that I hadn't.

"Pity," she said with her voice dripping sugary sweetness, "I know that Charles really likes women that can withstand the cold."

"Oh" I asked trying my best to sound confused as to what she was implying.

She laughed, "Oh that Charles is a charmer, isn't he?"

I smiled, "He's been very gentlemanly."

"He always is to the visitors," she smiled, "Always making sure they have what they need."

I nodded.

"It really is sweet, but I wish you could see the Charles I know. He's so amazing."

I couldn't help myself, "The Charles I met last night was beyond amazing."

Her face went completely white.

I smiled politely and for once was saved by Georgia who came out of the dressing room and did a little twirl giving the entire department an X-rated view of the television diva. Lena gushed over how pretty Georgia looked. Georgia was ecstatic and pranced back into the dressing room to try on another. Unfortunately, as soon as Georgia was out of sight Lena started in on me again. I understood what she was getting at; she wanted my Charles all to herself. I laughed on the inside. It was dangerous for me to be alone with or get close to Charles. For her, that type of contact would be almost suicidal. But she wasn't about to let her fantasy go. In a very real way I pitied her because I wasn't about to give up on that fantasy either.

"So, where were you two headed when I saw you last night?" Her hostility barely concealed in her inquisitive tone.

"Out," I answered simply hoping there wouldn't be any other questions.

"Did he take you out to that cabin of his?"

I was taken aback.

She saw it in my eyes and her smile was horridly sweet, "It's beautiful isn't it."

"Oh, it is," I answered. I smiled back at her sweetly, I would play her game if she wanted a fight, "I especially thought that the little stream that wound through back yard was precious."

She smiled at me and said desperately, "Well, did he take you to that darling little spot in the woods with the wooden bridge that stretches across to the other side. It's absolutely magical."

I smiled, I had been all through those woods last night and there were no streams anywhere near his cabin. Apparently, my smile had just a bit more smugness than it had before and Lena looked as though she was about to panic. This time it was she that was saved by Georgia stepping out into the main area of the floor. She looked miserable in the dress that covered her whole body. "Oh," Lena said compassionately, "That one just isn't you." She hurried to Georgia's side and cooed and primped the diva pretending I was invisible.

I sighed and resigned myself to a very long afternoon that was just getting longer with every passing second. Georgia, unsatisfied with her previous choices, needed to have dresses brought to her right and left and fortunately left no room for conversation with Lena. I was obviously distraught. I continued to wander around the dresses for what seemed like a millennia. Now I had two insecure women to fawn over, one of which was hoping for my demise. No wait, both of them were hoping for my demise. Lena was just far more obvious about it. Georgia had learned long ago that it was a much wiser idea to play nice with the person you hope to destroy. Lena could have used the tutelage. She needed to learn how to lure, not repulse her opponents.

After what seemed like an eternity, Georgia finally settled on a dark green spaghetti strapped dress that ended about two inches below her butt cheeks. She trotted out of the dressing room and a passing male sales associate started to drool. She smiled suggestively at him and he turned beet red and scampered off. I smiled and told her how wonderful she was going to look at the party. She simply looked smugly in the mirror.

After Georgia purchased her dress, Lena found her perfect outfit in record time. I wondered if she had been waiting for Georgia to find an outfit so that she would know what the lesser competition would look like. I, unfortunately, had to admit that she wasn't a hideous looking person. She, like Georgia seemed to have the ability to make men drool over her even though she was dead on the inside. She smiled contentedly as she strutted out of the dressing room in her purple scrap of fabric that someone had the nerve to try and pass off as a dress. She smiled condescendingly at me as if she knew she had a dress that would make Charles fall for her and her alone.

I couldn't find anything that I thought looked nice and of course neither of those two were any help. Lena giggled to Georgia every time I came out in anything. I, as I could plainly hear, was the topic of their conversation. Lena was smirking at my lack of enthusiasm and Georgia was whispering to her how I "never dressed well" and "couldn't get a man if I was naked." Lena seemed please with that analysis. I was sure, by the smirk that covered her face, she was thinking of Charles and how he would react to her naked. I rolled my eyes and walked into the dressing room yet again.

Luckily this dress was the one I finally decided on. It was a light blue silk dress that came across my chest into one shoulder strap and the full skirt came to my knee. I wasn't thrilled, but I figured that it was the best of my choices. To be truthful though, I never thought I looked good in anything, a fact that both Lena and Georgia capitalized upon. Neither one of them missed a single opportunity to lower my self esteem even more. We walked towards the exit and Lena started with "You know, that color might not be the best for your skin tone." Georgia nodded in agreement, but I stood firm on my decision. I was going to wear this dress no matter what and the more Lena tried to dissuade me from it, the more I started to like it.

We spent two hours looking for accessories and shoes. Lena and Georgia were insufferable. Absolutely everything they found, they invented something that was wrong with it. Those earrings were too dangly. Those rings were too tacky. That necklace was too distracting. And those heels were not tall enough. I found it most difficult to find a pair of shoes that would go with my dress. The jewelry was easy for me, a few understated pieces of silver made the outfit, and I finally settled on some silver strappy heels to go with it. Of course Lena and Georgia didn't miss an opportunity to tell me how nothing that I chose matched anything else and I had no fashion sense whatsoever. I had never wanted to disappear into oblivion more than I did at that moment. My mind kept wandering back to Charles and the little blue cell phone in my pocket. It didn't ring even though I desperately wanted it to. Why couldn't he just swoop in and save me?

As with all things, however, this dreadful day too did pass. After five hours of horrendous torture, I finally returned to the hotel. I felt so silly once I laid everything out on the bed. It wasn't that the dress, or the shoes, or the jewelry weren't pretty. In fact, this outfit was probably the nicest outfit I owned, but I had the vision in my head of me standing in the room looking an absolute mess. I shook my head to try to make the image disappear, but it was persistent. I looked in the mirror and stared at myself for a minute. My skin was pale and clear and my hair was a strawberry blonde that hung below my shoulder blades, but when I looked at me it all just didn't seem to fit. I fiddled with my hair for a moment. I pulled it up, let it down, pulled half of it up, piled it on top of my head, twisted it up, but nothing seemed to make me look any better. It was getting quite depressing.

I finally decided that there were other things to take care of and I headed out to meet with Oliver and Carter to discuss the soiree tonight and the upcoming press conferences. As always they were nothing if not on top of it. Much to my disappointment, they had already scouted out locations while I had been lost in the shopping world with Georgia and Lena. All of the locations were decided upon. All of the angles and the lighting had been discussed. The only thing left for me to do was to go back to my room and worry about how horrible I was going to look in that silky little dress and I would do anything to delay that little ego massacre.

Thinking fast I mentioned that Georgia had commandeered my morning looking for a new dress for tonight. Carter was instantly fascinated. He wanted me to describe it in detail and it wasn't long before Oliver caught the curiosity. As I described the length and neckline, they both became more and more amused.

We all wondered how the straight laced Alaskan news media would take Georgia. I couldn't wait to find out. I mentioned how the salesclerk was drooling over her and how the female clerk had the good fortune to be able to walk away. Oliver laughed and Carter looked placidly at me, but that was the extent of "The Georgia Story" and I almost panicked trying to figure out what I was going to say to keep them interested.

I mentioned that we had run into Lena Watters at the store and Carter's face went serious. My curiosity was definitely peaked. Oliver shot him a warning glance as if there was something there that he wasn't sure needed to be shared. I crossed my arms and leaned as casually as possible against the wall. I knew Carter wouldn't be able to resist telling me whatever juicy little secret he dug up. I waited patiently while a silent conversation took place in Carter and Oliver's eyes. I already knew who would win, but the complexity of the signals was intriguing. Their eyes were so expressive for not making a sound. I watched in fascination at the slight widening of Oliver's eyes and the slightly raised eyebrow of Carter. The spell was only broken by Carter blurting out, "She should know." He turned to me and said very gravely, "Nora, sweetheart, that Lena girl is a bad person." I stared back blankly. This was the big secret? Any moron who watched her for two minutes would have come to that conclusion. I laughed, "I expected more from you two."

Oliver cleared his throat and my eyes snapped over to him. "She was hanging all over Sgt. Bracken today. We had gone in search of a vending machine and there they were. It couldn't have been more than ten minutes after you left. She was hanging on him like her life depended on it. She looked desperate."

I shrugged and snorted, "And I care why?" Oliver looked down at his feet and Carter took my hand. "She was doing the same thing to Lt. Sullivan." My heart dropped. She had been hanging all over him? I couldn't even fathom his attraction to her. Granted she wasn't ugly, but she was hideous on the inside. I guess though, most men don't care about what happens on the inside, but I thought Charles was interested in more things than just sex.

Oliver must have seen my train of thought as it flashed across my face and he was quick to defend my Lieutenant. "He wasn't at all interested," he quickly spouted. "In fact, he almost insulted her." Carter was quick to pick up with that description.

"So," he said pulling me down on the bed next to him, "We went looking for the vending machine and saw her all over Bracken, then as we were heading back with our stash of chocolatey goodness, we saw her and Lieutenant Sullivan." I tried to look unconcerned. "I swear, honey, her shirt was barely over her nipples and she couldn't shove those milk bags at him forcefully enough. But Sullivan looked almost disgusted. She was babbling as best we could hear about how she knew he was just playing with you and that she would be here long after you left." I smiled and Carter laughed nervously. "Sullivan started to walk away, but she grabbed his arm. I swear the look on his face frightened me and it wasn't even directed at me. He removed her hand and gave her this look that was dismissive and almost rude. As he walked away, she stared behind him, but that hate sweetheart was directed straight at you." Apparently after that encounter she decided to track Georgia and me down. Unfortunately she succeeded.

Oliver seemed really worried. I smiled at him, but the lines between his brows didn't smooth out. "Sweetie," he said taking my hand and sitting beside me, "I'm worried about you. It's obvious you really like this man, but I can't put my finger on it." He looked at me seriously, "There's something off about him." I laughed and shook my head. Oliver looked even more concerned, "I'm serious Nora. I just don't want to see you get hurt."

I cleared my throat, "It's alright. I'm not looking for a commitment or anything. He's just been really nice, and he's hot."

Carter laughed.

Oliver scowled.

"Seriously, I'm just glad a hot guy is showing me some interest for once."

Oliver pursed his lips, "Be careful, Nora. Promise me."

I sighed, "I promise Dad."

"So," Carter cleared his throat, "What are you doing with your hair?"

"I don't know" I admitted, tugging at a stray strand.

Oliver smiled and walked over to the table and picked up a magazine. "Here, we figured you would need this." He tossed it at me with a roll of his eyes.

I looked at it and smiled, "A 'People' magazine?"

Carter laughed, "Use it, love it sweetheart."

I grimaced.

I went back to my room dejectedly and spent an hour and a half going through the magazine looking for the perfect hairdo that would go with my dress. I flipped through page after page looking for something I thought might be decent. I looked at the pages, looked in the mirror, looked at the pages again and finally just threw the magazine on the dresser and flopped over the bed. I decided that I should go over the press packet I had received the day before just to kill some time. If nothing else, Captain Dixon was thorough. The amount of maps and work that had gone into the packet was impressive. I never expected this level of professionalism from such a place. I finished with the packet and carelessly threw it on top of the dresser with the magazine. I picked up my dress from the bed.

That was when I noticed that there was something wrong. I had been in my room for two hours and hadn't noticed it before. I took a deep breath and there was the faint smell of that female vampire. She had been here, been in my room. The new dress I had just bought smelled of her. I took deep breath. The scent was so faint it wasn't a real surprise that I missed it at first. She mustn't have been here long. I followed the faint scent into the bathroom and my hairbrush and toothbrush were missing. What was she after? DNA? My hair color?

Upon further inspection I came across another scent near the door only, Sgt. Bracken. He had been here as well. The master and the marionette had stepped up their game. Before this invasion of my privacy it was all just a curiosity. But this was more than just a random coincidence. They were after something of mine and I had a sinking feeling that whatever it was spelled trouble. I growled and hurled my make-up bag into the door. It was childish, but for a moment I felt better.

Then the hotel phone started ringing. I already knew who would be at the other end of the line and Georgia did not disappoint. She screamed into the headpiece, demanding I come make sure she looked perfect. Of course the only thing she cared about was her. If she half-paid attention to anyone but herself she would have realized that something was wrong in my voice. I could hear it clearly even though I was trying to hide it. There was no way to disguise it, but she was as oblivious to anything if it didn't directly affect her. I could hear the blatant hostility in my voice as I told her I would be there after I got ready myself and slammed the receiver into the cradle. I looked sadly at my reflection in the mirror and the beautiful dress that lay stretched out on the bed. The silver heels were still in their box, the tags were still on the jewelry and dress, and they were screaming at me that I could still take them back. I hesitated, but I didn't really have a choice. I got dressed up.

I reapplied my makeup and started to mess with my hair. I couldn't decide if I should pull it up or leave it down. I twisted my fingers into the red mess and pulled it up, then I realized that pulling it up was going to reveal a lot of skin and I wasn't sure I was ready for that yet so I let it down. For twenty minutes I stood there. I pulled it up again, then I let it down again. I took a deep breath and decided that I was going to pull it up. I pulled it back into a French twist and decided that any skin I was going to show would be fine. If someone had a problem with it, they would just have to deal. I smiled and slipped into my dress and heels.

I stared in the mirror at my reflection and was completely dissatisfied. I felt stupid. I tugged on the skirt of my outfit and tried to adjust the one shoulder strap to cover as much as I could. I immediately regretted the up-do, but I didn't have time to change it now. I could almost feel Georgia tapping her foot in her room waiting for me to gush over everything that she was wearing. My stomach was tying itself in knots as I thought about what I was about to do. I looked down at the vanity and made a mental note to pick up a new hairbrush and toothbrush. If this pattern of theft was going to hold, it was going to get very annoying.

The large down-filled jacket I had brought did nothing to cover my half bare legs. The thought of how bitterly cold it was going to be took my attention away from walking and I ran straight into Sgt. Bracken. He was nothing but smiles and warm salutations for me. My eyes narrowed. I was immediately suspicious. What had he learned from my toothbrush and hairbrush that had put him in such a good mood? I quickly ran through my options. I could just show him my fangs and rip his throat out. That thought made me smile. But I figured that I should probably not show my hand just yet. Instead I smiled and excused myself to go and get Georgia.

I hadn't even let my hand fall on Georgia's door as it sprang open. Of course she looked wonderful. She always did. I knew that she would turn heads as she strolled into the ballroom. I could see the reactions of the men in my head. It was almost sickening. I sighed and looked down at the little blue cell phone I had acquired earlier that day. It hadn't rung, there were no text messages. There was absolutely nothing. I angrily shoved it back into my coat pocket. I had even checked to see if it was on. I was stupid to think he would get in touch with me anyway, and to top it off I looked like an idiot in this stupid dress. I was sure that walking into that room next to Georgia was just going to highlight my shortcomings.

Georgia was prattling on and on about her dress and her hair. She didn't even notice that I wasn't paying attention to her. The only thing she cared about was how much of a sensation she could create. I wonder if she ever had any idea that things occurred completely independent of her. No of course not, the world revolved around her; hence her never ending prattling about how awesome she was. Although thinking about self-centered women got me wondering what Lena was going to look like.

8. Dinner and Deceit

We walked into the hangar that was being used as a ballroom and all eyes seemed trained on the door as we stepped through. I felt so exposed without my jacket covering my shoulders. I glanced around furtively and was disheartened to find that Charles was nowhere to be seen. However, to my relief both Carter and Oliver were sitting at a table with two open seats and Lena was already waving to Georgia and the two empty seats at her table. The invitation was obviously not extended to me. Not that it mattered. Sgt. Bracken was at Georgia's side in a moment. His body language obviously excluded me.

I excused myself as politely as possible, not that anyone heard it, and hurried over to Carter's side. He made a point to stand up and hold my seat out for me. Champagne was on the table and I quickly emptied my fluke. Oliver and Carter exchanged a warning look and I shook my head. "I'm fine," I laughed, "It's just been a very long day." Oliver laughed and leaned in. He promised that we were going out tonight after this insidious dinner. He winked and whispered, "If you look like that, there is no reason to waste it."

I grumbled and looked for the wait staff to hopefully get a refill on my champagne. As I looked, I noticed Georgia out of the corner of my eye being romanced by every news anchor and serviceman in the room. It was fairly pathetic. The reason I couldn't find a waiter was because they were all male and being ruled at the moment by their pants instead of their heads. Private Tenor was staring at her and the look could not be mistaken. He was jealous. I could only assume the reason was his little clandestine meeting with her earlier. Sgt. Bracken was a fixture at her side, but I noticed that his eyes were constantly flickering towards me. I was beginning to just wish he would get it over with. In fact, I was hoping that he would. I wanted him to do whatever it was he and his little vampire puppeteer were up to, I was ready. I had a nasty little secret they didn't know about. I smiled at the thought and suddenly Carter popped his head up.

He looked disappointed after surveying the room and both Oliver and I looked curiously at his frown. He pouted, "I was just hoping that smile meant your dashing young Lieutenant came walking through the door." I made a low playful growling noise directed at him and smiled. He laughed and fake shuddered. If they knew what I really was, they wouldn't be pretending. I'm sure they would run as fast as they could in the opposite direction. The worse thing was that I so wanted to tell them what I was, but they wouldn't understand.

My gloomy thoughts were quickly lost in the smile I saw directed at me from the other side of the room. He did come. Lt. Sullivan came and he was standing in the doorway smiling at me. My heart skipped a beat and his smile widened. He heard it even that far across the room. I blushed a deep red and tried to focus on something other than his smile and the smirks of Carter and Oliver. I turned my head and surveyed the rest of the room looking for something to distract me.

I focused on a woman who was staring at me intently. She was a vampire. A blonde haired, deep blue eyed vampire and she was staring directly into my eyes. She was too far away and there were too many other smells for me to get a good breath of her scent, but at that moment I would have bet money that she was Bracken's puppeteer. Her mouth was twisted into a sneering smile. I couldn't place it, but whatever it was that she was thinking put me on edge. I heard a low growl rumble in her throat. I went to stand, but Charles was at my side in that moment. He caught me in his arms and whispered his greetings in my ear. I quickly looked back at that table, but the vampire was gone. She had gone, disappeared in the second Charles had taken my attention away.

I was immediately suspicious, but any uneasy feeling was quickly smoothed over with his irresistible smile. Carter and Oliver were amused. They nudged each other under the table but I don't think they knew what he was, they just knew that they had never seen me react like this to anyone else. I wasn't that easily swept off my feet, but I was enthralled and none of us understood why. He sat down next to me and whispered that I looked beautiful. I must have turned three shades of red. I fiddled with my dress self-consciously, but Charles took my hand and smiled so sweetly it took my breath away.

Lena was unfortunately not far behind Charles. She stepped right in between us, breaking the light hold Charles had on my hand. I looked away as she did her best to rub her bare leg against his.

"Hi Charles," she cooed throwing a nasty glance over her shoulder.

"Lena" he nearly growled.

"Hi Lena," I smiled deciding to be spunky.

She didn't even look, but Charles smiled as he saw the challenge flash in my eyes.

"Lena" I cooed sarcastically, "You must be so chilly with only a nightgown on."

Carter snickered and Oliver subtly cleared his throat.

"Well," she said without turning, "I would comment on your outfit, but I think that charm and class would be more appropriate for this type of affair."

"Oh," I exclaimed in mock horror, "Then you better leave before someone realizes you're here."

Charles bit his bottom lip in an attempt to not laugh, but a quick snicker escaped.

Lena was speechless. I almost felt bad. Well, almost.

She turned to me, "You suddenly got a personality."

"Pity isn't it, Charles knew all about it last night, sorry it took so long for you to find out."

I could feel the anger welling up inside her and for a moment I was glad. I readied myself for a fight, but Charles reached around her and grabbed my hand. I knew what he meant and I took a deep breath to steady my temper. He finally spoke up with "Have a good evening Lena." She looked hurt, but walked away without a word. She scurried back to Georgia's side and Georgia shot me a look that would have terrified me on a normal day, but I smiled back. Whatever was going on here, I figured I might as well enjoy it. It would be much more fun that way. Charles looked impressed.

The food was less than appetizing, but luckily the dinner did not last forever. The only thing that marred its ending was that Carter and Oliver were absolutely adamant about not wasting that dress. Charles, unfortunately, completely agreed with them. He smiled and whispered, "You look far too good to waste it on this." I grumbled half-heartedly. To be honest I was absolutely flattered that he wanted me to go out and he kept looking at me in a way that made my pulse race.

As soon as the dinner was over we were ushered out to a waiting car. Charles pulled me onto his lap and Carter and Oliver slid in beside us. Charles' lips brushed against my neck as he told Private Tenor where to go. The private's green eyes kept glancing into the back seat at me sitting on Charles' lap. He just kept grinning and whispering it into my ear so low that only I could hear.

"You really do look beautiful."

"We don't need to go play nice, you know."

"I want to get to know the people you care about."

"Why? Do you plan on sticking around?"

"Would you be upset if I wanted to?"

My heart skipped a beat and he smiled, "I didn't think you would be adverse to that idea."

I pursed my lips. I didn't want to feel as excited as I did because I knew it couldn't last.

"Nora," he whispered, a note of fatigue in his voice "I've never felt like this about anyone I've met in the last century."

I didn't speak.

Charles kept his eyes locked on Private Tenor's throughout our whispered conversation, "I don't want to lose you."

I didn't understand, but I wasn't given a chance to as we were pulling up to the club now. Carter and Oliver were out of the car in a flash and stamping their feet against the cold in the doorway.

The club wasn't anything to brag about, but it wasn't nearly as bad as what I had imagined. I mean seriously, a club in Alaska? But it was honestly just like any other club I had ever been in. As we walked in, the cop at the door waived the cover charge and drinks were free because of our escort. But the idea of going out after dinner was anything but an original idea. We were soon joined by three other cars full of people from the dinner. Lena and Georgia were, of course, among them.

Their unfortunate existence, however, did not interfere with my good time, laughing with Carter and Oliver, dancing, and having a few drinks. Charles fit right in, he seemed to be the missing part of my life, a part that I didn't even know I was missing. The music was pulsing through the club and the drinks just kept on coming. I tried to keep a level head, but my glass wouldn't get beyond half empty without someone refilling it. I could feel myself starting to get a little tipsy, but for once I was enjoying myself. Charles just sat on the bench against the wall and watched with an enigmatic smile on his face as I jumped to the beat with my two cameramen.

The female vampire was near, her scent suddenly assaulted my nostrils. I scanned the room, but it was pulsing with lights and people's heads bobbed up and down. I couldn't see her. Then I felt the sharp raking of her fingernails across my exposed skin. I spun around much too fast for human eyes to see and saw her. She stood at the exit door, a horribly wicked smile across her face. I went to confront her, but Charles spun me around and into his arms. He was smiling widely. I tried to explain to him what had just happened, but I was cut short by the spectacle that was beginning to gather momentum.

Georgia, in all of her scantily clad glory, had for some reason decided to start dancing on the bar. Not surprising, but the way Charles tensed when he saw the way that Bracken was staring at him was. I took Charles' hand and attempted to lead him to the back door. I needed to ask him about so many of these things that were happening and all I could do was hope that he would be honest with me. His fingers closed around mine, but the grip was broken by Lena Watters. I was caught off guard and the force that she charged us with nearly knocked me to the floor. She grabbed Charles around the neck and pressed her lips to his. Georgia cheered her on from the bar top, but Charles looked disgusted at best. She stepped back and Charles spat at the floor. Lena looked near tears as he stepped away from her desperate attempt to grab his attention and followed me into the night.

The cold air hit me like a solid right hook. It took the breath right out of me. My jacket was in the car, the car was out front. I considered going back inside, but I could feel Lena's eyes staring daggers in my back and more importantly I needed answers. Charles shrugged out of his suit jacket and wrapped it around my shoulders. I smiled at him, but his smile was not right. I reached out to touch his face and unexpectedly he pressed his perfect face into my palm and breathed in my scent deeply. He was acting like this was going to be the last time that we would ever be together. I opened my mouth to speak, but he was staring into the sky. I followed his gaze. In the darkness behind the club the green and yellow ribbons of the aurora borealis twisted above our heads. It was absolutely beautiful.

After a quiet ride being held in his arms while he whispered in my ear, Charles followed me down the hallway towards my room. I didn't know what to expect, but I knew I had never felt this intense desire before. He waited as I opened the door and turned to look at him. The intensity of his emotions nearly threw me off balance. His eyes were smoldering. I could feel the desire flowing through his body and felt myself lean forward. His pull was nearly magnetic. I cleared my throat stepping back and said, "Would you like to come in for a minute?"

He smiled, "Would that be proper?"

I sighed, "Are you just going to break in again later?"

He pretended to think about it for a moment and said, "Good point."

I led the way in and turned to lock my door with trembling hands. I turned and Charles was standing with his back to me. I hesitated. His body seemed to be pulling me closer. I tried to reason out what I wanted to do and what I knew I should do, but they wouldn't reconcile with one another. I took a halting step forward and reached towards him. He turned with his lightening speed and grabbed my hand. My eyes flew open and I felt me heart nearly jump out of my chest in surprise. He smiled as if he could see every emotion that ran through my veins.

He held my wrist for what seemed like an eternity as we stood there in the darkness. His eyes almost glowed with desire as he pulled me towards him. I felt my hips touch his, but I couldn't look away from his eyes. I was trapped and had no intention of breaking his spell over me. My breathing was shallow as he leaned towards me. I closed my eyes and took a deep breath before taking the plunge.

He pressed his lips to my jaw and moved down my neck. His lips were warm as they caressed the soft skin of my collarbone. My pulse was beating feverishly under his mouth and I could almost feel him smile against my skin. I twisted my fingers in his hair as his mouth moved down my collarbone towards my chest and his hands on the small of my back felt like fire through my thin silk dress. He pulled me closer and I could feel him getting harder against me. I moved my fingers down his neck to his broad shoulders. I hesitatingly reached down to find him.

In that instant he had me pushed against the wall, my hands pinned above my head. His strength and speed astonished me and I looked at my pinned hands in disbelief. He looked at me for a moment. He had a small smile on his face and his breath was shallow as mine. He looked like a god, but his intense stare was purely carnal.

I hooked my foot behind his leg and smiled. I leaned forward and pressed my lips against his. His lips moved against mine with a deep need as his hands slid down my arms and found my breasts. His fingers moved back up my collarbone and unsnapped the strap on my shoulder. I felt the silk slip away from my body as I explored his mouth with mine. His cold fingers traced their way down the center of my body from my collarbone to my waist as I fumbled with the buttons on his shirt. He broke away from me just long enough to slip his shirt over his head. The sight of his bare chest took my breath away. His hand came back down gently on my cheek. His eyes held me.

“I need you,” he whispered rubbing his nose against mine.

His mouth was against mine in a moment and he lifted me off the ground taking me to the hard hotel bed. He laid me back on the comforter and then just stood there staring. He just stood there looking at me on the bed. He was having some sort of conversation with himself, but I didn't understand why. He shook his head and moved to pick up his shirt. I was laying there in only a bra and panties and he stepped away. “Sorry,” he whispered, “I can't.” He grabbed his stuff and left.

He left! He walked out. The emotions spilled silently down my cheeks. I was embarrassed beyond anything I had ever felt before. I was hurt and I was angry. No, scratch that, I was pissed. I growled and threw the heels I had carelessly tossed off only moments before through the open window. I watched as they disappeared into the darkness then threw myself across the bed and smothered my angry screams with the plush pillow until I sank into darkness.

I was in the white room. My eyes were starting to open groggily and I heard a woman's voice order more sedative. It was a sing-song voice, a vampire voice. I tried to breathe and caught the faint scent of the woman who had been tracking me, but there was something wrong. I smelled me. I smelled my human blood and felt it rush out of my body and I smelled the immortal vampire. The smell was strong, stronger than just me. It had to have been my father.

I struggled to open my eyes. I fought against the sedative I knew they had put into my body, I tried to tear out the lines I felt running from my arm, but there was no way to move. My eyelids betrayed my efforts and drooped heavily. Try as I might I couldn't make out more than just the fuzzy outlines of dark faces with gleaming white teeth.

Suddenly I awoke screaming in my hotel room as a lamp clattered to the carpet. Charles was standing at the open window. The cold snapped me to my senses. I was still less than properly attired and pulled the comforter over my breasts. He glared and grumbled, "Suddenly so modest."

I blushed, "What are you doing here?"

"I needed to talk to you."

I snorted and glared, "Then talk."

His anger flared, "You don't have any idea what's going on here."

"So, enlighten me."

He growled and stalked towards me, "You have no clue who's after you. These people are the people you *don't* want to be found by."

I smiled, "This wouldn't have anything to do with Sgt Bracken and his vampiric female friend, would it?"

He looked taken aback and stuttered, "I didn't think..."

"What?" I hissed standing up, "That I would notice? That I would be able to smell her stench hanging all over him?"

"Look," he growled, "I'm not implying that you're stupid."

I laughed, "No, but you were hoping."

His eyebrows knitted together as though he couldn't understand something.

I growled, "I also noticed how every time she got close, you would distract me just long enough to let her slip away."

He growled, "You don't know what you're talking about."

I snorted and walked towards the door, comforter trailing behind me, "I think you should leave now."

He looked astonished, like he couldn't figure out how this was the outcome. He looked at me like he had before, but as though if he concentrated hard enough I would change my mind. I could smell the roses as the cold breeze wafted through the open window.

I swung the door open and shook my head, "Now would be good."

He stalked up to me and grabbed my chin roughly, forcing me to look up at him. His smile was smug and I could feel my knees tremble beneath me. His voice was soft and seductive, "What do you want?"

I closed my eyes and concentrated, "You. Out. Now."

He growled, but did walk out the door. I slammed the door shut behind him before I sank to the floor. I almost felt sick with the emotional tidal wave that washed over me. I wanted him, I hated him, I needed him, and I needed him to leave. I took desperate deep breaths to steady myself. I was trembling all over. I rose to my feet and walked to the window. I shut and locked it and just for good measure drew the curtains across the glass. I was too hyped up to sleep so I drew myself a bath and let the lavender scented bubbles smooth over my skin.

There were no more dreams tonight, just blackness. It was never ending. For being just darkness it was one of the scariest dreams I had ever had. I woke again at 3:13 and this time I was alone.

I woke to the prospect of a day of divas fighting for attention and big wigs blowing their own horns. I pulled my hair back and quickly threw on a tee-shirt and jeans and looked in the mirror. I had dark circles under my eyes and my lips were pale. I didn't care. Charles was the only person who I had hoped to impress and after last night that wasn't a priority. He was a part of whatever it was that was going on, but even knowing that he could not be trusted made my head swim with the emotions I couldn't sort out.

I growled under my breath, hoping that would quiet the nagging voice in my head, and stormed out the door. I was so glad that we were leaving tomorrow morning. I was ready to go. I was so focused on going home where none of this would matter, that I noticed with a start that the hallway seemed shorter than before; I was moving much more quickly than I should. If a human had looked out of their room and saw me moving like that there would have been a little bit of explaining to do. I stopped and took a deep breath to steady myself as I rounded the corner.

At first the lobby seemed calm and devoid of drama, but there standing in a corner was that bastard Charles Sullivan, Sgt. Dixon, and the mysterious woman. I tried to hone in on their conversation. It was no use. They had picked me up the second I had turned the corner. I didn't look over, just walked towards the front door. Carter and Oliver were already standing there. I smiled at them and tried to ignore the stares that were burning holes in my back. Oliver looked over my head and stared back at Charles, he wasn't afraid of the vampire and I admired him for that. I touched his shoulder thankfully and could almost hear the growl rush out of Charles' mouth.

I wanted to turn to him and his little friends, make them confront me, but this wasn't the place. I quickly surveyed the room. Oliver, Carter, a business man, and the desk clerk, four possibilities for innocent collateral and I wouldn't risk it. Bracken may have been human, but he was far from innocent. I wouldn't lose sleep over something happening to him. But the epic battle brewing on the horizon would have to wait. I needed to focus on the task at hand. I needed to get Carter and Oliver set up and then make sure that Georgia was looking good for her shoot. Forcing myself to do this was not going to be easy. I would rather have been anywhere else.

I heard Charles growl again and involuntarily glanced behind me. He was standing in front of the woman with his teeth bared. She was glaring over his shoulder at me. It was nothing to everyone else, but I noticed and smiled. She growled. If she wanted to play, I was up for the challenge. I let a low growl slip between my lips; it might be time for me to embrace my less civilized side.

The press conference went very well considering that Georgia was absolutely neurotic. She fussed over every little detail of her outfit, hair, and make-up. After about four minutes I excused myself and headed over to Carter and Oliver. They were a nice release from the idiocy. They were calm and methodical. I needed that in my life right now. It didn't help that I could feel Charles in the room. He wouldn't look away and I couldn't help but feel the ghost of the emotions that wreaked havoc on me. How I wanted to hate him, but somewhere inside I couldn't. But he was not the only person who seemed fixated with me.

Sgt. Bracken was standing not too far away from the stage and staring daggers alternately at either me or Charles. I understood the hatred towards me, but the hatred towards Charles confused me. They were both a part of this intrigue, but it was becoming obvious that there was some dysfunction in that happy little family. I tried my best to keep my head down and not draw any unwarranted attention to myself, but my eyes were darting restlessly around the room. The woman vampire was not there which surprised me. I would have thought that she would want nothing more than to see me squirm. I kept taking deep breaths, but never registered her scent. I did, however, pick up another scent.

It was animal and human mixed together. I had never seen one before, I had only ever heard legends, but I knew it was the scent of a werewolf. I looked around trying to find the source, but I couldn't be certain of where it emanated from. I glanced over my shoulder at Charles and he mouthed the word as discretely as possible. My eyes darted wildly around the room, but I couldn't find them. I didn't even know what they were supposed to look like. Then I felt another pair of eyes upon me.

I knew what to expect from a vampire, even from another dhamphir, but a werewolf was a completely new creature to me. Finally I located the pair of eyes that were boring into me. They were dark brown eyes set in the face of a young woman. She had black hair that extended to her waist and a pointed nose. She was pretty in an exotic sort of way, slight and dainty, but her stare was anything but friendly. She snarled at me. I smiled back bearing my teeth. Soon a man stepped to her side. It was obvious by their skin tone they came from the same background, but the point to their presence eluded me. I looked into the young man's eyes and was surprised to not see hostility. In fact, his eyes were dark and intense and very attractive.

To my relief Capt. Dixon finally took the stage to address the constituents who were hungry for information. I tried desperately to focus on what he was saying, but the many pairs of eyes that stared into me pushed the words of the conference far from my mind. I wanted desperately to think that it was just my paranoia that led me to believe they all kept looking at me, but it was unfortunately confirmed by Oliver. As we wrapped up all of our equipment he leaned over to me and whispered, "Who isn't looking at you today?" I just grabbed a bag and headed for the door. I wanted to get out of there. My gut was telling me there was something seriously wrong.

Charles was at the door being as polite as possible to everyone who walked out. I could tell that I was his real target, but when I approached he turned his head away and just said, "Be careful." I didn't want to leave things like this between us, but I didn't know how to make it right or if he even deserved it, but I whispered so low that only he could hear me, "I never lied." He took a deep breath and growled angrily. I walked away nearly in tears with the thought that I would never see him again.

Carter could tell that something wasn't right but had the good sense to wait until it was just him, Oliver and me in a room working with the equipment to ask about it. "So?" he asked quietly. I cleared my throat and shook my head. Oliver glanced between the two of us and his eyebrows knitted together. I ordered them not to ask and walked out of the room. I didn't see Charles or my mystery stalker after that.

The moment I set foot in Philadelphia, I made the conscious decision that the next time they came for me I would be ready. I didn't know when it would be, but I knew they weren't about to give up on their master plan whatever that was. I worked on controlling my "special gift." I figured that would give me an advantage against full-blooded vampires. I may be stronger and faster than any human, but I was still nothing to a full vamp. I was also concerned about the werewolves. There was something that wasn't right about them, aside from the fact that they were also monsters, obviously. It didn't make sense that they were there and that they seemed to know who I was. I expected I might be seeing them again.

9. Surprise Guests

After about a month of training, I could control what moved and when I moved it. It was a nifty little trick I perfected at work. When Georgia was being particularly obnoxious I found that I could move whatever she was looking for from the other side of the room. She would scream and yell and storm around until she found it whether it be lipstick or her purse. I was beginning to have some real fun with it. I just had to be rather careful when I did it. Carter and Oliver were starting to give me strange looks and I was pretty sure that they suspected something was wrong with me. I knew it was only a matter of time before I either had to tell them the truth or leave. For some odd reason, I didn't want to leave. It wasn't that I suddenly started to enjoy Georgia's ranting and raving, but I thought about leaving and realized that this place had begun to feel like home.

It was April when I stopped at a pretzel stand on the corner and Alaska was the talk of the day. The vendor was reading the Daily World News, a tabloid paper that I normally wouldn't put too much stock in, but the headline read "Vampires Ravage Small Alaskan Village." My heart stopped beating. This wasn't some made-up tabloid story. I was appalled. I acquired a copy for myself as soon as physically possible and sat in the empty studio reading the article. Carter and Oliver came upon me in that state. Their stares became more intense and they both pulled up chairs and sat down with expectant looks on their faces. I just smiled and tried to look as expectant back at them. They weren't going for it.

"What's going on, Nora?" Carter asked, breaking the silence.

"You tell me."

"Why are you reading the tabloids?"

"Because the headlines were all about Alaska."

Oliver cleared his throat, "Why are you still so interested in Alaska?"

"I don't know what you guys are on about."

Oliver sighed, "You're still stuck on Sullivan aren't you?"

I shook my head, "Surprisingly, not." I really wasn't lying.

Carter looked at me incredulously, "Really? You aren't still wondering if he'll come and sweep you off your feet again."

"No," I thought he was going to come back and try to kill me.

Carter opened his mouth to speak, but stopped suddenly. Over his shoulder I saw a sight I had hoped I would never see although I knew all too well that I would. Two werewolves were standing in the doorway.

No one else knew who they were or why they were here, but they picked up on my apprehension. The werewolves stood eerily motionless. At least the hatred in the woman's eyes hadn't dimmed even though it had been months since she saw me last. She stepped forward and the childlike voice that came from her took me by surprise. I had expected something more mature from her brooding appearance. "May we speak with Ms. Bell alone, please?"

Carter and Oliver didn't even look at me, they stepped away and left with unhappy glances back at the two new monsters. The door shut behind Oliver and a low growl erupted from the woman's throat. Perhaps this was really not my most brilliant idea. I just let myself be shut in a room alone with two beings designed to rip my throat out. So, I might as well prepare to spring, but the man stepped in between us. He spoke to the woman in Italian, I think. I didn't understand them.

"Please excuse my sister; she's not exactly comfortable being here."

"Well that makes two of us," I straightened up slowly, "May I ask why you *are* here?"

"It has to do with that little trip to Alaska," he cleared his throat nervously.

His sister spoke up, "Just tell her."

I was truly confused as to what they were talking about.

"You are in danger."

I laughed, "No offense, but I'm in danger every time I come to work, have you seen the woman I work with?"

He shuddered, "I have, but there are worse things after you now."

I sat down and looked at him expectantly.

"My name's Theodore DeMarco, this is my sister Jennifer."

"I'm…"

"Nora Bell, we know."

"I wish I could say I was flattered," I cleared my throat nervously.

"We mean you no harm," he said reaching towards me consolingly. I flinched.

"Maybe you don't," his sister growled menacingly.

I laughed, "Look sweetheart, if you want to have it out just go for it."

Her brother stepped between us again. "Ladies, please keep this civilized."

I muttered, "I'm not the one growling every five minutes."

Jennifer snarled.

Theodore turned to her and spoke to her in Italian again. She growled and walked out of the room, slamming the door behind her.

"Well, isn't she a little testy?"

"She has good reason," he pulled a chair up beside me and took my hand.

His hand on mine was like an electric shock and I pulled back.

"Sorry," he whispered.

"No, it's my fault," I was stunned "You touched me and it was strange. It was like there was a shock that ran through my body."

"I know; I felt it too."

I looked expectantly at him, hoping that he had an explanation. If he did, he wasn't about to indulge me.

"It just happens sometimes," he cleared his throat, "but the most important thing is that you know what is coming for you."

I didn't have any clue what he was talking about.

"Your trip from Alaska has unfortunately come with some lingering side effects."

"I read the tabloids today and it looks like there are some vampires running amuck in Alaska."

"They aren't just random vampires, they are engineered."

"Engineered?"

"Yes, they were made as failed attempts to create a perfect soldier."

"Wait, the government knew about this?"

"They paid for it, they hired a vampire to run the program, but there's a glitch with what they are doing."

"If that tabloid was right, there's more than a glitch in their plan, it's falling apart spectacularly."

"That's because they are missing something." He looked at me soberly. "They are missing you."

"What?"

"They need your blood to make this whole plan work."

"I'm not sure that I follow."

"Your blood is very rare."

I nodded.

"What they are trying to do is create soldiers that have all of the strengths of a vampire, but none of the bloodlust."

"But, I do have that."

"Your bloodlust isn't nearly as insatiable as theirs."

I was starting to feel a bit suspicious, "You don't consider me one of them?"

He cleared his throat nervously, "You aren't one of them, but you are still dangerous and you are still the key to their plan."

"I feel a *but* coming on."

"You are also an important part of our plan as well."

"I knew there was something. So what's your master werewolf plan for stopping them?"

"We need to use you to lure out their leader."

"Wow…so I'm bait."

"No," he snapped angrier than I expected.

His sister came shooting back into the room, "What's wrong?"

"Nothing," he grumbled.

They shared a look that communicated more than any words could have; the only issue was that I would have needed a translator to understand it.

I cleared my throat.

Jennifer's dark eyes snapped back to me angrily, "Don't think that I wouldn't rip your throat out in a minute if I thought it would do us any good."

I smiled, "I figured as much, but I think that there is something that your brother's not telling me that I may need to know."

She glared at him.

He dropped his eyes and refused to look at me.

"Tell me," I demanded quietly.

He took a deep breath and barely whispered, "If everything goes according to plan…One of us will die."

"How do you know?"

"None of your business," Jennifer snapped angrily.

"If there's a possibility I'm going to die, I would like to know how accurate that is before I decide to join your little crusade against the vampire horde."

"Just trust me," Theodore mumbled barely above a whisper. His eyes were remorseful as he stared into mine and I felt myself start to soften towards him.

Jennifer snarled in disgust. That was it.

I grabbed my stuff and shoved past them. Jennifer reached out and grabbed my arm. I looked down at it and smiled showing all my teeth, "You need to remove your hand or I'll remove it for you."

She snarled, "I'd like to see you try."

Theodore stepped in and breathed, "Jennifer don't." He gently removed his sister's hand, "She can leave whenever she pleases." He looked into my eyes and there was a burning intensity that frightened me as he whispered, "I can't protect you if you leave and they will come for you one way or the other."

Jennifer hissed, "It's not her choice."

"Theodore," I inquired quietly, my voice seemed to have no volume when faced with the intense stare that he refused to drop. His eyes held me in a way no restraint in the world ever could and it had a tangible effect on me. I could feel my blood start to burn in my veins and it felt like my lungs were being squeezed, my breath was short and fast.

"It is your choice," his voice was rough, "even if my sister refuses to believe it."

Jennifer grumbled something in Italian and a ruddy blush covered Theodore's cheeks as he broke our gaze. I didn't have any idea what was going on at all, but I was intrigued by whatever it was that seemed to be passing between them.

"May I walk you home?" When he spoke again his voice was soft and sweet yet the intensity in his eyes smoldered, but didn't frighten me the way it had before. It was warm instead of fiery. I nodded but didn't speak, afraid that my voice would break if I tried. For the first time in a long time, I felt truly frightened to my core. Whatever trance I seemed to be in was broken by a deep growl from Jennifer. My head whipped around, but I noticed that she wasn't growling at me. She was focused solely on the door.

I listened and heard the footsteps of Georgia approaching. I smiled. "You know Jennifer, for once I agree with you." She looked at me in disgust and threw open the door nearly knocking Georgia off her feet. The glare that Jennifer gave her quickly shut her mouth, but Georgia was only distracted for a moment. She turned to me with as much loathing as ever which was only made worse by the man standing at my side. Her eyes widened.

Theodore was handsome, a perk for werewolves as well, but Georgia nearly growled at him herself. I had to turn and look up at him before I realized that he was down right hot. I hadn't noticed with all the death and mayhem, but his arms and shoulders were thick and muscular. His face had the hard lines of maturity, but his eyes were soft and kind. He was a good six-four, but looked graceful as he stood slightly in front of me as if he were protecting me from her. It made me smile.

"Nora," she cooed sickeningly, "I think Oliver and Carter need to speak to you." She looked Theodore up and down as though she were a butcher eyeing some meat. I could feel the shudder run through his body. "Why don't you introduce me to your new friend?" she suggested.

I looked up at him and his eyes were worried. It was as though he had seen a ghost. I surreptitiously touched his arm. He looked at me and his expression warmed. Georgia noticed. I whispered hoarsely, "I'm not feeling too well, Georgia. This is my cousin, Theodore; I think he needs to take me home now." I gagged and Theodore pressed his warm hand against my forehead, playing along just the way I thought he would. I whispered a thank you that was so quick I'm sure only he heard it.

"Come on Nora," he murmured softly. "You need your rest."

I was holding my stomach and taking deep breaths as though I was trying to settle my stomach. Theodore carefully wrapped his arms around me in what may have been a little more than cousinly, but I liked it. It felt safe as he helped me out of the studio. Oliver and Carter came through the door as we were leaving. I nodded at them and whispered, "Sick." They crossed their arms and the expression on their faces just wasn't quite right. I just shrugged helplessly and let Theodore guide me out of the building into the street. I smiled as we reached the pavement and squeezed his hand appreciatively. He didn't let go of my hand as he helped me into their waiting car and seemed reluctant to let it go before he closed the door. I was puzzled, and intrigued, and flattered all at the same time, but Jennifer was in the car giving me no time to puzzle out my feelings.

Theodore climbed into the driver's seat and I asked him to take me home. He nodded, but of course Jennifer protested. She grumbled that we needed to meet up with the others and Theodore snapped at her in Italian again and I lost it.

"Stop the car," I screamed at the top of my lungs. They were instantly quiet and Jennifer's eyes momentarily flashed with fear. I growled in the back of my throat and Theodore pulled the car over. "What others? And what the hell is going on with you two and speaking in Italian?"

Theodore cleared his throat, but it was Jennifer who spoke, "The others are the rest of the pack and Italian is our native tongue. I wouldn't expect a leech like you to understand family values."

"Don't assume you know anything about me," my voice was hard and cold as ice.

"We didn't mean anything by it," Theodore muttered.

"No more speaking in anything except English when I'm in *ANY* way involved or I'm out." Jennifer opened her mouth, "I do have a choice and if I'm going to be bait, you two can at least make some concessions on your part."

Jennifer grumbled, but Theodore nodded solemnly and started off again in the direction of my apartment.

Theodore insisted on accompanying me up to my apartment although I assured him over and over again that I was perfectly capable of getting changed myself. He insisted that he go in first and look around. It was sweet; no one had ever really made sure that I was safe before, not even he who shall remain nameless. Theodore stepped back into the hallway and the look in his eyes made me feel completely vulnerable. He held out his hand to usher me inside and I thrilled a little as his hand touched my back.

It had been months since I had been rejected by he who shall remain nameless and no one since had shown any interest at all. It would have been flattering if that small part of my brain would stop wondering if the attention was a result of the pack's master plan for me. His eyes didn't seem to convey any fraud. In fact I would have believed it was almost admiration if I trusted it, but what the hell, I might as well ask.

I cleared my throat nervously, "So, why do you keep looking at me like that?"

Theodore dropped his eyes quickly, "I'm sorry."

"I'm not mad, I'm just wondering why."

"We should get going."

"No," I gently placed my hand on his forearm and it was almost as though he melted at the slight touch. I smiled, "Please tell me."

He laughed, "Another time."

He held the door open for me and I paused in front of him. I reached out and touched his shoulder. His breath caught in his throat.

I quickly changed into some faded jeans and a black blouse and hurried down the stairs to the waiting car. I knew I looked my best in dark colors and tried to convince myself that I was just trying to piss off Jennifer, but deep down I knew what I was doing. For some odd reason, it felt as though I had a connection to Theodore. I tried not to notice how it made me blush when Theodore's eyes roamed over my body. Jennifer had moved into the driver's seat and was impatiently tapping her long fingers on the steering wheel. I wondered if when she transformed her long nails turned into long claws or if her human appearance had no bearing on her werewolf form. From the way she was looking at me she was probably wondering whether or not I turned into a bat. Theodore slid into the passenger's seat and refused to look his sister in the eye. I didn't think much of it until I heard the low growl in Jennifer's throat. There was something going on that I was not privy to and it put me on edge.

It seemed like moments from my door to an abandoned warehouse near the river. It had nothing to do with the way she drove or the fact that I was hanging on for dear life the entire time. Theodore opened the back door for me and nearly laughed at the expression on my face and my fingers clutching my seatbelt desperately. Jennifer snorted and I muttered, "Stupid werewolf drivers." Theodore offered his hand and gently helped me onto the street. It felt nice to have his hand steady me. His touch rang of sincerity and a shy awkwardness that made him endearing where as he who shall not be named was completely enthralled with his own ability to knock me off my feet. I liked this feeling more.

Jennifer, on the other hand, roughly grabbed my arm and nearly dragged me into the warehouse with a growl never leaving her throat. I yanked my arm free and nearly knocked her off her feet. She was obviously not a fan as she regained her balance and spun to face me, crouched as though she was ready to spring. She was so earnest, I couldn't help but invite her to try. Theodore quickly closed the door and threw himself between us as Jennifer hissed, "half-breed."

I laughed, "You're one to talk mutt."

I could see her starting to shake and Theodore was trying to calm her.

"CONTROL YOURSELF." The voice boomed through the warehouse to the point that I fell into a defensive position.

"I'm sorry," Theodore stuttered.

I stood straight and lifted my chin defiantly in the direction of the voice, "It's my fault."

Theodore just stared as I stepped between him and the voice.

The voice laughed, "Well aren't you just a cheeky little hybrid."

I smiled, "I'm full of surprises."

The voice and the dark shape I finally discerned as its owner walked towards me, "I bet you are. Otherwise, you wouldn't be so valuable to their plan."

A deep growl involuntarily grew in my throat.

I could feel Jennifer snicker behind me and Theodore tensed, but the voice just laughed again.

I looked as a face materialized out of the darkness. I had seen this man before. He had been in Alaska. He had been sitting in the restaurant with a woman. As I watched his entourage was materializing out of the darkness, the woman among them. It suddenly started to make sense. That was why *he* had growled, *he* knew they were there, *he* knew what they wanted, and *he* really was a part of the entire plan. I smiled and turned to the door about to leave, but Theodore blocked my path. The pleading in his eyes stopped me in my tracks. The man behind me laughed and I heard the slight giggle of the woman as well. Theodore blushed and moved aside.

"He's very convincing isn't he?" the man asked with the slightest accent.

I turned, questioning with my eyes.

The woman spoke and her voice was a surprising childlike trill, "Some of us are special too you know."

The man smiled, "I'm sorry, my manners." He held out his hand, "I'm Alexander."

I took his hand firmly in mine, "Nora."

"I know," he laughed.

"I'm Julie," laughed the brunette who had been at the restaurant as she waved childishly.

"You already know Jennifer and Theodore," Alexander smiled, "Behind me is Jordan," he motioned to a tall man with long black hair and dark menacing eyes, "and Tonya," he motioned to a small blonde who was about as hostile as Jennifer.

I smiled, "I can see I'm well loved already."

Alexander laughed, "I like your sense of humor, I see why Theodore's been taken with you all these years."

I raised my eyebrows quizzically.

Tonya snorted, "He's had a crush on you since 1955."

My eyebrows knitted together, "1955?"

Alexander laughed, "Before you were Nora Bell, when you were the silver screen actress Savannah Childs."

I looked at Theodore and he hung his head shamefully.

"I can't believe that there is anyone still alive who remembers me like that," I smiled.

Theodore didn't look up. Alexander laughed, "He insisted we not harm you when we found that you were the one we were looking for." His eyes grew dark and his voice became grave, "Even when he knew what would happen." An interminable silence stretched out into the vastness of the warehouse.

"And we're back to me not understanding what's going on."

Alexander's voice brightened, "No matter, I just need to know if you are willing to cooperate."

"I think I need a few details first."

"But of course," Alexander accented stepping out of the way in a gentlemanly manner.

I smiled and stepped towards the room he motioned me to, but behind me I could almost feel the heat from Theodore's blush. Alexander was talking a low whisper to Julie in another language I didn't understand, I couldn't have even guessed at its origin, and I spun on my heel in the doorway to face a horde of werewolves. Tonya and Jordan smiled and dropped into a defensive crouch. I could see their skin almost vibrating, it was fascinating. I stared as their eyes lost a bit of their humanity and took on a hard animal edge. I smiled as I watched; I must have looked deranged as I stared at the pair of them, as their nails started to thicken into talons, but they didn't change.

I looked at Alexander, confused. He was looking at me with what I'm sure was a mirror image of my own expression. I almost read it in his face, I should have been afraid. He expected it, but I wasn't and he was as fascinated as I was. If they were already wondering what my major malfunction was, I might as well keep them guessing, "Show me." Jordan and Tonya immediately snapped into an upright position and looked taken aback. Alexander's eyebrows were knitted together, Jennifer's eyes were as wide as saucers and Julie looked concerned. Theodore was the only one who smiled at me.

To my surprise he started to strip down to nothing. He was quite well built to say the least. Alexander opened his mouth to stop him but he just said, "It's natural for her to be curious." His body started to vibrate like I had seen from Jordan and Tonya, but this time it only took moments for his body to explode. He was huge, at least seven feet tall. He stood unabashedly in all his buff glory. Most of his form was still human, but completely covered in black fur. His head was transformed into a snout and his pointed ears twitched towards me expectantly. His arms, which weren't scrawny before, bulged with muscles as did his legs which had taken on a more dog-like quality. I was impressed. I had never seen a werewolf in person before.

I smiled and cautiously stepped forward. I whispered, "Theodore?" and he dropped to my level and looked into my eyes. I reached out carefully and whispered, "May I?" He growled and I pulled my hand back, but he nudged his head up under my fingers. His fur was really soft and fine. He pulled back and flexed his arms as if he wanted me to feel his muscles. Rolling my eyes just encouraged him to grab my arm and place it on his bicep. Yet we were not alone. Five pairs of eyes were staring into my back. Theodore leaned back his head and howled as he started to transform back into a human. I looked away modestly, there was something different about him being a naked werewolf and a naked human. Not that it mattered to him.

I turned to the others and Julie was the only one who was smiling at me. Judging by his expression Alexander was concerned and upset, but he held his peace. I had a feeling that Theodore was going to be chewed out later. Jennifer looked disgusted and Jordan and Tonya looked at me almost with admiration as though they had expected me to run and hide. I smiled at them nervously and suggested that we continue to the office to discuss the plan.

It was pretty much what I expected. Theodore would keep an eye on me and wait for any of the vampires from Alaska to try and contact me. Jordan, Tonya, and Jennifer would keep an eye on the people I work with to make sure they were not informing to the others. I cleared my throat and asked the question I didn't want to know the answer to did they know who was in charge of the experiments.

"We know who his Lieutenants are, but the man in charge is known only as 'The Marquis,'" Alexander explained.

"The Marquis?"

Alexander smiled, "As in The Marquis De Sade, yes."

I thought for a moment, "Is he the real Marquis De Sade?"

Alexander chewed it over for a moment, "I'm not sure, but he may be a descendent if he's not. He definitely has the same penchant for torture."

I groaned, "Perfect. And he wants me?"

Alexander nodded.

I took a deep breath and paced restlessly.

Alexander cleared his throat, "There is one more thing."

A short hard laugh escaped my lips, "How could this get any worse?"

Alexander looked down, "One of his Lieutenants is Gregory Falls."

My stomach dropped, "My father."

Theodore gently touched my shoulder, but he might as well have been touching a wall. I completely turned inward on myself. The thought that my father was out there hunting down his own offspring made my blood boil. How dare he! I was so angry that I didn't realize Jennifer had moved towards me. She grabbed my arm roughly and before I realized what was going on I reacted. She went flying across the room and smashed into the wall. I turned, but apology was already too late. Jennifer was bursting into black fur as I opened my mouth. She growled and pulled back her lips in what I'm sure she thought was a menacing growl, but a laugh broke through.

Theodore jumped between us and begged his sister to stop. She obviously wasn't listening and I gently pushed Theodore aside. He looked at Alexander, but I could see him shake his head from the corner of my eye. Jennifer growled in what I can only assume was an all too happy manner. I cocked my head to the side. She took it as an invitation and leaped towards me. I put up my arms defensively and she smashed face first into my defensive wall. It must've looked strange as we both stumbled backwards from what looked like a collision with thin air. It didn't phase Jennifer. She growled and attacked again. I was caught off guard and only a weak shield materialized. Her claws ripped through my shoulder. I could feel the muscle tear and the blood gush down my arm as I moaned in pain. Even in her wolf form I could hear her laughing beneath the low growl.

My skin started to tingle in my rage and I focused as much energy as I could towards her hideous form. She leaped forward and didn't touch the ground again. She flew straight up into the air, smashing through the light fixtures until her head slammed into a steel support beam. She went limp and in the moment that distracted me she came slamming down into the concrete floor. I looked at Alexander, he looked astonished, I stood straight and defiantly, trying to hide how exhausted that had just made me. Jordan and Tonya ran to Jennifer's side as she rose painfully from the ground. They were quick to grab a change of clothes for her and usher her into the office.

Alexander took a deep breath, "They must never get your blood."

I bristled, "I think I can handle myself." I stormed towards the door.

"Wait," Theodore exclaimed grabbing his coat.

I turned furiously and he skidded to a halt, "I don't think that'll be necessary."

His brow creased, but Alexander knew what I had heard in his voice.

"I don't think I'll be protected by someone whose orders are to kill me if my father gets too close."

Theodore looked confused.

Julie kicked at the floor with the toe of her shoe and avoided eye contact.

Alexander didn't. He stared into my eyes and said, "I'll do what is necessary to make sure that this horrible scheme never works."

"Even if it means killing me?"

"Even if it means killing you." His voice was somber.

I glowered in his general direction.

He stared back with no emotion in his eyes.

I stalked out before I did something really stupid, glad I had worn black. The blood from my shoulder wound just made the shirt look wet as I stalked down the street in vague direction of my apartment. The muscle in my shoulder was beginning to heal, and I gritted my teeth against the pain. Theodore was faithfully only a few steps behind me, like a puppy. I could hear him taking deep breaths as though he were about to speak. He wisely never did. How was I supposed to trust a person who was ordered to kill me? I was so angry, I could barely see straight. Here I had thought that perhaps I had found allies in this debacle, but instead, yet again, I had found myself surrounded by enemies.

We reached my building before I finally turned to look at Theodore. The rage I had felt in the warehouse had subsided even if the pain had not. There was only a sinking hopelessness and the realization that I was absolutely alone. Theodore seemed to sense what I was feeling. I wondered idly if he could smell it like a dog could. He said quietly, “I would never kill you, no matter what my orders are.”

There was nothing but sincerity in his eyes, yet I couldn’t even smile back at him. All I could hear were Alexander’s words and to make it worse, I agreed with them. If it meant that my father would fail then I would have to come to terms with my impending demise. In all honesty, it didn't scare me as much as I thought it would. I managed a weak smile, but it didn't soften the look of worry that was etched in Theodore's eyes.

My Romanian neighbor just happened to be walking down the stairs as we entered the lobby. Her eyes flew open, her face drained of color, and she backed up the stairs slowly clutching her crucifix. My eyebrows knitted together as she started to mutter in another language and make the sign of the cross. She looked like she was about to have a heart attack. I began to step towards her, but Theodore's hand on my arm stopped me. I was confused, but he shook his head and led me up the stairs around her. When we reached my apartment he quickly stepped inside and pulled me behind.

“She knows what you are,” he whispered. His tone dropped, “and she knows what I am.”

I was astounded.

“I don’t know how, but she does.”

“How do you know?”

“She was speaking Romanian.”

I just stared.

“My mother was Romanian.”

I continued to stare.

“So I can speak Romanian.”

“I understand, but what was she saying? She sounded angry.”

He growled under his breath, “She asked for God to protect her from the monsters and may he send us back from whence we came.”

I nodded and added emotionlessly, "I always thought she wanted me to go to hell."

Theodore startled me by bursting out into a deep laugh. It was warm and seemed to engulf the entire room. I couldn't help but laugh too.

"How typical of my luck," I laughed, "I pick the only apartment in the entire city with a Romanian who actually does believe in vampires and werewolves."

He smiled, but his eyes were sad.

"What's wrong?"

"If that's your luck, then we may have an issue."

I thought about what he meant and I just couldn't help myself. I started laughing. Theodore was staring at me like I was losing my mind and I still couldn't help but laughing, in fact I was laughing harder. Maybe I really was losing my mind, but it was just so absurd I couldn't help myself. I looked at Theodore and giggled, "I, am supposed to take on my father's much stronger, much larger coven with a pack of werewolves that would rather rip my throat out…" I shook my head and could feel the pain welling into a lump in my throat. I cleared my throat and finished, "that would rather rip my throat out than actually stop what they are trying to do."

Theodore opened his mouth to speak, but the tears started to roll down my cheeks. That stopped him in his tracks. He wasn't sure what to do after that. I looked at him and shook my head. "I know," I said my voice thick with the tears, "its time to pony up." I motioned towards the living room. "You're more than welcome to stay on the couch." I walked into my bedroom and went to pieces on the floor. It all came crashing down on me at once. I was in big trouble. I dug my nails into my palm as the muscles in my stomach tightened to the point I almost threw up. I was not strong enough to do this on my own. I lay on the floor and stared into the low-pile carpet until I drifted into darkness.

The dreams never change; they just become more and more vivid. I woke from the horror of the white room and the staring white teeth only to crash back into the floor with a sickening thud. Apparently I had progressed from throwing objects across the room to levitating. I landed squarely on my shoulder and felt the wound from earlier reopen. Apparently that part of the folklore was very true. Werewolves have a certain genetic makeup that allows them to fight vampires. Annoyingly that meant it would take a while before I fully healed from Jennifer's attack and reinjuring it wasn't going to help the process. Once again the muscles started to knit back together and the strangled howl that escaped my lips echoed into the carpet. I frantically hoped for Theodore to come and help me, but there was no movement on the other side of the door. I dragged myself from the carpet and opened the door only to find once again I was completely alone. I glanced at the clock, six thirty-seven. I needed a shower.

10. Pleasantly Surprised

I stepped out of the shower and loosely wrapped a towel around me. I swung open the door and he was there. I screamed, he screamed. My heart started pounding so hard, I was afraid it was going to burst straight out of my chest. He completely caught me off guard. I sank to my knees and started laughing. Theodore ran to my side, but didn't touch me. He hovered like he wanted to comfort me, but wasn't sure how to do that. I made it easier for him and dropped my head against his shoulder. Almost instantly his arms closed about me, engulfing me. He held me to his chest and I could hear the rumbling deep in his chest as he relaxed and started to laugh with me.

"I went to get breakfast," he finally sighed as if in answer to my unasked question.

"Anything good?"

"I wasn't sure what type of doughnuts you liked so I got an assortment of a dozen." His brow wrinkled as though a disturbing thought had just occurred to him. "You can eat regular food, can't you?"

I pulled my head back and looked into his eyes. His brow was creased with worry as though he was afraid that he had done something bad. He looked so innocently concerned I couldn't help but smile. I looked down ashamed and laughed lightheartedly, "Are they filled with crème?" He laughed as I climbed to my feet and in my best Dracula voice said, "Come my doughnuts, I vant to suck your filling."

I had done it without thinking, but Theodore's husky laugh let me know it was alright. It was easy to be lighthearted with him around. He was sweet and sincere, but under it all I knew that he was still able to kill me and that thought gave me pause. It wasn't normal for me to be vulnerable, but at the same time, Theodore did everything he could to make me feel at ease. I couldn't say the same for his sister. She did everything she could to make it clear that she wanted me dead and out of the way. I took a doughnut. I could almost feel his eyes watching me as I bit into my Boston crème indulgence. I didn't think he had fully believed me when I told him I ate regular food as well.

He laughed and wiped the chocolate off my cheek. "Hey," I mumbled with my mouth full, "I was saving that." He laughed and licked the chocolate off his finger. I smiled, but then realized that I was still only wearing a towel. I blushed and started towards my bedroom. I heard him open his mouth as though he were going to say something, but thought better of it. I turned expectantly, but he looked away.

"What?"

"How..." he started, but he stopped and dropped his eyes.

"How what?"

"How do you blush?" he whispered.

I laughed, "Let me get dressed and I will answer your questions."

Theodore stretched out on the couch like he owned the place, but the minute he saw me he jumped up immediately and rearranged the throw pillows. I laughed and leaped effortlessly over the back of the couch landing with enough force to knock the throw pillows on the floor. He smiled, but the gesture didn't reach his eyes.

"Let the questions fly," I joked.

"How do you blush?" his eyes searched my face.

"I have a pulse," I could feel my face warming.

"How do you walk in the sun?"

"I'm half-human, but the whole vampires only come out at night thing isn't entirely accurate."

He looked at me inquisitively.

"Not all vampires are photosensitive." I hesitated for a moment unsure whether or not I should tell the enemy our secrets, but sighed and decided that whether or not I should, I would. "The ancients, the ones who are almost the original vampires, they are almost entirely photosensitive. I'm not sure why, but I think its one of those things that evolved as the species did."

"You evolved?"

"Well, *I* didn't."

"No, but your father had to of."

I grimaced, "Yes, the creature that fathered me had apparently evolved, but he did have photosensitivity."

"How do you know that?"

I went to the low bookshelf that sat beside my one window and pulled a leather bound book with yellowed pages. I caressed the front of the book, engraved with my mother's name. I brought it to the couch and read the excerpt I was looking for "*He comes to me only at night. His eyes nearly glow in the darkness and he leaves before the first light. It frightens me the way he looks at me, but I can not tell him no, I can not make him leave once he's here.*" Theodore was looking me with concern as I continued, "*He came to me again tonight, but unlike the nights before he didn't touch me. He stopped in my doorway and seemed to be listening to something only he could hear. The look on his face scared me. He touched my stomach and then left.* That was when my mother found out that she was pregnant. Pregnant with my father's abomination."

"What was her name?"

I blushed, "You already know that."

His brows knitted together.

"Savannah, Savannah Childress. I modified the last name to Childs." I blushed.

He smiled and held out his hand. I handed him the book. I watched as he traced the name with his long fingers, a slight smile danced around the edges of his mouth.

"Why?" he finally asked looking at me.

I smiled sadly, "So she wouldn't disappear."

He handed the book back to me and I put it back in its place.

"He used her," I whispered, "He saw something, he took it and he used it for his own purposes. I saw him once." I glanced over my shoulder at Theodore who sat very still on the couch listening intently. "When I reached twenty-five he came looking for me, but I apparently wasn't what he was looking for. I would've killed him then if I knew I could have."

"What do you mean?"

I looked at him inquisitively.

"You weren't what he was looking for," he clarified.

I smiled, "I don't know exactly. He looked me up and down like I was a horse at auction." I shivered at the memory, my father's blue eyes; paler than ice and just as warm had stared deeply into mine. His cold hand grabbed my chin roughly and jerked it up and down so that he could stare at my bone structure. He pinched at my cheeks and grunted, pulled at my lips. I was frozen, almost in a trance. I now understood what my mother had meant when she said she couldn't tell him to leave once he had come. When his cold fingers closed around my throat I tried to push his hand away, but he was much stronger than me and held me up against the wall. He poked at my stomach, arms, and legs before he released me and left me gasping on the ground for air. I watched as he walked to the door, he was as vivid in my mind as he had been that day as he hissed at me. "I should've known it would come out like her."

Theodore's head snapped up, "What?"

I hadn't realized I said it out loud, "My father." I cleared my throat, "Those were the only words my father ever said to me."

Theodore looked ashamed, as though my father's actions had somehow tainted the entire gender.

I smiled, "I've held on to those words. It let me know I had some of my mother in me, that maybe I wasn't a complete monster."

"That's why you used her name."

I sighed, "Enough about me I want to know about you."

Now it was his turn to blush beneath his olive skin.

"I've never met a werewolf before and pardon me if my views are somewhat based on Hollywood."

"What did you expect when I changed yesterday?"

"The big hairy dog looking thing." I took a deep breath, "That made absolutely no sense."

We laughed together and the sound of his laughter was like a blanket.

"Well, as with vampires, Hollywood didn't get too much right about us either."

"Bitten by another werewolf?"

"Yes and no, you can be bitten and transform, but most werewolves tend to stay away from human meat, I guess that's the wolf side of it. We prefer animal to people."

"So how then?"

"Mostly genetic."

"You're just born with it?"

"Most of us, like Jennifer and me, have the gene in our blood somewhere and every couple of generations it presents itself."

"So were your parents?"

"No. Both were completely normal, but the gene was there somewhere."

"I always thought of werewolves more as men than women."

"There aren't many she-wolves, the females tend to be carriers of the gene, but not presenters."

"So Jennifer?"

"Is kind of a freak of nature," he laughed.

I smiled, and asked "Do you always travel in packs?"

"No," he smiled, "We all came together about two years ago. Alexander was a professor of mythology in New York and he stumbled onto some messages about the army trying to create the Super Soldier. Afterwards, he sought out others like him. He's a bit of an activist." Theodore chuckled. "From what he can tell, however, the army isn't running the show anymore. The Marquis seems to have his own agenda. A scout in Alaska let us know that the attack they reported wasn't an accident. It was a test run."

"A test run for what?"

"We think its a smaller version of his master plan."

I must have looked confused as he continued to explain.

"Master vampires are supposed to be able to control their creations to an extent. The blood lust eventually breaks the mental link at least for the moment when the need takes over all cognitive functions."

I shook my head, "And that's why they need dhamphir blood."

He nodded sadly, "If he can control an army of dhamphirs he can control everything they create. In effect making him the ruler of an entire race and very possibly capable of ruling the world."

I stood up and walked to the kitchen. I fiddled around with the dishes for a moment before turning to him. He was standing in the kitchen doorway awkwardly looking down at his overlarge feet. It made me smile.

"Alright," I sighed trying to change the subject, "It's Sunday, so what do you want to do?"

"Go for a walk?"

It was a fairly nice day outside. There was a breeze coming off the river and the sun warmed my cheeks. Theodore stared at me like he was fascinated. I didn't understand why. I looked to him for an answer several times, but he would just turn his face away. We walked in silence for nearly twenty minutes. Finally I stopped and turned to face him. "Why do you keep staring at me like that?"

"Like what?" he glanced away quickly.

I reached out and touched his arm, "I'm fairly quick on the uptake here, Teddy."

He smirked.

"Jennifer hates me because you don't." It wasn't a question.

"That and the fact that you're a monster," he chuckled; a slight attempt at humor in what I was beginning to fear was a more than serious conversation.

That one stung a little bit.

"I didn't mean…"

I held up my hand and smiled, "It's alright, you're perfectly entitled to your opinion, but I must say as far as being a monster is concerned at least I don't sprout fur."

I turned on my toes and continued walking up the street.

"What's that supposed to mean?" he growled following behind me.

"Well, isn't it a bit awkward to morph into a giant dog and then morph back with absolutely no clothing on?"

He wasn't angry so I continued.

"I would think it would be especially awkward trying to go home and not having anything on except…well nothing. Especially with the Romanian woman who lives downstairs already eyeballing me like there's something off."

"Yeah," he mused, "I guess she would kind of notice that."

I smirked.

"I liked you before I knew what you were," he whispered embarassedly.

"Before you realized what a vivacious wit and robust character I have," I laughed trying to keep my tone light.

"Before I knew what a pain in the ass you are," he laughed.

"Ouch, that hurt," I laughed clutching at my heart in mock pain.

He playful hit my shoulder.

"It must be so boring being stuck on babysitting duty," I smiled half apologizing.

"Quite on the contrary," he laughed. "Everything about you is beyond interesting."

"Thank you," I snorted, "Like a science experiment."

He laughed and grabbed me around the waist, a little more possessively than I had expected and I wasn't completely sure how I felt about that. "No, you are much more than I ever expected knowing what you are."

"Well," I sighed resigning to let the light banter drop, "I guess you are much more than I expected too."

He blushed.

"You like soft pretzels?"

He nodded.

I grabbed his arm, "My treat." I walked towards one of my favorite street vendors and gave him a smile.

"Miss Nora," he laughed with his thick Philly accent, "I don't normally see you on Sundays."

I laughed, "Hey, Michael, this is my friend Teddy, he's in visiting from Alaska."

Michael shook his hand and laughed, "You're pretty lucky there, Teddy, you treat her right, eh?"

Theodore just smiled and nodded.

We got out pretzels and went to a little bench in the Liberty Bell Park. We ate in silence. I had the distinct feeling that this awkward silence was a predecessor to something big. I felt that there was some threshold that was waiting to be crossed, but I didn't understand why I felt the need to cross it. Still, I knew it would be inevitable. He seemed to sense my change in mood and put his arm around me. I was surprised at my reaction. I welcomed the contact. For a moment his arm was comforting, but a shock ran through my body again when his skin touched mine.

He whipped his hand away from my shoulder and jumped up dropping the rest of his pretzel to the dirt.

"What's wrong?" my voice was weak.

"I…nothing." He breathed slowly.

"Tell me," I demanded softly.

I touched his hand and a jolt ran through me, like I was being electrocuted without the intense pain. It was almost like a massage chair running through my insides. I took deep breaths to stop the dizzy feeling as the strange sensation coursed through my veins. It stopped when Theodore forcibly ripped his arm from my grasp. I lost my balance as he did and collapsed on the ground. I saw the remnants of my pretzel fall into a mud puddle and just stared at it in shock.

"I'm sorry," he whispered helping me back onto the bench. I noticed he made sure to keep his hands off of my bare skin.

"My pretzel," I whimpered.

He snorted, "That's what you're worried about? Your pretzel?"

I raised my eyes to his and they wouldn't focus properly on his face. I felt like the life had been sucked from my body. "What happened?" My voice had no volume.

"It's what I do," he whispered back.

"You electrocute people," I smiled at my weak attempt at humor.

"I…" he hesitated, "I…saw your…your…," he sighed and decided to tell me the truth, "your future."

I didn't understand and I'm sure that my face gave that away as he felt the need to explain.

"That's how I know one of us will die," he explained speaking so quietly I had to pay attention to how his mouth moved.

"You saw it?"

He nodded.

"You know who it's going to be then." It wasn't a question.

He nodded.

"Will you tell me?" I asked quietly.

He shook his head.

I stood and took his face in my hands. The current didn't start. I hesitated for a moment bracing myself against the current I thought would start at any moment, but there was nothing. I looked into his eyes and he sighed.

"It doesn't happen every time."

"Do you control it?"

"No, it comes in flashes, but I can force it if I want to."

I looked into his eyes and whispered, "What did you see?"

I could feel his face getting hot under my hands.

"Theodore, what did you see?"

He closed his eyes and clenched and unclenched his fists.

"Please?"

"I have to go," his voice was flat and even.

I nodded and dropped my hands, "Then go."

He looked horrified.

I turned and walked away. Well, it started as walking anyway. It ended up as a barely controlled at human speed sprint. I didn't look back. I just kept thinking, "How could you have been so stupid?" It repeated over and over and over again in my head. I felt so stupid. What was wrong with me? I knew better than this. None of them could be trusted. I ran up the stairs faster than I should have and hissed menacingly at the Romanian woman who opened her door just as I reached her landing. She cowered back and crossed herself in fear.

I slammed my door closed and nearly knocked the frame out of the wall. I was so angry with myself. I went to my closet and threw my suitcase on the bed. It slammed against the wall leaving a hole in the drywall. I growled at it and put my fist through the closet door. Literally *through* the door. That made me feel even stupider. I sank to the floor and started to cry. I couldn't help it. Somehow in my genetic anomalies my anger response was hardwired to my tear ducts. I let the warm tears stream in rivers down my cheeks and drop onto my folded arms. I hugged my knees to my chest and let it all go.

After a while I pushed my empty bag to the floor and crawled under the covers. I let myself fall asleep and hoped desperately that I wouldn't have that horrible dream again. I didn't. This new dream was worse.

I ran through the woods in Alaska. It was freezing cold and I could barely run for shivering. I was in a white halter-top dress in the style of Marilyn Monroe. My feet were bare and I knew rather than felt that my feet were cut and sore. I was being chased by wolves. I looked again, but I had been wrong. They weren't wolves, they were werewolves. One of them almost smiled at me. I knew it was Jennifer and she was looking for my throat. I ran and as I ran I knew I was nearing something I didn't want to get near, but if I stopped I knew I would be killed. I kept running. I could feel my heart beating quickly and I knew it wasn't in the dream, but I couldn't wake up. I ran until I found the white room, it was cold and the lights blinded me. I tried to wake up, but I couldn't. That was when I saw the gleaming teeth in front of me. The human teeth, the vampire teeth, the werewolf teeth, and then Georgia stepped from behind the light. I yelled for her to run, but she just stood there surrounded by supernatural creatures and certain death. I screamed at her to run yet again, but instead she smiled and I could see her elongated canines.

11. It All Falls Apart

My alarm hadn't gone off yet, but I was awake. I stared at the ceiling and counted the bumps in the popcorn coating. When the alarm finally sounded I moved mechanically over to it and tripped in the shoulder strap of my empty bag. I smacked my head against the closet door in a fumbling attempt to catch myself. The day already belonged to Murphy.

Work was even more disastrous than my morning venture out of bed. Carter and Oliver were there before I was which was unusual for them. They saw me as I saw them and walked in my direction. There was something wrong. They just didn't look right.

"Georgia's here," Carter whispered.

I felt the confusion on my face.

"She's been here all night," Oliver breathed.

"I'll deal with it," I sighed.

I walked towards Georgia's dressing room, Carter and Oliver's reactions leaving me uneasy. I took a deep breath as I steeled myself for the drama that was sure to ensue. That was when I smelled it. Her blood was suddenly sickeningly sweet, the smell of someone who was becoming a vampire. There was something else about it that was wrong. The blood smelled strongly of my father.

I backed away from the door and could feel Carter and Oliver staring into my back. I knew that she already knew I was there and that she would be strong while she was transitioning. She was more dangerous now than she ever had been or would be again. Fledglings had no self-control, and I could only imagine that for Georgia it would be even worse considering how little she had as a human. Options: I could take her out, but Carter and Oliver were standing nearby. I couldn't risk either of them getting hurt, I could get them out and then come back for her, but even as I considered it the elevator door dinged. There were more voices, more witnesses and potential victims.

I stepped back towards Georgia's dressing room and decided that I should probably try to talk to her first. To my surprise the flimsy wooden door swung open before I had the chance to lower my hand against it. Georgia stood there in little more than her underwear. She grabbed my arm and yanked me inside her dressing room. There was a pile of bloody clothes in the corner. A quick breath and I could tell the blood was hers. She hadn't fed. I looked at her eyes and noticed how quickly they were darkening. She was hungry, but she was frightened too. I hated myself for it, but I actually felt sorry for her.

"What's happening?" she whispered.

"Who bit you Georgia?"

"What?" she looked confused.

"Last night or the night before you were with someone and that person bit you, there" I pointed, "on your leg."

She looked down at her leg as if she was seeing it for the first time.

"Who were you with Georgia?" My voice was soft and gentle as though I were talking to a child.

"Alaska," she nodded. She was confused.

"Was it Sergeant Bracken?" I asked quietly

Her eyes flew open wide and she nodded fervently, "Yes."

Now it was my turn to be confused. When we had been in Alaska, Sgt. Bracken had been human. He was definitely not a vampire in any way. I wondered if the blonde had finally turned him. I looked closely at the bite mark on Georgia's thigh. The edges were smooth. Teeth don't make marks like that, tooth marks are jagged. He had injected her with my father's blood. Maybe he was actually still human.

I looked up at her and she was nervously fiddling with some clothes that hung on a nearby coat rack. What she was about to go through would be hell and she had no idea how bad it would get. Since it was my father's blood I could almost guarantee that she would have photosensitivity. So, added to the intense physical suffering she would soon endure, her anchor spot on the morning news was going to be her death sentence if she continued.

"Georgia?"

She looked at me like she was staring at some distant thing.

"You are going to start feeling strange."

She nodded.

"It'll be alright, but you have to stop working until you feel better."

Her eyes flared, "What!?"

"Georgia, you don't know how you'll react to what's happening to you and you don't want to be around people when this change is going on."

She grabbed my throat and I let her push me up against the wall with enough force to knock the shelving off the wall. A strange feeling told me to let her do it, that it wasn't her but my reaction they were after. I tuned out Georgia's ranting and raving and focused very hard on hearing any high-pitched noises in the room. There it was, faint at first, but the longer I listened the louder it became. Behind the mirror was a camera. They were recording this entire thing.

I started gasping for air. I rolled my eyes back in my head as though I were passing out. I went limp and Georgia threw me to the ground believing I was unconscious. I laid there, eyes closed, breathing shallow, just waiting for her next move. But it seemed that it wasn't her calling the shots. Sgt. Bracken step out of the closet and walk towards me. He leaned down carefully. His cold fingers pressed against my neck looking for a pulse. Apparently satisfied that I was alive, he turned to Georgia.

"You did well," he cooed and I could hear him kiss her.

"She said I'd have to quit my job," Georgia muttered and I could almost hear the pout in her voice.

"You don't have to do anything you don't want to," he whispered a little breathlessly.

"I want to, do you," she growled, there was a ripping sound and what I think was a button bounced off my forearm.

"Get her out of here first," he ordered poking my limp body with his foot before sauntering into the closet.

Georgia swung open the door and yelled for someone to get me out of her dressing room. Two warm strong arms scooped me up and carried me away. I took a deep breath to figure out whom it was that could carry me so effortlessly and the surprise made me nearly stop breathing. Theodore was holding me! I heard the barely audible chuckle in his throat as he whispered too low for anyone else to hear, "Little actress."

I waited until I was laid on the couch and someone put smelling salts under my nose before I "came to." I pretended to be disoriented, and didn't have full answers as to what had happened in there. Theodore stood back against the door frame watching as Carter and Oliver fluttered around me trying to make sure I was fine. I assured them again and again that I really was fine and they finally left to make sure the production was ready to go.

As soon as they left I turned my attention to Theodore, "They changed her."

"I could smell that."

"You need to tell the others."

"I can call them."

"Maybe you should tell them in person," my eyes felt cold even to me, "You don't want to have to deal with all of these monsters on your own."

"Look," he started, "what happened yesterday..."

I cut him off, "Don't. The look on your face said it all."

He opened his mouth to speak, but I breezed by him in the doorway and left the unspoken words hanging in the room behind me. I didn't look back, but I heard as he flipped his cell phone open.

Amazingly, the news went off without a hitch. Georgia appeared somewhat normal after some prep work from the make-up team. She seemed to exude sexuality and most of the camera men were panting after her as she stepped off stage. John, the idiot he was, nearly killed himself trying to stare over his shoulder at her. I wondered if that was her special talent, making men want her. She had certainly done enough of that as a human, now, as a vampire, her appeal was naturally enhanced. I could only imagine the bedlam that would ensue.

Oliver came towards me as I sat in the make-up chair, my face buried in my hands. Carter was not far behind, but seemed to be watching everything that went on around us with suspicion.

"Nora," Oliver started flatly, "What's going on?"

"I wish I could tell you," I didn't raise my head.

He grabbed my arm forcing me to look at him, "Nora, cut the bullshit and tell me what's going on."

Theodore was at my side in a moment.

Oliver glared at him and Carter walked up to his side.

I looked at Theodore and he started, "There are things that are happening here that are completely beyond your grasp."

Carter piped up, “Try us.”

“I’m 100 years old,” I blurted out.

Oliver was angry, “What the hell is this?”

Theodore sighed, “I told you there would be things beyond your grasp.”

Carter snorted, “You expect us to believe you’re 100 years old and look like you’re twenty-five?”

I smiled, “Yes, and none of it has been plastic enhancement before you ask.”

Oliver crossed his arms across his chest and stared at me.

I stood out of the chair and sighed. “Look, we can’t really discuss this here. If you want the full scope of the truth then meet me near the dog park tonight around six.”

I walked away with my head down, Theodore not two steps behind me. He went to speak, but I shook my head. He was clueless, but we walked to the elevator in silence. I gave him a meaningful look and he kept his mouth shut until we were outside.

“What?” he asked as we hit the pavement.

“There was a camera in the dressing room and Sgt. Bracken was there as well.”

He glanced back, “Is he..?

“No, they injected her,” I sighed.

He grabbed my arm and spun me to face him. “What’s bothering you?”

“Just cut to the chase why don’t you?”

His face was serious, “What?”

“First, where the hell do you come off coming back? And second, I’m going to lose every friend I’ve made in the last few years tonight and that always makes me a little upset.”

He dropped his head and looked ashamed, “It wasn't what you think.”

“How do you know what I think?”

He ignored that, “As far as your friends you knew that would happen eventually.”

“That doesn’t stop me from getting pissed off about it though.”

He took my hand in his and I stiffened in preparation for the inevitable shock, but nothing came. “None of this is your fault.”

“Oh god,” I growled ripping my hands away from his.

He threw his long arms around my shoulders and trapped me against his chest. I looked up in warning, but could see that he was just as agitated as I was and decided against provoking him. Him getting pushed away was something easily explained, him bursting out into a gigantic ball of fur on the other hand was a little harder to keep under wraps.

“Don’t look at me like you don’t like it,” he growled, “We both know you have the power to throw me across the street if you wanted to.”

I glowered, “Yeah, but that's a little hard to explain don't you think?”

He grabbed my chin so I couldn’t look away. “You infuriating child,” he growled, “Did you ever think there was a reason for all this?”

I snorted and tried unsuccessfully to look away. He was stronger than me without using my powers.

I growled disgustedly, “You really are an idiot you know.”

His fingers roughly entwined in my hair and yanked my head back. I stiffened as he rubbed his nose against my neck. “I can tell you want this,” he growled rubbing his teeth against my skin.

“I will throw you through traffic if you don't let me go.” I could feel my pulse racing, but it was fear making it work overtime, not desire.

He laughed a deep throaty sound into my collar, “Don't pretend you don't want to see where this goes?”

I smiled, “Don't think 'cause you're cute I won't kill you.”

A low growl echoed around us and we froze.

Theodore looked over my shoulder and whispered, “Jennifer.” I tried to take a step back but he held me fast. I watched as his side of the unspoken conversation unfolded on his face. He seemed to get progressively more upset until a low growl broke from his lips. I pressed my hands against his chest and he looked down as if seeing me for the very first time.

Without a word he took my hand and jerked me down the street. I could see Jennifer mirror our movements from the opposite sidewalk. She looked pissed off and wasn’t about to let us out of her sight. I noticed as we walked the click-clack of heels that seemed to be pacing us even though we were walking at an elevated pace. I squeezed Theodore's hand without a word and he nodded. He heard them too and I'm sure it was Georgia who was following just far enough out of range to avoid my being able to smell her.

We walked in that fashion until we reached my apartment. This was a safe place to meet considering Georgia already knew where it was and I would be putting no one in danger by coming here. Theodore locked the door behind him and turned to face me. "There's something wrong," he whispered, "I'm not sure what, but something is definitely wrong. Go pack a suitcase, we may need to move you." I silently obeyed.

I picked up the empty bag that I had thrown on the floor the night before and shoved some necessary things, including the money I had hidden in my lock box into it. I changed and stepped into the living room to see Theodore tensed standing by the window. In his hand was a cell phone. I knew there was something terribly wrong by the way he didn't turn. I could hear his heartbeat pounding through his veins, but I was afraid to ask what was wrong mostly because the answer to that question frightened me. I just stood there, waiting for him to acknowledge me, but I didn't have the pleasure of his attention. His sister burst through the door in a rage sending the chain lock flying across the room. I dropped to the floor and barely escaped getting a chunk of wood embedded in my ear.

If her eyes held any more venom they would have burned out of her head. She glared at me in disgust and then lunged at me, it caught me off guard and her fist smashed into my jaw with so much force I expected it to break. I fought the urge to fling her across the room and for my restraint caught a foot in the gut and a double fisted blow to the back of the head before Theodore could pull her off. She spit at me and lunged against her brother's arms. I slowly stood up and felt the blood drip from my nose onto the carpet and my vision was slightly blurred from the blow to the back of the head, but I was not about to let her see that. I stood confidently and wiped the blood from my face.

Theodore's eyes were strange. They held no concern, nothing. It was just absolute contempt. I watched him expectantly hoping that he would explain, but he made no move to speak. He just stared as if I were the most loathsome thing in the world.

I sneered, "What?"

Jennifer growled, "They're dead you bitch."

I was completely confused.

"I just heard from Alexander," he hissed.

Still confused.

"They were killed by a filthy leech," Jennifer screeched lunging at me again.

Theodore restrained her, but it seemed that he would rather have let her go.

"Who was killed?" I asked quietly.

His voice was ice cold when he spoke, "Jordan and Tonya."

I looked Theodore straight in eye. "Then let's not do this here."

He didn't move as I picked up my jacket.

"What?" Jennifer hissed.

"I know what your orders are," I spoke as emotionlessly as possible, "and I don't think that doing this here would be the best way to conceal our little secrets."

Jennifer smiled as she caught my meaning.

Theodore looked confused.

"Where does Alexander want this done?"

"I don't think he cares," Jennifer hissed, "as long as it's done."

"Just so you know," I hissed stepping through the door, "I had nothing to do with it." I looked at Jennifer meaningfully, "And it won't be easy."

She smiled, "Perfect."

We made sure we weren't being followed before we went to the warehouse. I stared at all of the sights I was fairly sure that I would never see again as Jennifer drove past them with lightening speed. I was going to die and decided that I would meet that fate with as much dignity as I could muster. I stepped out of the car with my head held high and no fear in my eyes although I could feel my insides trembling. I hoped none of them could feel it as well.

Alexander stood in the middle of the warehouse with his arms crossed over his chest. His face was blank, no sorrow, no hatred, nothingness which was so much worse. I could tell that he blamed me without saying anything, but in his eyes I'm fairly certain the fault did not fall to me entirely. He seemed to have an equal amount of indifference for Theodore.

"Miss Bell," he greeted me coldly.

"Alexander," I replied with equal frost.

"I suppose at this point you've figured out the verdict."

"I dare say I have," I smiled letting all of my teeth show.

"Alexander," Theodore squeaked at my side, "she couldn't have had anything to do with it."

"It wouldn't matter if she had done it herself, would it you traitor?" Jennifer started to tremble and I could tell she was barely holding her form together.

"You know," I whispered, "I still owe you for the bloody nose earlier."

Jennifer growled and I smiled in response.

"I'm sorry to break this up," Alexander growled, "but we do need to have this finished with as quickly as possible. We still have a vampire that needs to be killed immediately."

"Then perhaps," I smiled, "You might hold off on killing the dhamphir."

They all stared.

"Look, the original plan is still in tact even if your forces have been depleted."

I could hear Jennifer's breathing hitch and become indignant at that assessment of her friends, but Alexander seemed ready to listen.

"There have been other developments as well that I'm not sure you are aware of. Georgia Stone is transitioning."

"Theodore told me."

"Did he also tell you that it was my father's blood that was injected into her veins?"

"I didn't know," Theodore tried to defend his lack of knowledge, but I held up my hand to stop him.

"The point is she wasn't bitten, she was injected."

"And?"

"And that means that my father isn't stupid enough to walk into a trap like you have set up here. If you want him, you have to trust me and change what you're doing."

Jennifer growled, "Two of ours are dead because of you."

"And how many more do you want to die?" I snapped, "They know what you are doing otherwise how could one vampire be able to take on two fully developed werewolves."

"So, your plan is what?"

"Well, first we take this somewhere that we can control. I would prefer it be out of the city if we are going to have a throwdown."

"Where would you prefer?"

"Somewhere in the middle of nowhere would be good, so that there is nobody there to be collateral damage. I want to meet them on my terms and whether or not you join me is completely up to you."

Theodore stepped up beside me, "I would like to hear what else she has to say."

"Of course you would," Jennifer spat lunging at him.

He easily restrained his sister and pushed her away.

Alexander commanded her to sit down and she did with great affectation.

"There is something you need to know," Alexander stated flatly.

"Which would be?"

"There's a hunter in town."

"A hunter of what?"

"Vampires," the word hung in the air for a while and I let it fully sink in.

"How long has this hunter been here?"

"Longer than you have," he growled.

I laughed and they all stared at me in amazement. I couldn't help myself it just all continued to get more and more absurd. "I have lived 100 years and NEVER before have so many people been trying to kill me."

Theodore's eyebrows knitted together.

I headed for the door, a smile still playing around my lips.

"Stop," Alexander's voice boomed through the empty warehouse walls.

I obliged and turned to face him.

"I never said that you could leave."

"I never said I needed your permission."

"I should kill you," he growled, "for what happened to Jordan and Tonya."

"I should kill you for just being what you are," I countered, "And perhaps you could ask the lovely Julie to step out from the office above me."

I heard her bare feet slap against the bare metal.

"Nora," she whispered icily.

"Julie," I answered unable to keep the smile out of my voice, "Are you dressed to morph or is my imagination just running away with me?"

Julie laughed, "Clever child."

"I'm just over 100 years old Julie, don't you think that qualifies me as an adult?"

She leaped over the rail and landed gracefully in front of me clad in an old pair of cutoff sweat pants and a tattered tee shirt. It was perfect attire. I sighed and looked at Alexander. "I need to know right now whether you are going to help me or if I need to consider you as enemies."

Alexander stood in silence.

Julie stared at him waiting for his cue.

Jennifer's eyes were fixed on me her body slightly hunched forward as if ready to spring.

Theodore was frantically looking between us all with wide frightened eyes.

Alexander shook his head.

I smiled and turned my back as Jennifer morphed. I was on the cat walk before she had fully changed and her claws caught nothing but air. "Oh, Alexander," I laughed, "You didn't think it would be that simple."

"Stop it," Theodore thundered.

"Wow," I laughed, "I think that's the most authoritative I've ever heard you."

He shot me a look that actually frightened me slightly.

In the moment I looked down and smiled at him, Jennifer leaped on the catwalk and the whole contraption came crashing to the ground. My ankle snapped underneath me. Julie burst into fur and leaped into the fray. I tried to control myself, but for my trouble Julie's claws raked down my arm leaving three bloody streaks from shoulder to elbow. I effortlessly tossed her aside, but the blood was flowing too quickly. That movement made my head spin. I was losing too much blood too quickly. I could feel my head getting heavy. My vision was beginning to darken. Jennifer's claws ripped up my back and darkness began to close over me.

I heard a deep angry growl I didn't recognize and then there was nothing.

12. And Behind Door Number 2

I came to wrapped in my own sheets with Theodore standing over me. My head lolled back on the pillow as I tried to focus in on his face. He turned away. He wasn't wearing a shirt and his olive skin had angry pink streaks from his shoulder to his waist. I reached out and traced them with my fingers. He shied away from me like my touch had burned him.

"What happened?"

He turned towards me and my reaction to his face was audible. His eye had yellowish bruises around it and I think at one point his nose had gotten broken. Luckily he healed as I did. I reached out wordlessly, my mouth agape. My fingers traced his bruises and I could feel the horror in my eyes. He pushed me back and held his wrist to my mouth. I didn't understand. "Drink," he ordered emotionlessly, "You need to feed and this'll be better than if I let you out to hunt."

I shook my head. He grabbed my hair roughly and forced me to put my mouth on his skin. I clenched my teeth against him, but he was not to be deterred. He bit into his own wrist allowing the blood to flow and then shoved it against my mouth. I tried to resist, but had no strength to push him away. The more blood that I drank the more I felt my muscles return to their normal strength.

I pushed his arm away, "You taste terrible."

He laughed, "Thanks a lot."

I started to choke. I couldn't breathe, there was something wrong. I grabbed Theodore's arm, but he didn't seem concerned. My eyes lost their focus on my fingers and I saw Theodore, his face drained of blood, his eyes lifeless,staring. Then there was me, covered in blood standing next to him.

The vision faded and my fingers that were digging holes into Theodore's arm. I didn't have to look at him to know that he knew what I saw. He cleared his throat nervously and removed my fingers from his arm very carefully. I swallowed hard as he moved away from me, slumping against my armoire.

"Did I…I mean…Will I…?"

"I think so."

"Are you sure?"

"Not entirely. It could be anyone's blood."

"But you're pretty sure?"

"Yeah, I'm pretty sure."

"Then why did you stay?"

He moved to my side, "Isn't it a little obvious?"

I shook my head slowly.

"I'm sorry, Nora."

There it was, the threshold I had been dreading. He was going to cross it and his hand was offered for me to come along on the trip.

"Theodore," I breathed, "I can't let you." I couldn't let him care about me, not if I was going to kill him. It wasn't right.

He dropped his eyes and looked away, "It's not a question of letting me."

"No," I grabbed his face and forced him to look at me, "This is a question of letting you."

He grabbed my wrists, "I'm sorry if this makes you uncomfortable…"

"You idiot," I whimpered, "it's not that I'm uncomfortable or that I think you aren't worthy or that we're too different or any of those silly little things."

He smiled.

"There is the chance that I'm going to kill you."

"That's not certain."

"I *can't* take that chance. I know the future isn't set, but the course that we're on will lead to your death and possibly at my hand. I *can not* live with that."

"I fought off my friends and my sister to save you today."

"I know and I will *not* return that favor by killing you."

I felt the tear roll down my cheek, but I knew that I had no choice. He knew too. He kissed my forehead and left the room. I heard the door click shut before giving over to the sobs I had held back so bravely. It wasn't fair. I liked Theodore, why did he have to go and ruin it? I wasn't emotionally prepared for this. First it was Charles, then Theordore, who was next? What was next? The vague scent of roses wafted through my mind as I cried myself to a black and dreamless sleep.

When the elevator doors dinged, Carter and Oliver were waiting to confront me. I knew I had stood them up, but was afraid to tell them the reason without Theodore at my side. Still I thought they would understand, but instead of calm and compassionate Carter and Oliver, I was introduced to two people that I never thought could exist in the old Carter and Oliver.

Carter shoved me into the make-up chair and Oliver stood behind me with his hands on my shoulders. I was beginning to feel very uncomfortable.

Carter cleared his throat and began, "I'm surprised you're here this morning."

"Why wouldn't I be?"

"Oh, I don't know," Oliver whispered in my ear, "I was thinking blood loss would be a good reason not to show up to work."

"How do you know about that?"

Carter smiled, "We set it up."

My heart stopped, "Who are you working for?"

Oliver laughed, "Oh, we don't work for anyone in particular. We're part of an organization that calls itself the Van Helsing Group." He smiled.

"That's rather fitting," I replied flatly.

Carter smiled, "Although it's not exactly only vampires we hunt."

I snorted, "Werewolves fall into your domain?"

"Obviously," Oliver sighed, "It wasn't a vampire that took out your little werewolf friends the other day, and to be perfectly frank," he leaned in closer to me, "Alexander was rather fond of you."

I smiled, "That's how Alexander knew there was a vampire hunter around."

"So it would seem," Oliver smiled back.

"So, if I *had* met with you yesterday, that would've been bad, huh?"

Carter laughed, "Only for you."

"Do they know that it isn't only vampires you hunt?"

"No, no, but they soon will I can assure you."

They smiled at one another in a way that made my stomach turn.

"So I take it," I stated civilly, "Since you are obviously no more than human, and vampire hunters, that you are not working for my father."

Oliver came around and sat in front of me in another make-up chair. "Not exactly," he stated leaning back in the chair and lacing his fingers over his stomach.

"You see," Carter continued, "We got word of what was going on up in Alaska and we thought that you might be of use to us."

Oliver sighed, "Turns out that you really aren't. We've watched you since you started working here and in all honesty you are nothing special."

I smiled, "Well, you sure know how to make a girl feel good about herself."

"We need you to help us lure Georgia out before she becomes dangerous."

I was surprised, "You knew she was changing?"

"It's what we do."

"So, you need me to lure her out so that you can dispose of her?"

They nodded.

"What about the ones who changed her?"

Oliver sighed, "I'm fairly certain that there are no other vampires in the near vicinity."

As he spoke I smelled him, the soft scent of roses. I looked towards the door and nearly started laughing, "Who's your source?" I motioned towards the door with my head.

Carter and Oliver just stared in disbelief. Lieutenant Charles Sullivan stood in the doorway looking pleadingly in my direction. I stood to meet him. I glanced over my shoulder to see Carter and Oliver standing by the make-up station with their arms crossed. I wasn't sure which side I should fear the most.

I focused on Charles' face. He looked worn, not like he had in Alaska. He was hungry, but it wasn't just that. There was something bothering him and it was clear on his face that something was very wrong, but he may be my only chance of getting out of here alive and hopefully not as bait. I stood in front of him with my arms crossed and my lips pursed.

“It’s good to see you Nora,” he whispered reaching towards me. I flinched away and he dropped his hand with a hurt look on his face. I tried not to let it affect me in any way. He cleared his throat nervously and looked over my shoulder at the glares that were coming from my two would-be murderers. “Is there somewhere a little less public we could go to speak?” I couldn’t speak; I just walked towards the small editing office near the emergency exit.

He stepped in after me and I leaned against the back wall instantly regretting my strategic position. I was trapped. I refused to speak first and we stood there for what seemed like an eternity before he cleared his throat and said, “I’ve missed you.” I bit my bottom lip and looked away. I knew I couldn’t look him in the eye and keep my train of thought and at this moment, I knew, I needed all of my wits about me. It took him a minute, but he continued, “I really have missed you. I knew the moment you weren’t in my life anymore that it would only be a matter of time before I tracked you down.” He looked at me expectantly, but I couldn’t speak.

“I know you’re going to have trouble trusting me after all of the stuff that happened in Alaska,” he mumbled, “but I need to tell you everything even if you don’t believe me. I need you to know what was going on. I need you to know everything.” I stood very still. He took it as an invitation to go on while I started thinking of a way out of this mess as he launched into his explanation.

“I have never had anyone affect me the way you did in the little time you spent with me. I never even felt this way towards my wife.” He paused and looked up at me, but I made sure that nothing gave me away. “I was married when I was eighteen…I married a girl I grew up with in the town. I thought I was in love with her. I thought she was everything that I ever wanted in life.” He looked up. He looked tortured, but I simply slumped into a chair and sighed heavily.

He gulped, “We had a son.” He shot me another tortured look which I tried my best to ignore. “I named him Charles. I can still remember the day he was born and I held him in my arms. His eyes were hazel like mine, but he had his mother’s blonde hair. He was so tiny and helpless. It was so incredible to know that I did that. That I created that wonderful lively little human. He was the cutest thing I had ever seen and I loved every moment watching him grow up." Tears welled up in his eyes and I started to feel a pang of sympathy for him.

"He was seventeen when it happened. I was working that evening in a field we had near the edge of the town." He turned his back and his breathing accelerated. "I didn't even hear that monster get near me. I was just working and then before I knew it I was being thrown to the ground. It was a woman. She smelled like hay and freshly cut grass. I remember thinking how beautiful she looked. She was deathly pale and her eyes were a deep blue and her hair was golden blonde. It fell around her face as her lips parted. Her lips were blood red and her teeth became pointed as I watched. She smiled as she bit into my neck. There was a scorching pain that shot through me. I could feel my consciousness start to slip and I was getting cold. Everything started getting dark around the edges and I knew it was only minutes before I died and I couldn't move or fight.

"That was when I saw my son running across the field. He was only seventeen and he was rushing to save me. I felt so proud of him and so scared for him at the same time. I tried to find it in myself to move to tell him to run to save him. I couldn't. I was weak and helpless. I struggled to yell for him to run, but the only thing that I could feel was the blood in my throat. I heard the way it gurgled and I was so afraid that he would feel this pain too. The woman stopped and looked at him. She went to lunge at him, but then she stopped. She looked up like someone had called her name, but the only thing I could hear was my son's screams. Then she ran. She took off into the woods and didn't look back.

"He fell at my side and scooped me up in his arms. He cradled my head against his shoulder like I used to when he was little. I never realized how strong he was until he was running across the field with me in his arms like I was nothing, but then I guess half of me had been drained anyway. He ran in and my wife was cooking. She screamed and the tears started streaming down her face. Charles laid me on the bed and started to shake. I could feel the venom burning through my veins. They both looked so worried about me. I could never get that worried look out of my mind. I felt so guilty. I knew I was going to die and I knew that it would hurt them and that I couldn't do anything about it.

"For three days they watched me dying slowly. The venom burned through my body and I twitched and screamed non-stop. A priest came and gave me my last rites even. I don't think my wife stopped crying for seventy-two hours. Then I knew it was over. My heart started beating so fast I thought it was going to explode. My body rose up off the bed and I felt my heart stop.

"I closed my eyes, but it wasn't right. There was no bright light, no warm fuzzy feeling. It was just darkness and the high keening wail of my wife who was kneeling at my side. I realized after a minute that I hadn't been breathing. I took a deep breath and smelled the most delicious smell I had ever come across. It was intoxicating. I opened my eyes and immediately found the source of the smell, my wife.

"She looked at me in horror as I sat up and my son who had been at her side every moment didn't move. They both watched as the monster rose from where the man they loved had been laying. It happened so fast I'm not even sure that they knew what was going on. One second they were kneeling next to my dead body and the next I was at their throats. I drained ever last drop of blood from my son and tossed his limp and lifeless body to the side before I moved on to my wife. She didn't scream, she didn't try to run, she just stared at me open mouthed. I barely paused before I drained her as well. Their blood was the most delicious thing I had ever tasted.

He hung his head in shame and his shoulders hunched in around him. "I am a monster," he whispered. "I killed them and then I couldn't help myself. After the smell of their blood was gone my head cleared and I saw what I had done. I had killed my son, my beautiful baby boy and my loving wife. Their bodies lay at my feet as evidence. I couldn't believe what I had done. I sat there in that house for three days. The house that had been so happy just a few days before smelled like death and I sat there with my dead family and tried to cry, but no tears would come." He took a deep breath and tried to compose his voice that was dripping with pain and regret.

"I knew I couldn't be around people anymore," he continued. "I knew that I was too dangerous for that, so I ran. I ran into the woods and I hid. I found that feeding on animals was just as good as far as my strength was concerned. Of course it didn't taste nearly as good, but every time I think of the way their blood tasted it turns my stomach. I haven't ever tasted human blood again although I've been responsible for more than my fair share of deaths."

I tried not to look concerned, but I think I gave myself away. He smiled before he continued, "Honestly, for years I stayed away from humans, but I do have a human side. That human side made me crave the human world and human contact. I decided that the best job for me would be in a place that I could use my considerable talents." He half smiled and dropped his eyes. "I joined the air force. It took about 50 years before someone caught on. It was your father. He met me when I was transferred to Alaska about four years ago. He pegged me for exactly what I was and wanted to recruit me to help with this new project.

"The government knows we exist." He looked up to gauge my reaction. I kept my composure. He smiled. "They have an experimental plan that your father runs. He tries to track down people like us and get us to help." He paused and looked at his hands. "I'm ashamed of what I've done. I've let so many people die who didn't have to. I've killed humans and vampires alike to get this plan to work. Your father is trying to create a super soldier. Not quite a dhamphir, more powerful, but not quite a vampire, without the thirst. He wants a different type of creature and he's used my blood, and his blood, and the blood of every being I've ever lured to his clutches.

"I've killed so many innocent people in this crazy pursuit. I'm like their beacon. I search out the ones with the powers they want. They take your blood then they experiment with your DNA." His look was intense as he stared into my eyes. "They want yours." His voice was barely above a whisper. His perfect white hands reached for mine and I flinched away. He looked hurt, but continued, "I wanted to warn you that they were coming for you. I'm not sure when, but I know that they will be coming back."

I finally stood and looked at him with what I thought was indignation, but it didn't feel right. "Let them come," I hissed. He started to say something, but I held up my hand to stop the words. He grabbed my arm as I tried to walk past him. His touch sent that same feeling I had felt in Alaska and I despised myself for still allowing him to have that effect on me. I gently pushed his hand away as calmly as I could and growled, "Why are you really here?" He released my arm and I walked to the door. I wasn't waiting for an answer. In my head I knew that he was here to keep me busy while they moved in.

He laughed behind me and the sound stopped me in my tracks. There was something off. He was stressed and angry and it sounded like he would be crying if it was possible. He seized on my hesitation. He moved with lightening speed and flipped me against the door before I even took a breath. His lips pressed against mine and I melted into his arms. His mouth moved with utter desperation against mine and his fingers twisted into my hair forcing my face towards his. My body curved into his. I threw my arms around his neck as his other hand found the skin on the small of my back and pulled me closer to him. Adrenaline and desire raced through my veins and my heart pounded in my ears.

What was I doing? Last time I trusted him he betrayed me. My mind warred with my body. His hands felt so good on my bare skin and my lips reacted to his as though we had been lovers for years. I was intoxicated by his scent and wanted nothing more than to bury my face in his neck. But my mind won out. I pushed against him and nearly threw him into the wall. His breathing was as ragged as mine. He was confused by the completely mixed reaction I had to him, I could tell by the look on his face. I didn't know if he realized that I was just as confused. I stared at him for a minute and then muttered, "I need to think." I turned towards the door, but he was there. "Nora," he whispered, his breathing still not back to normal, "I want you."

"What about my father?"

"He doesn't know I'm here."

"What about Lena?"

He laughed, "I'm sure she and Bracken are just fine without me there."

I glanced down and noticed the tabloid someone had left on the counter, "And that?"

He sighed heavily, "A botched experiment apparently."

"How bad?"

"I saw that and immediately got on a plane to come here."

"That's pretty bad."

Charles reached out and took me into his arms. "He wants to make them with your DNA. He thinks that your blood, half breed blood, will keep them from being thirsty."

I shuddered.

"I'm never going to let them hurt you."

I stepped back and realized that tears were streaming down my face. I opened my mouth to speak but a pounding on the door stopped the words in my throat.

Oliver's voice was on the other side, "Nora sweetie, is everything alright?"

I opened the door, "Yeah."

Carter ran to my side and glared daggers at Charles who was standing in the doorway with a completely confused look on his face.

"It's alright," I whispered. I cleared my throat, "Charles is going to be staying for a little while."

A dazzling smile broke across his face, "For as long as she'll keep me."

My heart skipped a beat.

Carter and Oliver exchanged a concerned glance.

From around the corner, Georgia glared with absolute loathing.

13. The "Truth"

I opened the door to my apartment and a completely unusual sensation raced down my spine. I could hear Charles behind me breathing slightly. He fidgeted nervously with his luggage as we walked into the tiny living room. He set his bags down next to the couch and smiled, "I guess this is my bed?" I smiled and looked around. My breath was coming in short gasps and I felt the warmth of a blush creep across my cheeks again. That kiss this afternoon had made this far more awkward than I had planned.

Charles just sat on the couch and smiled at me while I fidgeted with my clothes and hair. I wasn't sure how much I should tell him. After a moment's thought, I took a deep breath and decided that I should just get it over with.

"I know you are here," I started, "to keep me busy while they move in."

"That's not…"

"It's fine," I interrupted, "I'm not angry about it, but if you think that you are going to lead my father to me like the butcher to the lamb, you are sadly mistaken."

"Nora," he plead coming to my side, "You have to believe me; I didn't come here to lead them anywhere. I don't want them to hurt you."

I pushed him back, "I *will* kill you if I find out you are lying to me."

"I'm not…" I held up my hand to stop him.

"Then you should know that Carter and Oliver are not to be trusted."

His brows knitted together.

"They're hunters, and now Georgia is transitioning."

He was silent.

"And…I've got a friend…He's a werewolf."

His stare hardened, "He's…"

"A werewolf." I crossed my arms and leaned against the wall.

"Will he be around often?"

"I sent him away. It seemed that I might be the cause of his death and I wouldn't be able to live with myself if that happened."

Charles looked at me as though he were seeing me for the first time. "How much blood did you lose?"

I clenched my jaw and looked away, I thought that I had recovered fairly well.

"That much? Was that courtesy of your new werewolf friend?"

"Your prejudice is only because you don't know any of them."

"*ANY* of them?"

I walked away, "I don't want to talk about this anymore."

He grabbed my arm and spun me around, "No, we need to talk about this."

I forced a smile, "It seems, my good Lieutenant that we are at some bit of an impasse then because it's NONE of your business."

"It is my business. You are putting yourself in danger so stupidly."

I stepped back, "Look, I can handle myself. Perhaps you should hurry back to my father and tell him that."

"What is it going to take to show you that I'm not working for your father?"

"Maybe he could write you a note," I smiled sarcastically.

He went to open his mouth, but I held up my hand to stop him, "Charles, you gave me that cell phone in Alaska in order to keep tabs on my whereabouts for my father. I know that you were working for him."

"You still have the cell phone."

"I know," I smiled, "is that how you found me?"

"No," he spat, "I knew where you were because this is where you worked before. I only went on what I knew about you."

I sighed.

He crossed his arms and slouched back against my couch cushions in full pout mode. I was about to say something, but we both suddenly jumped. I took a deep breath and registered that someone was on the other side of the door. I sniffed again and realized that there was more than one person on the other side of that door, one of which was the Romanian woman who lived downstairs. I took another breath and knew that Carter and Oliver were standing there as well.

That was when it registered this was how they knew what I was. They knew what I was because she had told them. A deep growl rumbled through the room, but the sound was so unfamiliar it took me a minute to realize that it was coming from me. I heard them hesitate, the sound of a gun scraping against a plastic holster. I crouched, ready to burst through the door. Without warning another scent wafted to my nostrils. Now it was Charles' turn to growl. Theodore was standing on the other side of the door as well, but he was farther away than the others. I couldn't tell if he was playing for the offense or defense.

"Theodore," I whispered my voice far too low for them to hear, "What are you doing?"

I had to strain to listen to his response, "I think explanations are best left for later. How are you getting out of there?"

"I'll get her out," Charles growled under his breath.

"Stop it," I hissed at Charles, "How heavily armed are they?"

"Very," Theodore answered, "and how are you Lieutenant Sullivan?"

Charles opened his mouth to speak, but after a warning glance from me, settled for a low growl instead.

I could hear Theodore snort softly.

"Look boys," I breathed, "I think it best if we both sneak out the window and then Theodore just go out the way you came."

I heard Theodore's soft footsteps as he slipped back out the apartment building and then the loud booming knock on the door frightened me into a standing position. They were using a battering ram. I froze for a second and before I knew what was happening I was in Charles' arms being whisked out the window. He tucked me to his chest like he did as we ran through the woods that night so long ago. His arms pulled me closer as we dropped through the air and hit the pavement without even the slightest shock.

"Great!" Theodore grumbled, "I think half of Philly just saw that."

"Argue later, move now." I growled yanking the two of them towards the corner.

Theodore scooped me up in his arms, "The car's this way."

Before I knew it, we were running down the street towards a car with Jennifer in the driver's seat. I nearly growled, but Theodore jostled me purposefully and I kept my peace. Jennifer, however, was not nearly so palatable to the idea of having us in the car. She wrinkled her nose is disgust and growled under her breath. Theodore shot her a warning look and she dropped her eyes to the road.

"Why did you defy the others?" I asked Jennifer suddenly.

"Theodore," she stated flatly.

"Can you still call them or get in contact with them?"

Her brows knitted together in the rear view, but she nodded.

"You need to let them know that it wasn't another vampire that took out Jordan and Tonya."

"What?" she growled angrily.

"It was the same people that convinced you guys to off me."

Theodore shook his head, "That's impossible."

I shook my head, "The hunters aren't just vampire hunters. They hunt everything. They said they were part of the Van Helsing Group."

Neither Jennifer nor Theodore moved towards their phone.

"Trust me damn it," I screamed pulling out my phone, "The others have to get out of there before Carter and Oliver get a hold of them."

Theodore pulled out his phone and dialed Alexander. He didn't say two words before handing the phone back to me.

"What are you playing at?" Alexander growled.

"Get the hell out of Philadelphia,"I growled, "Carter and Oliver are the ones who killed Jordan and Tonya."

There was silence on the other end.

"You have to trust me," I insisted.

There was still silence.

"Alexander," I demanded.

"We tried to kill you," he stated flatly, "Why should I believe you now?"

"Because I have no reason to lie."

"Revenge."

"Fine," I breathed, "When you get yourselves killed just remember before the life leaves your body that I told you so."

I hung up the phone and threw it towards the dash, fortunately, Theodore caught it before it shattered against the radio. I didn't know what to expect next. I didn't want to do this, but knew that I had no choice. I needed some allies and I had to make due with what I was given. I hunkered down in the back seat and waited for how this could get any worse.

It got worse when the car pulled into a driveway somewhere in Camden. I groaned and dropped my head against the pleather seats in despair. Jennifer glanced in the rear-view mirror and groaned, "For once I agree with you." I sighed and shrugged in despair.

Theodore ran up to the stairs and rang the bell. A man in a grungy wifebeater opened the door. He and Theodore exchanged words and some money. Then Theodore turned and nodded. Jennifer snorted and pulled around the back of the house where several other cars were parked. She turned and smiled at me, "Let's go and get this over with." Her tone was actually warm. I wondered if it was possible that she was beginning to warm up to me or if she was really just planning something horrendous in my future. In a way I was ready for that. If my life continued in its current pattern things were going to get far worse before they were ever going to get better.

I'm not sure how to explain this place that we were shown into. I would have called it a brothel, but that sounds too high end. It was really more of a crack house that doubled as a whorehouse. The man with the wifebeater showed us into a room upstairs, away from the costumers. Everything was stained, the comforter, the carpet, there was even a stain on the ceiling. I didn't want to know what had made that. I shuddered at the thought of when the last time this room had actually been cleaned. It seemed that everyone else was having the same thoughts. I could see everyone's eyes scanning the room and nostrils were flaring as they took in the scents. I tried very desperately not to smell anything, but sniffed in spite of myself. I instantly regretted that decision.

I cleared my throat and everyone's attention returned to the task at hand. I took out the little notepad I carried in my purse and wrote down my name, Theodore, Charles, and Jennifer. I looked up and challenged, "What else do we have?"

Jennifer smiled, "The element of surprise."

Theodore added, "And a cabin in North Georgia that is fairly secluded."

I smiled and Charles rolled his eyes.

I looked at Charles then to Jennifer, "And we have a way to lure my father in."

She didn't follow, but it seemed that Theodore was on target with my plan, "You," he nodded, "And you," he looked meaningfully at Charles, "will bring him down here."

"No," Charles leaped to his feet so quickly that I jumped, "I will not bring him to you."

I smiled, "Yes you will, or I will go and find him myself."

Charles slammed his fist into the window frame. It splintered.

Jennifer laughed, "Well, that's a little bit of an overreaction."

Charles growled and Theodore stepped between them.

I sunk back in the scummy chair in the corner and shook my head, "None of ANY of this plan will work unless everyone is on the same page."

Charles looked at me with such pleading, I almost lost my resolve. Then I remembered everything that had happened before and remembered that he wasn't to be trusted. I growled and stood up. "Look, I need to go take a walk because I'm starting to get really angry and when that happens things start to levitate around the room." They all just stared.

I stormed out of the room and nearly ripped the door off the hinges. I needed to get out and I needed to run. This was far too much for me to take in for one day. It was dark and I sought the seclusion. I needed to let myself go. I jumped to the top of a nearby building and took in the chaos that was Camden. The lights from the cop cars lit the place up like Christmas. Charles was following me. I could smell him even through the exhaust and garbage aroma.

"Hello, Lieutenant," I whispered, "Is there something about 'alone' that escapes you?"

In less than a second he was beside me on the rooftop. I shook my head, for some reason the fact he was quicker than me just got on my nerves. In fact, the more that I thought about it, the more he seemed to get on my nerves. I couldn't figure out why I had been so head over heels for him in Alaska.

He swung his feet over the side of the roof, "Why are you so upset?"

"Wouldn't you be?"

He was silent.

"My two best friends end up being vampire hunters, Georgia is turning into a vampire, I'm apparently supposed to kill my new friend who happens to be a werewolf, and the guy who broke my heart in Alaska came back and poured out his entire life story expecting me to just fall back into his arms. Now I'm on the run and about to lure my sadistic father and his minions into a secluded area with a werewolf that hates me, a vampire I can't trust, and a werewolf I'm apparently destined to kill." I leaped to the next building in my agitation.

Charles was right behind me, "I know you're mad at me..."

"I can't figure out what it was that made me so terribly attracted to you."

I could tell that one hurt.

He cleared his throat, "You're not the only person with talents."

"Is that so?" I was intrigued, what was his little secret.

"I can sense what people want."

I just stared.

"It's kind of like being an empath. I don't see it, but I know what the people around me want."

"So you played me," I laughed.

"It wasn't like that..."

"Yeah it was," for some reason I couldn't stop myself from laughing at the memories of it. "I got played."

"Well, it was at first," he stared incredulously, "I was supposed to gain your trust, but things changed."

I shook my head with a laugh still playing around the edges of my lips, "Just like in every sappy movie, right? End of Act Two you find out the guy you thought was the hero is really the jerk? Now what?"

He stood angrily, "Look, you want to confront your father, fine. I'll make sure he's here."

He was so close to me that I couldn't even smell the filth of Camden over the scent of his skin. I was starting to feel dizzy the scent of roses was so strong. My knees felt weak and my breath was labored.

He grabbed my chin and forced me to look at him, "You believe whatever you want about me."

I opened my mouth to speak, but he covered my mouth with his, literally taking the breath out of me. His mouth explored mine and I couldn't help but feel the same feelings that had overcome me in Alaska stirring in my chest. In spite of myself I kissed him back. He pushed me away and I turned trying to collect my thoughts. I heard him leave.

I turned in time to see him leap off the next building. I felt bad. Sure he had done some stuff that wasn't right, but maybe he really didn't want my demise. Maybe he did really care about me. I shook my head. It didn't matter anyway. I was pretty sure that in this confrontation with my father, I was not going to survive. I only hoped that everyone else did.

I waited watching until the sky in the east started to brighten and then went back to the hotel room. I had expected everyone to be asleep, but amazingly enough no one was. I closed the door gently and stared back at the three pairs of eyes trained on me. Jennifer was finally the one to break the silence.

"I think we're on the same page now," she said.

"Good," I sighed, "Now just please tell me which page that is."

Theodore stepped forward, "We decided that we are going to play this your way."

Charles chimed in, "However you want."

I sighed, now it was time to get the plan that was bouncing around in my head out on paper.

14. Alliances

I slept well with my impending demise spelled out in black and white on the pages of my notepad tucked in Charles' pocket. I dreamed a surprisingly calm dream. I dreamed of my mother. I hadn't known her, I had never even had a photograph, but over the years from her diary and my reflection, I had come up with a concept of her. She would sit with me in my dreams sometimes.

We were in a beautiful room that I didn't recognize, a stone tower draped with rich red velvet tapestries. She sat in a high-backed chair, her hand left to dangle gracefully over the ornately carved arm. I sat on a round ottoman covered in red velvet. She looked at me with her warm eyes and asked me softly what was wrong. I told her what was happening. She looked at me with love and asked me simply, "Why?" I had to. I have to stop him. There are lives at stake. Innocent people's lives are at stake here. She smiled, "Save the world." I looked at her earnestly and asked, "Mother, what does it feel like to die?" She didn't move. The more I looked the more it seemed as though she had been carved from marble and all I could do was stare.

She said something to me in a language I didn't understand, a single word "trean". I asked her to explain, but the light was starting to filter in through the red velvet curtains and flit across my mother's face. She closed her eyes and I watched as she started to dissolve into nothingness. I cried for her to come back, to not leave, but even as I reached for her she was out of reach. I woke up with tears streaming down my face and Jennifer staring at me curiously.

I wiped my tears away and sat up. Jennifer continued to stare as though she was trying to figure out why I could move. I knew she could hear my heart beat, but it was as though I wasn't living. She had seen me eat, but without blood I would shrivel. I could understand her confusion, but her open staring irked me to no end.

"What?" I demanded crankily.

"What are you?"

I smiled a half smile, "I'm a freak among freaks."

She laughed and sat down on the air conditioning unit.

I leaned against the headboard and sighed, "Are you?"

She shook her head, “No, the story books don't have that right either.”

“I've read every book, watched every movie I could find to try and figure out what I am, but I can't find a single one that has it right about either of us.”

“The story books are a little sexist aren't they,” she snorted.

“Very,” I smiled. “It's strange, since the beginning of time people have believed that we've existed. Vampires, werewolves, we're the stuff of legends.”

She smirked, “We were gods.”

“Now we don't exist to the masses. We are simply horror movie monsters. It's not like we actually exist in the real world.”

Jennifer snorted angrily, “You least of all.” Her expression changed and she stared at me as though she was trying to pry all of my secrets out with a look.

“What?” I asked after a moment, trying to keep the annoyance out of my voice.

“I don't understand why he can't stay away from you.”

“Well, to be honest,” I sighed, “that makes two of us. I would much rather none of you be involved.”

“Hey, the only reason I'm in this is because he is.”

“Trust me I know. I'm not stupid, and I'm pretty sure that you would much rather rip my throat out.”

She smiled.

“I guess we'll just have to hold off on that then,” I laughed.

A knock on the door broke up the slight treaty we seemed to have gained. We were both on our feet in a second. Jennifer opened the door and Theodore and Charles were both standing on the opposite side. Theodore looked at me and smirked leaving me to realize that I was standing there in nothing but an old T-shirt. I quickly grabbed a pair of jeans and pulled them on. I could feel my cheeks burning.

“We have a surprise for you too,” Charles announced with more than a little amusement in his voice. My face was on fire.

We stepped outside and Alexander and Julie were standing there. Julie refused to meet my eyes and Alexander looked haughty and unapologetic. I just crossed my arms and shook my head. Charles moved protectively to my right side and Theodore moved to my left. They both adopted my stance and Alexander growled slowly.

"How bad was it?" I asked.

"Bad," Julie squeaked.

"Sad that it took that for you to trust me."

Alexander glowered, "You may have been right about this, but if we are going to help you then we do this my way."

I shook my head, "Then have a nice trip wherever it is you are going."

Alexander puffed up to his full height as though that was going to intimidate me and thundered, "Look here..."

I was having none of this. I concentrated and threw my power out at him. In a second he was on the ground defiantly trying not to whimper. I could feel the three other werewolves tense, but none moved against me. I was the pack leader now.

"No," I said quietly, "You look here. You tried to kill me and in return I saved your life. If you want to be a part of this I would welcome the help, but things will be done my way. Otherwise, have a nice eternity."

Julie nodded, "I'm with you."

I allowed Alexander to stand and he begrudgingly agreed to my terms. Now our merry little band was slightly less horrendously outnumbered, but we needed to get moving. I turned back into the room and threw my clothes into the duffel bag. I pulled the little blue cell phone out of the side pocket of the bag. At the time I hadn't wanted to get rid of it for it's connection to Charles, but now I was glad for the connection to my father and not for sentimental reasons.

I was holding the phone when Charles walked in. I shoved it in my back pocket and could feel his smug smile without turning.

"So you kept it," he smiled.

"Yeah," I laughed, "it belonged to a guy I thought I was in love with."

"Ouch," he sighed.

"I don't know what I'm doing right now Charles," I confessed.

He stepped inside the room and sat down on the bed, "How so?"

I turned to face him, “I'm not sure we're all going to survive this.”

“We have faith in you,” he nodded, “Even Jennifer.”

I smirked, “Right.”

“I'm serious,” he said moving closer, “You don't know what you do to people. You are very possibly the strongest person, human or otherwise, that I have ever met and if you asked I would follow you to the end of the world.”

I shook my head, “I don't want to be responsible for someone not coming back.”

He stepped towards me and put his hands on my shoulders, “You aren't.”

I could feel the tears welling up in my eyes and tried my best to hold them back, “I am.”

He pulled me to him and wrapped his arms completely around my shoulders and whispered, “We all had the choice and we all believe in you.” He kissed me softly on the temple.

I wanted to say, I'm not sure about you. I'm not sure about Theodore. I wanted to say that I didn't know what my feelings were and I didn't want to hurt either of them and I knew that I was going to. I wanted to scream that I didn't know if I was going to survive this or not. I wasn't sure about any of this, but I wasn't sure how that was going to work out. But I didn't say anything. I just stood there and let him hold me. It felt nice, safe.

He took a deep breath and lifted my chin. His eyes had the same look they had in Alaska, that passionate smoldering that made my heart beat faster. However, he didn't move any closer. He was waiting. He wanted me to make a move, make a decision. I was so conflicted, but I ended up not needing to make the decision. Jennifer walked in and cleared her throat conspicuously.

Charles stepped back slowly and smiled sadly at me. I was so lost in this entire mess that I didn't know what to do. Jennifer was staring at me angrily. I stared back at her with a blank expression. She growled and grabbed her bag nearly knocking the lamp off of the nightstand. I almost said something, but she was just one other issue that I didn't want to deal with.

The drive to the North Georgia Mountains was excruciating to say the least. Eight hours of glares, growls, and awkward silence was not the way I wanted to spend one of my last couple of days. However, as with all things, this too did pass and we arrived at a small trail that wasn't even wide enough for one of the cars.

We all got out and grabbed our bags. Theodore smiled impishly as he took off running up the trail. The challenge was clear and honestly being able to get out of the car and stretch my legs was a welcome relief. I grabbed my duffel bag and shot up the trail after him. I could hear everyone else as they followed. The scenery was beautiful. Everything was so green and lush, it was a quite different scene from the gray concrete of Philly and the frozen beauty of Alaska.

It seemed like only seconds before we broke into a clearing. There stood a log cabin that held that title only by how it was put together. This house that stood in the meadow was two stories high. I took in the sight with awe. Gorgeous pane windows dotted the beautiful cedar logs covered with the natural knots that make cedar so special. A large wrap-around porch with ornately carved posts holding the railing curved around the edges of the house. I ran my fingers across the surprisingly smooth railing and smiled at the texture. Theodore stood at the door smiling at my expression. The outside was beautiful. The inside was no less amazing.

Inside the door was a large living area/kitchen. The open concept was not what I had expected from a cabin in the woods. All of the amenities of the modern kitchen were present. Cherry wood cabinets, stainless steel appliances, and slate tile floors stretched through the kitchen to a cozy breakfast nook. The furniture in the living rooms kept with the modern theme. Mission-style end tables and a coffee table accented the sleek leather furniture, a couch, love seat and arm chair. It was all arranged in a very conversation friendly pattern around a colorful area rug. I noticed that a television was nowhere to be seen. There was a staircase that was made from gnarled trees that led up to a loft style second floor that housed two bedrooms. However, the most impressive feature was a large stone fireplace.

"Wow" I marveled.

"Thank you," Theodore smirked.

"When was this built?"

"A couple of years ago," Jennifer broke in irritably, "when Theodore saw that we would need it."

I nodded and for the first time noticed the way that Jennifer was looking at Theodore. It wasn't sisterly at all. It was possessive and soulful and suddenly I understood why she hated me. This was weird even for me. I decided that I needed to try and puzzle this out as soon as possible. However, we had plans to set in motion first.

Charles was standing outside in the only spot where we could get cell reception with the circle of the rest of us standing around him. He was watching me silently, but he knew this needed to be done.

"Yes sir," he said, "I've located her."

A pause.

"No sir, she's left Philadelphia."

Pause.

"I don't know sir, I did not know that was a mission that was currently being played out."

Pause.

"Yes sir," a wicked smile broke out across his face, "I think that Ms. Stone would be an asset to this mission given her obvious attachment to your daughter."

The smile fell from his face.

"No sir, I don't mean to suggest that you have any qualms about what needs to be done."

Pause.

"I understand sir, I will prove to you that I have not abandoned the mission."

He nodded.

"Good-bye sir."

We were all waiting with baited breath. He closed the phone and slowly put it in his pocket. He sighed and looked at all of us before speaking.

"He doesn't trust me."

I smirked.

"He thinks that I have abandoned the mission and doesn't really believe that I'll hand you over to him." He looked at the others, “The good part is that he doesn't know anything about the rest of you or your special talents.”

Alexander growled, “I don't like this.”

I sighed, “You can leave at any time.”

Julie shook her head, “No, we're in this together. I just wish we could get those hunters in on the whole thing and be able to take them out at the same time.

Alexander smiled, “Well, if the one survived.”

I immediately felt defensive, but they were right. Carter and Oliver were snakes and I needed to remember that everything they had shown me of friendship was a scam to get close to my father. If I saw them again I would have to kill them as well, but I didn't hope for their involvement in this. “How many will my father bring?”

“Not many,” he said confidently.

“How do you know?” Jennifer asked.

“He said he was going to come down and handle it all personally,” Charles snorted, “When he says shit like that he means that he can handle it. He's too arrogant to think that he needs anyone's help.”

I smiled, “Hopefully he'll be in for a surprise.”

Charles didn't look happy. “Look, he won't bring many, but the ones he does bring will be powerful.”

That wasn't what we wanted to hear.

“How powerful?” I growled.

“Very,” he sighed, “His girl alone is the fastest creature I have ever seen.”

The circle grew very quiet. I didn't know my father had a mate. “The blonde?” My voice was a soft whisper at best.

“Yeah,” he whispered.

Theodore stepped towards me, but I shook my head. “How long have they been together?”

Charles fidgeted nervously.

“Tell me,” my voice was firm.

“They said,” he sighed, “that they had been together since the civil war.”

I bowed out of the circle and headed for the nearby woods. They knew better than to follow. I ran and ran up the side of the mountain until I reached the summit. The animals instinctively grew quiet as I rushed through the undergrowth. I wouldn't have messed with me either in the state I was in. I scrambled up to the top of a tree and screamed. I couldn't help it. There was so much to take in and all I could do was scream. The birds took flight through the leaves and animals scurried away in panic as my anguish echoed through the woods.

The civil war! Half a century before he even met my mother! I realized as I stared at the sky blazoned with pinks and purples that I had been holding on to the illusion that I had a father. That I may have been his mistake, but at least he had loved my mother. The knowledge that I was nothing but an experiment, a creation, an abomination, churned in my stomach. Although I hadn't been hoping to meet with my father when I went to Alaska, I had felt something just knowing that he had been near there. That maybe he would have felt it too.

No, I had never been anything more than a specimen to him. I could feel the trails of the tears I hadn't realized I was crying in the cool night air. I had been a fool and it had taken me one hundred years to figure that out. I stared into the sky as it darkened and a few flecks of light peppered the sky. It was strange. I felt my heart break with the knowledge that he hadn't even loved my mother let alone me. However, at the same time that this pain that ripped through my gut was at its worst, I felt a sense of clarity. I had been a fool, but that didn't need to continue. I needed to stop running.

I walked back to the cabin slowly. I realized that I didn't need to move quickly. In a strange way, walking quietly through the woods that had been here longer than I had been in existence was empowering. It felt as though part of me had died and that decaying portion of my soul had burned away to leave room for something stronger. I was seeing things with new eyes.

15. Surprise

There had been some changes at the cabin by the time I had fed. Charles was lounging on the front porch with a smile that signaled bad things for me. He looked like the cat that ate the canary. A very attractive cat, who seemed to know exactly how good he looked since he stretched as soon as I saw him. He had, of course, opted for the shirtless and jeans look which only made his rock hard body that much more impossible to ignore. Of course he also knew that. I had forgotten exactly how attractive he was. I could feel my heart jump as he "unconsciously" flexed his muscles and internally kicked myself for it. His smile only widened.

I grumbled under my breath and trudged up the front porch. The grin never faded from his face even though he wasn't looking at me. I reached for the door handle and he cleared his throat. I didn't want to look at him, I was still annoyed at him for even being there, but I did stop.

"You may not want to go in there," he smiled.

He smiled that quirky half smile and I wanted to either smack him or kiss him.

"Why not?" I asked leaning against the rail.

"It seems as though this mountain air has released the beast, so to speak," he smirked. I suddenly had the urge to wipe that smirk off his face. He seemed to sense that and found it hilarious. "You see," he explained sauntering to the corner of the porch flexing every muscle as he moved. He just exuded sexuality. "Your friend Teddy there has been a little less than truthful so it seems."

I growled, "Do continue."

He smiled slyly, "You see, Teddy and Jennifer aren't exactly siblings."

I snorted, "Figured that one out already."

He shook his head, "Guess I should've expected you to have figured that one out."

"Still hoping I'm just stupid?"

I just smiled, "They aren't only not siblings there pet, they are married and have been for quite some time."

I smiled back, "Well, that makes sense." In my mind I raced through everything that had taken place between all of us. This was a trap, but I needed to figure out just how screwed I was at this point. I figured the best thing to do was to keep him talking, so I quipped, "Well at least I'll have my room to myself tonight."

It was his turn to laugh, "But where will I sleep?"

I shook my head, "Oh, you have got to be kidding me."

I closed my eyes for a moment and suddenly he was there, pressed against me. I took a deep breath and his sweet scent filled my head. I tried very hard not to let it affect me. Then his lips traced my jaw and moved down the strong pulse in my neck and my breath rose in my chest. His hands slid under my shirt. I groaned as his lips caressed my collarbone and fingers massaged my sides. I felt my knees go weak. I twisted my fingers into his hair and yanked his face away from me.

He smiled, "Someone's feeling a little feisty."

I growled, "I don't trust you."

He groaned, "Not what I need right now."

I smiled, "And what do you need now?"

He pressed against me leaving no room for speculation about his intentions. I pressed my mouth into his, sliding my tongue across his lips. His breathing stopped and I smiled against his soft lips and pushed him back.

He sighed, "You needed to ask?"

I smiled, "No, but perhaps you should."

He looked up confused, "What?"

The smile slipped from my face and I growled, "Ask me, or has it never occurred to you."

He smiled, "I never asked because I can tell. I told you that. I can tell what you want."

I shoved him away from me, "Never assume anything."

I stalked into the house. Theodore and Jennifer were thankfully nowhere to be seen or heard. I don't think I could've endured that. I went up to the room I had been assigned and threw myself across the bed. I needed to think. This was a trap, but what was I going to do. My head was swimming and suddenly so heavy. I couldn't think. My eyelids fluttered and no matter how hard I tried, I couldn't help myself. My eyes closed and the last thing I remembered was the almost suffocating scent of roses.

It was dark when I awoke. I felt them in the room before I opened my eyes. I took a deep breath and recognized the scent. It was Georgia. I felt the muscles along my back tense. She wasn't alone. The blonde from Alaska was standing next to her. I could almost see it behind my closed eyes. They both stood in the doorway watching me and I knew my sleeping act wasn't fooling anyone. Theodore moved past them into the room.

My mind was racing. He kneeled in front of me and I opened my eyes slowly. He was staring at me intensely with a very strange and frightening smile stretched across his face.

"Good morning, Jesse," He grinned.

My heart skipped a beat. I hadn't used my given name in nearly fifty years, how did he know it? This did not bode well, they knew more than I had given them credit for.

Charles moved into the room.

"How did you know?" My voice was at least strong.

"Don't you think your father should know your birth name?" Theodore laughed and the sound slithered against my skin.

"You're all working for my father," it wasn't a question.

He just grinned and stood back making a large sweep of his arm as if to encompass the ever growing entourage in my doorway. I sat up slowly and took in the view. Jennifer had stepped up to join in the party. She was more than happy to move forward. She crouched forward menacingly and her skin rippled.

"Stupid, stupid, girl," she growled.

I snorted, "Why this time?"

Theodore answered, "Didn't you know Jennifer and I have been married for nearly sixty years?"

I looked sarcastically shocked, "Long time."

He grinned and I couldn't help but slap him as hard as I could. The sound of the impact acted as a starting pistol. Jennifer pounced before my fingers left his face. Her arms wrapped around my shoulders and slammed me into the headboard. I could feel her skin vibrating against me. I didn't want her to change holding on to me, I could only imagine that would be messy at best. She swung me around and I noticed that we were two short. Alexander and Julie were nowhere to be seen. It seemed that my thoughts were rather obvious.

"They are dead," Jennifer hissed in my ear, "They were expendable."

I snickered, "What's in it for you two?"

Theodore leaned in and ran his cheek against mine, "Money," he purred, "Lots and lots of money."

I spit in his face. For some reason I just couldn't stop making it worse for myself. I wanted to push him away with my mind, shove him into the wall, but this had been what I wanted. I literally couldn't do anything, most of all show my hand.

Theodore laughed menacingly, "Oh," he cooed, "Are you frightened?"

I breathed heavily. "No," my voice was trembling. Great, I can't even trust my voice anymore.

The blonde laughed and the sound twinkled off the walls. She skipped to my side. I struggled against Jennifer's arms, but the blonde just ran her fingers down my face and then flicked my nose maliciously. "Little bastard," she laughed, "didn't you know that you had certain weaknesses?"

I gasped as she pressed an amulet into my throat. It burned something awful.

She pulled it away and I could still feel the shape of it on my throat. A little heart.

I coughed, "What an interesting choice to scar me with!"

Her voice was high and almost childlike, not the voice I would have expected from a preternatural being that exuded sexuality, "I thought a cross would be too cliché."

I snorted, "I admire your attempt to be original."

She dug her nails into my throat and I felt the tiny rivulets of blood trickle down my neck, "Let's see how much you admire when we're through with you."

I took another painful breath,it shouldn't hurt this much to just be alive, "What is this?"

Jennifer growled and squeezed, "Just a little herbal concoction."

The blonde raised her hand and brought it down hard against my temple. The pain exploded in little flashes of yellow and white behind my eyelids. I tried to fight it, but there was something about this mixture that Jennifer was drenched in. I couldn't fight my way to consciousness. The darkness won and I slid into oblivion.

When you are waiting to die, you realize several things that are truly real. I discovered that I was able to stay far calmer than I had ever thought possible. I also discovered that I had horrendous taste in men as well as in friends. Not to mention the fact that my father was coming to kill me and I really did welcome the challenge even though my hands were tied behind my back and my feet were tied to the legs of the chair I was bound to and the rope had been drenched in the same herbal mixture from the cabin. I also discovered that I was certifiably insane and alright with it.

The drug they had given me to keep me unconscious wore off and I could see the taupe colored walls. Wondered if it was meant to be soothing. Heavy red drapes hung from the ceiling to the floor on one wall. I closed my eyes and listened. There was an opening on the other side of the wall. I could hear the faint rush of air whispering against the curtains. There were soft footsteps in the corridor. They were definitely not human. I listened closer. Two voices lowered in hopes that I wouldn't hear them.

"She's not going to be of any use if she's drugged." It was Charles.

"It will work its way out of her system." The high timbre of the voice could only belong to the blonde.

"Only if she's alive long enough for her heart to pump it through her system." Charles was angry.

"Then go and check on her." The woman was dismissive at best.

I kept my eyes closed and listened as his soft footsteps get closer. I knew I couldn't move even though I desperately wanted to throw him through the wall. He moved towards me cautiously. I let my head hang down on my chest and waited. He reached out and gingerly touched my neck even though I'm sure he could hear my pulse the minute he entered the room. He leaned down and whispered so low I had to strain to hear him from centimeters away.

"I can feel what you want and I can't really blame you for that, but I want you to know that I won't hurt you."

I didn't move.

"I'm so sorry," he whispered, "I need you to believe that."

I opened my eyes and just stared into his for a moment. He bit into his bottom lip and blood oozed out of the little cut he opened. Suddenly, he pressed his mouth against mine. I was completely taken off guard. I tried to pull back, but he twisted his fingers through my hair and held my face fast to his. His blood trickled into my mouth.

I nearly choked on it. I had to swallow. I had never tasted vampire blood before. It tasted just like all the rest. He let me pull back , but his lips lingered against mine as his breath came hard against my lips. It tickled. I took a deep breath, I needed to clear my head. Then he whispered, "Slam your head into my face."

That was perhaps the most off the wall request I had ever gotten, but far be it from me to disappoint. I swung my head full force into his mouth. I felt his teeth graze my forehead and his blood gushed warm down the bridge of my nose. He cursed at the top of his lungs and smiled quickly at me before help came rushing in. He didn't want them to know that he was the one who cut his lip, but I didn't understand why.

The blonde came rushing in and took his face in her very white hands. She looked at the blood dripping off his chin and then my face and stood very slowly. He didn't move, just sat there and stared. Then she turned her attention on me. I laid my head back and smiled at her. She was infuriated and it seemed the only outlet for her anger was to punch me in the stomach. I could feel the air rush out of me, but I couldn't help laughing as the breath came back into my poor lungs. I laughed and she just stared in anger. She flexed her fists over and over again until they slammed into the side of my face. I tasted my own blood and I couldn't stop laughing. Charles was standing in the corner with his hand on his mouth silently pleading with me to stay quiet, but I couldn't help myself. I was hysterical.

She hit me again and I could feel my eyes rolling back in my head. The laughter slowed, but that smile stayed plastered across my face. I rolled my head back onto the cold metal headrest and looked into her deep blue eyes. I gathered a mouthful of blood and spit and splattered it down the front of her light green shirt. Every eye in the room stared at me in horror as I whispered, "Bitch." She hit me so hard that the chair I was on tipped over and slammed me to the floor. The only thing I remember before the blackness closed in on me were her pointed red heels. I snorted and then fell into unconsciousness.

These were not my memories. In what should have been the peace of my unconsciousness, I was seeing images that I had never seen before. They came in flashes and didn't make sense. Then I saw me. I was backed against the wall and blushing. I was running through the woods. I was being carried to the jeep. I was sleeping, my face tear stained and sad. It was strange, I was laying on my bed in my apartment. I saw the reflection in the mirror. It was Charles, standing there. My bag from Alaska was laying on the floor. I hadn't even unpacked yet. I hadn't known he had come to me. I was watching a disjointed movie of Charles' thoughts.

I started to come to and realized that no one had actually taken me off the floor. I was still bound to the chair, cheek on the cold concrete. I easily could've lifted myself off the ground, the herbal concoction was losing it's strength. But I figured it would be better to suffer discomfort for a moment rather than begin the show again. Then there was the nagging question, why was I seeing images from Charles' point of view. I was a little groggy and not as quick on the uptake as I normally was, so it took me a minute until I realized that was why he hadn't wanted her to see that he had given me his blood. I could see his memories.

He had to have given me this for some reason. I just couldn't figure out why. I closed my eyes and tried to concentrate, to separate the images. At first they were nothing but a jumble with no sense of time, but then specific information began to emerge. He had given me the run down of the plan. It was like I was watching a movie that was slightly out of focus.

They were standing in a little room, I knew rather than saw that it was a room in Alaska. I could almost feel the chill. My father and the blonde were bent over some microscopes, Theodore and Jennifer lounged against a large door frame and Charles paced back and forth in front of a window. They were waiting, but for what I could only guess. There was a loud cry on the other side of the door. Charles raced through it with my father and the blonde not far behind him. Theodore and Jennifer seemed unfazed.

The sight I saw was unlike any I had ever believed possible. A human being was strapped to a table. In his memory I could smell the blood. The vampire blood was being pumped into his system while the human blood was being siphoned out. They had to have been at it for days to ensure they didn't kill their test subject. Not that it mattered. They watched as he screamed out in agony, the blonde jotting something on a clipboard, not one of them moved to help him. The poor human was scared to death. In a minute the heart monitor flat-lined. They all waited and watched. Not a one batted an eye.

Suddenly the man leaped forward, breaking the restraints and lunged at Charles. He easily sidestepped the fledgling and in a swift motion had it in a headlock. My father simply shook his head and Charles' muscles flexed snapping the creature's neck mercilessly. I felt a tear run down my cheek.

"Pure blood isn't working," my father announced after a moment. His voice was gruff, like I remembered, but there was something different about it. I couldn't place what sounded off.

"We need the dhamphir," the blonde hissed. I thought I noted a tinge of jealousy in her phrasing.

"She's nothing special," Charles grumbled, "She can even die, she said so herself. She's only slightly stronger and faster than a human."

It had been after our little romp in the woods.

"She's immortal," Theodore growled, "and her blood can't be any more pathetic than these displays are turning out."

"I'm telling you," Charles insisted, "She's not the answer."

My father seemed to be turning his options over in his mind and finally sighed, "We won't know until we try." He turned to the blonde, "Darling," he whispered, "Bring me her blood."

"No," Charles groaned, "I'll bring her to you. Her blood will be of no use to us if she is dead." He looked meaningfully at the blonde who showed her fangs menacingly. My father, however, nodded and Charles smiled. They were talking again, but I couldn't hear anything. His thoughts were jumping to different images so quickly I almost couldn't keep up with them.

The blonde, her fangs exposed, leaping from the woods, his hands covered in blood, humans and vampires alike strapped to that same table and suffering similar fates. The ones that didn't attack were put in a holding cell, but these weren't regular vampires. These were vicious monsters that attacked anyone and anything that got close enough, except for my father. I didn't have time to puzzle out what that meant before the images changed again. More blood. Screams.

Wait. Those screams weren't in my head, they were echoing off the walls. I opened my eyes and searched the floor. The screams were coming from behind the curtain and were getting closer. I would have thought that nothing would surprise me after the last few days, but yet again I was wrong. Lena Watters was being drug through the curtains. She was thrown carelessly on the floor in front of me. My chest became tight. I was near panic. I was breathing heavily. What was going on?

It took me a minute, but I remembered what Charles had said his special gift was. He could feel the emotions of others. Hers were frantic. Apparently a little of his power came with the memories. Georgia sashayed in a step behind her, I nearly gagged on her self-importance. She crouched in front of me and smiled a sickeningly sweet smile that made me want to puke. A growled rumbled deep in my throat and for an instant fear flickered across her face, but then it seemed as though she remembered that she was also not human and she straightened up and delivered a kick to my abdomen that left me gasping for air.

Georgia pulled me up and sat me straight. I gasped as she towered over me, triumph plain on her face. "Now" I gasped "you are...the monster." She lunged with her claws out, but Charles easily caught her around the waist and tossed her back against the concrete wall. She let out a horrendous hiss and screamed at him. It brought the rest of our darling crew into the room.

The blonde screamed for silence. The only one who was unable to comply with that was Lena, who whimpered quietly in the corner. The blonde seemed to take notice of her for the first time and moved with the supernatural grace that made her menacing scowl even more frightening. Lena stopped whimpering. Her bottom lip just quivered and tears ran down her cheeks. I was gasping and tears were escaping my eyes with alarming speed. Without pause, the blonde took Lena's head between her hands and twisted until I heard her neck crack. Then nothing. There was no more fear, nothing.

I looked up at Charles, but he seemed to be purposefully avoiding my gaze. I wanted to scream at him, demand he tell me what he did, but I had the sneaking suspicion that this strange turn of events might actually be helpful. There had to be something in his memories that would help me, there had to be. I kept my peace and let Georgia tower over me.

"I've hated you," she hissed, "since the moment you walked into the station."

I smiled up at her, "I've hated you since I saw you on the news back when you were fat."

Her hand came smashing down on my face.

I fake pouted, "Georgia, I didn't think you cared."

She showed her fangs and lunged. She was easily subdued by Theodore.

"Temper, temper," I laughed.

Theodore back-handed me and again the chair tipped over. My shoulder slammed into the floor and dislocated. I gritted my teeth and tried not to let them see how painful it really was. Charles obviously could tell. They were going to kick my ass until my father showed up. I really hoped that it would be soon. Charles strode over in two steps and roughly set me straight. He deftly cracked my shoulder back into place. I literally bit down on my tongue until I could taste blood.

It won't be long now.

I looked at Charles trying to hide the alarm in my face.

Don't look at me like that. They'll know what I did.

I could hear him. Hear him in my head. I guess I shouldn't have been so surprised. There were rumors that some vampires could do that as well. Guess I found one, lucky me.

Yes, I can hear you too.

Of course he could hear me, it wouldn't be fair for me to have my thoughts to myself.

I can help.

How?

When they release you to move you, I can get you out of here.

How?

Just follow my lead and do what I tell you to.

Why should I trust you?

Do you have a choice?

I snorted unintentionally and the blonde whipped around at me.

"Something funny?" She growled.

I snickered and Charles rolled his eyes. "Well have you seen your pet lately?" I motioned to Georgia with my head.

Georgia growled but was afraid to lunge. I raised my eyebrows at her tauntingly, but she still didn't attack. Thinking about it for a minute I should've been glad of it, but for some reason, I just wanted to be knocked out again. But no such relief was to be given. I dropped my head back against the cold metal chair and closed my eyes. There were sounds everywhere. Activities that I couldn't, and didn't, want to know about were happening in this building wherever it was.

What are you doing?

What do you mean?

Why are you provoking her?

I'm itching for a fight.

You know you're a bad liar.

I wanted to growl at him, but instead I looked at him. He pleaded with me silently to let me know how much trouble I was going to be in if I continued to provoke her. My mind was bombarded with images of things that Georgia had done. She had ripped people apart and laughed as she played in their blood. She was a far worse monster than anything I had ever imagined. I rolled my head back and closed my eyes again. I pulled into myself where at least the darkness was less unnerving.

I can't hear you. The feel of the thought was frantic, frightened.

I'm fine.

How did you pull away from me?

I don't know.

Can you do it again?

I don't know.

You should try it.

I concentrated on folding a shroud around me. I listened for a moment. There was nothing, not a sound from him. Radio silence. I let the concentration slip and there he was again.

Jesse? Jesse can you hear me?

I can hear you.

You shouldn't be able to this.

Then why can I?

I don't know. Maybe because you are part human.

So I need to call up my humanity?

I guess. He was confused and amused at the same time.

What is this stuff they put on me?

It's a common mixture made up of things that vampires are rumored to be allergic to.

So you put everything in there and just hope whatever vampire you come up against just happens to be allergic to something?

*Something like that,*there was amusement in his thoughts.

There was a sound unlike anything else that I had ever heard outside of the movie theatre. It was the whirring of helicopters. I could feel my eyes widen and I struggled as hard as I could against my restraints.

Stay calm.

A high pitched frequency bounced off the walls and made my eyes water. I watched as the blonde freaked out and Georgia scurried around close to the floor like the cockroach she was. Theodore and Jennifer were howling like the wolves they were, their hands covering their ears. The whirring of the blades got closer and closer. I didn't even see Charles as he slipped up behind me and cut the ropes from around my wrists. He was very careful not to touch them at all.

The mixture only works on vampires, his voice was soft in my head as if his blood was working its way out of my system, *touching it hurts you and takes your abilities.*

I felt like I could breath again, like I had recovered from an asthma attack. Every breath brought an exquisite clear-headedness with it. Charles looked angry. He grasped me by the shoulders and forced me to look in his eyes. He seemed like he was trying to tell me something but nothing was happening.

"Shit," he growled. "You can't hear me anymore."

The blonde screamed, "Grab her, we need to get out of here."

I didn't need to hear him in my head to know what I had to do. I threw him back against the wall, being sure not to hurt him. He crumpled to the floor like a ragdoll. I growled at the blonde, but before I could even think about throwing her around she was gone, behind the velvet curtain and out the door. There was a sound like breaking glass and then I felt the sharp shards rip into my skin. Charles sprang from the wall and protectively threw him self across me knocking us both to the floor. For a moment everything seemed to stop. Charles had me wrapped in his arms and I was going to be alright. Then he was violently ripped away from me.

I looked up to see the blonde grabbing Charles by the waist and throwing him against the wall. He hit hard and I sprang to my feet throwing myself against the skinny vampire, knocking her to the ground. I scrambled across the floor to Charles' side only to be thrown across the room. In all of the excitement, I had forgotten about our furry friends. Jennifer stood above me with a sneer that frightened me to the core. She was going to enjoy this.

I pressed against her with my mind, but it was weak. My leg was broken and I could feel the bone pressing against the skin. I was feeling groggy and my head was pounding. I realized that my head was bleeding, I was not nearly as worried as I knew I should be. For some odd reason I just couldn't bring myself to care. The vision at the corners of my eyes started to blur and darken. I was losing consciousness and I didn't care, I wanted this to end. I vaguely registered that there were gunshots going off somewhere close by as the blessed darkness closed in around me.

16. The Van Helsing Group

I awoke and instantly sprang to my feet. The searing pain in my leg brought me to my knees almost instantly. A strangled cry broke from my lips as I clutched the wound that stubbornly refused to heal. A sharp intake of breath accompanied the movement and in the air I caught his scent. Quickly, I used my good leg to push me back to the wall. I didn't know where I was, but I was not about to go down without a vicious fight.

I shivered as my back touched the stone wall, completely covered in shadows. The darkness was suffocating. My night vision was usually pretty good, but I couldn't see my hand in front of my face. I closed my eyes in an attempt to perceive some sort of outline of my new prison. I opened my eyes only to find that I could see no better now than I did a moment earlier. I needed some source of light. As if in answer to my needs a bare bulb hanging by a wire flickered to life in the center of the room and in its swaying light I saw the vampire who was at the moment my warden.

He was exceptionally handsome, even more so than Charles. But where Charles had seemed modest and unassuming about his appearance, this man reeked of conceit. Even so, my jaw nearly dropped at the sight of him. He wore tight black jeans that barely masked the muscles that leaped just below the fabric as he glided forward with liquid grace. He wore a black silk shirt completely unbuttoned revealing a trail of pale skin. His sleeves were rolled revealing muscular forearms and a strange marking on the inside of his left arm. It looked familiar, but I couldn't place it.

He knew I was looking and he laughed as he stepped into the center of the room. The sound was deep and rich and made me shiver to my core. I thought Charles' voice had been intoxicating, but he was an amateur compared to the vampire that stood before me. I had to concentrate to keep from falling into it.

"Come now *chere*," he whispered softly, the sound reached places a whisper shouldn't, " The old man will be pleased that you are not injured too badly."

I winced as I moved my leg and tried very hard not to let it show, but I could tell he saw it. He moved towards me in what must have been a painfully slow pace for him palms forward as if to disarm me. He stopped abruptly when I caught his eyes. He must have read the warning on my face. He smiled crookedly, the only mar in his otherwise perfect visage and it still managed to be beautiful.

"Who is the old man?" At least my voice was strong even if the rest of me was falling apart.

The vampire smiled again and the only word I could think of to describe it was dazzling, but his eyes gleamed with a self-assuredness that made me want to gag. "The old man," he whispered intimately, "Is the one who brought you here *chere*. The one who saved you." He squatted down near me so he could be at eye level. "Take my hand *chere,* let me help you."

His voice was dulcet, and every word he whispered was uttered as if in seduction. I wanted desperately to see if his lips were as soft as they seemed, but resolutely I put my hands against the cold stone behind me and pushed myself into a standing position. I gritted my teeth against the pain that pulsed through my body, but at least it helped me clear my head. "My name's not *chere*," I growled through clenched teeth, "Now take me to this old man."

The vampire looked up at me incredulously and laughed softly to himself. I was furious, but bit my tongue. He seemed to know that and it just amused him all the more. He stood gracefully as a cat and strolled towards me, his palms forward. "I know your name, Jesse." The way he whispered my name echoed with repressed desire and it ached through my body. He was good.

He held his hand out to me again and I snorted, "I didn't take your help before, what makes you think I will this time?"

He was even more amused and chuckled at me softly, "Now," he smiled, "you won't have the wall to support you, you must walk."

I defiantly stepped away from the wall and crumpled. I would have met the floor for the second time in five minutes if it hadn't been for the strong arms that locked around my waist. My leg was refusing to heal or hold weight and that frightened me more than being held up by a strange vampire.

His fingers brushed my hair from my neck and I shivered as much from desire as from the shock of his cold skin against mine. I turned to look at him and was surprised to see him concerned. I felt a small giggle start in the back of my throat and it escaped my lips as he felt my forehead. Like I wasn't warmer than him on a daily basis. I couldn't stop myself from giggling. I didn't mean to laugh in his face like that, but he didn't seem to mind. In fact he smiled as he swung me into his arms effortlessly.

He shook his head, "I see why everyone is so taken with you, *chere*."

He carried me out of the small room through a door I hadn't seen in the gloom. Normally, I wouldn't allow someone to carry me, but the pain in my leg was beyond intense. I realized with chagrin that I was gripping this stranger's shirt with iron fingers as the pain spasmed. I didn't understand why it wasn't healing. I needed someone who would be able to fix it and unfortunately this handsome monster who held me so carefully in his arms seemed to be my best bet. I relaxed my death grip on his shirt and realized that with him carrying me, the pain was subsiding.

He carried me through a corridor that was painted gray. It surprised me. Most hallways were painted taupe, but I guess soothing wasn't the mood they were going for. It was scary quiet in the corridor. It made me shudder and the vampire pulled me close to his chest. I could hear my heart beating, but the only other sound was the clicking of his heels against the pale gray linoleum.

I didn't look at him, "New Orleans?"

I could feel him smile as I shifted against his soft shirt, "What gave me away?"

"*Chere,*" I answered quietly, I was suddenly drowsy being rocked in his arms, "and you have a slight accent."

"Most women find it charming," he laughed, "but Charles told me you wouldn't."

I looked up at the chestnut brown stubble that covered his chin, "He did what?"

He smiled and pulled me closer. I tried to push away from him, but my hand met the skin on his chest and he gasped as if I had burned him. I pulled my hand away, fear in my eyes. He just smiled and took a deep breath, "He told me to take care of you and make sure you were safe."

"When did you talk to him?" He had helped me and I wanted to know that he was still alive. I surprised myself with the realization that it was nothing more than that, just a debt to be paid.

This vampire sighed, "Not recently." He chuckled at some memory and said, "He called us right before you decided to embark on your little scheme."

"What's so funny?" I asked suddenly insulted.

"Nothing *chere*," he smiled, "we are here."

He swung a door open. After my welcoming room, I didn't know what to expect but this wasn't it. The room we entered was filled from floor to ceiling with books. Cracked bindings and yellowed pages were the only wall decorations. The smell filled my senses. I was speechless as I looked up at the half balcony that ran the perimeter of the room. Another set of bookshelves went up from there. The ceiling had to be at least thirty feet high. The sheer volume was impressive, it must have taken centuries to build a library like this.

I was so busy staring at the books that I barely noticed as my handsome captor set me on a plush velvet chaise. I looked up as his hands slipped out from beneath me. He was smiling at me as though I was the only thing in the world and I couldn't take my eyes off of him. He dropped his gaze and I think would have blushed if it had been in his power. It was cute, more than cute. I took a deep breath to steady myself.

"Georges does have that affect on women it would seem," said a soft human voice with a slight German accent.

I looked for the source of the voice and saw him standing on a ladder on the second tier of bookshelves. He hadn't even glanced down at me, he was placing a book back on the shelf as though nothing out of the ordinary was happening. The vampire, who I assumed was Georges walked towards the door with that feline grace that emanated from him. I couldn't help myself. I enjoyed the view. The old man chuckled as he descended to the ground level. Georges was looking at me, grinning like an idiot. I expected to blush under this scrutiny, but I couldn't find it in myself to be embarrassed.

The old man stared at me as though I were under a microscope. I stared back and observed him as closely. He was nicely dressed, a pair of freshly pressed khaki slacks matched the argyle sweater-vest. He looked stately and refined. He was human, but not normal. There was something that I could almost smell on him that screamed supernatural. The corners of his thin lips twitched as I attempted to classify him as if he knew what I was thinking. He ran his hand through his snow white hair and stared intensely through his gray eyes. Then I realized what it was that shimmered around him. He was a mind reader.

"Yes *Fraulein*, I can read your thoughts."

"My name is Jesse," I growled. I hadn't noticed how much my leg had hurt while Georges carried me, but now the pain began to throb dully.

"I know," he laughed, "I'm sorry about your leg." He moved towards me and I tried to move away. He winced as I did. "Please don't move," he whispered as though the air had been pulled out of him.

I looked at him confused, "Are you alright?"

He smiled weakly, "The amount of pain you are in is amazing and you ask if I am alright? You are indeed a strange creature, Jesse Childress."

I must have looked confused because Georges stifled a laugh, "I don't understand what you mean." I tried to push myself up to a more sitting position, but my I crumpled from the pain, "Why won't my leg heal?"

The old man shook his head, "It doesn't normally take this long for you to heal?"

I shook my head.

He pondered for a moment, but at length replied, "I do not know. I would like to have our physician take a look at you if you don't mind."

I shook my head, "No one is going to touch me until you tell me who you people are and why you brought me here."

"Of course *frau*...Jesse." The old man nodded. He moved carefully to a matching velvet chair across from me. I glanced back at Georges who was uninterestedly picking at a piece of lint on his jet black shirt. The old man cleared his throat and crossed his legs. "We, my dear Jesse, are the Van Helsing Group." I immediately tried to get up, to use my powers to help me run, but I only succeeded in falling off the chaise and an incredible paroxysm of pain attacked my body. The old man screamed and grabbed the snowy white hair on either side of his head. Georges swooped immediately to my side and scooped me up into his arms again. The pain didn't matter, I needed to run.

"Let me go," I screamed, pounding my hands into the vampire's chest to no avail. I was starting to panic. Carter and Oliver had been a part of that group. Carter and Oliver had tried to kill me. I knew something was wrong, I wasn't healing, my powers didn't work, I was with the enemy. Despite myself, tears rolled down my cheeks as the panic gripped my chest and I started to hyperventilate.

Georges pulled my head close to his chest and started whispering to me in French. I struggled against him, but he was far too strong. He locked me in his arms and lowered me to the chaise still whispering. His voice was soothing and part of my mind whispered for me to give in to the sound, to let his voice lull me into peace. I couldn't give into that voice I pushed against him with my mind and nothing happened, there was no reaction at all. Fear silenced the voice in my head and I suddenly lashed out at Georges landing an open handed slap across his face. He easily caught my wrists in his hands as I screamed in fear and frustration.

"Stop," the old man cried, "You do not understand. We are not here to hurt you."

I looked at him incredulously, "Talk fast old man."

"My name," he panted, "is Gustavus Van Helsing. I am the several greats grandson of Abraham Van Helsing. He founded this organization."

"Why did you try to kill me?" I asked angrily.

"We did not," he protested, "the two of whom you speak were hired by the Marquis, not us. We would not stoop to such levels."

I looked at Georges who was carefully backing away from me. He was obviously unharmed, but made a show of being slow. "What was he doing to me?"

Van Helsing shrugged, "He was doing what he could to calm you. Georges has an amazing voice, don't you think?"

I stared into the vampire's warm brown eyes, "Never try to do that again."

He smiled and actually winked at me, "No promises, *chere.*"

Van Helsing shook his head, "Sometimes Mr. Moncrief can be incorrigible."

I looked at the old man without a shred of humor and he cleared his throat nervously.

"We mean you no harm, Miss Childress, you must understand that. We are here to prevent harm from coming to you. The Van Helsing Group was created to stop creatures like The Marquis from running amok. You are completely innocent of any wrong doing and we would not have any harm come to you simply for your birthright."

I didn't speak, but he took my expression as sufficient encouragement to continue.

"Your friend, Charles Sullivan, is one of our operatives. He has been working with your father so that we can find the Marquis and stop him. Up until recently, he was unable to locate the lab they were using. He has only been allowed into the secondary locations. When he realized your vitality to the Marquis' plan, he contacted us."

The old man shook his head disapprovingly, "You risked far too much with that little scheme you concocted, Jesse. You don't realize what would have happened if we had not come to get you." I looked at him confusedly. "Charles called for us to come and get you before they arrived in Georgia. The woman you used to work for had a very nasty idea about how you needed to be handled and it was less than appealing."

I smiled, "I thought Georgia might have something to say about that."

The old man shook his head again, but Georges was trying very hard not to laugh. "You are a strange woman," Georges chuckled, "You aren't at all worried about this?"

I smiled and laid my head against the chaise arm, "This thing between Georgia and I has been brewing for quite some time. In fact, I've really been expecting something to happen."

The old man winced again, "You need to get your leg attended to, would you allow me to have our resident physician look at you?"

I begrudgingly nodded and the door immediately sprang open to reveal a small woman with jet black hair and small beady eyes. She was prim and proper and nothing but business. She wore a no nonsense black blouse and a pair of straight leg jeans. Her black physicians bag, which had to be upwards of one hundred years old had definitely seen better days and from her expression this was not her happiest hour.

"Daphne LaRue," she said without the slightest intonation or friendliness. She was just there to fix my leg.

I held out my hand, "Jesse Childress."

She looked at my hand like I was going to bite her and said, "I know who you are."

I dropped my hand to my lap and rolled my eyes, "It seems like everyone around here knows me."

She didn't respond at all. She looked down at my leg and her eyebrows knitted together, "Do you normally heal this slowly?"

I shook my head.

She took my leg and viciously wrenched it back straight. I howled in pain. I couldn't feel it knitting back together the way it normally would. I didn't know what was wrong. I looked at the old man, but his face was crumpled in pain. "Get out of my head," I growled through gritted teeth, but I couldn't close myself off from him like I had from Charles. I couldn't muster the control I needed. It took me a minute to realize that tears were spilling down my cheeks.

Daphne set a brace on my leg to hold it still and gave me a shot that was supposed to numb the pain, but it was working through my system too quickly. My leg hurt so bad that I didn't notice the pain in my chest at first. She was tightening the brace when I noticed that I was suddenly short of breath. I grabbed Daphne's arm, but she pulled away quickly as if I was attacking her. I gasped for air like a fish out of water.

"Can't...breathe," I panted trying desperately to take a deep breath.

"Did they give you anything before you came here?" she asked stepping forward timidly.

I shrugged, I couldn't remember what they had done to me, I was hyperventilating. WHY WASN'T ANYONE

CONCERNED ABOUT THIS?! My lungs were beginning to burn with the lack of oxygen. I furiously dug my fingers into the velvet chaise. I was suffocating and the look in Daphne's eyes told me that there was nothing she could do. The edges of my vision were blurring and I could feel my heart slowing. I was going to die if I didn't do something soon. I didn't know what to do. Unconsciousness was licking at the edges of my mind. I tried to fight it, but I could feel my strength waning. I gasped for air as I lost the battle with the pressing darkness.

I didn't think that I would ever open my eyes again. I reached out to either side of me and couldn't feel either side of the plush bed. I was laying on a California king that was covered in Egyptian cotton sheets of at least 1000 thread count. I kept my eyes closed and traced my fingers over the softness of the sheets. If I was dead this wasn't too bad. The sheets were cool, comfortable, and soft. There was only a sheet covering me, it felt too light for a blanket of any sort. It was perfect for the temperature of the room.

I ran my fingers over my stomach. I was wearing a silk tank top. I hadn't been wearing that when I came in. My hands moved down to my thighs. I was wearing silk pajama pants. I wasn't wearing that when I blacked out either. Slowly I opened my eyes. It was a midnight blue matching pajama outfit. That definitely wasn't something I owned, it was way too pretty. It was also really soft, and I really hoped that it was Daphne who put me in it.

“You're alright?” asked a timid voice from a dark corner.

“Yes,” I answered hesitantly sitting up, “Who are you?”

“My name is Vicki Fuller.” A young girl stepped from the shadows. She was maybe sixteen at the most. She had blonde hair that reached down to her waist and emerald green eyes that shimmered curiously. Shimmer. That was the word that described her. She timidly stepped forward as if afraid to move too quickly unless she frighten me. The air around her nearly vibrated with her power.

“What are you?” I whispered.

She laughed and her voice chimed like bells off of the stone walls that surrounded us. “I'm amazed you noticed,” she laughed, "but I guess I really shouldn't be so surprised considering all that I've heard about you."

"Heard about me?"

She moved like a bird, her weight shifted forward as if she was about to take flight at any moment. She alighted on the end of the bed and stared at me intently. "Will anything freak you out?" She seemed genuinely concerned.

I laughed, "At this point that is highly doubtful."

She hesitated for a moment and then dove right in, "I'm a theriomorph."

I just looked at her.

"A shapeshifter," she explained patiently.

"Into what?"

"An eagle," she said excitedly.

She was adorable. I looked into her eyes and saw them go completely black. The air around her seemed to dance as she started to shift. I backed up to give her room, but she stopped having only changed the color of her eyes. She giggled and jumped off of the bed lightly. When she looked back her eyes were again the color of emeralds. So maybe fragile wasn't the word to describe her.

"I'll go get Georges," she laughed and the sound twinkled off the walls, "he'll be happy to know that you're awake."

I started to protest, but she was out the door before I even had a moment to take a breath. She was much quicker than I expected. I stood up and looked desperately around the room for the clothes I had come in wearing. They were nowhere to be found. The room was surreal, like a prototype for a hotel minus the Bibles in the drawers. There was nothing of mine anywhere.

I swung my feet over the edge of the bed, the deep blood red rug was plush under my feet. I tested my leg, slowly putting my weight on it. It held, but I reached out to a nearby chair for support just to be safe. The chair beneath my fingers was covered in a sumptuous black velvet with rich brass nails studding the back. The textured stone walls and gray slate floor in contrast to the soft regal red tapestries and fabrics that covered the room gave an imperial feel to the space. Having a chance to look around momentarily distracted me from my pursuit of clothing but then I noticed a large ornately carved oaken door. I cautiously made my way to it and slowly opened it to reveal the biggest closet that I have ever seen. I just stood and stared at the room covered with hanging outfits. I stood agape.

"Glad to see you are up and walking around," I jumped at the sound of the voice.

"Daphne," I sighed, "Is this all yours?"

She snorted angrily, "I'm not that girly."

"I am," laughed Vicki as she danced into the room, launching herself onto the bed.

"Well thanks for letting me borrow your room for a bit," I smiled and sat down in the large armchair. "Exactly how long did I occupy it?"

Daphne looked at me strangely, "You've been out for two days. We thought you were dead."

I looked at her expectantly.

"You were poisoned," she explained slowly, "that's why it was taking so long for your leg to heal."

"How?" I asked confusedly.

"In my expert opinion," she answered curtly, "They injected it when they scarred your neck."

I touched the heart-shaped scar that was still emblazoned on my skin.

She sighed, "Whatever it was they gave you, it pretty much tried to kill your vampire side. Obviously without that, you should already be dead."

"How did you know?" I asked quietly.

"We didn't," she admitted flatly, "I just tried some antidotes to several things."

"So you don't know what they did?"

She shook her head disinterestedly, but she didn't look at me. She knew what was going on, but for some reason she didn't want to tell me and I wasn't ready to push it just yet. She looked away quickly and went to lean against the wall as far from me as she could. I don't know why, but something about her put me on edge. I looked at Vicki who was staring intently at the pair of us. She knew something was off as well but seemed to be confused as to what to do. I could feel the tension. Not the preternatural tension that swirled in the air before someone's beast broke free, but pure unadulterated human tension.

"My aren't we serious," his voice was like detergent in a greasy sink, the tension just melted in its wake.

"Mr. Moncrief," I smiled, "Didn't your mother teach you to knock?"

"Ah, *chere*," he laughed, "Perhaps there are some lessons I can only be taught by you."

Vicki laughed. I didn't think the sound would ever cease to amaze me, "Poor Georges. I think this may be one woman who won't fall into your arms so easily."

I looked at her and her wide innocent smile was beaming in my direction. Daphne was the only person unamused. She growled, a completely human sound and not very intimidating. Georges glanced back at her with his perfectly imperfect smile.

"What are you looking at?" she huffed, "Shouldn't you be more concerned about your master's precious pet.?" She folded her arms and glared around the room.

"Your master?"

Georges looked at me, the smile gone, "My master." He looked angrily at Daphne, "I'm sure that Charles would have preferred you get the truth from him and not in this manner, but the cat's out of the bag so to speak."

Daphne stormed from the room angrily.

Vicki came to my side and alighted lightly on the floor beside the chair.

"Charles Sullivan," began Georges, "is not the man you know. His real name is Anthony Verchelli."

I could feel the heat of anger flash to my eyes.

Georges laughed, "You're one to be offended *chere*, or shall I say Savanah Childs or perhaps you prefer Nora Bell."

Vicki giggled.

Georges smiled and sat in one of the plush chairs. He motioned to the one opposite him and waited until I sat before he continued, "He and I fought together in the War of 1812, although he had been one of the first settlers of New Orleans nearly one hundred years earlier." I did the math in my head. He laughed, "He looks pretty good for being over three hundred years old, eh *chere?*" I shrugged indifferently, but I was pissed. I wondered exactly what else it was that Charles, or Anthony, had lied about. So far it had been everything. "Young Anthony was in the regulars. He was handsome and suave and soon caught the eye of a young woman whom I had recently come to know rather intimately. Needless to say, that was not what I wanted to find out as I called for her at her window one moonless night. Anthony was standing in the window frame." Georges sighed at the memory, "Originally, I wanted to kill him, but I decided against that as an immediate course of action.

"Instead I followed him, tried to find some weakness to him, some way to bring him down. I never went back to the young woman's room, to be honest, I don't know what happened to her after that. I found instead that this young charmer was a good man. He believed in justice, honor. The things that seem to have faded over the centuries. I was fascinated to the point that I joined the militia. Young Anthony was to command us and we hit it off immediately. He became a confidant and a friend.

"It was merely weeks after having become a part of the militia under Anthony's command that we had our first taste of war. We were not prepared as soldiers, nor was the city prepared to handle such an assault as was thrown against our doorsteps. There were more casualties than I would care to count. I was one of them."

I looked into his hypnotizing eyes, confusion in my face. Pain flickered across his face as he remembered. "I was wounded badly when he found me. I could feel the life seeping from my body. He whispered in my ear that he could save me and I begged him to. I begged him not to let me die so he gave me a life of sorts. He was my brother in arms and I was his child in the dark gift."

There was some hidden pain and it crept along just below the surface of his eyes. Haunted was the word that came to mind. He was haunted. When I spoke my voice came out more softly than I intended, "What does that have to do with our dear doctor Daphne?"

Georges smiled sadly at me, "Daphne was, until recently, closely tied to Anthony."

"I don't understand. They were lovers?"

He shook his head, "They were more than lovers. Daphne tied herself to him through her psychic abilities. Surely you must have felt them."

I nodded. I knew there was something about her, but I still didn't understand what he meant by tying herself to Anthony.

Georges seemed to sense my question before I could voice it, “Vampires can have very strong psychic links to their lovers, but with Daphne it was more. Her abilities blended with his abilities and they could communicate with one another from continents away. They could share in each others dreams.” I blushed at the thought of things she may have seen with me. Georges smiled sensing where my thoughts tended, “I do think that is why she no longer has that ability. It had been his choice as much as hers and Anthony's choices about you seem to have broken that bond.” There was something near to bitterness in his voice and I looked at him expectantly.

He held out his hand for me to follow him. I looked for Vicki, but there was nothing where she had been only a moment before. I looked up, but Georges was smiling bemusedly.

“She's quite sneaky when she wants to be.”

“Ya think?” I huffed.

Georges dropped his hand and stared at me intensely, “What is wrong, *chere*?”

“I don't like being left alone with you,” the words were out before I even had the chance to think them through.

“Why may I ask?” He stepped away as he said it.

I felt guilty, I hadn't meant to hurt his feelings. I had the sudden urge to press my hand against the stubble on his face and tell him that it was alright and the overwhelming urge to touch him scared me. It was more than I had felt with Charles. “You have an ability that frightens me.”

His face went completely blank, “I frighten you.” It was a statement, not a question, but I felt the need to explain myself.

“You affect me unlike anyone I have ever met before and that frightens me.”

He smiled quietly, “You have not been around long *chere*. There are a lot of monsters just like me.”

I jumped up from the chair suddenly very aware of the fact that I was in nothing but a silk pajama set. I froze and felt the warm blush reach across my cheeks. He looked away quietly and the pain that filled his eyes broke my heart. Without meaning to, I moved towards him. His face was in my hands before I even knew I had thought it. It wasn't normal for me to move as quickly as my thoughts.

Georges just stared at me, his arms crossed tightly against his chest. I was suddenly very aware of the way he smelled, like shampoo. It was clean and intoxicating and all I wanted to do was to get closer to it. I felt his body pull away from me. I stopped. What was I doing?

"I'm sorry," I whispered, if he weren't preternatural he wouldn't have heard it.

"Don't be *chere*," he smiled again, but it left his eyes untouched, "I know you can't resist my charms."

I stepped back slowly. I could feel my hard nipples brushing against the silk. I was suddenly very aware of my body and what it wanted. I wanted to feel him touch me. I wanted to touch him. I crossed my arms against my chest and whispered softly, "What have you done to me?"

"I'm sorry," he whispered, "but to be perfectly honest, I'm not entirely sure." He straightened his back and smiled at me sadly, "I'll wait for you in the hallway when you are ready."

He turned on his booted heel and left me to myself. As he walked out of the room, I realized that his hair reached down below his shoulders. It was tied back with a black satin ribbon. I wanted to brush it out, but kept my hands pressed firmly against my sides. I didn't know what was going on. I could control myself better than that.

Vicki was suddenly standing right next to me. I literally jumped and her laugh filled the room.

"I figured that you would want to get dressed."

"How do you know my size?" I was easily five inches taller than her and was far too busty to fit in anything that Daphne had.

"Anthony told us," she smiled guilelessly.

"How...never mind. I don't want to know."

She flitted to the closet and came back with a pair of jeans and an oversized T-shirt. "This is good for you right now." She looked at me appraisingly, "You should pull your hair back though. It will probably help you."

"What am I going to be doing?"

She looked at me and smiled, "Training."

17. Training

Georges led me silently down a darkened corridor. I felt awkward about my reaction to him in Vicki's bedroom and couldn't think of anything to say. I wasn't even sure how I felt about him. He was beyond attractive to be sure, but I had felt something that I just wasn't able to shake. Then again, I didn't know if maybe what I had been feeling wasn't completely me either. I had felt this same pull, this desire, with Charles and it wasn't anything lasting. I was confused and knew that somehow I had to speak with Charles, or Anthony, to get some answers.

Georges pushed a door open and ushered me inside. I turned to speak with him but he was no longer beside me. I suddenly became very nervous. I was alone in a pitch black room. I reached out with my senses trying to hear or smell someone nearing, but there was nothing but my pounding heart. I heard the slip of a latch and my heart stopped. A row of florescence lights hummed to life above me. The room was a large open area covered mostly by a large cushioned mat. It looked like a sparring mat. There was a pile of large free weights in the corner. I wondered what these supernatural beings needed with weights, but I had a feeling I wouldn't have long to wait to find out.

A large oaken door across from me opened with a huge gust of wind. Van Helsing stepped from the void surrounded by his entourage. Georges stood behind him to his left. I couldn't help myself, I stared. He was ripped. He must have known my eyes were upon him, but the only indication was the wicked way his eyes sparkled. I tried not to let my eyes wander down his abs and instead forced myself to look at the rest of the crew.

Behind the old man to the left stood a young man I had yet to meet. His hair was shockingly red and you could see the freckles that tinted his nose. His green eyes gleamed with intensity. Gung-ho was the only word that described his stare with any accuracy and still it failed to capture the full effect. He also had rippling abs, but unlike Georges his skin was a pasty white color that was offset even more by the black jeans that hugged his figure close enough to leave no doubt as to what he wasn't wearing underneath. His lips curled back in a smile that was for all intents and purposes the most frightening thing that I had ever seen.

Little Vicki stood behind them with Daphne at her side. They were both dressed in similar outfits. Leather was the fashion du jour. Both women were clad in skin tight leather pants and leather boots that reached about mid-calf. From the looks of it they laced up the back and had about a three inch heel. I hoped this was not the accepted uniform. As if that wasn't enough, the black leather haltertops that ended just above their ribs finished the ensemble.

"Please tell me that's not what you expect me to wear," I stated crossing my arms stubbornly.

The red head frowned at me disapprovingly.

Vicki and Georges tried to hide the smiles that played at their lips.

Van Helsing just guffawed like the old man he was until he started to cough. I reached out towards him, but he waved me off. It was several seconds before he could speak again.

"My dear Jesse," he sighed, "You will never cease to amaze. Tell me dear, what would a normal person have thought by my entourage?"

"Holy Hell!" I said with a smile.

Vicki couldn't help herself. Her laugh tinkled out from behind the old man, "You're awesome."

"Likewise," I smiled.

Van Helsing smiled softly, "Glad to see you are getting along with your team."

I looked at him expectantly, "My team?"

"Allow me to introduce you formally," he said with a flourish. Georges stepped forward. "As I'm sure you've noticed," Van Helsing announced, "Georges is a vampire, a very old and powerful vampire in fact." Georges bowed grandly. Van Helsing ushered the red head forward, "This is Richard Bicks, werewolf extraordinaire." The man stepped forward gracefully. The air around him positively buzzed. I could tell from across the room that he was not pleased to have me there. Great, what had I done to him? The old man ushered Dapne forward, "Our young Daphne here is a witch, psychic, and extraordinary doctor." I smiled at her sheepishly but she looked away angrily. Vicki danced forward and smiled brightly. Van Helsing smiled at her lovingly and put his arm around her shoulders, "And this bright young woman would be my niece Vicki, a theriomorph." I couldn't help by smile back ant the exuberant young woman.

Richard stepped towards me menacingly, but I stood my ground. It was going to take more than some macho posturing to scare me today. He smiled. Shit, he smelled my fear running in an undercurrent through my blood. Still I held my ground as his eyes turned amber and his skin started to vibrate. "When you change," I asked guilelessly, "will you be as red as your hair?"

His skin stopped vibrating suddenly and he looked at me quizzically, "You *are* scared."

"Ya think?"

"Then why are you so..."

"Sarcastic," Georges chimed in taking a step forward with his arms crossed over his chest.

"You look very bodyguardish," I smirked.

"I look a lot of things, *chere* and you are fully aware of every one."

I smiled wickedly, "Well isn't that just the pot calling the kettle black?"

He smiled, "Touche."

Richard growled, "Are you going to be a distraction Moncrief?"

Georges smiled at me, "Am I?"

I shrugged indifferently and Van Helsing laughed, "She may need your training gentlemen, but I fear she will not be the only one getting trained."

I landed flat on my back and felt the air whoosh out of my lungs. I struggled to my elbows and looked at Richard who was standing across the room picking at his fingernails uninterestedly. I rose to my feet painfully.

"I don't know why we have to do this," I gasped.

"Because," he said with disdain, "some people can resist your particular brand of witchery."

"It's not witchery," I protested rubbing my sore back.

He grumped at me, “I don't give a damn what it is, some of the creatures we come up against will be able to resist your whatever it is.”

“I haven't met one yet,” I grumped back.

“Well when you do, you're going to get your ass kicked.”

“Stupid monsters.”

Richard moved at blurring speed. It was almost to the point that I couldn't see it, but at the last second I blocked the roundhouse kick aimed for my head. It still managed to knock me off of my feet even though I knew he had held back. He nodded and tried for a punch that I blocked. He threw a series of combinations and I moved just fast enough to avoid being slammed into the concrete wall again. That one had hurt like nobody's business.

I countered with a punch of my own and hit him squarely on the jaw. It didn't even phase him. He stopped swinging at me and I landed another punch of my own. He smiled, hands dropped to his sides. He was taunting me. I did it again and he started to laugh. I could feel my insides vibrating as the sound of that laugh irked my last nerve. I lashed out at him again, hitting him squarely against his chest. I knocked him to the ground.

He looked up from the ground with a smile, “Good.”

“But it wasn't...I don't...” I didn't know what had happened.

“You did what I wanted you to do,” he smiled jumping to his feet.

“But...”

He put his hands on my shoulders and looked into my face, “You can harness your power and the result should be truly preternatural strength.”

“How?”

We sat on the mat and he looked at me intensely, “What triggered it just now?”

“I was pissed,” I sighed, “you wouldn't stop laughing at me.”

“What did you feel physically?”

“My insides vibrated and then I hit you and it was gone.”

He smiled, “Have you ever felt like that before?”

I shook my head.

"Good. You are used to pushing your power off of yourself and into something else. My guess is that is the feeling of pushing your power into yourself."

"What if I can't do it again?"

"We are going to make sure that you can."

"How?"

"Practice," he lithely jumped to his feet and held out his hand.

I looked at him uncertainly, but reached out and took his hand anyway. I could feel his power pulse down my arm. It was like holding on to a low voltage wire. I jerked my hand back and he let me.

"What were you doing?" I asked nervously rubbing my arm.

"I projected my power onto you."

"Why?"

"You have to defend against it," he smiled in challenge, "I only brushed you with my power, you wouldn't be able to handle the entire thing."

Far be it from me to back down from a challenge that could kill me. I defiantly held out my hand. He took it and again the vibrations of his power slithered up my arm. I closed my eyes and concentrated. I could feel my power like an animal waiting to be unleashed. Richard flew back. Apparently I had flung open the cage door without the ability to control the beast.

Richard stood slowly, "We need to work on that."

Vicki's part of the training was vastly different. Where I was beaten and tossed around by Richard, I was primped and prodded by Vicki. She sat me in front of a mirror surrounded by light bulbs. It looked like one of those Hollywood dressing rooms they showed in movies. I had never seen one that actually looked like that. It didn't seem to bother Vicki any.

"Stop wiggling," she huffed twirling my hair into a very tight curl.

"Sorry," I whined. "I just haven't been poked and prodded like this in decades."

"Which is why your hair is such a disheveled mess."

I smirked, "Points for good word usage."

I heard her huff behind me, "You could be a very beautiful woman if you wanted to be."

I tried to behave myself and do as I was told. I watched as the young lady moved around me pulling strands of hair in every direction. She amazed me. She was only sixteen. Truly sixteen, not sixteen in the way that I was twenty-five. She still went to school had homework, was worried about getting a date to prom, and trying to get into college. Yet she handled all of the strangeness within her with an air that was far beyond her years.

The constant drama of high school made her the perfect person to teach me how to make an entrance. This was an area I desperately lacked in. I had tried for decades to just blend in and not attract much attention and now I was supposed to be vying for attention and screaming to be noticed. I didn't like it and Vicki kept scolding me that my scowl gave that fact away. I tried to keep my disdain to myself, but it was difficult.

"You're doing it again," she growled.

"Sorry," I plastered a large fake smile on my face and she dropped her hands to her hips in frustration. "Can't we work on something other than my hair?"

"Fine," she dropped the curling iron on her vanity with a huff. She stood up and stalked out the door. I followed with my head down like a bad puppy. She took me to stand at a large floor to ceiling mirror. "Look at how you stand," she scolded, "You hunch your shoulders down around you like a dog waiting to be hit."

"Thanks for that," I grumbled.

She let her breath out in one big huff, "You do. You need to stand up straight. Be proud of who and what you are."

I rolled my eyes and Vicki yanked my face forward, none too gently. She stalked around behind me and thrust my shoulders back. She put her hands against my sides and pressed, forcing me to stand up straighter. She stalked around me and slapped me in the rear. "Tuck it in woman," she commanded like a drill sergeant. I felt the need to salute. "Now look at yourself," she muttered in a martyred tone. I obliged.

She was right, I did look a lot better if I stood up straight, but I felt so tall like this. To make things worse, I was supposed to do this in three-inch heels. I was beginning to miss getting the crap kicked out of me by Richard. She seemed to sense my feelings and rolled her eyes at me. "It's just a little primping, it won't kill you." She muttered under her breath, "but I might." I stuck my tongue out. It wasn't necessarily dignified, but it made me feel better.

I ran into Georges on my way to Van Helsing's library. He had been avoiding me since the scene in Vicki's room nearly a week ago. I had just come from Vicki's primping session and felt completely foolish and overdone as I caught Georges eye. He smiled and lounged against the wall, giving me plenty of room to pass.

"Vicki's working wonders on your wardrobe," he smiled.

I smirked. Vicki had managed to get me into a pair of skinny jeans, high heeled boots, and a corseted tank top. Nothing I would have chosen for myself. "Was there something wrong with my big T-shirt look?"

"Nothing wrong with it *chere*," he purred in that voice that made me melt. "This look just makes you so much more...fierce."

I snorted and went to walk past him, but he caught me around the waist and forced me to look into his gorgeous eyes.

"Do I still frighten you?"

My heart was pounding against my ribs, "No."

He leaned down and whispered in my ear, "Liar."

"So?" I took a deep breath, he smelled so fresh and clean. I just wanted to wrap the smell around me.

He smiled, "What will you do when it's my turn to train you?"

I stared defiantly into his eyes, "There's nothing you can teach me that I don't already know."

He smiled and let his eyes wander down my body, "Oh *chere*, there are a great many things that I could teach you."

I laughed and pushed away from him, "Don't flatter yourself."

I headed down the hall, excited. My heart was pounding. I was playing with fire and liked the game. The thought of it gave me the most exquisite feeling. I could feel his eyes upon me as I walked away and wondered if he was having the same forbidden thoughts about me that I couldn't help having about him.

Van Helsing sat me down in his library and stacked a pile of books on the floor in front of me. “These, my dear,” he said with a smile, “are the books I have that detail what you are.”

I looked around the vast room, “It's not much in the scheme of things is it?”

He sat down next to me and patted my hand softly, “No my dear, it is not. You are something special in our world.”

“So I'm a freak in a world of freaks,” I sighed, “tell me something I don't know.”

He looked at me sadly, “That's not what I meant.”

I nodded and picked up the first book. It smelled old and the paper was heavy. The spine creaked as I cracked it open. Van Helsing took up a book of his own as I began my reading. There wasn't much I didn't already know in that one. Then I came across the reason I was twenty-five. I looked up at Van Helsing with a smile, “I had always wondered why I stopped getting older at twenty-five.” He stopped reading and looked at me expectantly. “It says here,” I showed him the passage, “that a dhamphir will only grow as old as its mother was when she died.”

He smiled at me knowingly, “You will find a great many things in these books that you did not know before.”

“Will I find out why this little organization of yours exists?”

Van Helsing smiled quietly, “You have read Dracula?”

I nodded.

“Most of it is true,” he smiled. “My many greats grandfather was a great doctor. The Count was unfortunately not his first encounter with the supernatural, but it was his most famous. He published the journal entries under another name, but what the journal did not tell you was what happened afterwards.”

He settled back in the chair so I tucked my feet up underneath me looking at him expectantly. He continued, “The Harkers were adamant about helping him track down evil and at first, the group was set on extermination of every preternatural being they could find.” He shook his head, “After a while they realized that not everything that wasn't human was evil. They started recruiting preternatural beings to help with their cause, hence our current situation. There are many creatures that are evil just as there are many men who are evil, my dear. Our job is to make sure that the things that go bump in the night are stopped."

He stood and patted my hand. "You read now, my dear. You need to learn what you can about what you are. We will talk later."

He walked out of the room and left me there to absorb as much of the books as I could. I learned that you could kill a vampire, but it was difficult. All of the things that people thought would do it were pretty much ineffective. Things like garlic and silver would weaken some vampires, but it wouldn't kill them. There were apparently only two ways to truly be certain that you killed a vampire. One way was to burn them. The other was to bleed them. Burning them was simple, light them on fire. Bleeding them was the much more difficult route to take. There are very few ways to cut a vampire to make them bleed. One was simple, another vampire's fangs, or a werewolf's teeth and claws, were sharp enough to break the skin, but there were apparently issues with that. If you bled a vampire dry by drinking their blood either you would gain their powers or their powers would overtake you. Either one was not good from what the books said. The other option was a carbon steel alloy blade thrust through the heart. It wasn't the blade thrust that did it, it was the bleeding. It took a long time for the bleeding to be fatal and once the blade was removed the wound would heal. You had to be sure they were dead before you pulled the blade out. Even a drop of blood left in their system would be enough for them to regenerate.

I read about the special ammunition that was used to hunt preternatural beings. It was made of a carbon steel alloy with a tensile strength of 122,000 psi. It wouldn't kill a werewolf or vampire, but it would definitely stop their advancement and make them think twice. I also found the compound that had seemed to strip the strength from my body. It had been made by a witch in the early sixteenth century. She had created it at a time when vampires had been bound by the sun and werewolves by the moon. Although those parameters no longer held any power, the witches potion still maintained it's bite. However, to recreate it you needed a very powerful witch. It wasn't just a mix of herbs and garlic or silver, it was bound together by some very powerful magic. The magic was responsible for drawing the ability to heal out of the vampire it was placed upon. If a vampire was weakened enough by this compound, they could be killed by a regular bullet, or even just a broken neck. I wondered how powerful Daphne was.

Feel free to think I'm strange, but I have always had the tendency to get lost when I'm in a library. I have no sense of time when I'm floating through the pages of a book. It must have been hours before Georges finally walked in and announced that I would be late for dinner if I didn't hurry. I marked my place and hurried after him.

It was not long before I was taken to the "range" by Georges and Richard. It wasn't much to talk about, really just a ditch that had been dug into the side of a hill, but it served it's purpose. We trekked out into the woods for half an hour before we reached it. From the look on Georges' face you could tell that it was his baby. As I approached the firing line I noticed a folding car table littered with different weaponry. Georges walked straight to the table and lovingly ran his hand across the table top.

"These," he announced, "are an assortment of the weapons we have on hand."

I looked at Richard, "Why do we need weapons?"

Georges explained, "Because *chere,* sometimes we come up against things that we can not fight with our hands or our abilities."

He motioned for me to come to him, "Pick a weapon. I would like to see what you know about weapons before we get started."

I looked over the options. There were six guns laid out on the table. It may be hard to believe, but in a century I had never used a gun. So, I went with the choice I had seen most women use on television. "I'll try the revolver."

Georges smiled at Richard over my head, "Then let's get started."

Richard tossed the duffel bag he had been carrying onto the table. From it he produced large earmuff looking things and safety glasses. "Eye and ear protection," he explained. "Normal humans need to wear these when they practice, imagine how painful it would be for us without them."

Georges put on his gear and picked up the revolver, "Step to the firing line, *chere.*" I followed. "Now what do you know about guns?"

I looked at the gun in his hand, "I know that's a revolver, it has six shots, you pull the trigger and the bullet comes out the other end. It's not that hard."

Georges smirked and handed the gun to me. I took it and stood with my feet shoulder width apart. I took note of the cool grizzly bear that was etched into the side plate before I raised the revolver to eye level, I even used both hands. I closed my left eye and looked at the target. The sight on the end of the gun was pointing at the center of the target set up maybe twenty-five feet away. I tried to pull the trigger, but it was harder than I thought. I pulled harder and the gun went off. I stumbled back and my arms jerked upwards. Georges and Richard laughed as Georges took the gun out of my hand. The target was completely unscathed.

"Easy?" he laughed setting the gun back on the table.

"Why do you even have that?"

"To teach people like you that you don't know everything."

I opened my mouth to speak, but Georges jerked my shoulders around. I figured it was probably just better for me not to speak. The severe look on his face confirmed that. He put his hands on my hips and moved my center of balance back. "This," he explained repositioning my leg, "is called a modified weaver stance." He picked up a pistol and brought it to me. "Take this in your right hand," he commanded. I obeyed. "Raise it up and use your left hand to support and stabilize the gun when you shoot." I nodded and closed my left eye. Georges shook his head, "No, No, No. Don't close your eye. Focus on the sight at the front of the gun and you'll see two targets. Aim in the middle."

I aimed and pulled the trigger. This one was easier to pull than the revolver and the shot went off without the gun trying to fly out of my hands. I looked down range and saw the hole. It was much higher than the bullseye, but at least this one actually made it on the paper. Georges reached from behind me and steadied my hands, "Squeeze the trigger, don't pull. Gently *chere.*" I steadied my hands and aimed again. I took a breath and squeezed the trigger steadily. The gun went off. It wasn't dead center, but it was closer. Georges nodded in approval.

The next few hours were spent with me trying to find that sweet spot in the center of the target. Georges said that my grouping was good, but I was still having trouble getting it dead center. The sun began to fade and we set about packing up the gear to head home. I looked at the pistol I had been firing. It was all black, but after the hours of firing the end of the barrel was a grayish color. George saw me looking and explained it was because of the muzzle flash. I nodded and read the etching, XD-9 Sub-compact. Georges smiled and put the gun in its foam lined box, "It's a Springfield XD nine millimeter. Each magazine that we have holds 13 rounds."

"So," I asked as he packed everything up, "You are the weapons expert."

He nodded. "I am the expert, but by the time I am done with you, you will have a working knowledge of every weapon we use here."

He wasn't kidding. In the weeks that followed I was introduced to every weapon that the team carried. Georges was adamant that every person on the team was able to use every weapon carried. His answer as to why was simply, "What if you have to use it in battle." I found my groove with the XD and now just needed to become proficient with everything else. Richard was first to step up and let me play with his gun. His had been his father's weapon brought from Ireland. It was a Browning High Power with cherry wood grips. An ornate Celtic Cross adorned the wood. He smiled proudly when I noticed and told me how an old man in his father's village had hand carved them specifically for his family.

Vicki's weapon of choice, and since she was underage, was a PSE Reaper Crossbow. It shot a one hundred grain carbon crossbow bolt at three hundred and ten feet per second. The first shot hit the ground, twenty bolts later and I was on the paper at least. It took two hours after that for my aim to be anywhere near reliable. Daphne, who was not thrilled to be helping, stood watching me with her arms crossed. But luckily the Ruger single action revolver, high gloss .45 colt, only took me about thirty minutes to master. I asked her what the stag carved onto the grips meant but she just snatched the gun from my hand and stormed off into the woods angrily. Richard explained later that the gun had been a gift from her grandfather, an heirloom so to speak.

Georges was a completely different story when it came to weapons. He carried a Colt Delta Elite. It was a 1911 pattern pistol in ten millimeter. It was quite a piece of work, all metal with fleur de lis etched in the ebony wood grips. However, that was the most normal of his weaponry. He also had a British flintlock pistol, Brown Bess musket, and a cavalry saber. They were of course vintage, from actual wars. He smiled when I joked that this was all he had and answered simply, "You haven't seen my house."

As the weeks progressed I not only became much better with all the "service weapons", but I also became much better at harnessing my power. I had pushed through the limits of what I had believed possible. I had gained a measure of control and with that control came an increase of power. I could move objects twice my size or multiple objects at the same time. With that also came a certain amount of acceptance. Richard, Vicki, and Van Helsing had opened their world to me without reservations. Daphne and Georges, however, dealt with me as little as possible. I expected it from Daphne, she obviously had a few issues she needed to work out about me. She would get up a leave when I entered the room. In a way I really wanted to talk to her. To let her know that Charles/Anthony, and I had a connection months ago in Alaska when I thought he was someone else and he thought I was someone else. That I didn't even feel that way about him now, that I didn't know how he felt about me, that I didn't want things to be awkward because of this. I wanted to be fully engrossed in this group, but she wouldn't give me the chance.

Georges dealt with me in a different way. He tried to avoid being left alone with me, but he was always there. He watched, and commented, during my training sessions with Richard, and my sessions with him were likewise observed by Richard. Yet physically he shied away from me. It didn't really matter, he was always in my head. I will admit that I contributed to the avoidance and tried to have someone else present when I had to come to him for anything, but he was always on my mind. It was hard to stay away. Just a glance from him would send my heart into overdrive. Dinner every night was the worst.

Van Helsing found it necessary for all of us to eat together. A family that eats together and all that. Georges, obviously, never ate. So, we all sat in the great dining hall while Georges occupied himself by seeing how many times I glanced at him. I swear he really did amuse himself with his little game. He was infuriating. I could feel his eyes roaming over my body and he always made sure to wear an outfit that would draw my attention to his. I wanted to be ashamed of my feelings, of my reaction to him, but all I could bring myself to feel was exhilarating desire. It made for an awkward relationship.

18. Boundaries?

Richard and Van Helsing had a new limit they wanted me to push. Levitation. I hadn't ever tried to do that on purpose before, I had only done it by accident. Saying that over and over again didn't seem to help my case any, it only made them all the more willing to make me try. I stood in the middle of the mat in the six story training room and looked straight up. I had gotten better at this whole telekinesis thing. I could make myself as strong as any vampire by controlling it, but this was different. Everything I had lifted before was inanimate, there were no consequences if I dropped it. There were going to be major consequences if I dropped me.

"Just relax," Van Helsing cooed.

I closed my eyes and released the tension between my shoulder blades. I was still nervous.

"Remember what we talked about," Richard commanded.

I nodded and concentrated on making myself feel weightless. I thought about floating, but nothing happened. I could still feel the mat under my feet.

"Keep trying," Richard grumbled.

I did, I kept trying to picture myself flying, but nothing.

"Concentrate," Richard growled.

He was starting to get on my nerves and I could feel the power start to trickle through my skin. The hairs on the back of my neck stood. I thought, "Up." I shot into the air before I could even think to stop. My eyes flew open and I realized that I was at least four stories into the air. I could feel myself panic. The power abruptly stopped vibrating through my veins and I plummeted to the mat. I hit hard and the air evacuated my lungs in one gigantic exhale.

I felt like a fish out of water, my lungs were deflated. I took stock of all of my bones and realized that my wrist was not holding any weight. I attempted to tell them that, but my two teachers were too busy contemplating and exclaiming over the possibilities of my new trick to notice that I was in pain. If I hadn't been struggling for breath, I would have been pissed they were treating me like a trained poodle.

Luckily for me, Georges came bursting into the room. He saw me on the ground still catching my breath, gripping my wrist in pain, and was by my side in a movement too fast for me to see. It was then that Van Helsing and Richard finally turned to me. They both had a moment of confusion as Georges attempted to scoop me up. I was getting my breath back and shook my head. He apparently understood what I wanted and just helped me to my feet.

"My wrist," I breathed.

He nodded and led me to a room where Daphne was stretched out on the couch reading. She looked up and rolled her eyes, "Now she's ruining my reading time too?"

"I fell," I said softly, "and tried to stop it with my hand..."

"And shattered your wrist," she cut in impatiently.

Georges left without a word.

"What did I do to him?" I muttered.

She huffed, "Probably the same thing you did to Anthony."

I whimpered in pain as she reset my wrist. "I don't follow."

She huffed and I winced as she started to wrap my wrist, none too gently. "If you had belonged to any other man, Georges would have swept you off your feet with all of his little tricks."

"His tricks?"

"If he touches your skin, Georges has the ability to project emotions into you."

"Like he could make me angry or happy?"

"Or lustful."

"Ok, but I still don't understand why he won't even talk to me."

She yanked the bandage tight and I bit into my lip. "Well, I'm not going to spell it out for you."

She picked her book back up, in effect dismissing me. I walked to the door and paused, "I want you to know that I didn't know anything about you when I met him."

She didn't look up from her book, "It doesn't change what you did."

"If I had known, I wouldn't have..."

She snarled at me, "Wouldn't have what? Wouldn't have acted like the whore you are?"

I smiled at her, "You know, I never understood why people don't blame their partner for being unfaithful."

She glared at me.

"I didn't know that he had you, but he did and he made the choice to try to get with me."

She turned her head away angrily and I could see the tears welling up in her eyes. I didn't want her to cry, I hated it when people cried. A broken sob escaped from her lips as she ordered me out of the room.

"I really am sorry," I whispered, "I just want you to know that nothing happened between us. I didn't mean to hurt your feelings."

I hurried out into the hallway and nearly ran smack into Georges. He looked embarrassed and went to walk past me into the room with Daphne without a word. I put a hand on his shoulder, being very careful not to touch his skin. "Did you hear what she said?"

He shook his head, but didn't look me in the eyes.

"She said you could project emotions onto someone by touching their skin."

He looked confused for a moment, but nodded, "I can also feel their emotions."

"Like Charles...Anthony could?"

He nodded, "He can feel emotions without contact, but the emotions aren't nearly as strong."

"Tell me the truth," I took his chin in my hand and forced him to look at me, "was what I felt for him real?"

He took my hand from his face and looked at it sadly, "I don't know. He can project."

He dropped my hand and walked away without a glance back. I suddenly felt very cold and alone and angry. I sunk to the floor in the corridor and every emotion I had seemed to leak out of my eyes and drip down my chin. I couldn't stop crying. I wasn't sobbing, in fact I was angry, but the tears just wouldn't stop. I heard the door that had concealed Georges and Daphne open and I ran down the hall, away from them, like a five year old.

I ran out the back door and into the woods that surrounded us. I ran and ran until the ground ran out. I skidded to a halt, falling backwards to avoid being thrown out over the abyss. I stood up and dusted the dry leaves off of my jeans before cautiously looking over the edge. I was standing on the edge of a precipice that dove jaggedly down into the lapping waves of the ocean, just like in my dream. As I stared down at the whitecaps that lashed against the rocks, I felt the wicked urge to jump. Nothing suicidal, if I dove off the cliffs would I be able to land safely in the ocean, I wanted to see if I could levitate. All I had to do was to keep my concentration. I kicked off the sneakers I had been wearing and folded my clothes on top of them. I stood at the precipice in nothing but a tank top and underwear, if I landed in the drink I wanted dry clothes to walk home in.

I gripped the jagged rock with my toes preparing myself for the leap. I was terrified, I could feel my heart beat racing, but I was not about to back off. If I could levitate this way, I would be able to levitate anywhere. I could feel the power respond to my fear. It crept along my skin raising the hairs on the back of my arms. I prepared myself for the jump and thought "feather." I took a deep breath and bent my knees. 3-2-1, I launched myself into the abyss. I fell quickly. The air was deafening as it whooshed past me . My hair trailed behind me as the force pushed it back from my face. "Feather," falling, "Feather," still falling, "STOP," no more falling. I didn't realize I had closed my eyes, but in the darkness of my own making, the spray from the waves crashing on the rocks trickled across my legs. Slowly, I opened my eyes. I was only about five feet from impact, but I was levitating. I could feel the power under my skin. It was exhilarating. "Up," I thought, "gently." I rose slowly towards the cliff. I closed my eyes and felt the world moving around me.

"Jesse!"

The scream startled me completely and there went my concentration. I fell into the waves back first. I didn't even have a chance to hold my breath before the blue expanse closed over my head. The current pulled me under and toppled me head over heels. For a moment, I didn't know which way was up. I started to panic. I concentrated on going up and I was up, hovering just above the lashing waves. There was a figure hurtling towards me from the top of the cliff. I reached out and willed it to stop. I heard it howl in pain as it slammed to a stop in mid air.

"Sorry," I called, "I'll have to work on being gentle."

"Are you alright?" I looked up on the cliff to see Van Helsing and Vicki staring down at us.

I looked at the figure dangling above me and it was Richard.

"Well, I see you got out of the water," Georges voice huffed from below me.

I looked down to see him floating back and forth on the waves.

I closed my eyes and concentrated very hard on raising him up out of the water. In my mind I pictured the three of us rising up towards the edge of the cliff, envisioned our feet touching the rock. Then I could feel it under my feet. A violent shudder ran through my body and I felt the rock beneath my knees, but I somehow knew it wasn't beneath them. I concentrated very hard on bringing them to me. I reached out my hands and felt the seam of their pants brush against my fingertips. They were safe, they were over solid ground. Then the rock was beneath my cheek.

I could feel that I was wrapped in a big blanket. It was warm. I had a vague awareness that I had been very cold, but I felt better now. I moved, but then froze. Someone was holding me. There was far too much fabric between us for me to feel who it was but a deep breath and it was Georges. He knew I was awake and I knew that he knew I was awake. It was very awkward.

We sat like that for a few moments in silence, but in the end I couldn't help myself. I started giggling. I couldn't help it. I started full out laughing. I could feel his chest rising and falling against me as he attempted not to laugh. That only lasted a few minutes. He couldn't resist. I rolled over and looked in his face. He was smiling that goofy smile of his and I just smiled back at him.

"So how long were you going to let me lay there pretending to be asleep?" I asked stretching out across his lap.

"As long as you wanted to lay in my lap, I was not going to discourage you," he smiled.

I rolled my eyes, "How gentlemanly of you."

He bowed his head, "I do try."

He looked at me for a minute and then nervously cleared his throat.

"How did you find me?" The laughter had died in my voice.

"I saw you run from the hallway."

"Why did you follow me?"

He looked towards the door, "I should go now."

I struggled out of the blanket and grabbed his arm as he tried to stand. "Tell me what is going on." He was silent. "You treat me like a pariah, you ignore me and barely speak to me and then you follow me out into the forest and jump off a cliff after me. There is something that I am missing here."

He looked at me sadly, "You are unlike any woman I have ever met, Jesse Childress." He took my hand gently and brought it to his lips. My body tightened at the brush of his lips. "That is why I can't be near you and can't stay away from you."

"I don't understand, you want me so you can't be near me?"

"Yes," he laughed, "it sounds silly, but you don't understand. You belong to another and I will not do that."

I growled, "Would you all stop saying that?"

"Saying what?"

"That I belong to him, whatever his name is today. I belong to no one."

He smiled, "That I believe, *chere.*

I smiled sarcastically, "So the main point to this presentation is basically, you can't even be friends with me because you won't be able to control yourself?"

He looked confused.

"Look," I sighed, "I'm not going to lie, you'd be able to tell anyway. You are very possibly the sexiest man I've ever met." I think he would've blushed if he could. "Having said that," I continued, "I don't want to sleep with you."

He snorted and kissed my wrist suggestively, "Don't lie *chere*."

"Ok," I breathed, "so I would physically love to have sex with you, but I'm not about a quick fling. The last person I even considered having a fling with set an entire coven of insane vampires on my ass."

He smiled.

"I know that you all think I'm somehow desperately in love with Anthony, but I'm not. He can't be trusted, all he did was lie."

Georges nodded his head, "Know I never lied to you *chere*."

"I know," I said extending my hand, "Friends?"

He took my hand and pressed his lips to my fingers. A wave of desire jolted through my body. "Friends?" He asked wickedly.

"You can't do that if we're going to be friends."

He laughed and nodded, "As you wish *chere.*" With mock solemnity he held out his hand, "Friends."

My training continued, much more inclusive and extensive than before. I could lift myself now with relative ease. I didn't even have to close my eyes and concentrate anymore, I only had to think up and there I went. Raising other people was a completely different issue. I had to concentrate very hard to get anyone else in the air and once they were up it was even harder to hold them suspended for more than a minute or two. The longer I had to hold them up the weaker it made me. Van Helsing was not pleased with my progress.

All of my other trainers, however, were. I even started doing my hair and make-up in a way that gained Vicki's approval. And as it turns out, I was pretty good with the weapons once I got the hang of them (even that blasted crossbow). My hand to hand still wasn't awesome, but it was good enough and I was finally able to control my abilities to give me full preternatural strength. Still, I was itching to get going. But Van Helsing had apparently received no word from Charles-Anthony since my extraction. They didn't even know where The Marquis was hiding the facility he was using. I understood, but it didn't make the waiting any easier to bear.

To help pass the time, and for "research purposes" of course, Richard had bought a mixed martial arts pay-per-view. He invited everyone to watch, but Daphne and Van Helsing both opted out. I think Richard was disappointed. The night passed with Vicki and I sharing a bowl of popcorn and laughing at the bad tattoos while Richard and Georges hushed us. I'm sorry, some of the tattoos were horrendous. Your nickname across your stomach or a gigantic sword down your chest, really? Who told these people this was a good idea? Still, I have to admit there were some moves that I definitely wanted to try on the training mat. Of course, if I had to use those moves, I wouldn't have any sort of referee to stop it before someone got hurt.

As it got later and later Vicki curled up next to me and drifted off to sleep. A few times, I started to drift off myself and was abruptly brought back by a the sharp thump of Richard's middle finger on my knee. “Pay attention,” he growled, “some of these moves will be helpful. God knows you need all the help you can get.”

I rolled my eyes, “I can handle myself.”

He laughed.

At some point during the fights I drifted off to sleep. It must have been nearly an hour before I woke up stiff and pinched. Vicki had been laying on my leg for so long that I couldn't feel it anymore. My toes were completely numb, not even the pins and needles feeling. Georges was sprawled out across the floor haphazardly, his eyes were closed even though I knew he didn't need any sleep. Richard, however, was fast asleep at my feet, curled up like a dog. He looked so innocent laying there. I wondered how long he stayed in wolf form to pick up these little canine idiosyncrasies.

I had noticed it while we trained, more often than not he would raise his upper lip in a grimace like a dog baring his teeth. He didn't even seem to notice that he did it, it was just natural. He even moved like a dog when he attacked, he would drop his head and hunch his shoulders forward like his hackles were raised. Even now in his most unguarded moment he moved in the attitude of a dog, curled up with his hand and foot twitching slightly. I smiled as I watched him like a beloved pet and thought, “I wonder what he dreams about.”

I heard Georges husky laugh, “So that's who catches your attention.”

“As a friend,” I smiled looking sleepily at him, “I would tell you when I found 'the one' so that you could congratulate me on being happy.”

He growled, “There is only one man I know of who could make you happy, *chere*.”

"Really," I yawned, "then do tell us who it is so I can get on with the business of being happy."

He smiled and rolled towards me, an impish grin on his face, "You know quite well who will make you happy and when you decide to accept that then I will congratulate you."

I growled wordlessly, unable to come up with any comeback, appropriate or otherwise.

The next morning, Richard was more than enthusiastic about attempting some of the moves we had watched the night before. So, the morning sparring session consisted of Richard, Vicki, Georges, Daphne (even though she hadn't been there the night before), and myself. I sparred against Vicki and Daphne as Richard and Georges went at it like two pros. I attempted an arm bar and ended up just smacking myself in the face with Vicki's arm. Daphne couldn't stop laughing. After our little chat she hadn't exactly warmed up to me, but I don't think she loathed me quite as vehemently.

We were all rolling around on the floor laughing when the doors opened and a beautiful vampire I had never met before stepped onto the training mat. She was taller than me, but that may have been because of the eight inch heels she seemed to be wearing. Her silken brunette hair reached her waist and she swayed her hips as though the world was moving underneath her feet. Her air as she entered the room was as if she was the only thing in the world that mattered. I immediately felt Vicki tense and her power began to vibrate off of her skin. Daphne also seemed to draw back, leaving the more powerful creatures in front of her. Richard and Georges, however, both stood protectively in front of the rest of us. I already didn't like her.

"Is this your new whore, Georges?" Her melodic voice vibrated through the room.

He snorted in disgust, "That does not concern you, Lilith"

"Oh," she laughed, "but it does. Especially because your darling little Anthony has been out of contact for so long. I am the one who gets to question that," she looked at me as though struggling to define what I was, she settled on "thing."

Both Richard and Georges moved to protect me. I stood from the mat and stepped between them. Each of them grabbed my arms and tried to warn me with their eyes, but I shook my head.

"It's alright," I laughed nervously, "you don't need to stand up for me."

Georges looked at me sadly, "You don't understand what she plans on doing."

I smiled at him, "I know better than you think."

They both reluctantly released my arms and I strode up to this succubus. "Lilith?" I asked with a smile.

"Whore?" she growled at me.

I laughed and folded my arms across my stomach, "My guess would be not nearly as big a one as you."

Her hand whipped out in a movement almost too quick to see, but I knew beforehand what she was going to do. This was just a vampiric version of Georgia and I easily avoided her little flare of temper. She smiled sadistically and in a flash she was flying towards me. She anticipated me stepping away from the attack and smashed into me. We rolled to the floor and I could taste blood in my mouth from where I had bit my cheek. She smashed her fist towards my face.

I rolled out from under her and she smashed her fist into the mat. It was hard enough to break through my skull. She was incredibly pissed and she was incredibly strong and I was incredibly screwed. I pushed her off of me and attempted to roll to my feet only to get a fist to the kidney. I whipped around and smashed my forehead into her nose. It didn't break her nose of course, but it did take her by surprise. She stumbled backwards and gave me just enough room to land an awesome kick to her ribs.

She didn't fall, in fact, she laughed. I didn't back up even though every fiber of my being was screaming for me to run like hell. Georges and Richard were standing behind her looking at me expectantly. Lilith rolled her neck and looked over her shoulder at them.

"This is Van Helsing's little prodigy?" she asked disgustedly.

"Leave her be, Lilith," Georges warned, "She doesn't know the rules you use."

"Then I'll enlighten her," she growled focusing back on me. The smile she gave me made me wish I had some sort of weapon.

"She plans on hurting you badly," Georges called to me. "According to her rules, you threw the first punch because you stood up to her. In her mind that's a challenge."

I smiled nervously as Lilith stalked towards me, "So what am I supposed to do?"

She growled, "You're supposed to submit to me."

I stood up straight and cemented my stance, "You are just like every other bitch I have ever dealt with and let me tell you that I am completely over it. No matter how hard you hit me, you will never submit me."

She grinned with the challenge and swung straight at my face. I stood there and stared at her. I didn't move, didn't blink. I felt the power surge through me until it raised goosebumps down my arms. I watched as her hand moved towards me as though it were in slow motion. At the last moment I moved back. She had moved too far into her swing and I let her momentum carry her straight into my elbow. Her nose made this sickening crack and blood exploded across her upper lip. She stared at me, holding her nose in horror.

Everyone was staring at me in horror. I didn't know why. Georges was just standing there with a small smile across his lips. I didn't know what I had done. Lilith stared at me as her nose started to knit back together.

"How did you do that?" she hissed.

"What?"

"How did you break my nose you little bitch?" she pulled out a gun and pointed it at my chest. I didn't see that one coming.

"Wow," I backed away slowly, "I just...I did what I normally do...I don't know what you want me to say..."

"I don't want you to say anything," she screamed, "I want you to die you stupid whore."

I opened my mouth to ask why, but the gun went off. I felt like it all happened in slow motion. I saw the muzzle flash and I saw Georges and Richard leap at her. From my peripheral vision I could see Daphne and Vicki heading towards me. I saw the door fling open as I felt the bullet rip into my shoulder. Luckily for me she was a lousy shot and missed everything vital. I just couldn't figure out why she wanted me dead. I hadn't done anything to her.

I dropped to the ground and felt a strange numbness spread through my arms. I wasn't here, I was floating. It was getting hazy. My mind felt clouded, then out of nowhere I felt the power rush through my body. My head snapped up, suddenly I was alert. Vicki and Daphne were stepping back from me as Lilith swung the gun around frantically. Van Helsing stood behind her palms towards her attempting to placate the lunatic.

"Lilith," my voice was calm and measured. I stood slowly, "Stop pointing your gun at my friends."

She stared at me in horror.

Everyone else seemed to move slowly towards the walls as if they were expecting something and they were afraid of what it was. Lilith just stood frozen staring at me. The power almost seemed to roll in waves off my skin. Vicki moved towards me and Lilith swung the gun in her direction. That was it. Every atom of the power surged off me and slammed full force into Lilith She hurtled towards the wall as the last of the power left my body and I sank to the floor. Lilith crumpled to the floor opposite me.

The bullet wound was throbbing and I slipped to the ground, "Daphne," I whispered hoarsely, "Could you help me?"

She nodded nervously, "Are you in control?"

I had never been out of control. "Yes?"

Vicki ran to my side and cradled my head against her shoulder while Daphne examined my shoulder. The three men just stood there and stared at me. I managed a weak smile, "Do I have something on my face?" I grimaced as Daphne probed the wound.

"Sorry," she whispered, "but this going to hurt."

I nodded and went to take Vicki's hand, but she stopped me. "If you squeeze too hard, you'll break my hand."

Richard stepped in, "I've got you."

I smiled at him and took his hand. Then Daphne went to work. I was glad that Richard took my hand, it would've been awkward to break poor Vicki's fingers because this hurt. Daphne's adept fingers reached into the wound and searched for the bullet that hadn't exited out of my shoulder. She pulled it out and dropped the lead mess onto the mat. My shoulder was already starting to heal, but I had lost a lot of blood. Human half downside, I need blood to survive.

I noticed that Georges wouldn't get near me, but that no one had bothered to check on Lilith I looked up at Richard, “Is Lilith alright?”

He snickered, “Of all things to be worried about right now.”

“What else should I be worried about?” I asked quietly while a little voice inside me whispered that I didn't want to actually know the answer.

Richard patted my hand softly, “We'll talk about it later.”

Vicki helped me stand. My legs felt like jello and I hoped we weren't going very far. Daphne took the other side and both supported me with an arm around the waist. I thanked them quietly and allowed myself to be led into the room I had come to regard as my own. They laid me down on the dark silk sheets and Daphne tucked the soft comforter up to my chin. She whispered that I needed to sleep and I would hunt when I awoke. I nodded and snuggled down into my fresh pillows.

I awoke to cool fingers stroking my hair and a long muscular body pressed against me. I smiled and looked up at Georges who was smiling back at me. “You know that as a friend it's really creepy to wake up with you next to me.”

“As a friend,” he smiled whispering in my ear, “I think this is a fine way for you to wake up.”

I laughed, “You're still fuzzy on that whole friend boundary thing aren't you?”

He nuzzled my neck and my heart rate picked up exponentially. “You never said anything about boundaries,” he whispered.

I was afraid to speak for fear that my voice would squeak out and loose the force I needed to command. He brushed his lips against my jaw and I could feel my body tighten. He pressed his lips against the soft flesh where my neck met my collarbone and I pushed him away. “And that's the line,” I announced rolling from under the covers.

“Oh,” he laughed rolling to all fours on the mattress, “That's the line?”

“No,” I tried to control my breathing, “the line was when you climbed into bed with me while I was not conscious.”

He crawled towards me on all fours, “So next time I have to ask permission?”

I nodded.

He continued to crawl towards me, “Will you deny me, *chere?”*

His eyes widened with such mock innocence that I had the urge to smack him as he settled back on his heels. He was dressed in blue jeans and open shirt. His body was so distracting, and he smiled knowingly. “Yes,” I finally announced, “I will deny you until you figure out that you are not the end-all be-all.”

He smiled, “But I am.”

I smiled back, “So you'll never be invited to my bed. However, I am going to invite you to dinner.” I pulled on a pair of jeans and wondered at how comfortable I was being half dressed in front of him. I noticed the pulled skin where the bullet wound was finishing the healing process and remembered his strangeness. “Why wouldn't you come near me when I was shot?” I asked looking for his reaction in the mirror.

He dropped his head ashamedly, “You don't know the draw of blood to a full vampire.”

“But I've bled around vampires before and they haven't had this reaction before.”

He smiled at me in the mirror, “Do you really want me to explain this to you?”

I held his reflected gaze and let that be my answer.

“Blood has a certain draw, you know that, you've felt that before.” I nodded. “But you can resist it even though you can taste it in the air and on your tongue.” I nodded, not wanting to admit to myself how right he was. “You know how fulfilling it is when you drain that last drop of blood, how utterly forbidden and tantalizing it tastes. I could smell your blood across the room and added to that sweet scent was you. I was afraid if I got too close to you, I wouldn't be able to control myself.” I broke his gaze and pulled a sweatshirt on over my tank top. In an instant he was next to me. “Don't pull away from me *chere*,” he whispered softly,

"You don't understand what it means that you challenge my control." I looked up into those intense eyes and saw nothing but sincerity. "You are the only person in nearly half a century who has challenged my self-control."

"Half a century?" I questioned.

He smiled impishly.

I smiled and shook my head, "You are something. I don't know exactly what, but you are something."

"Thank you *chere*," he smiled leaning towards me. He took a deep breath inhaling my scent in a sensually enticing way. He seemed to drink me in like a fine wine and I noticed I seemed to be leaning in to his magnetic pull. He smiled and I hated him for it. He sensed my disdain and he stepped back grinning like a Cheshire cat, "Shall we hunt?"

I grumbled incoherently and watched as he gracefully loped to the door. I had a feeling the most dangerous thing I was going to have to deal with here was him and part of me was fine with that prospect.

19. Forbidden Desires

We were well satiated as we walked back towards the compound. Georges had a faint smile on his face and felt the warm buoyancy of blood flooding through my veins. I didn't want to go back to the compound just now. I wanted to enjoy the beautiful clear night.

It was as though he read my mind, “Want to play a little hookie?”

“Is it really hookie if we're not required to be there?” I teased.

He laughed and the sound caressed my body, “Ah *chere* you and I should hunt more often.”

He took off running into the night and I followed with ease. He wasn't moving quickly enough to pull ahead, or maybe I was moving as quickly as he was. He smiled happily as he ran into a clearing and slammed to a halt. He spun quickly to stop me and only succeeded in knocking the both of us to the ground. I rolled away uneasily but he just laid there and stared up into the sky.

“I used to do this all the time,” he sighed.

“Do what?”

“Look at the stars,” he smiled at me and the look was guileless and soft. For a moment he wasn't the sexy man who seemed to pull all women to him without care, he was a young man enjoying the sensation of the grass on his arms and the lights in the sky.

“I was always afraid to lay out where it was dark enough to do this,” I laughed laying just out of arm's reach from him.

He snickered.

“What's so funny?”

“You,” he raised up on an elbow and stared down at me. I felt a flutter in my chest, “You are very possibly the most powerful person I have ever met and you were afraid of the dark. What you did to Lilith was scary.”

I looked at him earnestly, “What did I do?”

“You broke her body against a stone wall.”

I didn't understand.

“You shouldn't be able to break a grown vampire. You shouldn't be able to crush her nose with your elbow. She should have shattered your arm with her face. You aren't a full vampire, you are...breakable." He said that word so softly it broke my heart.

"Apparently I deserve more credit than I've been given," I laughed nervously.

He rolled back to gaze at the stars and I followed suit. All was quiet for a moment before he said, "You have never shown power like that before. I guess we are all just a little concerned about how powerful you really are and how that's going to affect you."

"What do you mean 'affect me'?"

"Even vampires can go insane, *chere*, and you being part human only gives us that much more reason to be concerned."

"Us?"

He rolled back towards me and smiled, "You know that we all love you in our own ways. Even Daphne respects you if nothing else."

I rolled my eyes and focused on the darkened sky.

He laughed, "How modest. You are more wonderful than you think, and not just as the amazing weapon you are. You are a wonderful person and you don't even see it."

I smiled, "You aren't so bad yourself."

"Ah *chere,* don't say that" I could hear the smirk in his voice, "You don't know what I'm thinking."

The trouble was I did know what he was thinking because I was thinking the same thoughts. He was so close to me. I could feel his magnetic pull and was fighting the urge to trace my fingers across the muscles in his arms and across his chest and stomach. The thought made my body tighten. I knew he could hear my heart beating in the night like a parade drum.

He whispered, "Or maybe you do."

Part of me wanted him to move towards me, part of me wanted to move to him, but neither of us moved. We both just laid there in the darkness listening to each other breathing.

I closed my eyes and tried to sort out what I was feeling. Georges scared me because I wanted it, everything he had to offer. He was a strange combination of sex and sincerity that made him completely irresistible, but how could I trust him. I didn't know him. I had never been into casual sex at any point in my long existence. The desires I felt with Charles/Anthony had been so strange for me. Then again, he apparently had the power to make me feel however he wanted me to feel. That worried me more than I cared to admit.

"I would never do that to you," Georges whispered.

I started.

"Didn't mean to startle you."

I sighed, "You would never do what to me?"

"I would never use what I can do to make you do something you didn't want to."

I rolled onto my side and looked him in the face, "Would you use it to help influence my decision?"

He smiled, "Never. I would never use what I can do to take what I would have you give willingly."

I got to my feet and wiped my hands on my jeans, "I can't trust that."

He stood behind me, "Why not?" The pain laced his voice with a bitter edge.

"I don't want to feel like this again, confused and...dirty."

He touched my shoulder and I spun to face him. I pulled away, but he grabbed my shoulders and forced me to look at him. "Do you feel anything but my hands?" he demanded.

I concentrated very hard and there was nothing, no pulse of power, just his hands on my shoulders. He moved his fingers slowly to my bare skin and the breath caught in my throat. I grabbed his arms, frightened and he stopped for a moment. "Trust me," he whispered. I didn't drop my hands, but he slowly traced his fingertips across my collarbone. I felt that desire well up inside of me, but it was pure carnal lust, not a trace of power.

"Just relax," he smiled, "I'm going to use some of my power on you."

I gripped his arms tightly, but he shook his head. "Please," he whispered.

"Why?"

"I need you to feel how it feels when I do this so that you will always know whether or not I'm using it."

I nodded apprehensively. He took a deep breath and let the the power trickle from his fingertips. The power was overwhelming. My body reacted violently as the power washed over me. My knees buckled and I had to fight the urge to pull him to the ground with me. Somehow I knew he wouldn't resist, couldn't resist. I could smell honeysuckle in the air then suddenly he pulled my his arms away from me and stumbled back. I sat on the ground and took a few deep breaths before I was able to speak.

"What..."

"Have I ever done that to you before?" He asked breathlessly.

"No."

"Then I have never used my powers on you before."

"I smelled honeysuckles?"

He smiled, "I've heard that before."

"You didn't smell it?"

He shook his head, "No, I never can. I guess you can never smell yourself."

I laughed, "Well I guess that depends on how much you stink."

He smiled back at me and reached out to help me up, but I shook him off. He looked hurt. "Please don't be afraid."

I smiled and climbed to my feet, "I'm very afraid of you now, Georges."

He dropped his eyes.

"You have no idea what that felt like or how desperately much I wanted you."

He smiled, "Where do you think I pulled the power from?"

I couldn't help but laugh, "Then we really need to work on boundaries with you."

He sighed and smiled that innocent smile that could melt ice, "Shall we return home?"

Home, it was strange to think that this odd place I had been kidnapped into was as close to a home as I had ever gotten. It wasn't perfect. I knew the old man was using me and Daphne only tolerated me, but Georges said it best, they all loved me in their way. I loved them too. "Yeah," I sighed, "Lets go home."

The moment I walked through the doors Vicki grabbed me and drug me into her torture chamber. Daphne was sitting on the plush bed with a strange look on her face. I was quite apprehensive as Vicki sat me in front of the mirror and started to pull out her bag of tricks. "Night Out!" she announced starting to pull my hair into some sort of half updo that I would never be able to do on my own. I looked at Daphne for help, but she just shrugged her shoulders. From the looks of her she had already been subjected to Vicki's chair of torture.

An hour later there was a strange creature staring from the mirror. I had done my make-up and hair to fish in bars and such before, but I had never looked like this. She had made me look innocent and tempting, sensual and sensational all rolled into a light green dress that reminded me of a slip. To be perfectly honest, I was highly impressed. Vicki's fashion sense never ceased to amaze me.

Daphne slipped up beside me and pulled out a necklace. It had that symbol I had seen tattooed on the inside of George's arm twisted in gold.

"What does that symbol mean?" I asked as she slid it around my throat.

Vicki smiled, "It means that you are one of us now." She wore the symbol as a pair of earrings and Daphne showed me the charm on her bracelet. I smiled, I had never felt like that before, like I actually belonged to a family. Vicki seemed to sense that and threw her arms warmly around my neck. Even Daphne smiled and touched my shoulder.

I touched her hand and looked into her eyes, "Are we good?"

She smiled, "Yeah, we're good." I squeezed her hand and she sighed, "You really aren't that bad."

I snorted, "I'm not so sure."

Vicki laughed, "You're amazing and everyone here thinks so."

I looked at Daphne and she nodded, "Even me."

Vicki couldn't help but throw in, "Especially Georges." She snatched her little purse and opened the door before I had a chance to respond. Little imp.

Richard and Georges came walking down the hall looking absolutely scrumptious. They strutted towards us like they were coming down the runway, and between the two of them they could totally own it. Richard's sheer light blue shirt shimmered as he moved towards us. He held a hand out to Daphne who took it with a smile. She glanced back at me and smiled, which led me to wonder if she had forgiven me due to a new romantic interest. Whatever the reason, I'm glad she did.

Georges stepped forward in a dark red silk shirt buttoned to his waist where it met his tight jeans. I looked at Vicki and she winked, I just shook my head. Too wise for her years. He politely held both hands out to us. Vicki didn't hesitate, but I ignored his hand and just walked at his side. He smiled, but Vicki rolled her eyes at me. I fought the urge to stick my tongue out at her.

I don't know why we bothered to take cars, it was only minutes before we pulled up into a parking lot outside of a club named "Forbidden Desires." I looked at Vicki, but she just laughed, "Where do you think we get the money to keep going?"

I hadn't thought about that.

Vicki danced up to the bouncer that frankly frightened me. He was nearly seven feet tall and maybe four feet wide. He smiled at me and I could see the slight point of fangs beneath his smile, but he wasn't a vampire, in fact he was human, well human-ish. He also wasn't shy by the way he eyed me up and down. It was so blatant I wanted to slap him.

He didn't take his eyes off me and I couldn't help myself, "You got an issue gigantor?"

He snorted, "You got a really big mouth for such a little girl."

I crossed my arms, "Compared to you, I think an elephant is little."

He stepped towards me, "You looking to find out just how big I am?"

"You looking for an ass kicking?"

He laughed, "No wonder you're causing such a stir around here." He offered me his hand with a huge smile, "I'm Jackson, I'm the usual bouncer here."

"And a theriomorph?"

He smiled, "Yeah, shift into a tiger, hence the fangs." He pulled his lips back to reveal the full length of his canines. "It makes me a little more intimidating to normal people."

"You saying I'm not normal?" I smirked.

"Hell, yeah," he laughed, "from what I've heard about you, you are one scary motherfucker."

I held out my hand, “Jesse, unnatural scary motherfucker.”

He shook my hand and smiled, “Pleased to meet you. Van Helsing is upstairs in the office if you need him. Otherwise everyone enjoy themselves.”

We were all seated at a plush booth in the VIP section. First time I had ever been in one of those. As I glanced around, most of the waitstaff were not exactly human. I did notice however, that none of them were wearing any form of the symbols we were. Yet they all seemed to know who we were and treated us with the utmost respect. They also knew that Vicki was not old enough to drink and made sure that she didn't have anything containing alcohol. She was rather annoyed by that fact.

Everyone else made their way to the dance floor while I marveled at the decor inside the club. It looked a lot like other clubs, but almost classier in a way. It reminded me of Van Helsing's library back at the...actually, I'm not sure what to call it...the hideout. I watched as Vicki danced and laughed, for once looking less like an adult and more like a junior in high school. Daphne and Richard were laughing and having fun spinning around the floor in each others arms. Richard wasn't exactly the best dancer, but he was trying. I had to smile.

“Are you enjoying yourself?” Van Helsing had apparently materialized out of the shadows to slide into the seat beside me.

I smiled at him, “I didn't know you were an entrepreneur.”

“Yes,” he laughed, “'Forbidden Desires' is my child.”

I glanced around, “You must be very proud. From the look of the crowd, you are doing very well.”

He smiled, “It does help finance our little operations, but more importantly it has become a rather popular spot with all sorts.”

“I never knew there were this many preternatural beings in any one place.”

He smiled and nodded.

“Where are we anyway?” I asked softly. I had been here months and no one had ever told me.

“We are in a small town about two hours from Washington, D.C.” he smiled.

“I guess I shouldn't be surprised we're near D.C.” I laughed.

He held his hand out to me as the DJ switched to a slower song, "Shall we dance?"

I took his hand and smiled, "I would be honored."

He spun me out onto the dance floor. He was surprisingly light on his feet for being as old as he was. He seemed so debonaire in this atmosphere and he guided me around the floor with ease. Richard and Daphne smiled at us as they slowly circled the floor, Vicki smiled at me as well, but Georges turned his head away and seemed to be concentrating very very hard on something.

I leaned to Van Helsing's ear and whispered, "Is Georges alright?"

"Mr. Moncrief," he laughed, "He is more than alright and miserable at the same time."

"I don't understand."

"Neither does he my dear," the old man laughed.

The DJ switched tempo and Van Helsing took me back to the booth. "Thank you for the dance, my dear." He looked up at a woman who was standing agitatedly near his office door, "But I'm afraid my managerial duties await me." He bowed slightly and took leave.

The waitress brought me a drink and I sat in the booth watching as everyone enjoyed themselves, but my solitude was short lived as Vicki came pouncing up the stairs with a martyred look on her face. I knew that look and it meant that she was going to scold me for some reason or another. I thought perhaps I was wrinkling my dress.

"I didn't get you all dressed up to see you sit there by yourself," she announced.

I laughed, "Go back to Georges and enjoy dancing."

"Oh," she laughed, "You think Georges wants to dance with me?"

I rolled my eyes and looked away.

"Well, I have someone else who wants to dance with you anyway," she giggled, dragging me from the booth.

I followed her down to the floor only to stop dead in my tracks. Standing before me was none other than Theodore DeMarco. My skin started to vibrate as my power rose to meet his. Vicki pulled her hand away from my skin as though I had shocked her. And every other preternatural being in the place sensed the sudden rise in power and looked in my direction. I shook my head slightly and they continued with their actions, but didn't stop watching warily out of the corner of their eyes.

I forced a smile at Vicki, "Please go back to your partner."

She nodded and moved away without a word. As I glanced at Georges I saw Jackson and Richard approach him. Theodore was holding out his hand for a dance. I realized suddenly that the music hadn't stopped. I took his hand and let him lead me to the floor. I bristled as he touched me familiarly and Georges took a step towards us. I glanced at him quickly and he stayed put.

"Yes," Theodore sneered, "call off the dogs, you wouldn't want something unfortunate to happen to any innocent bystanders."

"Where are the others, Theodore," I demanded with a sneer.

"Now, now," he laughed looking me up and down, "why so serious? Dressed up like that you should be in nothing but good humour. You look good enough to eat."

"Touch my skin, dog," I growled, "lets see if I still stand over your dead body."

He grinned, but there was no humor in it now, "You promised me you wouldn't."

"I lied," I laughed, "like you and all the rest of them. I should have known that I wasn't what you all were interested in, it was always just my power."

"You think your little Van Helsing group is any different?"

I shook my head, "No, I don't, but they don't lie to me about it."

"Oh really?" he laughed and the sound was hollow. "You're telling me that Georges over there hasn't done exactly what Charles did to you? Seduce you until you're stupid enough to fall for whatever it is they have in store for you? After Charles had such an easy time with you, he passed it on. All you have to do to get you, is convince you you're wanted." I didn't speak and he laughed, "After all of this you can't still be stupid enough to think you are desirable. You're nothing but a freak."

I could feel the weight in my stomach. "I can't argue with that, but tell me...how do you know their names?"

He laughed and the sound made my skin crawl, "It's amazing what people tell when you torture them long enough, even vampires."

My voice hissed out, "What have you done?"

He smiled and pulled a small jump drive out of his pocket, "It's all on here." He dropped the drive into my hand being very careful not to touch my skin.

I looked down at the drive. Theodore started to walk away, but I reached out and grabbed his bare wrist. His eyes fluttered back in his head and he tried to keep his feet as the visions pressed against him. His skin paled and his breath came in short gasps. "What do you see?" I whispered, "I promise you this, Theodore. I will find a way to kill you and I will enjoy every second of it."

I released his arm and he stumbled towards the door, tears in his eyes. The blonde vampire and Jennifer were standing in the night waiting for him. They were smarter than that. I smiled at them and mouthed, "Bring it." As I said it, I could feel my team move up behind me. He wisely left without further ado.

20. Hearts

I sat out on the cliff edge and looked down into the lapping waves. I didn't know how to feel. That jump drive held the most horrific thing I had ever seen. I pulled the light jacket I had brought with me close around my throat. Charles/Anthony was dead, and brutally so. The drive held an account of the entire thing. The torture, the death. Georgia had participated with enthusiasm in the whole affair. She seemed to take a wickedly sick pleasure in it as she sunk her fangs into his throat. That was aimed at me, she couldn't help looking into the camera while she did it.

Still, I didn't know how to feel. Everyone expected me to break down, to start crying. Daphne had. The tears had started for her shortly after they began torturing him. I had just stared, through the seemingly endless gruesome torture, it was all I could do. Georges hadn't cried, but he seemed to have been in pain. I just felt numb. As the blood drained from his neck, I left the room. I wandered out into the woods and found myself here looking into the ocean wondering what I was supposed to feel. If it had been right when I returned from Alaska I would have been devastated, but I wasn't that person anymore. I had changed. He had changed me, his lies had changed me, his betrayal had changed me. I knew they would think I was being cold, but he was dead and that was it. I stood and headed back to the house. Vicki was standing outside waiting for me. She looked concerned.

"Georges locked himself in his room and won't come out," she blurted as soon as I got near her.

"Then let him be," I answered calmly. "He needs to deal with his grief."

She grabbed my arm as I tried to move past her, "I'm worried about him."

"Why?"

"I think he might do something stupid," she admitted.

I nodded and walked to his room. I could feel the anger on the other side of the door. Vicki stayed at the end of the hallway looking like a scared rabbit. I didn't want to, in fact I was sure this was a bad idea, but I knocked on the door. There was no answer.

"Georges," I called softly.

No answer.

"Georges, it's Jesse. Everyone is worried about you."

"I'm fine," he growled from the other side.

"Please open the door," I whispered, "You're scaring Vicki. She's afraid you're going to do something stupid."

No answer.

"Georges, you're starting to worry me too. Please open the door."

"I can't," his voice broke in a sob.

"Let me come in, please."

No answer.

"Georges?"

His voice was soft and fatigued, "Just go away Jesse."

I stepped away from the door, "I'm sorry." I walked slowly down the hall, my bare feet softly slapping the concrete. I could hear the sobs coming from Daphne's room and the soothing voice of Richard. I could almost sense Vicki and Van Helsing in his library trying to come to terms with what they had seen. I felt the tears start rolling down my face as I sat on the edge of my bed. I could feel the hearts breaking around me and I couldn't let them feel this way. They had hurt my family and the Marquis and his pets were going to have to answer to me.

The morning found me in D.C. I was standing on the steps of the Lincoln Memorial. I knew they were here. When I had grabbed Theodore's wrist I had seen flashes of the monuments. This was as far as I had gotten. I wasn't sure where to go next. I slumped down on the stairs and stared at the hustle and bustle that was beginning around me. I hadn't thought this through. I was in D.C., alone, tired, and without a clue as to where I was going or what I would do when I got there. I thought about going back, but I was exhausted. I still had my credit cards and honestly, if Georgia wanted to find me this would be the perfect breadcrumb. I went to a nearby hotel and checked in.

The room smelled funny, but I as exhausted as I was I didn't even care. I dropped back against the pillow and waited. I wasn't sure what I was waiting for, but I didn't care. I laid there thinking about the note I left. I felt so guilty about leaving them, but I needed them to know why. I needed the Marquis to come after me and honestly, he was going to one way or the other. At least if I was here, my team would be safe. Still, I felt like I had run away. I hoped they understood. I didn't want my friends to come after me but at the same time I was afraid they wouldn't. I finally fell asleep in that state of complete agitation.

The knock on the door was insistent. I was deep asleep and at first didn't know where I was, but then I noticed the floral printed comforter and realized I was in a cruddy hotel. The knock on the door continued. I stood groggily and noticed how messed up I looked in the mirror. The knocking on the door became angry and suddenly I was apprehensive about opening it. I debated in my head whether or not the Marquis or his henchmen would bother to knock.

"Jesse Childress," Georges roared from the other side, "If you don't open this door in two seconds I am going to bust it down."

I swung the door open to reveal a very agitated vampire who looked about as bad as I did, "What are you doing here?"

He strode in and slammed the door shut, "What are you doing here? What the hell were you thinking?"

I stumbled back and ended up sitting on the bed, "I'm sorry?"

He pressed his fists to the sides of his head, "Sorry? Did you even stop to think how worried everyone was going to be when we realized you were gone?"

I started to get angry. There was no way he was going to stand here in a room I paid for and lecture me like I was a child. "Don't lecture me," I yelled at him standing up.

He continued as if I hadn't even spoken. "Vicki started crying hysterically, Daphne couldn't stop blaming herself, Van Helsing was beside himself trying to figure out where you could have gone, and Richard was about to transition and start tracking you by smell."

"I didn't want anyone coming after me, enough people have been hurt. The only one they're after is me."

He shook his head, "You don't even understand do you?"

I looked at him angrily, “No, you don't understand. I am what they're after. If I get hurt, that's it, no one else needs to get hurt.”

He postured up to me, towering above me, “You are stupid. You....”

“What?” I demanded getting into his face, “What? A stupid little freak and you came out here to get me because the Van Helsing Group isn't done with me yet?”

He looked like I had slapped him.

I walked to the window and looked out angrily crossing my arms across my stomach, “Just go.”

He didn't move, “You really did love him didn't you?”

I shook my head, “No, I didn't.”

I heard him sit on the bed, “Then why did you come on this suicide mission?”

My voice was cold, “I'm responsible for his death. He got me out and I got him killed. This is the only way I can think of to pay him back for saving me.” I took a deep breath, “You can think I'm a horrible monster if you want, but I didn't feel anything until I realized how bad it hurt all of you. I'm sorry.”

“I'm sorry,” he whispered, “I didn't want to talk to you last night because I was confused.”

I turned to face him.

“I don't know how I'm supposed to feel about this, but you don't deal with it by running away.” He stood up and walked towards the door. “We all love you. We want you to come back, and against my better judgment I'm leaving the choice up to you.”

I nodded, but didn't answer.

“I'll wait ten minutes,” he whispered walking out the door.

I stood there for eight minutes, knowing that I would absolutely go down there and get in the car. I didn't know exactly how I would be received, but if he wasn't lying and they were that upset, I couldn't leave them like that. Still, I was so angry with Georges. Who was he to tell me what to do?

I let my anger be known as I got into the car and slammed the door shut behind me. He didn't say anything, he just drove. I watched as the landscape flashed by. We were barely twenty minutes outside of the compound before Georges said anything and then it was just, "Apologize to Daphne and Vicki, they were really worried about you."

I growled, "Yes dad."

He just stared like I was the biggest bitch he had ever met and I was fine with that for the moment. He could hate me all he liked, I hated myself enough for everyone involved. It seemed like no matter how much I tried to keep people out of danger, it didn't help. I had gotten Charles/Anthony killed and Georgia turned into a monster. I needed to quit being stupid and start fighting back.

Georges got out of the car and stormed towards the Van Helsing Group who were standing there staring at me. I walked up to Vicki, but before I could open my mouth she threw her arms around my neck and started sobbing. Daphne was not far behind. It seemed that everyone accepted me back with open arms with the exception of Georges who was standoffish and cold at best. That was fine, I was pissed at him too.

That night, Vicki insisted on staying with me. She wasn't about to let me out of her sight. As she curled up next to me I realized just how young she was. She looked up at me with those big green eyes like pet. She watched every move I made, every readjustment, every shift of weight, everything. I didn't understand.

"Vicki?" I asked softly, "How did you end up here?"

She sighed, "I am Van Helsing's niece."

"That explains nothing."

"My mom didn't like what I am." She turned her face away. "It was a thing on my dad's side, but he died when I was little. Long before I presented."

"I'm sorry," I whispered.

She smiled, "The funny thing is, my mother's the Van Helsing. The entire family in some way or another is involved with something that isn't exactly natural and she sent me away because I wasn't."

I hugged my knees to my chest and looked at her, "What does your mother do?"

"She does research for my uncles." She saw the next question coming and smiled, "Just two, but I do have a brother and a sister as well. They're both normal and my mother won't let me talk to them without her there. My other uncle has two boys. They aren't normal either. It was nice to have other people in my family that aren't."

I smiled at her, "You have an entire family here who loves you and there isn't a one among us who is anywhere even hinting at normal."

She didn't smile back, "But you left."

My smile faded, "I thought it would be the best for you. For all of you."

She shook her head, "It was a mess when we realized you weren't here." She sighed, "Georges was about to freak out when he read that note. He started pacing and literally tore the note into pieces."

I smirked, "He was still pretty pissed when he found me."

She looked confused, "He wasn't angry."

Now it was my turn to be confused, but she had apparently decided that she was done with this line of conversation. She rolled over and pulled the blanket close around her.

"Tired?" I whispered.

She nodded, but didn't speak.

"I'll be here when you wake up," I said softly.

She reached back and squeezed my hand, then drifted off.

Georges was standing outside the door when we awoke. He was less than pleased, but Vicki seemed absolutely thrilled that I was there. Georges just growled, "Van Helsing wants to see you."

I walked into Van Helsing's library alone as he fiddled with some books, "What was the matter?"

"You saw the movie," I said settling on the couch, "that was my fault."

He sat in the chair opposite me, "How was that your fault?"

"Wouldn't have ever happened if he hadn't tried to get me out."

"You can't blame yourself, my dear," he whispered sadly.

I was angry, "Why not?"

"Because we are all to blame," he stated with authority. "You share the blame with all of us. He would never have been in this position if Georges had not wanted to join us in the first place and believe me he is feeling the full weight of his guilt. He never would have been there if I had not recruited him and I feel the fullness of my decision every day. Daphne feels that if she hadn't loved him, he would never have stayed and Vicki believes that she made him leave on this assignment to begin with."

I looked at him and shook my head, "We aren't all responsible."

He smiled and leaned forward, "Indeed we are, my dear. You have always been on your own, you have never been a part of a family and when something bad happens in a family we all stick together and be the support for one another. We are family here Jesse Childress and you are a part of our legacy."

I didn't respond.

"We know where they are," he said quietly, "We are going to avenge him."

I looked up confused, "How do you know where they are?"

He held up a manilla envelope and sighed, "He sent it to us before he was killed. It gives us detailed maps and everything we need to know."

21. Kicking Ass and Taking Names

I stood looking at myself in the mirror and thought I was going to puke. There was no way I was going to go out that door wearing this. Vicki stood behind me impatiently tapping her toe and pursing her lips disapprovingly. She had spent hours primping my hair and torturing me with hairspray, not to mention the hour she spent on my highly dramatic make-up. Still there was no way I was stepping out in this.

Vicki stood in a very similar outfit and seemed fine with it. We looked like something out of a bad action movie. I was in three-inch heeled leather boots that reached three quarters of the way up my calves. They laced up the back and took me five minutes to even get them on. As if that wasn't enough I was in a pair of black leather short-shorts and a leather halter-top. I had two knife sheaths attached, one to each wrist and my XD in a hip holster strapped to my thigh in low drawl style. It wasn't ideal for a quick drawl, but it was dramatic and that was what Van Helsing wanted. To be honest the cold steel of the slide against my leg was comforting. The rest of the get-up, not so much.

"I look like a dominatrix," I groaned.

Vicki rolled her eyes, "You look frightening and dramatic. You will make an entrance."

"Why do you get to wear pants?" I whined.

She sighed exasperatedly, "Because I'm sixteen and to be perfectly honest you have better legs than I do."

I groaned again, "I'm not going out there."

As if in answer to my declaration there was a knock on the door. Vicki smiled, "Tell them that."

She swung open the door and everyone was standing there. I didn't know that Richard's eyes could get that large. Even Van Helsing's jaw dropped. Vicki bounded out and waited for me expectantly. I took the long leather trench-coat from the vanity and pulled it reluctantly around my shoulders. I stepped out of the bathroom. Only Georges seemed utterly unfazed by my appearance.

"Someone is getting their ass kicked for this," I growled.

Van Helsing laughed, "Perhaps my dear you should channel that aggression in the proper direction."

Van Helsing was dressed in a jet black suit and white shirt with a silk tie. He looked as though he was about to go into a board meeting. I didn't like the idea of bringing him along at all and had made my sentiments known when the plan had been announced, but as with every other part of this scheme, outfit included, my opinion was disregarded.

Van Helsing led the way to the awaiting chopper. At least we got to ride in a chopper. I crossed my arms and legs and scowled in general. Georges wouldn't look at me and Richard didn't seem able not to. Daphne just shook her head while Vicki sat there quietly. I watched as she closed her eyes and took a few deep breaths. When she opened her eyes they weren't green anymore, they were black. She was ready. I looked at Richard and his eyes were yellow and his teeth were pointed, all his teeth. Georges looked at me and I couldn't breath. The hostility was like nothing I had ever felt before. He curled his upper lip back and I could see the points of his fangs. I smiled, I was not the only scary motherfucker in this group.

Then the chopper stopped moving. I looked down and saw a clearing in the midst of the woods. Vicki smiled and moved to the jump door. She leaped into the air and I nearly had a heart attack, but she landed as though she had stepped down the stairs, she looked up and smiled. Richard and Georges leaped out the door both landing gracefully. My guess was that it was my turn. I stepped out of the door and lowered myself carefully to the ground. It would have been just my luck to break an ankle jumping out of a helicopter.

The chopper blades hummed above us, but there was another sound that had our attention. From the wood line there was the sound of clapping, a slow sarcastic clap. The blonde stepped out from the shadows and laughed, “Impressive.”

We all took defensive stances.

She smiled, “Did you really think that we didn't get this information from your little vampire spy?”

I suddenly had a very bad feeling about this. I listened very hard and could hear things moving very quickly through the woods. This was definitely going to be bad. I smelled the air and knew who was coming. The rest of them seemed supremely unconcerned, but they didn't know what was coming for us. I could hear they had changed. The two werewolves that burst into the clearing growled menacingly. We weren't outnumbered, but I was sure they were ruthless.

“You bring two puppies to fight us?” Georges laughed.

Richard vibrated with power, “You don't bring pups to fight the big dogs.” I could hear his clothes ripping as he transitioned.

I could feel Vicki's power vibrate at my back as she smiled, “The odds aren't so good for you.”

I noticed someone was missing, “Where's Georgia? There's no way she would sit out on something like this.”

She stepped from the trees, my father at her side, “Of course I wouldn't miss my chance to get even with you for all the little bitchy things you did over the years. When I looked back the blonde was gone. That seemed to be the signal as everyone attacked at once. Jennifer leaped at me but a ball of red fur intercepted and they rolled into the leaves, Georges had his hands full with Theodore's snapping jaws and amazingly enough, Georgia did not attack me. Instead she dove for Vicki whose fingers had taken on a sort of claw-like quality. That left only my father for me.

I locked eyes with him and he ran into the trees. I sprinted after him and the last thing I heard was Georges screaming, “Jesse No!” I couldn't stop, I ran after him. He flew through the woods but I was barely a few steps behind him yet he was still just out of reach. Suddenly he slammed to a stop and close-lined me. I saw the sky and the tree trunks and then met the ground. Hard. The air whooshed out of me and my father's foot slammed into my side. It lifted me off the ground enough for me to get my feet under me. I stumbled back against a tree and managed to duck a punch that splintered the trunk in half.

“Just hold still,” he roared.

“What's the matter, Dad? Not as easy as you thought?” I landed a right hook that threw him back a bit.

“Not bad for a half breed,” he laughed throwing another punch.

“You're the one who bred me for my blood, now deal with it.”

I attempted to hit him again, but he easily caught my hand and sent me flying hard into a tree. I pulled my power into myself and didn't break anything, but there was definitely going to be bruises in the morning. He was moving towards me at incredible speed, I pulled my gun and fired. I only got off one shot before a small tree landed across the back of my head. I struggled to keep my consciousness as the blonde stepped out of the tree line.

"She isn't so tough," she laughed kicking my gun out of reach. As it disappeared into the darkness I felt my heart sink.

I stood and faced them, "I guess you're like my evil stepmother then?"

My father laughed, "Vanessa is my daughter. My real daughter."

She smiled and sneered, "Not the bastard child you are."

I bum rushed her and we tumbled to the ground. Two powerful preternatural beings were reduced to a cat fight. We pulled at each others hair and scratched at each others faces. Greg stood there with a strange look on his face, but didn't even attempt to break us up even as we tumbled to the dirt. He just stood there and let it all happen. She opened a gash on my cheek with her nails and the sudden pain seemed to clear my head. I felt the power build and unleashed it against her chest. She flew into the woods.

I got to my knees weakened by the push of power and my father attacked. He took a lazy swing at my face and I was able to lock my teeth around his wrist. The blood flowed into my mouth. I locked on with a vengeance and stuck my heel into his throat. He struggled, but it didn't seem right to me. I continued to pull his life into me. He was weakening and I could feel it. The last drop was coming. I was about to let go of his wrist as he mumbled "You're as weak as your mother."

The last drop of his blood flowed down my throat and with his last breath he whispered, "Thank you."

I tried to stand but the world shifted under my feet. I couldn't see straight, there were two of everything. I grabbed handfuls of dirt trying to make sure at least the earth stayed beneath me, but it didn't seem to matter. The world just kept spinning. I tried to call out, but nothing would come out of my mouth. I was sweating and beginning to feel nauseous.

Vanessa, my apparent half sister stepped out of the tree line. I knew the end was here. I couldn't even tell exactly where she was. She kneeled down in front of me and I watched as her mouth stretched and distorted as she spoke. It sounded like it was coming out in slow motion. Suddenly the world lurched forward and I fell to my elbows. When I looked up, Anthony was standing there with her. He laughed and pulled me to my feet. I could feel his hands on my shoulders, I could smell the roses surrounding him, I could feel his power seeping into me. His face stopped twisting.

"You know what the best part of this is?" he sneered, "No one will believe you when you say you saw me."

"Why?" That one word was slurred even to my own ears.

"Oh pet," he cooed pushing a stray strand of hair out of my face, "I'll explain it all to you when you feel better."

I looked at Vanessa who was growling behind him.

He glanced back then looked at me, "It's alright, she's not going to attack you now. I need you."

"No," I slurred pushing him back.

He laughed and dropped me back to the ground, my legs wouldn't support me and without his power to clear my head I fell to the ground and vomited. Vanessa laughed and held out her hand for Anthony to come with her, but he had some more parting words of wisdom for me, "We'll be in touch."

I lunged towards them but the ground just refused to stay under my feet and I fell face first into the dirt. I looked up into the cold dead face of my father. He was rotting away faster than any normal body should. I tried to scramble away from it, but I couldn't get solid ground under my body. It hurt everywhere.

I laid there and closed my eyes hoping that the world would return to normal, but it didn't. If anything, closing my eyes only made it worse. All of the sudden I kept seeing colors swirling around behind my eyelids. I tried to focus, but nothing would stay in one place. Even the colors wouldn't stay straight. I heard feet approaching me but the only thing I could do was try not to vomit again.

I slowly opened my eyes and realized quickly what a bad idea that was. Feet running in my direction were not the best things to try and focus on. I squeezed my eyes shut and horrendous pain pulsed through my body. I heard voices, but they were distorted horrible voices. I tried to crawl away and only succeeded in rolling over. It sounded like monsters. I curled into a ball and willed them to go away. There was this awful sound like an animal dying and I couldn't make it stop. When I covered my ears it only got louder and louder.

Georges voice came softly at my side, "Jesse, Jesse it's us, calm down."

The noise was me. I closed my mouth and heard the whimpering start.

"Is she alright?" Vicki asked tears in her voice.

I suddenly lifted off the ground and went flying into the trees. I wrapped around a tree and could feel bones snap, but even knowing they were broken wasn't enough to dull the pain of the fire rushing through my veins. I tried to struggle to my feet, but when I opened my eyes the world flipped out from under me again. I landed face first in the leaves.

Georges scooped me up in his arms and it was all I could do to not vomit on his chest. His hands slipped under my coat and made contact with the skin. I squeezed my eyes shut and smelled the honeysuckles as Georges tried to calm me with his power. I felt my heart slow, but it did nothing for the pain or the sickening dizziness.

I heard the chopper.

"She killed him." Georges.

"How bad?" Daphne.

"Dizzy, but no hallucinations yet." Vicki.

I opened my mouth, "Charles was there...Anthony...not...he's not dead."

"It's starting," Van Helsing sounded stressed.

I insisted, "He was there."

They didn't believe me.

"It's not crazy," I demanded trying to open my eyes.

I realized with a start that my eyes were open. My eyes were open and I couldn't see. But I could. I wasn't seeing the chopper. I was seeing a field. I was hallucinating. I was standing in a field. It was beautiful. I reached my hand out, but instead of the soft waves of golden wheat that I saw there was a warm sticky liquid. I looked at my hand and blood was dripping from my fingers. I screamed and tried to move but I couldn't something was holding me down. I thrashed out at what was holding me, but couldn't shake it.

"Calm *chere*," I could hear Georges whisper frantically in my ear, "It's only me, it's only me. Be calm *chere*." I stopped thrashing and the field of blood started to flicker into black. "That's it *chere*," I could hear the relief in his voice as started to caress my face, "You are hallucinating, stay with me now. I am real, stay with my voice."

I tried to stay with his voice but was pulled under again and again no matter how hard I tried.

I was in a small house in Scotland, it was beautiful in its simplicity. There were stone walls and sturdy furniture still knotted from where the maker took it from the tree. A woman was setting the table. She looked happy. The blonde vampire stepped into the room carrying a pot of stew but she wasn't a vampire now, she was just a girl. The door to the cottage opened and two men stepped inside. Unfortunately, I knew them both. One was my father. The woman ran into his arms and they embraced lovingly. They seemed happy.

The other man that stepped into the small cottage was none other than Anthony. He wasn't human, he was a full blooded vampire. I'm sure that only made him more alluring to the family. He was a handsome young man who could work the land and perhaps take over for my father when he could no longer handle the burden. Anthony smiled at the blonde, Vanessa. She blushed and smiled back, she was beautiful. You could see the wheels turning in her parents eyes. "What a match!" They sat together and began dinner. It was idyllic.

Then Anthony opened his mouth and his fangs started to elongate. Blood splattered everywhere, but Vanessa only lifted her chin and let him take her blood. My father tried to fight back but only ended up infected. Vanessa knew this was coming, this was what she had wanted, this was her plan all along. Her mother screamed and tried to run, but Anthony broke her legs with one hard kick and left her to wail under the table.

They left her mother and our father there for what seemed like days, I guess it was long enough for Vanessa to transition.

Vanessa glided back into the cottage, fully transitioned minus the all important first feeding. It was obvious who she intended for her first meal. She grabbed our father's hair and pulled his chin up, but Anthony quickly stepped in to stop her.

"He's changing," he explained, "It's dangerous to drain someone who is transitioning."

She growled and forced Anthony to look at her, "No, this is supposed to be mine and mine alone."

He stroked her hair as though he were comforting a small child, "Be content love," he cooed, "Take your mother. Your father may be of use later."

She growled, but obeyed and sunk her barely sharpened teeth into her mother's flesh. Her scream made me cringe in horror, but what was worse was the look on Anthony's face. He seemed to be feeding with her, feeding off her mother's terror and horror. He was completely enthralled, willing her to pull that last drop of blood from her mother's form. I felt myself vomit.

"Is she going to make it?" Georges sounded very far away.

"It's up to her," Van Helsing sounded old and tired.

"We can't lose her." There were tears in his voice; why would he be upset?

I tried to speak, but the movement of my lips seemed to open up a scream that was kept somewhere deep in the darkest part of my soul. The sound was horrendous and I clamped my mouth shut. I realized with a start that my blood was still burning in my veins and every atom of my body was screaming in pain. Somehow I had been able to block it out, but it was like looking at a cut, it didn't hurt until you acknowledged it was there and then the suppressed pain came back with a vengeance.

"Jesse?" It was Van Helsing, "Jesse, listen to me, you have to control it, you have to fight it. Don't let the power overtake you."

Georges cool hands were touching my face. That was weird, I felt like I was thrashing around, but his hands stayed in one place on my forehead. Maybe they weren't real. I started shuddering and pulled myself into a ball, but I'm not sure that really happened. Suddenly I was floating in this abyss that was nothing but blackness and I was watching me like I was watching a movie.

"Stay with us Jesse," They were whispering, but it wasn't real. I knew it wasn't real. It was strange, they were whispering and it was bouncing off the walls in my head. I screamed for them to stop but they just kept whispering until it became nothing but gibberish.

There was a low growl and I jumped up in this room of nothing. In the corner of this apparent emptiness was a wolf. She was beautiful and white with pointed ears that flicked towards me curiously. Her fluffy tail flicked back and forth expectantly, but she just sat there staring at me. She moved her front paws impatiently. She was waiting for something, I could see it in her amber eyes. I wasn't sure exactly what it was but the way she was looking at me made me nervous. I backed up until I felt my back hit something rough and cold. The wolf lowered her head as she looked at me. She didn't look aggressive, just incredibly interested and it was starting to freak me out. As I looked into her eyes, I felt pulled towards her. She whimpered impatiently and that sound broke whatever trance I seemed to be in.

I stood and ran. I could hear the padding of her feet behind me. My breath was coming quicker and quicker, she was gaining on me. I looked over my shoulder and could see her breath fogging in plumes into the air that suddenly seemed very cold. I spun to face her and there was nothing there. I stepped backwards and felt myself spin into the darkness, falling backwards into nothingness.

Vanessa and Anthony were brutal and ruthless and the murders were many and bloody. I understood why people passed them off as animal attacks, but what they had done was so much worse than just careless feeding. They toyed with their food, made friends with them before they ripped their throats out. They disgusted me, but I was viewing this from my father's perspective. He was watching as his daughter, his flesh and blood, massacred these innocent people. It had to be killing him. I thought they couldn't see me, I thought it was just memories, but Vanessa looked up and saw me, she met my eyes and lowered into an attack position. I backed against a wall and watched as she changed. Her body started twisting and morphing into this horrible creature. Her face elongated, pulling the skin tight across her bones. Her eyes still that startling color sunk back into her skull. Her lips pulled back to reveal a row of sickeningly protruding teeth. She was Nosferatu.

It was like a horror movie. They stalked forward. My blood was racing through my body and with it came the searing pain of my father's blood. Vanessa's mouth twisted as I screamed in pain and dropped to my knees. It took me a minute to realize the grimace was supposed to be her smile. She was enjoying this way too much. I could see the excitement in her eyes, but I couldn't move, the pain was so intense. I was just waiting for my heart to burst. I was going to die and Vanessa was nearly salivating at the thought. Anthony seemed less concerned about my fate and was instead staring lovingly at Vanessa as she circled me hungrily. I closed my eyes and felt the tears roll down my cheeks. I wasn't even sure I would feel her killing blow above the pain pulsing through my veins. That was when I heard it, the low growl of the wolf.

I slowly opened my eyes to see the white wolf I had been running from, head lowered and hackles raised. Vanessa and Anthony froze. I could feel the tension in the wolf's body as she lowered her head for the charge. I could feel her paws flex against the dirt as she got purchase on the ground for her spring. The monsters around me began to hiss and growl. It was going to be a fight to the death. I closed my eyes and listened to the initial clash of bodies. The wolf howled, Vanessa screeched in pain, Anthony bellowed in anger. I could smell the blood and hear the ripping of flesh. My breath was coming in short gasps as the battle continued, my soul ached as I heard the wolf whimper in pain and yet I still could not open my eyes. Suddenly, there was silence. Not a sound echoed through my self imposed darkness.

I waited and softly the sound of drums rose to my ears. They grew louder and louder. My mouth was dry and my breathing quick until I realized the sound I was hearing wasn't drums at all. It was my heart. I laughed nervously at my fear and slowly opened my eyes. Sitting in front of me, waiting patiently was the wolf. Her snowy fur was matted with blood, both hers and theirs. I quickly glanced around to find that the two monsters were nowhere to be found. Cautiously the wolf moved forward. She was within arms reach and looked at me with her amber eyes. In the back of my mind I knew I was in pain, but her eyes were mesmerizing. Without knowing I was doing it, I reached my hand out and could feel the warmth of her breath on my fingertips.

She growled and leaped before I could even blink. Her paws slammed into my chest, just above my heart. The contact burned as I slammed back against the ground. Colors exploded behind my eyes. I could feel the sheet beneath me and the comforter over me. It was my bed and I wasn't in pain. I took a deep breath and suddenly felt calm. I moved my hand slowly and touched the place above my heart, right where her paws had hit. I could feel the warmth, but for some reason I wasn't worried. I felt at peace.

22. Battles

I was alone laying on the bed in my room. I could see everything. Everything. I had always seen everything with more clarity, but this was different. I could see the specks of dust on the dust specks. This was strange. I didn't understand what was going on. This wasn't normal even for me. I had never been able to do anything like this before and it was quiet. I realized that I could hear leaves rustling outside without trying. I took a couple of deep breaths and could smell...Carter and Oliver.

I sprang from the bed much quicker than I anticipated and ended up with my feet tangled in the sheets and my face in the carpet. The carpet smelled like shampoo. I struggled out of the cocoon I had inadvertently made and heard the first sound that horrified me, their steps on the porch. I yelled for someone, but no one came. I paused, but then there was the knock.

I slammed through the door, literally through the door. It splintered out into the hallway and I fell flat on my face. I looked straight into Daphne's shoes. I thought about standing and was on my feet before I finished the full idea. Daphne looked frightened.

"I'm alright," I whispered.

She stepped back and shook her head. "No, your not."

I was confused, I was alive, I was fine.

"Your eyes," she whispered taking another step back.

I was going to ask her to explain, but I could hear the latch on the door being thrown. I was skidding around the corner before Daphne blinked. "No," I screamed as Vicki opened the large door. They were on the other side. They would kill her. I reached her and spun her behind me protectively. Carter and Oliver stared incredulously from the other side of the door. They both stepped forward apprehensively.

"We come in peace," Carter announced.

"Bullshit," I countered.

"Miss Childress," Van Helsing called from down the hall behind me, "if they come with no intent to harm us, we will not be the first to offer violence."

I turned to him and heard the sharp intake of breath as he, Richard and Georges saw me. Van Helsing recovered the quickest and cleared his throat authoritatively, "Mr. Moncrief, please show these gentlemen to my study." He turned to me, "Miss Childress will you and Mr. Bicks please report to the informatory."

I stalked down the hallway with Richard holding my arm as though he needed to support me. I didn't understand why they were playing this game with me, then I saw it. We walked around the corner of the corridor and in the picture of Abraham Van Helsing, I saw my eyes. They were beyond not normal, they were glowing. It was like a blue flame had replaced my irises. I stopped in the center of the hall and Richard didn't try to prod me forward. He let me stand there for what seemed like hours staring at what was supposed to be me. I thought I had looked fearsome when I had dressed to hunt, but this creature that stared back at me dwarfed that memory. It made me look like I wasn't human, at least before I had always been able to pretend. Most people hadn't been able to tell the difference. I couldn't breath, I felt my heart race, I couldn't breath.

Richard reached out and touched my hand, "Jesse?"

I looked at him and amazingly enough he kept his composure, "This isn't normal?" My voice was barely a squeak.

He smiled and shook his head, "No, even for you that isn't normal."

"Maybe it's just my sparkling personality shining through," I laughed nervously.

The look on his face said it all, totally failed attempt at humor. He was worried and that wasn't good. Van Helsing had even been shocked and there had to be little to nothing he hadn't seen or dealt with before. I shuddered at the thought that I might actually be the monster I had always feared I would become.

When we reached the infirmary, Daphne was sitting in her chair with a look of absolute shock on her face. Richard ran to her side quickly and she collapsed into his arms sobbing hysterically. I had a pretty good idea why she was so upset, so I stepped back into the hallway to not frighten her any further.

"What is she?" Daphne asked, her voice quivering.

Richard looked at me over her shoulder and answered, "I don't know."

I looked up at them and it was then that I realized I was seeing things differently. I could see the warmth on their skin. I backed away further. I wasn't sure what was going on so I ran down the checklist in my mind. I wasn't thirsty, in fact the burn I had become so used to was practically nonexistent. At least there was an upside to this strange change I was experiencing. I could feel all of my appendages. I was breathing. I closed my eyes and listened hard for my heartbeat, there it was, there was something else.

I heard Georges footsteps on the carpet. He was moving slowly towards me, trying hard not to startle me. I looked in his direction. I could see the warmth in his skin as well. That wasn't right. His skin was cool to the touch, but he was glowing like they were. I needed to touch him, make sure that he was real and that he wasn't suddenly human again. I reached out towards him, too quickly, he flinched away.

"Sorry," I whispered, dropping my hand to my side.

He smiled, "It's alright, your eyes just have us all a little worried."

I laughed out loud, "Tell me about it."

Richard came out cautiously, "Is everything alright."

I nodded, "Is Daphne?"

Her voice came out weakly, "Yeah, you can come on in."

I walked in with Richard and Georges at my flanks. I turned back at them too quickly again and the glow that was on their skin became more pronounced. I made a point to turn slowly back towards Daphne so as to not frighten her. Her glow was different. It was softer than theirs, and almost a yellow-orange color. I stared at her for a moment and I could see her muscles tense and hear her inaudible intake of breath. I was fascinated by the way it stirred the dust molecules in the room. I heard Georges move up beside me. He reached out slowly and took my hand.

"What are you seeing?" He asked me like I was insane.

I pulled my hand back insulted, "The dust that's moving as she breathes. I couldn't see that before." I muttered under my breath, "I'm not crazy."

Richard stepped forward, "What do you mean that you couldn't see that before?"

"I didn't see this much detail before. I can also hear more than I could before."

Daphne's glow diminished slightly and she turned into the clinical doctor she needed to be, "Describe it in more detail if you wouldn't mind."

I nodded, "Shouldn't someone go back to Van Helsing and make sure he's alright?"

Georges cleared his throat nervously, "Um, Lilith is with him."

I felt the power trickle across my skin, "Lilith?"

The glow that surrounded Georges and Richard intensified tenfold. Daphne stepped away from me as if instinctively. I took a deep breath through my nose and could still smell them there. Van Helsing's heartbeat was heightened, as soon as I knew where he was it was easy to pinpoint every change in his breathing, his heart, his sweat. He was scared, I could smell it on him. My eyes widened and as I lunged for the door both Richard and Georges tackled me to the ground. I was caught in a tangle of limbs as I tried to get up and get to him. They grabbed at my arms and legs, screamed for me to stay down, but I couldn't let Van Helsing be hurt. Not by those traitors.

I listened beyond my current struggle, beyond the panic in the boys' voices and concentrated on Van Helsing. His voice barely wavered as he spoke. They were talking about The Marquis, he wanted something. Van Helsing was telling them no. They couldn't have it. The Marquis couldn't have what he wanted. What did he want? I couldn't tell. I needed to get closer, but they wouldn't let me up. Let. Me. Up. Georges and Richard flew backwards and I scrambled out into the hallway. Georges was behind me, I could hear him, Richard was not far behind that. I stopped dead in the middle of the hallway. Georges slammed into me in the hallway. We both tumbled to the floor. I looked up and saw only the black heels of Lilith.

"Don't you normally save that for the bedroom, Georges?" she sneered.

I stood, throwing Georges to the ground behind me, "You left Van Helsing with them?" I roared the words at her and for a moment the breath left her body.

"I'm fine," Van Helsing whispered stepping out of the room behind her.

I was so relieved he was alright. I could feel the tears start to creep down my cheeks and I sank to my knees. I could feel the power in me recede. I was suddenly tired, like an adrenaline dump. I looked at Van Helsing. He was glowing. Lilith was positively on fire. I looked at my hands, but there was nothing. I wasn't glowing. I looked at Van Helsing and he was on his knees in front of me, staring into my eyes. He was trying to read my thoughts, but his brows were furrowed. He didn't understand why he couldn't read me. Wait. He couldn't read me? Why couldn't he read me? His glow was fluctuating, it was getting stronger the more it seemed he tried to concentrate on me.

"Why is everyone glowing?" I whispered wiping the tears from my face.

"Glowing?" Van Helsing asked, his voice quivering slightly.

"Yes," I answered with a smile, "As if you didn't already think that I was losing it. I can see you glowing."

Van Helsing's face relaxed, "Am I glowing now?"

I shook my head as his glow diminished, "It's gone now." He concentrated again. "Oh, it's back now."

He laughed, "Look at Mr. Moncrief."

I turned to look at Georges who was towering above me, "It's dull. I can tell the glow is there, but it's subdued somehow."

Van Helsing looked at Georges, "Mr. Moncrief, would you be so kind as to use your powers on Mr. Bicks."

Richard stepped up and let Georges put his hand on his neck. I watched as Richard's beyond intense expression relaxed and the corners of his mouth twitched up. Georges glow intensified and I could smell the honeysuckle. It was then that it dawned on me, "You have got to be kidding."

Van Helsing chuckled, "I think you know what you are seeing now."

"I'm seeing their powers?"

Van Helsing nodded.

"So that would explain why they are all different colors?"

Van Helsing held out his hand for Georges to help him up, he looked down on me and shook his head, "I don't know, but I know someone who will."

I stood slowly. “My father,” I whispered, “That's why he kept my father. He could see.” Then I remembered. When I saw my father it was dark. He only came to my mother at night. I assumed that he was photosensitive, but his eyes glowed. I walked past everyone, this time no one moved to stop me. I laid my hand on the heavy wooden doors and slowly pushed them open, out to the light.

I woke up in Daphne's office, strapped to a bed. I laid there staring into the darkness. I could still see the dust and the scars in the stone walls, but I remembered everything that had happened. I started to cry. I had taken for granted every day I walked in the sun, every time I laid in the grass and felt the warmth of the sun on my skin. I closed my eyes and sobbed silently in the darkness. The pain in my head had been so intense there was no way that I could possibly spend any amount of time in the light. Who was I kidding, there was no way I could be seen by humans with eyes that glowed like fireballs. A soft cry broke through my lips.

“Are you still in pain?” It was Daphne's voice, soft and frightened.

I sniffled and tried to clear my throat, “No,” I whispered, “I'm alright, you can unstrap me now.”

She snorted, “You already did that.”

I looked down and realized that I had indeed unstrapped myself from the bed. “I didn't mean to. I didn't want to scare you guys anymore than I already have.”

“Really?” It was Lilith at the door. “Because your little suicide stunt was really relaxing for everyone.”

I stood, “Lilly, right?”

She glared, “It's Lilith.”

“Oh, I'm sorry, I guess you just weren't important enough for me to remember.”

She was in my face in a nanosecond, “I will rip you apart, I don't care what Van Helsing says.”

I smiled, “I can see your power is rising up to meet your temper, but honestly, if you were going to attack me you would have done it instead of standing there talking about it. Kind of like when you shot me.”

Georges stepped into the room and ordered Daphne into the hallway. His glow was intense.

I smiled, "Here to save your girlfriend, Georges."

He took an audible breath, "Jesse, just take a step back and take a deep breath."

I laughed and pushed past Lilith, "Or you'll what Georges?" I looked back at Lilith, "She's the one who got in my face and the one who SHOT ME, but your right...I mean I can't possibly be trusted now."

"That's not what I meant."

"But it is." I walked past him into the hallway. Daphne was nowhere to be seen. "Tell Daphne I'm sorry, I didn't mean to frighten her." I turned to the pair in the room. Lilith moved up and put her hand possessively on Georges shoulder. "As for the two of you," I smiled, "You both can go to hell."

I walked down the hallway towards the front doors, it was night now, I could sense it. I needed to run. I needed to hunt and I needed to be able to control whatever this was inside me. The doors opened before I reached them. I could get used to this.

23. What now?

Richard and Van Helsing stood in my doorway. I hadn't slept. I hadn't felt tired. This wasn't right. I could sense the morning light. It was almost like I could smell the light, the atmosphere changed. These new senses were interesting, but I was already beginning to miss the sun. Still, I did my best to smile at the pair of them. Van Helsing wasn't glowing at all, but Richard was almost bright enough to hurt my eyes.

"Why the high alert there Richard?" I asked uninterestedly.

He laughed, "It was your first night, we weren't sure how you would do." His glow relaxed.

"I'm fine," I sighed realizing for the first time that we were missing someone, "How is Vicki?"

Van Helsing pursed his lips, "Safe."

I smirked, "Away from me."

He nodded, "We can't be sure you're safe and I can't risk my niece."

I stretched and walked towards them, "I don't blame you. I wouldn't risk it either."

Richard held out his hand to stop me. I obliged, it's not like I could really go anywhere anyway. He cautiously stepped forward and leaned towards me. He nosed at me and took a deep breath. His power fluctuated and he took another deep breath, closer, at my neck. I tensed and the power trickled down my arms. I could almost feel the hair on Richard's neck raise up as he backed away. He looked at Van Helsing and cleared his throat. "There is something really wrong."

I snorted, "Thank you Captain Obvious."

"No," he shook his head, "Worse than we thought."

I crossed my arm and waited.

He cleared his throat again, "You smell like a Lycan."

I was confused, "Like a werewolf?"

He nodded.

I looked at Van Helsing, "What does that mean?"

"That's not supposed to happen."

"Why not?"

Van Helsing closed his eyes and took a deep breath, "Have a seat my dear." We both sat on the bed and Richard took a protective stance over Van Helsing's shoulder. "We were all pleased that you survived your ordeal with your father's blood, but we were afraid the blood was tainted and it seems that we were right."

"I don't understand."

"Werewolves and Vampires have never been compatible as species. There were wars between the species for centuries before a grudging regard for each other was established. There were experiments, atrocities where scientists from each species tried to interbreed the species, but the offspring never survived, at least not for very long. The blood between Vampires and Werewolves does not blend. It's like giving someone who is O negative an AB positive blood transfusion. The body should reject it." He paused and looked at me, "Killing the host."

I stood up and started pacing, "Why not me?"

Van Helsing stood, "I don't know."

I could feel my blood start to pump quicker and quicker, my breath was short. Richard could sense my stress and started to move Van Helsing towards the door. "Richard," my voice broke, "get Van Helsing out of here, I can't control it."

He moved quickly and the door was closed before I knew it. I sank to the floor and pulled my knees to my chest. I concentrated on the power, tried to pull it back, but it refused to obey. I could feel the things lifting off the floor. My eyes were squeezed shut, not that it mattered. I could see the things just as clearly as if I had had my eyes open. I heard the door open and could smell Richard as he came in. I could hear the clicks on the floor. He had transitioned. He thought I was that dangerous. The nightstand exploded in mid air. I looked up angrily, but all that Richard did was sit back on his haunches and look at me curiously.

The expression on his hairy face made me smile. I could feel the power start to subside and the furniture started to settle back down. The door started to creep open, it was Georges. The lamp that had been on the now destroyed nightstand shattered into the doorjamb. Richard jumped to his feet and stuck his nose out at me. I just smiled and shrugged as all of the other furniture settled back into place. Richard just shook his head and walked out the door.

I stood slowly and felt out my powers, they were going to behave for the moment, "It's safe for the moment."

Georges slowly pushed the door open, "Are you sure?"

Angry pink lines from the shattered glass were healing over on his face, "Sorry about that, I can't really control it when I get upset."

"So I see," he grumbled feeling the lines on his cheek.

I smiled, "Was there something you needed?"

He closed the door ominously, "What was the deal last night?"

I sat on my bed and looked expectantly towards him.

"Don't sit there and pretend you don't know what I'm talking about."

I shrugged, "All I remember from last night was your girl getting in my face because she thought I should be afraid of her and you jumped in to defend her honor. I must say it was quite admirable of you."

I could see his jaw flexing as he tried to keep his temper in check, "So you told me to go to hell because you admired me so much."

I jumped up lightly, "If I remember correctly, I told the both of you to go to hell."

He huffed, "Van Helsing let her come back."

"She shot me," I said calmly, "Don't expect me to welcome her with open arms."

"You broke her body against a wall."

"Did you forget the whole, she attacked me first thing?"

He shook his head, "No, which is why I've been trying to keep you apart."

"I understand your need to protect her." I walked towards my door, "Now, I'm going to go to the training room to attempt to control this...thing. If you would please see yourself out."

I left him standing in my room, but he didn't follow thankfully. I didn't know why I was suddenly so hostile towards him. I knew that he had slept with Lilith, the first time I met her I knew that. She had been far too angry at my mere existence for just a friend. I had no claim on him, I had no reason to think that he had any feelings for me. I had no reason to be angry at him and honestly, I was a little eradic lately and he had obviously known her for quite a while longer so I shouldn't be hurt that he trusted her and not me. But logic aside, I was pissed.

I went into the training room and sat in the middle of the floor. I stared up into the ceiling. I was angry and the power was swirling around in me with my emotional state. I tried some yoga and deep breathing and felt myself calm down. My heart rate slowed and the power settled. I sat there for nearly an hour just thinking about this strange turn of events. Finally, there was a soft knock on the training room door, it was Richard and Daphne. I didn't even have to look anymore, I just had to concentrate and the image became clear to me.

“It's safe,” I called out softly.

“Good,” Daphne called coming in softly, “I have some questions to ask you and...” she hesitated, “A blood sample to take.”

I rolled up my sleeves, “Alright, take whatever you need.”

Richard stepped up, “Would it be alright if I hold you down, just in case?”

I laid back on the mat and spread my arms out to my sides, “If it'll make you two feel any better.”

Richard cautiously moved forward and clamped his hands down over my wrists. Georges stepped in behind them, “I'll take her legs.”

I looked up at Richard who was hovering inches above my face, “Really?”

He shrugged, “Better safe?”

I growled and stretched my legs out, “If you must.”

I flinched at Georges' cold fingers on my ankles. He smiled, “Just relax.”

“Right,” I grumbled, “Although, thank you for not being on high alert. You're all much more relaxed around me today. Even after my shattered bedroom furniture.”

Richard smiled, “You knew you weren't going to be able to control it and you reacted appropriately.”

Daphne pulled out a much larger than necessary needle, “Now, this may hurt slightly, but just remember to remain calm. I'll be done in just a minute.”

I nodded and closed my eyes. I felt the needle go into my arm and then the cold fingers around my ankles warmed. I looked down at Georges to see that he was using his powers. I could feel the heat and smell the honeysuckle, but I didn't feel any differently. He was concentrating very intently on projecting something into me, but I wasn't feeling it. Daphne pulled the needle out and hurried away to her office.

The boys let me up, but I grabbed Georges arm, "What were you trying to make me feel?"

He looked confused, "Calm."

"I didn't feel it." I looked between him and Richard, but they both looked lost and confused.

Georges reached out and touched my cheek, "Tired," he said as his power rose to meet me.

I just stared at him, nothing was happening. I could smell the honeysuckle, but nothing was happening. I pressed his hand to my cheek firmly, but again there was nothing. I shook my head. Richard reached out and took Georges wrist as if to check and make sure that Georges powers weren't weaker than normal. Almost instantly his eyelids drooped and his knees sagged. I reached out and caught him before he fell. He was coming out of it groggily, but it was clear that Georges powers were not diminished in the least.

"What's this?" Lilith's voice was shrill in the doorway. "You getting freaky without me Georges."

I hadn't realized that Georges was still touching my face, I pushed his hand off roughly and helped Richard to his feet, "You alright, pup?"

Richard growled, "At least we know it's definitely you."

I laughed, "Like that was ever in doubt."

Lilith grimaced in the doorway, "How cute. Now if you're done Georges, I believe we have some..."she smiled seductively, for my benefit I'm sure, "business to discuss."

I snorted, "Run along Georges, I've got Richard." I leaned towards him as though I had a secret to tell him, "Besides, she may not be in heat later."

Lilith flew at me, but I was far too quick and a simple sidestep left her beyond me. "Bitch," she spat lowering her head for an attack.

"Look pet," I hissed, "As I said before, I've dealt with people like you my entire life and you don't frighten me. You run around here like a bitch in heat after Georges trying to show your dominance, I'm surprised you haven't marked him the traditional way for a dog." She lunged at me, but I knocked her back without even putting a finger on her. "No, you will listen to me. The moment I met you, you tried to assert your dominance and I broke you. Do NOT try me." I glanced at Georges who was smirking slightly, "As far as your love interest is concerned, I don't know why you are even worried about me. Women always make the same stupid conclusion with men. If he is yours then he knows it and if he strays it is his fault, not the woman's. I didn't even know you existed until you pulled out your bitchy claws, so take it up with him."

She pulled herself to her feet, "Well consider this your notice that he is taken."

"Shut up Lilith," Georges growled, "You have no claim on me."

She was about to retort, but I didn't care to listen to their lover's quarrel. Richard, fully recovered, and I both excused ourselves to Daphne's office to see what she had found out about my blood.

It seemed that Van Helsing had the same thought. We walked in to find him and Daphne bent close to the microscope analyzing a slide of my blood. They both looked perplexed.

"Well at least I know your looking at my blood," I laughed.

"Usually the thing that makes us perplexed," Daphne admitted.

"So what about my blood this time?" I asked moving closer.

Daphne went all clinical on me, "Well, you see vampire blood and werewolf blood shouldn't be able to mix. Each blood type considers the other to be a virus and attacks it." I nodded and she motioned for me to look through the microscope, "Look at the different cells in your blood."

"Some look like half moons and some are full circles and some look like shriveled up circles."

She nodded, "The full circles are human blood cells, your original human blood. The shriveled up circles are vampire blood. When you were born, your genetic make-up allowed for these two cells to coexist without one taking over the other." She switched slides and motioned for me to look again. "This slide is your father's blood."

"How did you get my father's blood?"

Daphne smirked, "You weren't exactly neat and tidy when you drained him. We found you very soon afterwards and the blood you had spilled wasn't dry yet."

I laughed, "Next time, I'll try to be a little more aware of my dining etiquette."

I looked through the microscope, "Do you see the half moons and shriveled circles?" I nodded. "Well the half moons are werewolf blood. Look at how much of the circles and moons are missing, they were deteriorating each other." I looked at Daphne expectantly. "You ingested more vampire blood and that wouldn't hurt you except that you drained him dry and transferred his powers. The nearest I can figure is that the werewolf blood that should have killed you was apparently absorbed by your human cells."

"Shouldn't they still try to attack one another?"

"I think because your blood was already conditioned to coexist it did not have the normal reaction."

"So, I'm alright?"

Van Helsing nodded, "Physically you should be fine. We are a little worried about you emotionally and psychologically still."

I paused, "Will I transition now?"

Richard stepped up to answer, "Not necessarily. Some people are carriers of the gene, but they never actually transition. In two weeks is the full moon and that will be when we can be sure that you will or won't transition."

I nodded, "Will I be able to walk in daylight again?"

"We are working on a solution to that problem," Van Helsing assured me.

"And the reason people glow different colors?"

Van Helsing patted my hand, "I have a friend who is on his way to try and explain it to you. Hopefully he can figure out the nuances of your new powers."

"What about the new addition to our team?" I asked quietly.

Van Helsing cleared his throat, “I have my reasons for putting her on the team temporarily.”

“But she tried to kill me, actually tried to kill me.”

He nodded, “I know, but suffice it to say that we need to keep her close.”

I nodded, wasn't happy about it though. The sun was still high in the sky, I could sense it. I couldn't leave. So, I wandered through the corridors to Van Helsing's library and picked a book out of the stacks. I wasn't even paying attention to what it was, I just wanted to get lost in something. I opened it up to find the words, “It is a truth universally acknowledged...” I couldn't help but laugh. This love story had always been my favorite. Only there was no Mr. Darcy in my story, just one creature after another after another. None of them worthy of that title of utter romance. So, I curled up on the Velveteen chaise and lost myself in a century long past and out of my reach.

24. Me time

The day waned and I hadn't been disturbed, not by people, not by hunger, not by sleep. It worried me that suddenly and for no apparent reason I no longer needed to eat or sleep. I walked out into the corridor and listened, felt out for movement. There was some down the hall, but it was minimal. Daphne and Richard were walking out into the evening air, a romantic rendezvous. I smiled and walked to my room, I figured it was time to give Forbidden Desires another chance.

At least I got to choose my own outfit this time. A pair of jeans, a tank top and leather jacket complete with pair of sunglasses. I would fit right in. I walked out into the night and smelled the air. This was a new perk, I could smell the club, the heat of the bodies pressed together, the perfume and cologne all mixing in the night air. I made my way to it's arms letting the scent lead the way.

Jackson stood out in front of the club in all of his theriomorphic glory. His fangs seemed a little more prominent than before, but his muscles hadn't changed at all. I stepped out of the woods and he immediately tracked me, showing all of his teeth in a big goofy smile as I walked up.

"We were all more than a little worried about you," he smiled.

I laughed, "What's to worry about?"

"I heard your eyes are wicked."

"You heard right," I slipped my glasses down on my nose.

He smiled, "Damn they weren't kidding."

I walked past him, "I need to know where you get your intel."

He laughed as the doors swung shut behind me. The music surrounded me instantly. The release was exquisite, no one watching me like a ticking time bomb. I relaxed and took a seat at the bar. The bartender was human, cute, but with a slight glow unlike any of the others I had seen. He brought me an amaretto sour without me even needing to ask. I raised an eyebrow at him, but he just smiled knowingly and motioned up towards Van Helsing's office. I turned to see the old man standing on his balcony and motioned towards him with my glass. He smiled and motioned back with his wine glass as he went back into his office. At least he wasn't worried about me being in public. Maybe he should have been, that bartender was looking rather tasty and he just kept looking back at me.

"You're Jesse," he said, "I've heard about you."

I laughed, "You guys gossip more than any women I've ever been around."

He smiled, "So you talked to Jackson."

"Yeah," I laughed, "So what else do you two know about?"

He leaned in, "I heard that you beat the shit out of Lilith."

"Wow," I sipped my drink, "There was an altercation and really it was all because she thought I wanted Georges for myself."

He smirked, "I think all the ladies would like to have Georges for themselves."

I leaned towards him, "Too much drama."

"Really? You're not interested in the irresistible Mr. Moncrief."

I smiled, "Have you seen his entourage? No thank you."

He sighed, "That's really good to know."

I smiled, "I think your other patrons have need of your drink making services."

He glanced around and shrugged, "I've been off for the last five minutes."

He got me another drink and then came to the other side of the counter and sat with me. He was definitely a cute young man. His shirt was slim cut. Just enough to see all the definition of his stomach. His smile was wide and guileless, he looked so incredible it had to be a trap. He ran his hand through his shaggy blonde hair and laughed, "So why don't you trust me?"

I smiled, "I don't even know your name,"

"Riley."

"Well, Riley. There are a lot of things going on here that I don't think you're privy to."

"Why don't you tell me?"

"Not my place."

"Well what can you tell me about you?"

"Not nearly as much as I could," Georges voice was right behind me.

“Riley,” I said politely, “ I'm sure you know Captain Buzzkill.”

Georges chuckled and held his hand out to me, “Please, Jesse.”

I looked at Riley, but he only smiled, “Maybe next time Jesse.” He walked out and I liked the view.

Georges' fingers traced across the back of my hand, “Please Jesse.” He looked so intense that I took his hand and let him lead me out onto the dance floor. Of course he had the perfect timing to lead me out to the beginning of a slow song. He draped my hand across his shoulder and slid his hand around my waist, under the jacket. My heart skipped a beat. It wasn't power, it was just him and I couldn't help my reaction to him.

“What do you want?” I asked as his body moved against me.

“Do you really have to ask, Jesse.” The way he whispered my name made my knees melt.

“I thought we already talked about all of this. We decided that we were friends and besides, I'm not about to keep fighting with Lilith.” I smiled as he dipped me back, “Especially since all I'm getting is a headache and no benefits.”

His lips brushed my jawbone, “It doesn't have to be like this.”

He spun me so that my back was to him, “It does. I mean you can't trust me anyway, right?”

“I do trust you,” His hands moved down my legs, “You don't trust yourself.”

“Well, that's the truth.” He spun me around to face him again.

“Why not?” He demanded, “You're stronger than you think you are.”

I sighed, “Not strong enough.”

“Let me help you,” he whispered longingly, “I would be yours completely.”

I leaned back to look him in the eye, “But I could never be yours. I won't belong to you. I'm not that person. You wouldn't be happy with me.”

“Don't you think we should give that a chance?”

I noticed Lilith standing in the corner, "She doesn't think so." I walked away and back into the night. So much for a night out with no drama. I could feel Lilith and Georges staring into my back. Like I didn't have anything else to worry about.

Jackson was at the front door, entertaining a few young ladies with the way he could make his muscles jump. He was smiling, showing the canines to full advantage. I smirked and patted him on the arm as I left, "Have a good night, Jackson."

He followed me out of hearing range of the young women, "Hey Jesse, wait up."

I turned to him.

"You sure you're alright?"

I smiled, "Yeah, I'll be fine, why?"

"You seemed a little upset."

I snorted, "For once I'd like to have a drink without anyone watching me like I'm about to burst into flames."

He slapped his business card into my hand, "Call me before you come and I'll let you know if anyone's here."

I laughed and smacked his arm, "You're a good man Jackson. I'm going to take you up on that."

I walked back into the woods, but my mind wasn't right enough to go home. I wandered in the night listening intently to the night sounds. The crickets, the rustling of the trees, the sounds of the night birds. They were soothing. I walked through the trees and took in the scents. I explored the woods for hours until I finally wandered to the cliff and sat on the precipice. I loved the sounds of the waves crashing against the rocks, so powerful and yet so beautiful. So lolling gentle when it wants to be, so vicious when it suits. I adored my little spot in the woods. I closed my eyes and just felt the waves moving beneath me.

I was lost in the movement of the ocean and then, just to interrupt my me time, I could feel them approaching through the woods, quick footsteps. Barely at a walk, just below a run. It was Richard and Georges, at least Georges had the good sense not to show up alone. They both quieted all the night sounds.

I sighed softly, "You're frightening the wildlife."

They both ran past me and plummeted into the openness. "Sorry," they yelled as they fell.

I watched them get smaller and then swallowed by the waves.

Daphne and Lilith walked out of the tree line and stood on either side of me. “Men,” Daphne muttered, but there was a smile in her voice.

“You want to join them?” I asked holding my hand up to her. She took it with a smile, I looked up at Lilith, if I was going to be forced to deal with her it might as well be as painless as possible, but she just growled and looked the other way. “Ready then?” Daphne nodded and we pushed off from the cliff. I slowed our decent just enough that we wouldn't hurt ourselves, but I could see her exhilaration in her smile. I whispered, “Hold your breath,” just before the water closed over our heads. We came up laughing.

Richard came up beneath us and grabbed Daphne around the waist, throwing her up into the air. She screamed happily and splashed down a few feet from us. It was fun, just playing. I laid on my back and just floated for a moment. Daphne swam up from beneath me and grabbed my waist pulling me under. I hadn't seen it coming and must have swallowed a good gallon of water which came sputtering out as I broke the surface in giggling gags. I felt like a kid.

We splashed each other and dunked each other beneath the waves and laughed so hard that my sides hurt. Richard and Daphne were so in love, you could see it the way they played. Her eyes were glowing too, just in a different way. I smiled and realized that George was staring at me. I smiled back at him right before I dunked him under the waves. He pulled me under with him and locked his arms around me. We came back up splashing each other. For a moment it was perfect and I could forget all of the bad that was surrounding us. Unfortunately we had forgotten one very important person.

Lilith came splashing down a moment later. It was no longer just good fun. It became a contest the minute she met the water. She came up and attached herself to Georges almost completely. He pushed her away and both Daphne and Richard looked uncomfortable. I swam up to them and whispered, “Is it time for the kids to get out of the pool?” Daphne nodded.

I pushed back and floated for a second, “Do you want spin dry as you go up?”

Richard laughed and shook his head, “Don't even think about it.”

“Fine,” I sighed, “I'll send you up the regular way.”

Richard reached out and took Daphne's hand and I concentrated on lifting them up. I laid back and waited until I could feel their feet touching the rock. I turned my head towards the other two, that hadn't tired me at all. “You want a ride or are you two going to do the freaky vampire climbing the rock face thing.”

Lilith growled, “I think we'll just hang out down here for a little while.”

Georges looked at me, “I'll take the lift.”

I smiled and held out my hand. He took it and I closed my eyes. I concentrated on pulling the two of us up. I didn't think that it would be hard, but I was wrong. I felt the ground close and suddenly started to falter. The vision in my head wasn't clear anymore. I opened my eyes and dropped us both to the ground rather unceremoniously. The world spun for a moment and I gripped Georges hand for support.

His arm was around my shoulder in a blink, “Are you alright?”

I nodded, “Just a little dizzy.”

Daphne took my face in her hands, “Has this been happening often?”

I smiled and patted her hand, “No, this is a new development, but I may just need sleep?”

She looked concerned.

“I didn't sleep at all last night.”

“Richard,” she commanded, “Get her back to her room and make sure she sleeps.”

I smiled at Richard, “Are you gonna hit me in the head with a two by four?”

He laughed, “Maybe if you ask nicely.”

Georges moved to follow, but Daphne detained him, “I need to talk to you, Richard take her home.”

Richard took me by the elbow and led me back towards my bed. The more I thought about it, the more sleepy I became. I wondered idly at what Daphne was saying to Georges. Then I just wanted to sleep. As soon as Richard opened my door, I climbed beneath the sheets and was gone within seconds.

I knew I wasn't alone the minute I woke up. Georges was in the darkness as was Daphne and Richard. I almost laughed. "Was I having a slumber party and no one told me?"

"We didn't think you should sleep alone," Daphne explained.

I looked to see her and Richard curled up together on the small couch on the other side of the room. "I appreciate the concern, but honestly you couldn't have just asked?"

Georges smiled, "It was my idea, but they wouldn't trust me to be here alone."

I laughed, "I wouldn't trust you to be here alone either if we're being honest with each other."

He smiled, but held his tongue.

Daphne smiled, "I wouldn't trust him either."

Richard growled playfully and pulled Daphne closer to him.

"You want my bed?" I asked stretching out.

Daphne looked at me strangely, "No" she whispered, "you need more sleep."

I shook my head, "No, I feel fine."

"Good," Van Helsing announced from the corridor, "Because I have a friend you need to meet."

24. Messages, Moons, and Men

The old man was standing in the middle of the training mat. He was wearing a blanket. It was embroidered in vivid reds, oranges, and yellows. He had it fastened somewhere beneath his long gray hair and it reached to the floor where it hung in a puddle. He smelled strange, like dirt and saltwater mixed together. Van Helsing stood at my side.

He opened his mouth to introduce me, but the old man held up his hand to stop Van Helsing. "She is strong," he said appreciatively, "Much stronger than you led me to believe."

Van Helsing smiled, "That's why we needed your help."

The old man was pulsing, "Indeed you do for she is fragile as well."

"My name is Jesse," I announced.

The old man turned, "I see that."

He was blind. His facial features were decidedly Native American, but above his high cheekbones were eyes glassed over as if someone had spilled milk in them. He laughed at my silence, "I do not need to see to know the look on your face."

I dropped my eyes, "I apologize, sir, I just expected..."

He laughed, "Don't worry my dear everyone does." I smiled. "She does light up the room."

I looked up and Van Helsing was smiling at me, "Indeed she does."

The old man motioned for me to come forward and I obeyed. He reached out and touched my face I closed my eyes as his fingers moved over my features. He felt my nose and eyes and chuckled as he felt my mouth, "How often do you smile, Jesse."

My lips twitched, "Often."

He nodded, "I can tell."

He held his hand out to me, "My name is Thomas."

I shook his hand, "Nice to meet you Thomas."

"Likewise, Jesse." He sat on the floor so I followed suit. He reached his hands out towards me, but didn't touch me. It was strange, but it looked like he was feeling the air around me. He smiled as though he felt my confusion. "You are right to be confused and I can feel it."

"How?"

"I am blind, but I can see. I can sense your power. You are far more powerful than even you know, but you are not in control of it."

"Tell me something I don't know," I joked.

He smiled, "Do you know what you can do?"

I shook my head and then realized the mistake and answered, "No."

"You can move objects with your mind which you know, but what you do not know is how much you can do. You are still new to this power, so it tires and weakens you. You do not know how to train with it, how to make it stronger."

"Why was I so tired after using the powers yesterday?"

"You still have a human element to you and your body was not used to the strain you were putting on it."

"I saw my blood under the microscope and I saw the human blood in me."

"You are indeed unique because you have two of the most powerful beings coursing through your blood and the most frail as well. You have to balance your demons." He took a deep breath and then commanded, "Tell me everything you saw while you were unconscious."

I hung my head, "I have no idea what was real and what wasn't."

He patted the back of my hand, "Why don't you start at the very beginning and we'll go from there."

I started at the part where I thought I saw Anthony and Vanessa in the woods and continued through the crazy jumble of memories and nightmares. Thomas agreed with everyone else's assessment of my experience. Everyone thought I had hallucinated the two vampires, but I wasn't so sure. Still no one seemed too interested in my theories about Anthony. But when I got to the part about the wolf, Thomas seemed to gain interest.

"The wolf would be your spirit animal, but it symbolizes many things. Sometimes it symbolizes strength which I think could be one reason why she presented herself to you, another possibility could be the symbolization of death and rebirth. You died as your old self and were reborn as the creature you are now."

I nodded, "Why did people start glowing?"

"Glowing?"

"Yes, people started glowing after I woke up. They aren't all the same color though."

"What do you know about your father and his abilities?"

"Nothing really," I admitted. "I know that his eyes glowed like mine do and that he was photosensitive."

Thomas laughed, "Your father was photosensitive because of what he passed on to you."

"Freaky eyes?"

"No, the ability to see. People are glowing because you are seeing their powers. I would think the different colors are the different types of powers."

"You could see my powers without sight, how did you know what each power was?"

"For me it isn't color, it's taste. You taste a certain way and that means I can tell what you can do."

I nodded. This strange man seemed to understand what was going on with me so I was willing to give him a chance. I just hoped I wasn't falling for a fool's trap.

The days past with training unlike any I had ever done before. I was exhausted after every session. I would fall into a deep sleep every night and I would dream of my mother. She was trying to tell me something in every dream I had. Just as I would feel myself waking up she would tell me "trean." I didn't know what that meant, but I didn't tell Thomas about it. It was my mother and she was my secret.

Thomas was teaching me to "taste" the power coming from others. Richard was the first guinea pig.

"But I can see the color," I complained, "Why do I have to 'taste' it?" The quotation fingers were lost on Thomas.

"I will teach you to pull the power within yourself so that it does not cloud your vision, and then you will need to taste the power of your enemies. Your eyes are a dead giveaway that you are nothing normal."

"That's awesome, thank you."

He laughed, "You are not normal and you know it as do we all."

"Fine," I growled, "Then here we go." I walked up to Richard.

He stood there awkwardly, "What are you going to do?"

I shrugged, "Hell if I know."

Thomas groaned. "Close your eyes." I did. "Lean towards him." I did. "Now breath in through your nose and let the taste roll around on your tongue for a moment." I did. "Now what do you taste?"

"Um...I don't know. He smells like a warm dog."

"That is not what you are supposed to be concentrating on." I rolled my eyes. "I may not be able to see, but I saw that."

I sighed, "I'll try again."

I leaned towards him again and smelled Richard's neck. I closed my eyes and took a deep breath through my nose. I concentrated on rolling the smell in my mouth like a fine wine. It tasted kind of nutty. I started laughing, I couldn't help it.

"What?" Richard asked indignantly.

"You smell like a nut."

Thomas pinched his nose between his fingers and groaned in exasperation.

"No," I insisted, "I'm serious. He tastes nutty, like the woods."

Thomas just threw up his hands and walked away. However, he was not finished. Many of the wait staff of Forbidden Desires were brought in to see if they also had the same tastes and colors. It was a long and arduous process, but fruitful. I had a notebook full of powers and their tastes and colors and scents. Yet the most important thing that Thomas was teaching me was how to pull the power into myself, how to turn it off so to speak.

He told me to visualize a containment system. I chose a steamer trunk with many little compartments to hold as much or as little of my power as I wanted. With more training I became more and more comfortable with locking away my bits and pieces. I was getting so good at it that I was able to go out into the daylight for almost an hour at a time, but nothing could stop the dreams of my mother.

That word continued to roll through my head until I finally made my way to Van Helsing's library to ask him, uninterestedly of course, what he thought. He didn't know what it meant but of course wanted to know where I had heard it. I just brushed it off as something I had heard in passing somewhere years ago. He seemed to buy that explanation and did tell me that he thought it might be Celtic in origin. Of course he did have a Celtic to English dictionary, but for some odd reason, Georges had it.

I knocked on his door and he opened it in nothing but a tight pair of jeans. He was beautiful, utterly amazing. I did my best to control my facial expression and not drool.

He smiled impishly, “You know you can have all the power in the world, but I can still hear your heart.”

I rolled my eyes. “I'm not here for you, I'm here for a book.”

“You'd rather have a book than all this?” He flexed his muscles and flashed his best come hither smile.

I laughed, “The book there hotshot. It's the Celtic to English dictionary.”

He stepped back from the door, “Entree vous mademoiselle.”

Against my better judgment I willingly walked through the door. I looked around the room and could barely keep the surprise from my face. It was nothing like I had expected. Part of me was looking for the heart shaped bed, disco ball, and Barry Mantalo. Instead, the walls had been left natural, only a few iron sconces dotted them. A large oak armoire sat on a deep red rug that ran under the California King and the few short bookshelves that were overstuffed with leather bound novels.

“You were expecting what? An open bar?” He grumbled walking to his bookshelf.

“Actually,” I admitted, “Kinda yeah.”

“So that's what you think of me?” He turned his back on me and that was when I saw it. I had never seen him without a shirt before and the long gash on his back was horrible. Without thinking I reached out and touched his skin. He spun lightening fast and grabbed my hand. “Don't.” He walked to his bed and threw on a shirt.

“What is that?” I asked softly.

“Battle scars.” He growled grabbing the book and shoving it at me.

I set the book on a table by the door, "Tell me what happened." He didn't answer so I crossed my arms stubbornly and insisted. "Tell me, I want to know."

He laughed a short hard sound, "You can't always get what you want."

"No, but you just might find you get what you need."

He smiled, but shook his head, "It's something I don't want to talk about."

I nodded and reached for my dictionary, "I get it," I shrugged, "but if you ever want to talk about it, I'll listen."

He smiled sadly and stepped towards me, "Am I allowed to give you a hug as a friend?"

I put my arms around his neck and let his arms wrap around my waist. I laid my head on his shoulder, and suddenly I didn't want to leave. In fact, it felt right to be wrapped in his arms and he didn't seem too eager to push me away. I leaned back and looked at him.

"Am I allowed to kiss you as a friend?" His breath lifted the hair from my neck.

I smiled, "No," and gently pressed my lips to his.

They were as soft as I had imagined they would be. He moved against me slowly, carefully, as if he didn't want to frighten me, but I wanted more. I twisted my fingers in his hair and pulled him closer. It was all the invitation he needed. His fingers slipped under my shirt and his fingers against my skin sent chills up my spine. He seemed to feel it too. The desire took on a life of its own and we were only too eager to take the ride. His mouth moved down my neck and I could barely breath. He moved so quickly I almost didn't notice before my back was pressed up against the rough wooden door. He hitched my leg around his hip and I couldn't focus on anything except his hard body pressed against me as his mouth explored mine.

That was probably why I couldn't hear her heels clicking down the hallway. In fact, Georges had just thrown his shirt to the floor and I was intent on tracing the muscles down his stomach as his fingers slid across the top of my bra when her insistent knock resounded on the door. We both froze for a moment. Then she knocked again.

"Georges," she trilled, " I know you're in there."

He looked at me unsure what to do, but the moment was gone. "Answer her."

"Oh my god, Georges! Do you have that bitch in there with you?"

I fixed my clothes and picked up the book I had come to get. Georges just stood there with a rather awkward look on his face. I opened the door slowly and stood there looking at Lilith who was nearly steaming from the ears. "Hope you weren't talking about me."

She just glared, guttural incoherent noises issuing from her.

I turned to Georges as cold and unemotionally as I could muster, "Thanks for the book."

He straightened up and met me with the same icy politeness, "Your welcome, just make sure to bring it back when you're done."

I nodded and walked past Lilith who was nearly vibrating with anger. I barely cared, I was too busy trying to catch my own breath. I can't believe I just let that happen. Still, I couldn't get the feel of his fingers to stop burning in my skin and my lips were sore from the urgency of his kisses, but I hated that even now I could feel it slipping away. I glanced back to see Lilith still standing at Georges door. I smiled as he glanced my way and continued down the hallway to nowhere in particular. I was floating too high to care about such mundane things.

I threw the book on my bed and grabbed my jacket. I needed to get out. It wasn't that I was running away, but I needed to sort out what just happened and for that I needed some space from Georges. In a way, I should have thanked Lilith. If she hadn't interrupted us, I'm not sure exactly how far I would have let it go. I thought about how far I wanted it to go and felt my cheeks warm. I needed a drink.

Forbidden Desires was there to oblige me. Jackson wasn't at the door. There was a lycan standing there, arms crossed and an overly serious look on his face. He didn't even crack a smile when a couple of girls tried desperately to flirt with him. I stared from the woods as he let them inside with a scowl. He could have been a handsome man, but that scowl gave his face a pinched and twisted almost evil look. He pulled off the bouncer look though, at least he definitely had the body of a bouncer. His golden blonde hair was shorn close to his head but his eyes were so dark they were nearly black. I considered just slipping back into the woods when I caught his attention. His head snapped up as though he was sniffing the air and then his eyes found mine.

I walked forward and held out my hand cordially, "Hey, I'm Jesse."

He scowled, "I know."

I dropped my hand, "Where's Jackson?"

"It's his night off," his voice was completely flat, "I'm Norman."

Then I heard Riley's voice behind me, "Jesse?"

I turned and smiled, "Hey! You working tonight?"

He shook his head, "No, I was actually just coming to talk to Van Helsing, but after that meeting I would love to buy you a drink."

He offered me his arm and I took it with a smile, "I would love that."

Norman growled and let us pass, but he didn't look happy about it.

Riley showed me to a table and disappeared into Van Helsing's office. I don't know why, but I wasn't exactly at ease with that. I ordered a drink and sat watching the people dance. Couples were all smiles as they moved against each other. Supernatural beings, humans, mingled together like it was nothing. They didn't have a care in the world. Before I knew it, Riley was back, all smiles, and holding out his hand for a dance.

I smiled, "You know I really don't dance very well."

He leaned in and whispered in my ear, "What if it's just an excuse to hold you?"

I blushed.

"You're beautiful when you blush," he whispered. He brushed the hair back from my face and I could feel my heart flutter.

I took his hand, "Then I guess I have no choice."

He led me out onto the dance floor. Unlike Georges, Riley didn't get me out there for a slow song, but that didn't stop him from holding me as close to him as possible. It was fun dancing, letting my hair down, but I wasn't fully at ease. I suddenly realized that I didn't know what I was doing. I had just come from Georges' room. I had just made out with him and now here I was with Riley's hands running over my hips. This wasn't me, I never acted like this before. Riley seemed to sense that something was amiss and smiled at me sadly. He took my hand and led me back to the table.

"Tell me what's wrong," he said sitting very close to me.

I moved away a little, "I just don't normally act like this."

He smiled, "Don't have fun and let your hair down?"

It was like he had read my thoughts, "Well, that and I don't flirt like this."

He smiled and took my hand, "You do it very well for not doing it."

I smiled, "I just..."

"Hey," he interrupted, "You're a beautiful woman. I'm surprised you don't have more men falling all over themselves to get near you. If you want to flirt some, you should. You don't have to be afraid."

And there it was, the bald faced truth. I was scared. I was scared of the way I was feeling, the desires. I smiled at Riley as he kissed my hand softly. He wasn't afraid.

We had been trying to control the power for weeks, but tonight was the moment of truth. The full moon was going to rise and with the new addition of lycan blood to my arsenal of oddities, the prognosis was not good. Richard was so worried he had the doors of the training room chained shut and padlocked. He insisted on being with me for this. Unfortunately he couldn't talk Georges out of it either. They both stood there staring at me as the sun dipped below the horizon. I had felt the moon rising into the sky since about six, Richard said that was normal, that he could feel it too. It wasn't until the final rays of the sun disappeared though that I could feel it's full power.

It was like a magnetic pull in the sky. I could feel my blood rushing around with it's calling. It was making me dizzy, light-headed.

"Richard," I whispered, "I don't feel so good."

He smiled and kneeled in front of me, "That's normal. This is your first full moon since the...infection."

I nodded.

"I can feel it too," he assured me, "the rush of the blood, the calling of the moon."

"How do you control it?"

He smiled showing a full row of pointed teeth, "I've been doing this for years."

I grabbed my stomach, "I think I'm going to be sick."

Georges stepped forward but Richard waved him back, "It's normal."

I watched as Georges stepped back to the wall, "I won't be able to hurt him if I change will I?"

Richard smiled, "Possibly, but he'd deserve it."

"Will I be able to hurt you?"

He shook his head, "Not really, you won't have an urge to if you transition. The scent will calm you."

I smirked, "Has Daphne ever seen you transition?"

He laughed and sat in front of me, comfortably, "Yes she has. She told me I had to if we were going to have a relationship."

"I don't blame her."

"Neither did I, so I showed her and we've been together ever since."

"That's nice," I groaned and doubled over in pain. "My mouth hurts."

Richard looked concerned, "I think you're going to transition."

I laid down on the mat, "Because my mouth hurts?"

He laid down next to me, "It starts with the gums hurting, then it's your back and your arms. Well, your hands really."

I took a deep breath, "My hands?"

"Yeah," he sighed, "When you transition it's an actual change in your bone structure. It's not like you just sprout fur and are good to go."

"How long does it last?"

"Well that depends. You can change quickly or slowly, but the pain only lasts with the transformation. When the pain ends the transformation is over."

I nodded, my breathing was becoming labored.

Georges' voice was hushed, "Is she going to be alright?"

Richard shrugged and answered, "I hope so."

I could feel the sharp prick of my newly sharpened teeth. My back and arms and hands were beginning to ache. I was wondering how badly it was going to hurt when everything was said and done. I wish Georges hadn't been there. I didn't want him to see me burst into a gigantic fur ball. I was going to change and I didn't know how that was going to work or whether or not I was going to hurt someone. I was starting to panic and I tried very hard to pull the power into the steamer trunk, to keep everyone safe. It fought me every second, it did not want to obey. I concentrated to the point that I didn't even hear Richard and Georges calling my name, but the power whipped out at the walls. I felt the door splinter and then I heard my name, said in panic. Suddenly the power quieted. I opened my eyes and there was nothing. No pain at all.

Richard and Georges were crumpled on the floor in the opposite corner of the room. I scrambled to them as fast as I could. They were on the floor, but they were fine. They were fine. I nearly cried, they were fine.

Richard looked up at me and smiled, "Well that was interesting."

"Sorry," I nearly sobbed.

Georges laughed, "It's never a dull moment with you."

I flopped on the floor next to them, "So glad I could entertain you."

Richard sat up and looked at me quizzically, "You seem to be rather cheerful."

I sighed, "I don't hurt anymore."

He grabbed my face and roughly jerked my chin in his direction.

"Ok, that hurt genius."

He smiled and pushed his finger under my lip, "It's just your teeth."

I snapped at his finger and he pulled back startled, "Easy there sweetheart."

Georges had been surprisingly quiet through all of this and couldn't help but wonder why. He just kept staring at me, "What's up Georges?"

He stood up and held out a hand for me, I let him help me up, "You're what's up."

"What do you mean by that?"

He smiled kind of sadly, "You're different now."

"Ok?"

"You just are." And with that, he walked out of the room and I was left wondering what that meant.

The next morning Richard and I walked out into the hallway. My teeth had receded and I felt completely normal again. Thomas was waiting for us in the corridor. He looked tired and I wondered if he had been waiting out here all night.

"Yes," he answered my unasked question, "I have been waiting all night to see what the outcome of this would be."

"It was nothing too terrible," Richard explained.

I smiled, "Just some freaky teeth."

Thomas nodded knowingly, "That may be a very valuable asset as time moves on."

I sighed, making sure that he heard it. This was great for me, just one more thing that I was going to have to control. As if in response to my thoughts Lilith came flying up the hallway at vampire speed and threw me through the training room doors before I could even register what was happening. I was on my feet almost as soon as my back touched the mat. I immediately adopted a defensive stance, but she just stood, hand on hip, defiantly staring at me.

"I warned you," she growled angrily.

"Are you serious?" I asked in utter amazement.

I was so angry I couldn't see straight. That stupid bitch thought that she could treat me like this? Well, she was quite mistaken. I could feel the power roiling in waves across my skin. I growled, a deep animalistic sound and flung the power out at her. The sounds of the power hitting her cracked like a bullwhip and she flew across the room. She didn't even have time to think about moving before I was on her.

I crushed my heel against her chest, "That wasn't even all my power."

She screamed and literally clawed my leg. Blood spotted my pale skin, but it was surreal as if it wasn't even happening. The power had taken over. It had covered the pain and I hesitated in amazement. It gave her just the time she needed to sweep my legs. I slammed to the floor. Lilith didn't wait for me to recover from the shock of her take down. She sprang towards me, claws out. We tussled on the floor for a moment, but our fracas was cut short by Van Helsing's booming voice.

"Stop," he yelled and the sound reverberated off the walls.

Lilith and I both scampered away from each other.

"What is this?" He demanded.

I looked at Lilith expecting a quick answer, but she hung her head in shame instead.

"It's apparently some sort of misunderstanding," I answered quietly.

I could see Lilith tense in defiance, but she wisely kept her mouth shut.

"What," Van Helsing continued, "is this misunderstanding pertaining to?"

Georges stepped through the training room doors, "It's pertaining to me sir."

Lilith glowered at him, "Really sir, it's none of your business."

"None of my business," Van Helsing hissed angrily, "If it threatens the well being of my team then it is definitely what I would call 'my business.'" He walked around the two of us angrily, "You two have been at each others throats since you met and I can only imagine that the reason has something to do with your feelings towards Mr. Moncrief. If I do say so that is very possibly the most childish reason to be unprofessional."

"I'm sorry, sir," I muttered softly.

Richard stepped in for me this time stating in no uncertain terms, "Jesse did nothing wrong here sir. Lilith came racing down the hallway and attacked her."

Lilith was glowering, "Thanks for sticking up for the person you've known the longest."

Richard laughed, "And what? That means what? The truth is still the truth."

Van Helsing sighed sadly, "Lilith, I think you need to leave."

I knew what she was going to do barely a split second before she acted. I jumped in front of Van Helsing as she flew across the room. She hit me harder than I had anticipated and we slammed into the wall. I felt my shoulder dislocate. Not good. Lilith seemed to somehow sense that something was wrong and pounced on my moment of weakness. Her claws raked against my face and brought the red stain of blood to my cheek. I tried to push her away with my power, but nothing happened. I was going to have to resort to Richard's training. I swept her legs out from under her and she slammed into the floor. I was moving at superhuman speed, but the power had been sucked from my body; somehow I felt weak. I could barely move. Her fist flung out and smashed into my jaw.

I smashed into the wall and slid to a pile on the ground. I watched her coming towards me as though it was slow motion in a movie. In my head I heard a low growl and felt a tingle rush down my spine, but there was hardly any power in it. I tried, but there was nothing but a faint spark. I closed my eyes and waited for her blow to come and wondered vaguely if it would knock me out. In a way I hoped it would. I was pretty much sick of this. I waited, but nothing happened. There was no hit, nothing, just an eerie silence that hummed in my ears. Then I could smell it, honeysuckle.

Lilith was in front of me, passed out on the ground while Georges kept a steady hand on the back of her neck. Richard was coming towards me with Daphne only steps behind. Thomas was holding on to Van Helsing's arm as they made their way towards me as well. I tried to stand and realized that my arm really was dislocated. Tears sprang to my eyes as the pain shot down my arm. Georges looked as though for a moment he might let Lilith go, but thought better of it and just stared from across the room.

Daphne ran to my side, "What hurts?"

I grunted, "Everything."

Richard chuckled and scooped me up in his arms, "At least she still has her charming personality."

Richard laid me gently on Daphne's table and she took my hand in hers. Her voice was cold and clinical, "I think you've dislocated your shoulder."

I nodded, "I think you're right."

Richard took my hand, “It's gonna hurt when she pops it back into place.”

I gritted my teeth and nodded.

“Hey,” he laughed, “Nice leg sweep though.”

I smiled and that was the moment Daphne chose to snap my arm back to where it belonged. I squeezed Richard's hand and howled in pain. He laughed and patted me on the head like a puppy.

“Easy now pup,” he laughed.

That was when it hit me, “Pup? That's why.”

Daphne sat on the edge of the bed and took my other hand, “What do you mean?”

I sat up, “I couldn't use my power. There was a small spark, but nothing would happen. It was dampened.”

Richard sat down and looked at me, “But you hit Lilith with your power when you first got up.”

I shook my head, “But that was it, it was like the after you turn off the hose there's still a little water left in it.”

Richard looked perplexed, “You would have thought it would make your power stronger.”

Daphne was sitting there pensively, “Do you think it will come back?”

I nodded, “I'm feeling better already, but nowhere near full strength.”

She looked at Richard and he nodded. “You need to be careful, Jesse,” she whispered, “You aren't Wonder Woman regardless of what you think.”

I smiled, “Don't tell me you're worried.”

Richard squeezed my hand, “Listen to us. We've been talking about why they tainted your father's blood.”

I was confused, “To kill me.”

Daphne shook her head sadly, “I don't think that was why they did it.”

“It doesn't make sense otherwise.”

Richard sighed, “Think about it. You were damn near indestructible until last night.”

“So?”

Daphne groaned, “Are you really so dense that you aren't getting this? Your father was dying when you drained him because his blood was tainted with werewolf blood, you were powerful before that because of your mother's apparent telekinesis that was only enhanced by your father's vampire blood. It would stand to reason that if you survived the induction of the werewolf blood that would only strengthen your powers. It seemed to work for a while, after you drained your father your powers were enhanced even more and you took on his powers as well. You were literally a powerhouse."

Richard took my face in his hands, "The Marquis was making you a weapon."

I shook my head, then I thought about it for a minute and realized that it actually made sense. That would be why Anthony had been so interested in my powers, why Alexander had been so against any of them finding me. The Marquis, that I was becoming more and more convinced was actually Anthony, had tried to make me into a weapon. Daphne tapped my hand softly. Oops. They were both levitating. I did my best to lower them as gently as possible, but they both bounced against the mattress. At least they were smiling.

Richard smacked my arm, "Hey your eyes aren't glowing anymore."

Daphne nodded, "You might actually be able to survive in the sunlight now."

I stood up and started pacing around, "This isn't good though."

"Why?" they asked in unison.

"Anth...The Marquis thinks that I'm a weapon and his pets have seen me with those eyes."

Richard nodded, "And they will be expecting what they saw before."

I nodded, "And I'm going to have to deliver."

Thomas' voice piped up, "And now aren't you glad that I taught you how to taste powers?"

I smiled at the old man and even though he couldn't see me he smiled back. "Thomas, I am very glad for everything that you've taught me and I'm afraid that I'm going to need all of it."

Van Helsing stood with Thomas and shook his head, "I know what you're thinking."

I smiled, "I think I can handle playing bait."

Georges was waiting outside my room. It was clear from his scowl that he was not happy. It only made me smile more.

"Keep your little Creole temper in check there Georges," I laughed as I walked up.

"I would chere if you would stop provoking me," he growled.

I snorted, "Really? And how exactly am I provoking you now?"

"Aside from you running around with Riley the other night?"

I laughed, "Well you were busy."

He growled, "You left. You were the one who walked out, not me."

"It was your room and you seemed like you had business to take care of with another woman."

"So you ran into the night? Ran away into *his* arms?"

"Maybe I'm just getting used to being a little reckless."

"Reckless?" He roared, "You don't know anything about him. Do you always put yourself in danger? Idiotic danger?"

I slumped against the wall opposite my door. He was so cute when he was angry, "Yeah I guess I do. I'm alone with you aren't I?"

He sighed letting go of his sudden flare of anger, "Do you have any idea what you've just done?"

"Gotten your girlfriend kicked off the team?"

"Gotten yourself an enemy, a powerful and pissed off enemy."

"You talking about Lilith or are you talking about you?"

He pushed off my door and was standing so close I could smell his cologne rising with the heat of his anger, "If you don't know who your enemy is then you are worse off than I thought."

I walked past him and into my room slamming the door behind me. It wasn't exactly the most mature thing I had ever done. Come to think of it, it seemed the more I was around Georges the more I acted like a juvenile high school girl. I could feel my power responding to my emotions and suddenly realized that I was glowing. I could see my own power. I ran to the mirror, but my eyes weren't glowing. I could still see, but my eyes weren't glowing. Oh this was good, very good. I took a deep breath and let the calm rush over me. I smiled at my reflection, I was beginning to like the new me.

25. The Other Shoe

I knew in my heart we didn't have long to wait. The Marquis had to be planning something, they had left me alone for far too long. I laid in my bed staring into the the ceiling wondering when they would come. I listened into the night. Richard and Daphne were in her lab. I could almost see them, her looking into her microscope frantically trying to figure out what was happening with my blood and him sitting on the metal table, feet swinging awkwardly over the edge. Van Helsing was in his library, as always, sitting in his overstuffed leather chair reading, I could hear the rustling of the pages as he turned them. Georges was pacing, he seemed to be doing that more and more since Lilith had been so unceremoniously dismissed.

I hadn't been back to Forbidden Desires and I hadn't been alone with Georges since we had it out in the hallway. I didn't know what to do about him or about Riley. Of course Riley hadn't exactly been blowing up my phone so maybe that wasn't something I needed to worry about anyway. Georges on the other hand would barely look at me anymore. He still made my heart beat like no one I had ever come across before and it was real, it wasn't some parlour trick like Anthony had used. Georges was gorgeous and sexual and the most infuriating man I had ever met. And somehow despite myself, the more infuriating he became the more attracted to him I was.

Riley was different, he was definitely hot, but he had this sweetness that was so cute. The way he had danced with me though was anything but. I blushed remembering the way his hands had moved across my body and felt my heart flutter. I had given him my cell phone number that night at Forbidden Desires, but had only gotten a single text message, "Thought about you today." That had been over a week ago. With thoughts of the two of them, I fell asleep.

I awoke to the sounds of gunshots. They were here. I jumped up and tripped over some shoes that had somehow made their way right into my path. Ever the graceful one, I stumbled forward and through the door. I sniffed the air and it was apparent that they were in the training room along with everyone else, but what was worse was that I could smell blood, purely human blood. It had been spilled and there was a lot of it.

I busted through the double doors to find Thomas on the floor, dead. He had been shot once through the heart. His gray hair mingled with his blood to form a matted mess on the floor while his lifeless eyes stared into the next world. I ran to his side and in my concern forgot about situational awareness and missed the tackle coming from Jennifer. As I reached for Thomas' cold dead body, she slammed into me, fully transitioned. We slammed to the floor and before I had even a moment to react I heard his voice.

"Well then," Anthony called. Jennifer backed up growling menacingly as she did. I looked up to see Anthony perched on the window's ledge with Vanessa. She held Van Helsing over the side by the back of his neck. "I would have thought you would have seen Jennifer coming."

I smiled and leaped to my feet, "Bad situational awareness I suppose."

I surveyed the room. Richard was being held at bay by Georgia. She hadn't raised a finger to him, but instead had Daphne in her arms. A twitch would snap Daphne's neck. Georges had apparently been fighting with Theodore, but was outnumbered by two apparently fledgling vampires and the werewolf.

Vanessa smiled wickedly, "We've been waiting for you pet."

I stood defiantly, "Come and get me."

Anthony laughed and brushed Vanessa's hair back from her face, "No, you will come to us."

It was then that I could smell it. Roses filled the air. Richard fell to his knees, calm and sedated. Daphne soon followed suit and Georgia lowered her to the ground. They both looked at me as though through some drug induced haze. Georges was unaffected and struggling to escape from the clutches of the fledglings. Anthony turned his eyes to me and the scent became stronger. I let my eyes flutter and dropped towards the ground. Georges looked at me with furrowed brow, but a quick wink let him in on my game. I wasn't affected, I was playing. Let them put their guard down.

"You can't control me like this," I choked out.

Anthony laughed, "Why are you fighting it? If I remember correctly you used to like it."

Vanessa growled involuntarily.

Georgia and Jennifer were both making their way towards me, "You can't make me your pet."

Anthony laughed and leaped off his perch and sauntered towards me, "My pet? Why would you think that?"

"Isn't that why you poisoned me," I bowed my head to him, "Marquis?"

He smiled and ran his fingers down my neck, "I knew you'd figure it out."

"Didn't take much. You needed me to be your weapon."

He sighed and took my chin in his hand, "I need you for many reasons." He brushed his lips against my cheek and I could see Georges struggle. Anthony growled, "Always the one to ruin a romantic moment, Georges."

"What about those memories you showed me? My father running everything?"

"I was trying to get you to trust me. Did you know you can lie in your memories?"

"And apparently in your life story as well."

He ran his fingernail down the side of my face, just enough to draw blood, "Yes, but that can all change if you only ask."

"Please," I whimpered, "Let my friends go."

Anthony sighed, "Will you come willingly then? Without me needing to use my powers over you?"

I nodded.

"Do you know why you hold such a fascination for me?"

I smirked, "I couldn't imagine."

"Aside from your obvious physical allurements," he took a moment to take them in, "You are the only person I have ever met that has been able, in any way, to resist my powers."

"I don't understand."

He stood behind me so that I could look up at Vanessa holding Van Helsing, "Do you see her?"

I nodded, "She's beautiful."

"And weak," he growled, "Not like you are."

"She's your mate."

"And if you wanted that position," he smiled, "I would have her throw herself into the flames of the hottest fire and she would do it willingly."

"Why would you do that?" I looked into his eyes.

"Because you always want what you can't have, mi amour, and you are that for me." He stepped back and leaped with ease to his perch beside Vanessa. "I can't even pretend to control you anymore."

I jumped to my feet, "You knew."

He smiled, "Of course, love, but how else was I going to get you to listen to my proposal without you struggling?"

He released Richard and Daphne, and I growled, "Get Daphne out of here." Richard didn't have to be told twice. They were out of there as fast as Richard could move. The two fledglings released Georges, but he stood his ground. He didn't advance, but he didn't retreat. I admired him for that, but apparently Anthony did not.

"This is who you are?" Georges growled.

Anthony smirked, "You wouldn't listen to her, would you?"

Georges looked at me, "No. None of us would. We thought she had hallucinated you."

"That's what I wanted. Our very own Cassandra."

I hung my head, "Very well planned."

"I do what I do. "

I smiled, "You haven't let Van Helsing go yet."

Vanessa released her grip on the old man's neck and he plummeted to the ground. Georges ran lightening fast and caught him right before impact. He had Van Helsing out of the room in a blink.

Everyone was safe. I could feel the power creeping along under my skin. I smiled, "Fuck you Marquis."

My voice was like a starting pistol. Jennifer and Georgia leaped forward and with a easy wave of my hand I sent them flying. The two fledglings took their chance to attack, but that was dumb on their part. Their bodies slammed into the walls. I gave a little extra push for good measure and in the time it took for me to do that Vanessa, Jennifer and Georgia piled on top of me. I looked up to the ledge, Anthony blew me a kiss and was gone. I thought I saw Lilith in the window, but I couldn't be sure.

“So sad,” I grunted scattering them away, “The Puppeteer won't be here to watch you die.”

I reached out with my power. I could feel their hearts beating even as I had them pressed up against the walls. I could almost taste the blood in their veins. A deep guttural growl broke from my lips as the power took over. It reached out and latched onto their beating hearts slowly squeezing the life from them. I watched as Georgia's eyes fluttered. She clutched at her chest. Jennifer was yelping in pain, I glance about for her protector, but it seemed that Theodore had disappeared with his master. One of the fledglings grasping at his chest in desperation dropped to the ground. He was dead. I screamed in my head to stop, but the power had a mind of its own. It liked the death and carnage it was creating.

The other fledgling dropped. I tried to pull back but it wouldn't obey. The power just wouldn't obey. Georges burst into the room and in my momentary confusion the power lost its focus. Vanessa and Georgia didn't wait for an invitation. They scrambled up the wall and were out of the window before I could blink. Jennifer,however, was slightly slower and the power whipped out at her and snapped her neck in mid air. She dropped to the ground and her body began the bone crunching transformation back into her human form. I took a deep breath and tried so hard to control it, but it was hungry and it hadn't been satiated. Georges walked towards me carefully with his palms out.

“Walk away,” I croaked.

He shook his head, “No. You can control this I know you can.”

I whimpered, “I can't. I'm trying, but I can't.”

He stepped towards me and the power locked onto his movement, “Let me help you.”

I shook my head, “I just killed them.”

His voice was soft, “I know.”

“It wants blood and I can't keep it in check. Get out.”

“It's alright.” He took off his shirt and held his arms out, “Give it what it wants then.”

I started to shake, “That's not all the power wants.”

He smiled and took a slow step forward, “The power or you?”

"This isn't a joke, Georges. I'm trying really hard here."

"I'm not kidding." He came up to me and laid his head to the side, "Take the blood and we'll sort out the rest later."

My lips brushed his neck, "I could kill you."

"I trust you, Jesse."

His voice was warm and the scent of his skin was so sweet. I let my fangs reach out and sunk them deeply into his neck. I heard the sharp intake of breath as my teeth broke the skin. He slipped his hands around my waist and pulled me closer to him. Then I felt it, calm. The power was losing its pull. Georges sank to the ground and I went with him. I focused very hard on pulling the power into the steamer trunk I had visualized, just like Thomas had taught me. I understood why Georges had wanted me to drink his blood. He took the gamble that even though his powers didn't work from the outside, maybe it would from the inside. He was right, I closed the lid of my metaphorical trunk and was me again.

I pulled back and licked my lips, "Its under control now."

He smiled, "Good."

He looked tired. "Thank you for trusting me."

He smiled wickedly and I realized that I was straddling him. "You know how hard I had to concentrate on calm?" He asked.

"Sorry," I blushed trying to stand, but he held me fast to him.

He pressed his lips to mine. I wanted more. But he pushed me back roughly and whispered, "God help me."

Richard cleared his throat conspicuously from the doorway, "I can come back if you two need a moment."

"Perfect timing," Georges quipped, "You can help clean up."

I stood and helped Georges to his feet. He was weak. I had taken a lot of blood and my emotions were completely out of whack because of it. Of course everyone wanted to know what happened. Georges and I recounted the whole episode. I was terrified. What I had done was scary as hell. I could crush someone's heart from a room away. What kind of freak could pull off something like that?

I sat on my bed that night with my knees pulled up to my chest thinking over everything that had taken place. A soft knock on my door pulled me out of my revelry. Daphne opened my door hesitantly and stepped inside. She came and sat down on the bed next to me. "Are you alright?" I didn't even need to answer. She just threw her arms around me and let me sob. Like a true friend she sat there and let me get it all out. I couldn't believe that Thomas was dead and I was the reason. I had only killed two people before this and they had been accidents. I killed three people today. Three. And I did it in a way that scared the hell out of everyone who I cared about. I was so scared I cried until I fell asleep.

That night I dreamed of my mother and the word "trean," it means strength.

26. Going Through Changes

Thomas' funeral was a solemn affair. His family accepted us with no question, but by their glances and whispers, they knew we were not normal. Still, nothing was said about it. As it was, I couldn't stop crying.

We returned to the compound and waited. Van Helsing had asked us to wait for him in the training room and we of course obliged. My eyes were puffy from crying, but Daphne just stood against the wall with her arms crossed. She looked worried. She chewed on her bottom lip and glanced nervously at the door in intervals. I discreetly sniffed the air and picked up the scent of another person, it seemed strangely familiar. I sniffed again and was greeted by the scent of other less-than-human beings. It was not going to be pleasant, I could feel the tension vibrating through the air. Georges and Richard took their places near us and adopted the same cross armed stance. I felt like I was missing something so I just stood there and stared at the door as well.

We didn't have long to wait. Van Helsing came in and looked at each of us sadly. He walked towards Georges and shook his hand, "You are the head of this team." He took Richard's hand, "Protect them." He hugged Daphne, "Keep them healthy and safe." Then he took me by the shoulders, "Jesse," he smiled, "be yourself." I didn't know what he meant by that other than that he was saying goodbye. He was leaving us. He walked towards the door and then turned to face us. "This compound has been compromised and it's far too dangerous for us to stay here. I am going to spend some time with my family and your operations are being transferred to Savannah. I will be handing you over to my nephew." We all looked at one another with the exception of Georges. He just hung his head as though he knew what was coming. "He will be here in a moment," Van Helsing continued, "It's been my pleasure to know you all." And with that he was gone.

We all looked at Georges waiting for some sort of explanation, but there was none forthcoming. The door creaked and we looked again to see two large werewolves already transitioned walked through the opening. One was tall, taller than any I had seen before and his fur shown a golden blonde, it reminded me of the coat of a golden retriever. He slunk forward and I watched out of the corner of my eye as everyone started to tense. Somehow, I couldn't find it in me to react the same way. After everything that had happened the last few days, I just didn't have it in me. The werewolf seemed to sense that and moved towards me with renewed purpose. He didn't wear the tatters of his clothes for modesty as Richard always had. In fact he seemed proud of his manhood flapping in the wind as he greased his way towards me.

When he reached me he pulled himself up to his full height. My nose only reached his ribs. His lips curled back from his teeth. Pointed canines greeted my gaze and eyes so dark they were almost black appraised my figure. He laughed a throaty deep sound and leaned down towards my neck. I didn't even flinch. His breath was hot against my neck as he growled in my ear.

"Are you afraid little girl?" he growled menacingly.

I laughed, "Do I look like Little Red Riding Hood to you?"

He stepped back and snarled, "Cocky little bitch aren't you?"

I smiled tiredly, "I've had a hell of a week and if you think some big bad wolf routine is gonna make me shiver, you're working on the wrong girl."

He backed up and tensed for a leap, "I'll rip you apart."

I held my arms out to my side, "This isn't bravado, I just genuinely don't give a shit right now."

"And why would that be?" I froze. I didn't need this too. I knew that voice even if he hadn't stepped through the door yet. The wolf stepped back and Riley stepped into his place before me. This was the new Van Helsing. His wolves stepped back until they flanked him.

I could feel my bottom lip start to quiver with rage and the power struggled against the restraints I had placed upon them. "So you would be the new Van Helsing."

He smiled at me appeasingly, "My name is Riley Van Helsing, but you didn't answer my question. Why would you let Norman rip you apart?"

I looked at the overstuffed golden retriever, "I should've figured it was you there Norman."

He grinned showing his teeth.

Riley stepped up to the rest of the crew, "Daphne La Rue, witch and doctor extraordinaire. Richard Bicks, werewolf and my uncle's leading combat instructor. And of course Georges Moncrief, vampire...among other things." No one missed the look that passed between the two of them. He turned to me, "My uncle told me what happened."

I nodded but didn't speak.

The other wolf came forward. He was covered thankfully. After realizing that was Norman, it was making me horribly uncomfortable to have him here completely unclothed. The other wolf sniffed at me carefully. He reminded me of a pup who was asking permission to play with the big dogs. I looked down at him and growled. He backed up with his ears down. He was slightly shorter than me which, combined with his attitude gave me the impression that he was young. Perhaps a teenager. It made me sad because I thought of Vicki who I hadn't seen in weeks. The pup halfheartedly bared his teeth, but he seemed to shiver just at my sent. The power seemed to sense his fear and rattled against the box again. This time I barely had to concentrate before it quieted. Maybe it was finally getting used to its box or maybe it was just biding its time until it could escape and crush someone else's heart at forty feet.

Norman was staring at me, hackles raised, Riley just smiled. He was impressed, but I had no time for him or his games. I slumped against the wall angrily. He dismissed us all and sent us to go and pack our things. We were going to leave the next morning.

I stood at my bed and slumped against the bedpost. I was leaving again. It never seemed like I could stay in one place, but at least this time I was able to bring my friends with me. I heard the footsteps long before they stepped into the room.

"Van Helsing," I greeted him coolly.

"It's still Riley," I could hear the smile in his voice.

I turned to see that Norman was with him, still in the buff. I threw a bathrobe at him. "God, Norman at least cover yourself."

He shook his hips, "You like what you see?"

I smiled and picked up the gun that was laying on my bed. I leveled it at his crotch, "You want to keep it?"

He laughed and pulled the pink terrycloth bathrobe around himself. I must admit though, Norman did have some killer abs.

Riley motioned for him to wait outside and he obeyed without question. After the door clicked shut, Riley looked at me, "I didn't want to lie to you."

I sighed and threw some clothes into my bag.

"I'm serious Jesse, I didn't want to lie to you."

I didn't even look up, "And yet you did. I thought you were this sweet guileless man, but I was wrong again."

"I had to get to know you like this."

I spun towards him, "Excuse me?"

He sighed and ran his fingers through his hair, "When I saw you the first time, I wanted to know you as just a random guy, not the next Van Helsing. I didn't think I was going to have to step in this quickly."

I shook my head, "Just get out of my room."

He stepped towards me, but apparently got the hint from the sudden glare I gave him, "Jesse, I really didn't mean to hurt you."

"Yeah well, the road to hell and all that."

He took the hint and left me to my packing. This was a change I had not foreseen and I wasn't sure I was ready for this.

I wandered out into the woods. I wasn't particularly attached to this place, but I was going to miss the scenery. I didn't have any idea as to where I was going, but found myself on the familiar path onto what had become my favorite spot. I was standing on the precipice again looking into the waves. They were calm, almost sad. I felt the sadness grip my heart. Maybe I did like this place. I thought about the times I had jumped and remembered the exhilaration as I rushed down towards the water.

I scooted my toes over the edge of the rock and closed my eyes. I wondered what it would feel like if I didn't have the power to brace my fall. I could feel the power start to rumble in my chest. I didn't know if I could control the power with the pure exhilaration of a free fall. Perhaps it was too many years of repressing my desires and delaying gratification, but I wanted to be reckless tonight. I spread my arms out to my sides. I wanted to fly.

"Don't jump," Norman growled from behind me.

I slowly opened my eyes but didn't turn, "If I jumped, I would fly."

"That would be a sight," Riley scoffed from behind me. It seemed that in public at least he was going to pretend there was nothing going on.

I looked down at the waves, "It wouldn't be safe for you to be so close."

I heard him slump against a tree right behind me, "You don't scare me."

I smiled and snorted, "That's because you're stupid."

I heard Norman growl behind me. I fake pouted. "I don't think your pet likes me much."

"Astute," Riley chuckled, "how your intellectual prowess amazes me."

I smiled, really smiled for the first time in a long while. "Touche." I turned to face them, "So, if my amazing intellect didn't draw you out here, what did?"

"Nothing too special," he smiled. "But you may want to finish packing, we roll in ten minutes."

I nodded and turned back to the ocean, "I have everything I came with."

I listened as they walked away and heard the waves crashing below as if they were saying good-bye. Riley had made it a point to tell us nothing about Savannah or what we could expect from it. None of us were terribly thrilled about it. Van Helsing had been theatrical when it came to confusing the enemy, but Riley was theatrical just for the hell of it. It was really starting to piss me off.

We had all been piled into the SUVs with all of our belongings. The ride was quiet to say the least. Finally, we pulled up to a majestic house on one of the city's many squares. The soft glow of the street lamps cast shadows through the Spanish moss that clung tenaciously to the limbs of the giant oaks that lined the squares. In the night breeze the shadows seemed to dance across the house in a strange ballet. I stepped from the van and stood before the ornate iron gate that kept us out. The hairs on the back of my neck stood up and Sean, Riley's pup, huddled close to me, begging without words for my protection.

"It's alright," Riley laughed, "You are just feeling the presence of the spirits."

I growled, "A little warning might have been nice."

He smiled impishly, "Why spoil the fun?" He took a deep breath flung out his arms, "This is my domain." With a flourish he spun to face us and bowed grandly, "I am a clairvoyant and Savannah is my city."

I unconsciously shuddered. What had we gotten ourselves into? I looked up at the house and noticed it's strange color. I asked quietly, "What is that color?"

Riley smiled, "H'aint blue. It h'aint quite gray and it h'aint quite blue, but it keeps the spirits out." He sighed tiredly, "I need a place where they can't reach me."

Georges and Richard stepped out to stand near us and I could hear Daphne take a sharp breath as she stepped to the sidewalk. For whatever reason, the spirits hit her the hardest. She nearly collapsed. Richard caught her effortlessly, but Riley only laughed and swung the large iron gate open. He was enjoying himself far too much. I thought Richard was going to kill him, but Georges placed a calming hand on his shoulder. Richard understood, no powers needed. This was not the time or place.

I turned my attentions back to the house. The old fashioned porch was adorned with old rocking chairs and conversation tables. The wooden planks creaked in protest as we all ascended the stairs and stepped through the hand carved wooden door. The glass in the door was a beautiful stained glass in blues and reds and yellows. I turned back towards the streets and noticed the row of broken glass that went across the top of the sand-stone wall that enclosed the lot.

"It's a guard," Jackson explained stepping into the square of light from the open door behind me. I turned and couldn't help but smile. Jackson, fangs and all, was standing in the doorway. Big goofy grin on his face. He held his arms open. "Surprise."

I threw my arms around him, "Jackson, with you here he needs a guard from what?"

"Spirits." He answered stepping back from the door for us to enter.

I stopped for a moment and noticed that I didn't feel the spirits at all. I guess that Riley's safe house really did work. We were ceremoniously shown inside and the decor was breathtaking. The wooden floors were polished to the point that I was afraid to step on them. To one side was a large sitting room complete with red Victorian sitting set. Iron sconces on the wall flickered with electric candlelight. To the other side was a large dining room with an oak table that could easily sit a dozen people. A large curving staircase reached to the second floor and Jackson led the way. I could feel both Georges and Riley looking at me, trying to gauge my reaction. I tried very hard not to let my amazement show in any way.

Jackson opened a large oaken door, "This is your room Jesse." He walked in and opened an interior door, "You have a his and hers bathroom."

"That I'll be sharing with?"

He stepped into the hallway and to the next door, "Miss La Rue, this is your room. You and Jesse will be sharing this particular bathroom." I breathed a sigh of relief loud and dramatic enough to make Daphne giggle.

My room was opulent to say the least. A large oak four poster bed with black velvet draperies stood against one wall opposite two large french doors that opened to a Juliet balcony. I dropped my bags on the bed and stepped through the doors into the cool night air where the night breeze caressed my face. The darkness crept up the walls of the house to where I stood, beyond the reach of the street lamps. I closed my eyes and listened to the night sounds here. People were laughing by the river, a couple was in the square across from the house, sitting on a bench. There was a dog barking at something a few blocks over. I would have to get used to these new sounds, not the wood sounds I had become so familiar with.

Here I was, a new city, a new Van Helsing, a new family. Out there somewhere was a horde of vampires being trained to destroy me, not to mention a rather angry werewolf who I'm sure would love to join the fray. Inside me the power rumbled and it knew as well as I that we were going to have to make peace with one another if either of us were going to survive. I closed my eyes and took a deep breath letting the salty scent of the ocean and the damp earth fill my lungs.

Slowly I opened the lid of the box and the power whimpered in excitement. I let it seep from its prison and creep down my arms. The air crackled as the power licked freedom at the end of my fingertips. I called it back, but it resisted at first. I concentrated and with a growl the power grudgingly obeyed. I let it wash over my body and it wrapped around me, covered me in power. It was exhilarating. I opened my eyes and stared out over the courtyard. I was in control, I was finally at peace.

Afterword

Yes, there are vampires. Not all vampires burn in the sun, none I've ever met sparkle. Crosses only ward off the superstitious ones. Garlic will only make their breath smell. You can stake a vampire in the heart, but it'll just stake you back. A bite will not infect you, drinking their blood will. Some have extra powers and you can't help it.

Yes, there are werewolves. The full moon does not control them. Silver is a fashion statement not a weapon. They don't transform into cute dog-like things, and some of them are less than modest about that fact. If you getting bitten, its a crap shoot as to if you'll be infected. They are faster and stronger than you, deal with it.

Yes, there are things that go bump in the night. Yes, there are things that bump back. I am not a vampire. I am not a werewolf. I am faster and stronger than you. I have powers you could never hope to match, conquer, or understand. I am Jesse Childress and I am no longer afraid.

Made in the USA
Charleston, SC
10 June 2014